A 190-Degreee Horizon

A Novel
By

Larry Murley

To Jason

Happy Trails
hope you enjoy

www.larrymurley.com
www.facebook.com/A190DegreeHorizon

3

Forword

About 1976 I moved to Colorado. I had never been to the state but it was love at first sight. I spent the next few years driving truck hauling fuel for the most part, then moving Mountain Bell's equipment and supplies around the state. I spent a lot of time in the high country. Then, at end of the day, I would come back down to the Front Range, where the magic disappeared. In 1980 I moved away for 3 years and went back trucking. My youngest son's imminent birth brought me back in the fall of 1983.

In 1987 I was able to buy a piece of mountain property in Cherokee Park, in Larimer County. I felt as if I was able to touch the life that one of the early settlers must have lived. It was a great experience. Then, sadly, I moved away again. I wound up writing my second book and based the characters on that piece of property. The book was entitled "After Texas Sank".

Finally in 2003, my wife and I were living in Texas. It was February, we were mostly financially embarrassed at that particular time. But more than that, we were bored. Bored with living in Gulf Coast Texas, where you can barely see the sky for all the "East Texas Pines," as mentioned by James McMurtry in his song *Angeline*. We longed for the broad vistas, the lofty peaks, the *rarified air* in Colorado.

So I googled Colorado vacant land. The first piece of property that popped up was a 4 acre plot in NW Fremont County in the region known as South Park. We called the Realtor that had the property listed and asked if it was still available. He said yes, but it would probably be April before it could be shown, as it probably had about 8 foot of snow on it at the time. That was probably the longest 3 months in the history of the earth. It was affordable, and it was empty, and it was a place to spend our summers. We had been visiting Colorado in the summers doing arts and craft shows, living in State Parks and National Forest campgrounds. But here was a place we could light for the weekdays between shows, and hike and explore and maybe even build a summer home, who knows? Anyway, moving forward. Time passed, and we found ourselves winding up a narrow mountain road from the town of Salida, up over the top of Cameron Mountain and then down two miles until a small park emerged into view. Then we rounded the corner, and the parcel we were searching for came into view on the side of a gentle sloping hill with pines and aspen above. We loved it. We bought it immediately.

We went back to Texas, and at the end of May began our show season. Over the next two or three years we built a small outbuilding and explored the area. Then, in 2005, we opened a small business in Salida and moved there for a year. We became involved in the history of the area, especially in the history of where our property was located. You see, in the small park at the foot of our place once lived a town called Whitehorn, a mining camp that lived from 1896 to 1925. It had at one time a population of about a thousand souls. It had all the amenities that any small town of its period would have had - a couple of stores, a café, two hotels, a brothel, a post office, a stage stop, a telegraph office, etc. etc. We walked the town site looking for relics. Oh, yes, I forgot to mention it also had a newspaper, *The Whitehorn News*, which has been archived. We fell in love with that bit of romantic western lore. We studied the area avidly.

In 2013, I developed a condition that prohibited me from living at 9500 feet, (the elevation of our place). So with heavy hearts, we sold our beloved piece of land that was backed into the San Isabel National Forest on two sides, and left Colorado, for what would probably be the last time for me.

In 2016 I decided I was going to bring Whitehorn back to life. In literary form at least. I looked around for four characters who would or who had already fallrn in love with the Colorado High Country, particularly South Park. My first was Marsh Redmon, a Texas Cowboy. Then Sarah Burns, a widow, and Sean Kelly, a young Irishman running away from the law in New York City. And, oh yes, you will love tall, blonde, Hanne Clausen, a young Minnesota prostitute. Together they were to meet and make a home in that world and build a future there. Before the book is even finished, both a prequel and a sequel are already planned in the Authors mind. The scope of the land and the people, have made it mandatory to turn it into a multi-generational saga.

Come, let us go west, young man, young lady, and get a breath of that pure mountain air! Go up high and look around, where everything is down. Go to the land of the *190-Degree Horizon*!

Larry Murley
2018

WHITEHORN

The Buckskin was frisky this morning. The thin air of South Park was chilled. Even though the early morning sun had risen just a bit to the right side of Black Mountain, the air glistened with white crystals that flashed reds and yellows like tiny diamonds someone had hung in the air. As he rode west toward the spot where Willow Creek entered the Park from the side of Cameron Mountain, a figure emerged from the hotel and raised his arm in salute. Marsh returned it. It was George Alexander, the telegraph operator. They had shared some time last evening and couple of drinks at the small saloon in the middle of Whitehorn. The conversation had been varied, but hinged mostly around the Bruce dig. Marsh had worked for several days doing odd jobs, earning but a few dollars from the owners. They were busy men, but seemed to be stressed for some reason. Maybe the assays weren't as good as expected. He shook his head, *Who knows....*

He turned his horse up the trail alongside the creek. About a half mile up

he emerged from the timber into a fairly wide meadow. It was easier going now. His thoughts went back to the Bruce. As he had ridden by, his eye had picked up the sparkle in the sand at the foot of the hill below the mine. It looked promising to him. As he rode, a flock of turkeys beat a hasty retreat toward the timber. He thought about pulling his gun and bringing one down, but decided he needed to keep moving. As he rounded the curve a herd of a dozen or more elk, almost as one, bolted from the meadow and vanished into the timber. There were many elk here. He glanced ahead about a hundred yards; there the trail would top the hill and head down toward Salida. Marsh Redman, stopped at the top of the hill to let his horse breathe for a moment. The two mile climb out of the valley from the little town of Whitehorn was enough to make his horse puff a bit on a good day, but with three feet of good March snow, it was even more so.

Marsh looked ahead. The lofty head of Mt. Antero glistened in the bright sunlight of another Colorado morning. The thin air was bracing and already the sun was

warming things to a point to make his heavy coat uncomfortable. Spring was in the air up here in the Colorado Rockies.

Marsh's thoughts turned to his parents back in the little town of Elgin, Texas. They would have their garden in by now. It was probably one of the best times of the year down there. Flowers were blooming everywhere. The Blue Bonnets and Indian Paint Brushes would start to blanket the rolling hills with contrasts of blue and orange. The grass was turning green, and young calves would be frolicking next to their mom's. Marsh had left home three years ago, hoping to make himself rich as a miner. He had heard of the strike in the little valley above Salida, Colorado, and headed for it almost as soon as reaching the state line. He spent the first summer in a tent just beyond the town on the east side in a small grove of trees. He panned along the little creek than ran down into the valley. He soon found out that the ore here was not in the creek but in the ground itself. He decided then to move over a bit to the north side of the ridge. There, he selected an outcropping of rocks, a ridge of stone that ran like a terrace along the mountainside. He was told that the gold and silver would be on the uphill side of the stones, and so his dig started on there. Since winter was approaching, he dug himself a dugout and built himself a small cabin about 6 foot by 10 foot to protect himself from the severe winters up here at 9500 feet elevation. He was rather proud as he built the entire thing with nothing but an axe. Iron nails were expensive and hard to come by. When finished it gave him room to sleep and eat in and protected him from the cold. Not a place to spend a lot of leisure time in, but Marsh wasn't the type to sit around much anyway. He guessed that mighta come from his old man. His father was a Civil War soldier, and had spent much of the war in the 8th Texas Cavalry, known as Terry's Texas Rangers, till a bullet had stopped his life at the Battle of Bentonville. His mother married about a year after the war to one of his father Jess's best friends and comrade-in-arms. Marsh hung around Texas until his early thirties. He had followed a few cattle drives up the Chisolm Trail when he was 16 or 17 and later, but realized he needed to broaden his horizons before he found himself getting too old.

Cowboys branding a steer, turn of the century

After tying his heavy coat behind his saddle, he kicked around in the leaves, knocking snow from his riding boots and stimulating the blood in his legs. It would be a little chilly until he got down to the levels a quarter mile distant. Marsh remounted and headed down through the thicketed aspens that grew on the downhill side of Cameron Mountain. It was downhill all the way the 14 miles to Salida.

Marsh reflected on the warm bed and a bath that could be had at the rooming house on G Street, a little ways from the river. Most usually one could enjoy a hearty breakfast to start the day right. Ham or bacon or both, and eggs and biscuits with gravy was standard fair, along with numerous jams and jellies. It took him home to Texas every time he sat at the table. And then there was Miss Laura. Oh, my! She just made his heart go flitter flutter! Miss Laura ran a convenience house down near the railroad station by the river. They had met at a general store up on F Street, then once more on the bridge crossing the Arkansas River. It was some months before he actually found out what she really did for a living. He was a bit taken aback, but then, damn, she was such a fine woman. He didn't delude himself though. Although he was quite fond of Laura, he pretty much knew she wasn't the type to settle down with, to raise a family. And he did want that.

As he rounded the first turn of the trail he jerked his horse to a stop. There, in the sandy mud along the trail was a footprint.

Massive and a missing toe, one at least. Above the trail, a large aspen tree was ripped badly at least 10 feet from the ground. Marsh reached and pulled his saddle gun clear and levered a shell. This was all very fresh. The Buckskin was sniffing the air, he smelled it too. Marsh knew instinctively that this was Ol' Mose. Probably the only grizzly left in a hundred miles, maybe in the state. He had eaten half the stock in Fremont County and maybe half a dozen men had disappeared and later been found, torn to shreds. He was a bad bear.

He nudged the pony into a walk and carefully watched all directions for the next hour at least. He had relaxed some when he reached the little open area about two miles from the top of Cameron. A herd of elk, maybe 40 or 50 cows, and a couple of bulls, grazed off to the right of the stage coach road. He kicked the pony into a lope now that he could see a distance around him. He climbed back over the ridge that started leading down to the creek that led into the town of Salida. Up ahead, he saw a couple of mules and two horsemen coming his way. As they approached, he recognized one of the men as Mr. Mills, who worked for Mr. Cole that ran the store in Whitehorn. The men met and greeted each other.

Cole's Grocery, Salida
picture faces west, sometime about 1900

"Howdy Marsh! How's the road up on the hill? Still snowed in?" Mills had a tooth missing, and it gave him a slight whistle when he talked.

"Yes'sir, all th' way to the top of the hill. You boys keep your guns handy, and your eyes open. I'm pretty sure it was Ol' Mose that left his mark up there in the aspen." His eyes were taking in the mule that was bearing a good part of his load, over his withers, seem to be uneasy. Marsh swung down and walked over to him and ran his fingers up under the packs. He pulled out a piece of a dead pine branch about the size of his wrist. It was digging the poor mule on the top of his shoulder. Marsh patted the mule, and rubbed his long ear. The mule thanked him by trying to take a bite out of his arm. *Damn you mule!* Marsh jumped away.

Mills remarked, "Huh, wonder where that came from? I know it wasn't there earlier, probably fell out of a tree or he rubbed it in. He tries to rub his packs off, the damn old asshole. Anyway, Whoee! I shorely don't want to tangle with that old boy! Okay, we gotta keep going. I damned sure want to be in town by nightfall, now that you tole me that."

The string of mules started their upward climb and Marsh turned his sights toward the lower part of the Ute Trail leading into Salida. An hour or so later, he caught the railroad and followed the tracks to the Arkansas River, then down to the foot of the hill near the train station. He crossed the bridge and headed up F Street. A chill had filled the air, and the clouds had spilled over Mt. Antero. It was plain it would snow tonight. He left The Buckskin at the livery stable on H Street near the stage stop. After making sure he was rubbed down and given a scoop of oats and some fresh hay, he patted him on the rump. The horse barely noticed when he left.

Stage Stop, "H" Street & 3rd,
somewhere near the present day Safeway Store, Salida, CO

He pulled his coat around him and headed back toward town and shortly walked into the Denton Hotel. As he was signing in he noticed the name a couple above his own. William Wells, from

Austin, Texas. It sounded vaguely familiar.

After a hot bath and clean clothes, he headed for the dining room. Several people greeted him,

"Hey Marsh, struck it rich yet?"

"Hello Marsh, your lookin' fit!"

"Welcome back to civilization stranger!"

The little Mexican waitress smiled her flirty dark eyes.

"*Como esta, Señor Redman!*" as she swished by with a platter of sizzling t-bones and mounds of mashed potatoes and gravy. She reached out and ran her fingers up his arm as she breezed by. Marsh caught the smell of the food and his taste glands reacted accordingly. The Senorita would possibly be for later.

After dinner Marsh found himself at the bar. He ordered a whiskey and after feeling the relaxing warmth spread over his body, he found a seat in the corner where he could watch the room. He had always enjoyed the actions of others more than becoming the center of attention himself. He thought perhaps it came from being his father's son. His father must have been a very private person. His mother often told him he would seldom talk about himself or his feelings.

Marsh watched as a man dressed in dark clothes with an overcoat stepped inside the bar. His collar was turned up against the night air, his dark flat brimmed hat sat low on his forehead, almost seeming to rest on his shaggy eyebrows. He appeared to be in his late fifties. His manner and bearing suggested he was not a miner, or acquainted with hard labor. He walked to the bar and ordered a drink. The snowflakes that had rested on his hat were fast turning to water and dripping on the sawdust floor. He turned his back to the bar, his dark eyes scanning the room. His eyes met Marsh's, and he walked toward Marsh's table. He stopped a respectable distance away.

"Evening, suh. Mind if I have a seat?" His soft southern voice seemed to have a familiarity to it.

"Free country." Marsh returned. "I'm Marsh Redman."

"Please to meet ya, Mister Redman. I am William Wells, of Mississippi. My father spoke of a man he once knew by the name of Redman, said he rode with the 8th Texas Cavalry."

"That could have been my father, he rode with them."

"If he was, then it is my honor to meet ya, suh. He was a brave man. He saved my daddies life during the Atlanta campaign. May I call ya Marsh?"

Marsh nodded to the positive.

"Call me Will, if it's agreeable to ya Marsh. Are you a resident of these here parts?"

"I have a small claim up at Whitehorn. Trying my hand at mining."

"Well, I hope that is working out for ya." The older man smiled.

"Well, I ain't planning on buying my own railroad car to travel in quite yet." Marsh replied. "How about you? You don't resemble a miner much, if I might be so bold."

Will grinned. "Naw. One of the mining companies up to Leadville has hired me for security. I'm only here for the night. I'm catching the train up there come morning."

The two men sat and conversed for a couple of hours. Their conversation varied from cowboying to families and places they had been. They had both worked as drovers with the herds of cattle moving north from Texas, but never the same drive. Still, they seemed to have a common bond. Sometime before midnight they shook hands and each went to their respective rooms.

Stepping out onto 1st Street next morning, Marsh was thinking it was one of those blue sky mornings so typical in the Rockies. Not a cloud in the sky, and the air so sharp it cooled the lungs. The sun was already warming the grass across the street. No traces, almost, of last night's light snow. He looked across F Street at the row of cribs for the girls who entertained the travelers and railroad men who visited the small town of Salida. Later, he would walk down and see Miss Laura. He would welcome some female company. Off in the distance the shrill whistle of an inbound locomotive cut the early morning air. He could hear the chug of the engine, pulling the grade up along the canyon of the Arkansas River from Canon City and points east. He had ridden alongside those tracks a few years ago when he first came to the area. He knew of no more beautiful place than that canyon. He was brought back to moment by a yell from across the street.

"Hey Marsh! Ya gotta minute?"

He nodded and walked across the street. It was Bob Bennett. Bob had a small claim up at Whitehorn as well.

"This train coming in has 250 cows on it, headed up over into the San Luis Valley. Feller is offering ten dollars each for 5 riders to drive them over. Ya game?"

"Hell yes!" was Marsh's reply. Marsh walked to the livery stable. The little buckskin mustang pony nickered his recognition as Marsh walked through the door. "Hope you got your relaxation over. You are going to have to work today, my friend." He patted his horse and pulled the apple he had swiped off the breakfast table that morning, cut it into quarters with his sheath knife and fed them to the anxious pony, one at a time. Then he brushed the animal thoroughly before saddling and bridling. He loped back to the railroad yard across the Arkansas where he spied Bob and an older man with a grey beard and goatee. The old man wore a Spanish style flat brimmed hat. His name was Trujillo. His family had been one of the original settler's way, way back in the late 1700's. They had been successful, but had endured much persecution from Anglo ranchers trying to steal their land. As Marsh rode up, the older man spoke.

"Buenos dias, Señor Marsh! Are you here to help us today?"

"Sí, Señor Trujillo, por favor, si me necesita!"

"Bueno. If you would, head up the drive and take them as far as possible today. I realize we are getting a slow start."

"We can probably get about where the railroad heads over Marshall Pass. We can bed them there tonight and take them over tomorrow."

"Bueno, amigo. You do it."

By late morning they had the impatient cows headed up the trail toward Poncha Pass. They were almost all Hereford heifers, with the exception of a couple of big Longhorn bulls. It seemed Señor Trujillo was going to do a bit of breeding. The Hereford produced more beef, but weren't as tough as the Longhorns. The drive went easy the six or seven miles up to the foot of the pass. They waited until a train came down before turning south and up the hill. The Little Arkansas was a great little stream alongside them with plenty of water for the thirsty cattle to drink. The spring grass hadn't really gotten started yet, so the push was easy.

It was nigh onto dark before they pushed them up above the narrow canyon that headed out toward Marshall Pass. They drank, and were content to graze on the grasses around the creek. A couple of the drivers volunteered for first shift and the rest settled down to have a dinner. Señor Trujillo had one of his ranch hand/cook meet them and already had food ready when the small herd arrived. The men finished dinner and proceeded to get acquainted. Marsh knew a couple or three, but the two strangers who sat together a bit off from the rest seemed a bit aloof. They had performed well during the afternoon drive. Marsh decided he needed to have a talk with them. He got up from his rock and walked over and introduced himself to them. One of the young fellows stood up and spoke.

"Marsh, you don't recognize us do ya? My brother Billy here said you didn't this afternoon. I am Tim Madison. We made a drive up from Texas 'bout five years ago. We were purty wet behind the ears back then."

Marsh was a bit taken aback. "Crap, Tim, I'm real sorry. I can see ya now. You boys weren't sporting chin hair back then. Billy, how are you? How's yer Pa?"

Billy looked down quickly, and Tim turned his face away. He seemed to choke for a moment.

"Marsh, Pa died. Then Ma died a few days after. Folks said she was broken hearted and just didn't want to live without him."

"Aw, boys, that is too bad, I am so sorry. Your Pa was a fine man, and your Ma was an angel. Did your Pa just fall sick? He was gettin' on up in years."

"Naw," Tim answered, "He was fine. He was out moving some cows out the woods down there at their place near Richmond when a big old wild boar came chargin' out of the brush. He spooked the horse and it threw Pa, and the boar gored him good. Coupl'a hands from the place next door saw the whole thing."

"They shot the hawg!" Billy chimed in.

"Worst thing that could have happened to Pa. He told stories about hawgs eatin' wounded soldiers at Shiloh, it was his worst nightmare."

"The boys said he didn't move after he hit the ground so maybe he didn't know. 'Least, that's what we hoped."

The men moved a little closer to the fire. It was a cold evening, but Marsh took the time and chatted with Billy and Tim for some time. Then they all turned in for the night. Next morning after breakfast they continued on to the top of Poncha Pass and over into the beautiful San Luis Valley. By early afternoon the lofty peaks of the Sangre De Cristo's towered over them to the east. Far to the southwest the snowcapped peaks of the San Juan's showed their splendor. Even from almost a hundred miles away, they were impressive.

Marsh yelled at Tim. "Hey, Tim! Did you know the Rio Grande starts down south there, little less than hundred miles?"

"You're jokin', really?"

"Nosiree. It does."

"Well, I'll be damned. Always wondered where it came from. I'll haft'a tell Billy when he catches up."

Down the road ahead Marsh could see the community of Villa Grove. It was to be the terminus of the trail drive. At this point Señor Trujillo's hands would take over and take the herd to their pastures farther south. As they pushed the little herd through town, Marsh took notice of some riders sitting in a bunch on the porch of a saloon. They were giving the herd some real hateful looks. He wondered if they were some of the boys that had been set on taking the Trujillo's ranches away from him. *Best not to get drawn into something not my business.* Señor Trujillo rode up and passed Marsh a twenty dollar gold piece.

"Muy gracias mi amigo! Bueno." He smiled and rode by the other riders. As he paid each of them for their work, they peeled off from the herd and the vaqueros took their places.

Marsh and the boys turned and headed back to Salida. It was late by the time they hit the top of Poncha Pass. The sun had dropped below the mountain, and the Sangre De Christos were lit up with the evenings last rays, making the snowcapped peaks look as if they were capped with gold and copper.

The boys rode slow down the pass for the first hour or so. As the moon started to rise, the valley below lit up from the reflected light. By the time they reached Salida, it was so bright one could almost have read a newspaper by its light. They headed for the saloon on Second Street. Even at near midnight it was alive and busy. As they entered, Marsh recognized some of the miners from Whitehorn. Two of them were employed at the Bruce Mine. They had found a vein of silver at the Bruce, down at about 140 feet and the vein was about 40 inches wide. The owners had run out of money and were searching for investors. *So that was why the owners had been so glum, money problems.* Marsh had never asked, but it reinforced his resolve to get out of mining business. *But how?* Jobs were scarce, at least good ones. Money was scarce at that time, too. There had been a run on some of the banks, and they weren't having much luck the last he had heard.

July 4th, 1898. Marsh sat on the spiny ridge just on the south east side looking down on the small town of Whitehorn. Everyone, at least everyone that could, had taken the day off. Children ran up and down the dusty streets, waving tiny American Flags. A war was on. *The Lusitania* had been sunk. Off to the right, a squad of men with rifles at shoulder marched, drilling for the time they would be called into service. The Whitehorn Rifles they called themselves. Earlier that morning they had held shooting practice. Marsh sighed. This truly was a beautiful place to live. On a clear day, if one rode to the top of one of the ridges around the town and looked to the east and just a bit north, you could see Pikes Peak, almost a hundred miles distant. A slight breeze passed through. The aspens leaves shimmered and chattered to each other. Or at least they had always seemed to be chatting. He leaned back against the granite boulder and shuffled his seat into a more comfortable position. Back to his right, on the same ridge, about 75 yards or so above the Bruce Mine, a small hastily built cabin had been erected and was surrounded by several shallow digs. He smiled. Seems like owner got tired a lot, and quit often. Marsh didn't blame him. His place was at about 94 or 9500 feet elevation. The air was quite rare up here. The man had just moments before tossed his spade over on his tailings bank and gone back inside the cabin.

Marsh leaned back against the huge chunk of boulder behind him just in time to look up and catch the last bit of conversation between the aspens above him as a breeze passed through. He had decided that he didn't like the prospecting thing. He had never minded hard work. He liked being outdoors, but the whole idea of digging up dirt and busting rocks to maybe chance finding a piece of gold or silver, just seemed to be a little out of his character.

He had ridden out early that morning to the north east of town toward Black Mountain. He stopped at Badger Creek and let The Buckskin drink. Just a ways back he had passed an overhanging cliff.

Even years later it was easy to see that the Utes and Arapahos had used it to drive Buffalo over to slaughter their winters cache. This place had once harbored thousands of the shaggy creatures, but now they were gone. It seems that Americans had to change the face of the earth wherever they went. The buffalo and the Indians seemed to go together, and they perished together. All except those poor creatures living in squalor on reservations totally lost from their way of life....

As he rode, he watched the grasses. This is excellent cow country, maybe he should try for some land. Surely it was not all taken. He had been around cattle since he was a pup, it was his second nature.

He skirted the eastern flank of Black Mountain, circling it around to the north. The Buckskin snorted and pulled up short, searching the dark shadows of trees on its north side, nostrils flared and ears up. Marsh had ridden the little mustang too many miles to not trust his judgement. He pulled his binoculars out of his saddlebag and searched the trees above him.

Nothing. He squeezed his knees together, and The Buckskin moved on slowly, still nervous. A couple of minutes later, there in the soft dirt, was a very large bear print. Then another above, then one with the missing toe. Ol' Mose! Shit, now he was worried. He glanced back along his trail, didn't want that bruin sneaking up behind him. He nudged his horse down off the skirt of the mountain toward open country, heading back southwest toward Whitehorn. He kept watching his back trail for some time after recrossing Badger Creek and heading up over the ridge. Finally he pulled The Buckskin up and dismounted, allowing her to graze as he sat on the rocks and watched the street life in Whitehorn. Tomorrow he was headed out to Fairplay. The stage had brought a letter from William Wells, asking if he could to meet him there on the 6th as he would be there on business. He was curious; it was a long ride, maybe 50 miles or so, maybe more. But then, he had not been to the little mining town, but had heard much of it. Besides, it would be a change of scenery.

Both pictures turn of the Century, Whitehorn, CO.
Bottom believed to be on a July 4th

The next morning early, Marsh saddled and rode down into Whitehorn to the Miner's Café on the ground floor of the hotel closest to the stage stop. He ordered ham and eggs over medium, biscuits and gravy, and some jam and coffee. He was waiting for the food when in came two young men. They were dressed in coarse work clothes and a kinda slouch caps. They looked at Marsh, then talked to each other for a moment, as if trying to make a decision. They finally walked over to Marsh's table.

"Sir, is your name Redman?"

"Depends on whose asking" Marsh answered.

"Oh, pardon me sir, I am Arnie Johannson. This my brother, Jon."

Marsh motioned for them to sit.

"Sir, we were told in Salida that you were interested in selling your claim."

"Yeah, I suppose so. I am not real inclined to that type of work, it seems."

"Would you take $200 dollars for it?"

"I was kinda lookin' at $300."

"Mr. Redmon, all we have is $275, but we really need to keep $25 of it for some food and supplies."

"Ok, deal. Two-fifty it is. But I am on my way out for a few days. We will have to go get the paperwork done when I get back, if that is acceptable. Go ahead and you can use the little cabin."

"Aww, thank ye Sir. You are too kind." Can we shake hands on it?" Marsh extended his hand to both men. It was a done deal.

Marsh had continued to consume his breakfast as they talked, anxious to get on his way. The sky back over the general direction of Suckerville Springs was just turning a rosy pink and he had a long ride ahead. He arose and shook hands with the two men. As they turned to head for the door, the door burst open and two men entered carrying a third, his leg was all bloody, his clothing torn, and he was moaning and crying. The two placed him on a long table in the center of the room. Someone was sent to get the doctor. Marsh got a good look at the man's leg. It was laid open to the bone from just below the knee in two separate straight lines down to the ankle. His guess was an animal of some sorts. One of the men that had carried him in backed away from the table and was standing next to Marsh. Marsh leaned over and asked what happened.

"Me and Bob was coming over from Turret by the low road over cross there," pointing at the hill on the west side of the park where Whitehorn set, "when we heard this guy yowling at the top of his lungs. We topped this ridge and looked down and saw this guy up a fairly large aspen tree, just a hangin' on for dear life! And down at the bottom was the biggest damn bear I ever saw in my whole life! He was a shakin' that tree and clawin' at it, for all he was worth. Bob, there, he pulled his scatter gun out of his saddle boot and pointed into the air and blasted off a load, an' the old bear stopped and went down on all fours and looked up at us. Bob gave him another blast. Well, he growled and turned off and headed north kinda in the general direction of Black Mountain."

"Shit, and I gotta head that way myself." Marsh replied.

"Well, we got him down outta the tree and put him onto Bob's horse and we headed this a way as fast as we could. He is in some kinda pain. His horse got lucky and got away after throwin' him. He shinnied up that tree but the old bear got one swipe at him a'fore he got high enough. It was Ol' Mose for sure, had a track with that missing toe."

"Damn, I need to be ridin' right now! Gotta be in Fairplay day after tomorrow." Marsh filed the information away about where Mose was last seen and his direction of travel. He took one last look at the man on the table and resolved that he would keep both eyes open all day today.

Marsh topped the little saddle in the hill on the northeast side of Whitehorn. Just to the right, more to the east was Black Mountain, He thought to himself *If I hold to the left of the Mountain and follow the stagecoach trail to Hartsel, that would be my best bet.* Riding across the hills he could see Badger Creek where it drifted down from the hills.

He was thinking about it when the Buckskin seemed to shy to the right a bit.

41

He slid off his horse. There was what he first took for a badger hole or maybe a coyote den. But no, it was bigger. Big enough to almost crawl into. He leaned down to take a look, first glancing around to make sure Mose wasn't sneaking up on him. The morning sun lit up the inside of the cave and he could see bones of all sorts. He didn't recognize many of them. A couple of the skulls looked a bit like small horses, but surely not. He shook his head and climbed on his horse and headed on toward the creek, still puzzling over the strange bones. He made a mental note to investigate later. Fifteen minutes later he rode into the yard of a dugout cabin on the north side of Badger Creek.

"Hello, anybody home?"

A few minutes later a skinny woman appeared in short doorway.

"Howdy Ma'am, your husband home?"

"Ain't got no husband. My Pa lit out this morning to go to Trump ta get ta mail. 'Spect he won't get back here 'till later."

"I see. This your Pa's place here?"

"Naw, this's part of the IM ranch."

"I see. Well, thank you for your help. I'll be on my way now."

Marsh shifted his weight to the right, and The Buckskin stepped out toward the bank of Badger Creek and loped off over the rolling hills. He felt like he should have told her about Mose, but she probably knows about him, living out here. For the next hour or so he kept a wary eye. As he slowly put Black Mountain in the distance he started to breathe easier. He headed down into a little valley surrounded by black cluster of trees and aspen groves to let The Buckskin get a drink. When suddenly the horse stopped and snorted loudly. An instant later a brown colored bear nosed its way up out of the creek. Marsh had his saddle gun out and was bringing it up when he realized it was just a big cinnamon bear, not a grizz. The bear saw him and immediately loped off to the east towards Black Mountain. Marsh grinned, *I wouldn't go up there, sir, you might get your ass in trouble.*

Later he came across the Stage Trail and started following it. It was getting dark when he saw the town of Hartsel. After taking a room and stabling his horse for the night, Marsh found the Café and settled down for a meal. He had not eaten much all day, and the roast beef and vegetables really hit the spot. The lady who had brought his food poured him a last cup of coffee and asked "You going to the springs and soak out some of the saddle soreness?"

"What springs?" Marsh replied.

"Why, just across the street there is a wonderful hot springs. The Indian people have come here to use it for as long as they remember."

"Hmm, might just have to investigate that."

After coffee he strolled across the narrow road and headed toward the springs. A young man met him at the building.

"Would you care to bathe, Sir?" he asked.

"That I might do"

He was handed a robe and a towel and a fence off area was pointed out. After removing his clothing he made his way to the pool. He lowered his body into the water. *Cripes!* He hoped his skin stayed on!

Another figure emerged from the shadows.

"Pretty hot, huh?"

"Yes Sir, indeed."

The two men sat and talked as the hot mineral water relaxed muscles and soothed their minds. The stranger remarked, "If you get down in the San Luis Valley, over at the foot of the Sangre de Christos about 20 miles down, there is another series of springs that come down off the mountain. About four of them if I remember correctly. They are not quite as hot as these, though."

Marsh said "Yes, I visited those once several years ago. Found them by accident, late one evening. I wonder what causes these?"

"Comes from deep underground, volcanic I suspect. I got all shot up at Chickamauga in '63. These springs are about the only things that keeps me at ease. I am much grateful for them."

"My respect for you, Sir. My daddy was at Chickamauga."

"Which side, son?"

"He was Confederate. Texas Cavalry!"

"I was a Yankee. Michigan Infantry. Your Paw and his boys wailed the tar outta' us. *MY* respect goes to them. As I have had time to think on it, they was just trying to defend their land and families. I would had done the same. It was a black time for our country." The stranger shook his head.

"Indeed it was, Sir. And my daddy never held any grudges for you boys either, said you were a brave lot. So my mom told me. He passed at North Carolina, never made it home. His last letter to my momma said a lot of things like you just remarked."

"God Bless him, young man. And may God Bless you and your momma."

"Thank you, Sir. And I bid you a good evening. If I don't get out of here they are going to have to carry me out in a tub. I am going to be melted entirely."

The older man snorted.

Marsh awoke the next morning feeling totally renewed. He silently resolved to watch for more hot springs. He could get used to them easily. After breakfast he came out to find The Buckskin brushed and saddled and tied to the hitching post. He checked the girth, and did a walk around, picked up his horse feet and found they had been picked clean. He swung into the saddle and rode around to the stable. A young man, obviously part Indian, was loading horse dung into a wheelbarrow.

"You take care of my horse?" Marsh questioned.

"Si."

Marsh flipped him a half dollar, "Thank you, I appreciate it."

The young man nodded and said "Gracias, señor!"

The ride to Fairplay was less than exciting. He waded a stream a couple of times that he later found out was the beginnings of the South Platte River, and he found an old fort of sort. He made a mental note to himself to inquire about it at some point.

It was just after noon when he tied his horse and walked into the small restaurant. At a table sat a woman and two men. One of the men jumped to his feet. Marsh recognized him as William Wells. He made his way to Marsh, his hand outstretched.

"Marsh, so good to see you. I would like you to meet Mrs. Sarah Burns, my boss. And this is Clinton Markam. Folks, this is Marsh Redman."

As the introductions went around, Marsh thought *Your boss... how interesting*. She didn't seem like a mining tycoon. He kept silent, but found himself strangely attracted to the lady. Dressed in riding clothes and a big hat, something about her bespoke confidence and...and... what was it? Something he couldn't put words to. And what was his roll, why was he here? *Ok, Marsh, just shut up and listen.*

William sat forward in his chair, his elbows on the table, his eyes intense under the dark brows.

"Marsh, Mrs. Burns' holdings have prospered. But knowing how mining works, I have advised her to diversify, and one of my ideas is to start up a ranch. And I would like to see it done here in South Park. I would kinda like to see you do it, and ramrod it. With Mrs. Burns blessing, of course."

"Well, that is a great idea! I have ridden the length of this valley in the last two day, and my mind has been full of ideas about ranching up here. It supported countless buffalo for hundreds of years. What is my part though? Just a foreman or such?"

"No, Sir. I was thinking maybe more of a stake partner. It gives you more incentive that way."

"Yes." Marsh replied without hesitation. He turned to Sarah. "Mrs. Burns, if you will have me, I will give you every effort."

"William, Marsh, this has been a dream since I was a small girl in California! Yes, let's do it! I am totally in favor! What can I do?"

The next morning, after breakfast, William was busy tending to the various details; getting funds transferred to a bank in Fairplay, checking Park County Land records. Clinton had left and headed back over Mosquito Pass to California gulch. Marsh was surprised when he suddenly found out Mrs. Burns - Sarah, she insisted he call her - was going to accompany him on a land search. Well, that was just fine. He hoped she was able to take the hours in the saddle. But she seemed a capable woman.

Marsh headed down to the livery stable. They needed supplies, a tent or maybe two, a pack horse, or mule, cooking gear.

As he walked around the corner, a shrill whinny greeted him. The Buckskin was rested and ready. Marsh rubbed his nose, and slipped a half apple into his lips.

"Hang loose, ol' son. You can rest today I expect."

He asked the stable man if he knew which horse belonged to Mrs. Burns. A big black was pointed out. Fine animal, he thought. He wanted to make sure she was mounted properly. He asked if a pack animal was available and was referred to a big mule over in the corner of the corral. Marsh looked him over, dropped a lead rope around his neck and turned to walk. The mule followed obediently.

"Give him a good feed and rub down, and check his feet. Do what is necessary to make him fit for a prolonged trail, and find him a pack saddle. We'll take him." Marsh remarked.

"Ye can't go wrong. He is a good old mule. He rides well, I'm told. Answers to name of Jed." the livery attendant remarked. "We will have him ready for tomorrow morning, if you need. I'll put him in a stall and give him a bit of grain."

Livery stable, Fairplay, CO

The next stop was the mercantile store. He went around picking out needed items; a pot for coffee, couple of frying pans, a cast iron pot, some iron work for cooking, a couple of lanterns. He asked the proprietor if he had a couple of small tents, when from behind him a voice interrupted.

"Marsh, I believe we could share a tent to cut down on baggage."

He turned to find Sarah Burns looking up at him. He studied her for a moment before answering.

"Miss Sarah, I would not presume to impose myself on your privacy. And I am concerned with a perception of sullying your reputation, should someone take notice."

"Marsh, I appreciate your concern, but we are going to spend a lot of time alone, just the two of us. So let's not concern ourselves with image. We can work it out without having two tents to put up and take down every day."

Marsh smiled, "Miss Burns, you are the boss. One tent it is."

It was then the proprietor remarked "Good thing, we only have one at the moment. But it is large enough to make you both comfortable."

The three of them laughed. Marsh asked, "Miss Burns, have you had any training with firearms? This is still a wild enough country that one should arm themselves."

Sarah looked at him, "Yes, I was taught at an early age to shoot, and bagged my first deer at sixteen. I have shot a handgun, but I much prefer a rifle."

Marsh turned to the storekeeper, and asked if he help Sarah pick out proper firearms and a knife. After some haggling and discussion, Sarah settled on a Winchester 44-40 and Colt .38 caliber revolver, and a good skinning knife complete with holsters and carrying gear. A bit more shopping brought them to the end of their quest. The proprietor agreed to have everything delivered to their hotel that afternoon.

When they headed back to the hotel they both had seemed to relax and conversation had become a bit easier. They spent the afternoon planning their trip. Their anticipation ran high. Sarah had little idea where to start. The selection of the direction to proceed was left to Marsh's discretion.

The next morning found the duo loaded with supplies and mounted, their horses pointed in a northeasterly direction. Marsh knew that most of the northern section of South Park had been settled earlier, even as early as the 1860's.

Ranching along Tarryall Creek back then had been fraught with dangers for the early settlers. Indians, both Ute and Comanche, had raided. And then there were the Mexican banditos that were every bit as savage as the Indians. But Marsh figured to give his boss a through tour of the big valley that was seated high up in the Colorado Rockies.

It was afternoon when they crossed over Red Hill. Sarah was constantly admiring the sculptured hillsides that were bare of timber, green with grass, and appeared to have been landscaped, with all the fallen limbs and underbrush removed. As they rode, she was taking notes and writing little snippets as they rode casually along. They had no reason to hurry.

They made their first camp that evening along Tarryall Creek, south of Jefferson.

Sarah made herself helpful setting up camp and helping with the tent. Then she noticed that the cooking fire just seemed to appear, all complete. And before she knew it, food was simmering in the big cook pot. She smiled at Marsh.

"Mr. Redman, it is plain to see that is not the first time you set up a camp!"

Marsh looked at her with a scowl. "I am going to refer to you as Miss Burns, if you continue with this Mr. Redman crap. The air is too refined up here to waste breathing on unnecessary words." His scowl faded into a grin. God, she was so pretty! She had faded into a sad face when he made his remark, now the smile returned.

"Yes sir. Please forgive the formality, it won't happen again, sir!" Now she smiled sweetly. "Marsh, you seem quite familiar with setting a grand camp, is there a story about that?"

Marsh leaned back against his saddle. He took the match stick he had been chewing and tossed it into the fire. "Yes, I went up the trail when I was just a bit wet behind the ears. Sixteen or so. Did several drives. One thing I had to do sometimes was help the cook set up camp. The first two drives I went on for Mr. Saunders, he was from down below Bastrop. He had a cook, a big black man, everyone called him 'Cleaver Ike'."

56

Sarah interrupted, "Cleaver Ike?"

"Yes'm. He could take a steer and in just a few minutes have the whole thing divided up and prepared for meals with what was left salted down and put away for later use. That big ol' meat cleaver was like magic. One night we had some Osage braves try to get into camp for some mischief, Ike grabbed his cleaver, killed 2 outright, then threw it about twenty paces at one who was running away and stuck it square in the back of his head."

"Owie," Sarah grimaced, "I am not sure I was ready for that. But go ahead, I guess you must have had some close calls doing that for a living."

"Sorry about that Ma'am, I probably shouldn't have been so blunt, but that was just the way I remembered it."

"That's ok, Marsh. I don't want you to spare the details at all. If I am going to write about this place and the people who have built it, I want the whole truth, and not some white-washed glob of cow hockey. And you may also drop the Ma'am, makes me feel old. I know I am a widow,

but I am a young widow." She smiled
again, one of those smiles that just melted
his insides. Lordy, this trip might get just
a bit tedious in the days to come. He
sighed. But he wouldn't have missed it for
nothing.

Leadville

Sarah stood looking off to the southwest. A herd of elk grazed in the distance. She could see the stagecoach bouncing along the rutted road headed for the town of Leadville behind her. Maybe she should get on it and head to Missouri to her parents. Tears came to her eyes. She looked down at her husband Jess's grave at her feet. What was she to do now? Leadville wasn't a safe place for a young, unattached woman to be in 1898. Rosie, her friend, clasped her arm.

"Sarah, hon, we need to get you home. There is a chill, and you aren't dressed for it. Besides, Mr. Martins, the city Attorney, wants to speak with you."

"Today?" she answered.

Rosie nodded yes.

The short ride passed quickly. She seemed chilled as she reached her house on Poplar Street just off 7th, down from the church. She had left just a short hour or so ago for her husband's funeral services. A buggy was drawn up out front, with two men sitting wrapped in a blanket. The temperature was starting to slide down as the sun lowered in the spring sky.

"Good Afternoon, Mrs. Charles. My deepest condolences, I am so sorry to hear of your loss. I know it is a difficult time, but it is very important I speak with you now."

"Of course, Mr. Martins. You and the other gentlemen, please, come inside. It is bound to be much warmer than out here."

The other gentleman sprang from his buggy to quickly assist Sarah in getting down from her carriage. His warm blue eyes smiled as he held her arm, and a soft southern drawl whispered "There you go, young lady." He bowed, removing his wide brimmed hat.

Inside, in front of a crackling fireplace, jackets were removed and soon Rosie had prepared tea and some ginger cookies for the guests. Mr. Martins leaned forward in his chair.

"Mrs. Charles, firstly, thank you for your warm hospitality on such a trying day for you. I will be as brief as possible, and leave you to rest from your ordeal. Although I believe what I am to tell you is going to effect your thinking somewhat."

"Indeed, you are welcome," Sarah replied. "I apologize for the humble repast. I have been forced to serve you, but time was short. Please, continue. I am curious to know what is so important to bring you out."

Mr. Martins removed a folded sheet of paper from his inside jacket pocket. "Mrs. Charles, your husband was playing cards the night of his demise. There were several onlookers present, one of them was myself. So I was witness to all of this. This piece of paper, is the deed to a mine back east of town a ways. The evening of the game, its owner wagered it at the table. Well, he lost. As well as another player, who was the one who killed your husband. The next day the claim struck a rich vein of silver....very rich. I not only have that but this as well." He handed her an envelope. She opened it. Inside was a stack of money about a half inch thick. She looked up questioning with her eyes, her voice refused to work.

Mr. Martin spoke, "Mrs. Charles, there is well over $5,000 in that envelope. It was the winnings from the table, including the poor losers. It is all yours now. Now, Mr. Wells here has something to add."

"Mrs. Charles, I was hired just a short time ago as a sort of a security and foreman for the said mine you just inherited. I was the one who brought the news of the strike to Mr. Martins. I would like to offer my services to you. I would be honored to continue to operate the mine, under your direction, of course." Then there was that flash of eyes and the warm smile.

Sarah breathed a deep breath. "Mr. Martins, Mr. Wells, I am at a loss of words! I'm afraid this is all just a bit much to process. I don't believe I can comment, other than to express my warmest appreciation for all this. Would it be convenient to meet at your office tomorrow, to further discuss this? Mr. Wells, I would like you to be there as well.

You seem a sincere person, and if you are to continue in your position, we have much to discuss."

The next morning Sarah walked down to the street where a carriage sat waiting. She was assisted to her seat by the driver, and shortly was sitting in Mr. Martin's office across from the attorney. Mr. Wells sat to her right, leaning forward in his chair, intent on what might come from the lawyer. In detail her holdings were laid out, various deeds and claim papers were set before her for signing. She set back and looked at Mr. Martins.

"Sir, I wish I might revert back to my maiden name. Myself and my late husband have no issue, and indeed, he has no family. His parents have long since gone on to their reward, and his last remaining sister perished last fall from a fever. So I would like to have this all in my maiden name, which is Burns. Would that be a problem?"

"I would have to check on the legality of that, Madam. But I think it can be done. I will get back with you. Meanwhile, sign the papers with your married name to settle the transactions. We will see about it later. You can, of course, use whichever name you choose."

"Thank you, Mr. Martins. Now, Mr. Wells, we need to negotiate your salary and your responsibilities, if you wish to remain. If you would, relate to me what you might be willing to take on as your duties. And in a few months, when the weather abates a bit, I would like to take a trip and visit my new holdings."

The men smiled. After the business of the day was settled, Sarah returned home and sat down to write her brother and sister. She had so much to tell them.

Sarah had sorted through the various riding habits at the Mercantile in downtown Leadville. She liked several, but was not happy with the idea of riding sidesaddle for the next several days while overlooking her mining interests. Her overseer, Mr. Wells, had literally turned her holdings into a very lucrative business. He was very wise man, and a hard worker. She had decided early on to make it worth his while. Instead of paying him a wage, she had Mr. Martins make him a minor partner, so that as it all grew so would his wealth grow as well. Now, at 27 years old, she was fast becoming a person of means.

"Grrrrrr," she growled, as she picked through the limited selection of clothing.

"Madame, may I be of assistance?" the tall, slender lady from behind the counter called. The lady walked to Sarah's side.

"Well, I am going to be in a saddle for several days, and the idea of sitting side saddle in rough country in a dress just doesn't sound comfortable or safe really." Sara replied. "Back on the farm growing up I would just jump on like the boys, although momma would just get all over me for it."

The lady smiled, "I understand. Here, let me show you something that I do when my husband and I go riding or when I join him to hunt an elk in the fall." She led Sarah around to the men's clothing. She selected a pair of men's trousers, a course riding skirt that was split, and a buckskin jacket. "Here step into the changing room and try these on."

Sara emerged minutes later. She stepped in front of the tall mirror. Looking back at her, she saw a tall young lady, her hair dark and wavy, falling a bit around her face. Her face she thought a bit long. Her eyes slightly far apart, full lips, a strong chin, she got that from her father. Her slender long legged, high-breasted figure, well, that was from her beautiful mother. She gasped. She would have hardly recognized herself. She completed the outfit with a wide belt to gather the buckskin jacket around her, a pair of tall riding boots and a flat crowned, wide brimmed hat. She thought to herself, *Mr. Wells is going to be surprised!* It was just a short walk back to their office.

She stepped inside the office. His back still turned, Mr. Wells called out.

"May I be of service?"

He turned to face her, and she couldn't help but laugh as the expression of astonishment and recognition both coincided on his face.

"Well Mrs. Burns! I do declare, I didn't recognize you! May I say, your choice of attire is both quite becoming, and quite sensible in the same breath."

"Thank you, Mr. Wells. I simply could not abide wearing a dress for a trip such as we are to embark upon. I also would prefer a regular saddle as well. Do you have any objections to this?"

"No Ma'am, I do not. Many of the ladies back home in Mississippi rode astride. And for some of the country we will be in, it is a sensible thing."

"Then I will be ready at daybreak tomorrow. I wish you a good evening, Mr. Wells."

"And the same to you, Mrs. Burns!"

The next morning Sarah finished dressing, walked out her door and down the steps to a waiting William and another man, both dressed in jeans and boots and large wide brimmed hats.

"Mrs. Burns, I would like you to meet Clinton. He will be riding with us this morning, at least part way."

"Good morning, Clinton. Nice to meet you."

Clinton mumbled something and touched the brim of his hat, smiling briefly. Sarah stuck the toe of her riding boot in the stirrup, then taking a little hop she swung up on the big black gelding. It was a long step, as he stood a bit over 16 hands. As soon as her foot connected with the other stirrup and her bottom settled into the saddle, the black was ready to go. Not disobedient or anything of the sort, but she could tell he just came on duty. She smiled. *This is going to be a good day.* Sure thing, he had stood patiently as William tied her bags on behind her saddle. But as he straddled the bay he was riding, The Black was stepping out at the lead. Nobody was gonna be ahead of him. She laughed.

"William, did this racehorse have a name? That I might call him back, case he gets away."

Clinton called forward, "Yes Ma'am. His name is Bolt, like lightning bolt. Cause he is so quick. But never worry, he is a solid, smart horse, not prone to shying from anything. And I'll give you a silver dollar if we get to the end of the road and you say you are tired. I thought you might like him. You probably don't remember, but I used to get horses for you and your husband when you needed to ride."

"Oh, please excuse me, Clinton, I do remember you now! It's just the last little while has been rather....."

"It's awright ma'am. I understand. You've had pretty good plateful of late."

Sarah nodded. The horses were ready to go in the crisp morning air and in no time they were winding along up a narrow canyon trail. No one talked much. It was a bit of a climb, so Sarah gave Bolt his head. The big black horse lowered his head and picked his way up through the rocky trail. Her mines were in the Dyer Mountains, Mt. Sherman area. It was noon when they reached the first mine. After looking at ore samples and taking a bit of a tour inside one of the digs, Sarah sat down on the porch of a little cabin near the mine. The men had gone up to the higher dig, but had told her it was ok to wait. She took her bags off Bolt and opened one of them.

In it was a package containing two biscuits and ham and scrambled egg, and a cinnamon roll. Sarah sat and looked down the valley. This was a rare occasion. She munched her biscuits and ham and washed it down with water from her canteen. How beautiful it was, as if heaven had stored all the beauty in the world here for further building. The air thin, with a fragrant mix that would drive a New York perfumer mad with envy. The sun high in the sky penetrated your skin with tiny spears of heat that were difficult to feel because of the coolness about you. Along the rocks were larkspur and paint brush, and little wisps of yellow arnica flowers. Lower down great clusters of aspen followed the little pretend streams that held no water, except, just occasionally. There were stands of tall conifers, lodge pole pine, Douglas fir, and a few Blue Spruce sprinkled in for color. She was lost in time! She wondered, *How many people in America will ever be able to see this, to smell the air, to experience the elation, how many will ever know that it exists? The trails are hard, making it difficult to reach these places. It takes time and money and effort.* She reached inside her jacket and pulled out a folded paper, worn thin with creases and scuffs.

It read, "The writer's pen poised above the paper. It was a keyboard of black and white. He lowered his pen, and as it connected, music flowed onto the page, until the air was filled with sound that drifted into the air, becoming an easel, and the notes brushstrokes that painted a portrait, expressing pain and pleasure, joy and despair. Thoughts that would at a later time be given to debate, or for lecture by a teacher to inspire the yet unlearned."

She had woke from a dream many years ago with this thought in her mind, and had arisen from her bed on a cold winter night and gone to her desk and written it down. She didn't know why, but she felt she had to do it. She had taken it out and read it many times. Now she knew why. She was to become a writer, and tell these stories and describe this wonderful place. She had money now, and security. It was time to give back.

William and Clinton rode up and dismounted.

"Sarah, are you enjoying the day?"

She smiled, "I have been inspired!"

Will laughed, "This is my third trip to the Rockies. I was about 14 or maybe 15 when my daddy rode off to join the Confederacy. He came home in '64. He was all worn out and sickly, so I stayed home 'til about '75, or maybe '76, when I hired on to a trail ride as a drover. We took the herd all the way up to Wyoming for a guy trying to start a ranch up there. So after we got paid off, I drifted back down through the Rockies, following the old Indian and mountain man trails down through the parks to the Arkansas River. Then went home to Mississippi. I just couldn't get it outta my head, and couldn't find anywhere I liked better. I made another trip, got a job in a mining operation, learned a bit about how to run one, and decided I wanted to live here. So I went back one more time and said my goodbyes. My daddy and momma had gone on to their rewards, so it was just some sisters and nieces and nephews left. It took me a couple of years to get back up here. I went to Austin and became a deputy sheriff for a couple of years, and well, just gained a bit more experience in life. And, well, I am here to stay now. These mountains got a hold on me!"

"Well, Sir, I am very glad you did. And so pleased to make your acquaintance!"

Sarah turn. "Clinton, is this horse for sale?"

"Bolt? Yes Ma'am. We could let him go, although I would miss him!"

"I suspect you would. Well, when you get back to Leadville, go to the office and have the secretary to write a check. I love him."

"Yes Ma'am. Ma'am, you didn't enquire for the price."

Sarah smiled, "No, I didn't, did I?" She smiled again to herself. It was new feeling, to not have to ask the price. She wouldn't misuse it though.

The afternoon sun was soon hidden by the mountains behind them as they descended through Mosquito Pass into South Park. They made early camp along a stream in a grove of aspen. Clinton hobbled the horses and gave them a measure of oats he had carried with them. They backed up under a overhanging rock as a summer monsoon shower refreshed the hillside. As soon as it was over, the smell of wet earth permeated the forest around them. Their evening meal had been furnished from the mining camp above; some chili and beans, a loaf of bread, and coffee. But somehow it seemed a magical meal, in such a majestic spot. As they sat around the campfire, Sarah asked the men to fill her in on the mining operation and about this country as well. William was the first to speak.

"Well, the mine up above today is producing some high grade ore. Here..." he handed her a palm size rock. "See the small hairline veins? See the black rock embedded in the granite? That black is hematite, the white is quartz. All that adds up to great promise. The main mine we saw earlier is making you money, and the other two claims are starting to produce. But...." William grew serious, "you have got considerable money in the bank. I would suggest that you start to invest some of it, maybe into property. I have seen too many mines play out quicker than a rattlesnake strikes, leaving their owners high and dry. Anyway, that's my thoughts."

"Miss Sarah, I agree with William on this one. I have lived in Leadville since I was a pup, and what he says is true."

"Gentlemen, I was brought up to be frugal, and have no quibble with your advice. This sudden windfall came easy to me. Well, it's true I did lose my husband. But even if he was with me today, I am sure he would agree with you. So let us keep our mind open and see what comes along. William, you asked earlier if I was enjoying my day. Well, I am starting a new career, something I have wanted to do for years. And yet, with having to deal with my life, was unable to find the mindset to accomplish. I am going to become a writer!"

"Sarah, I have some thoughts on a bit of diversity. I have a man that is going to meet us in Fairplay, and soon as I talk with him I will tell you what is on my mind. And, Sarah, that's wonderful, what are you going to write about?"

"This country. It is now so pristine, and its earliest history is so reachable. It is just now coming to be civilized, many of its original citizens are still alive and able to be interviewed and their stories captured before they are lost forever. And the images need to be described and preserved so the world will have a record of it. I sat on that mountain side and realized so few in our lifetime will ever see these mountains. I want to tell Colorado's story."

Daylight found the three out of the pass and riding into a huge expanse of a valley. Far to the east a range of mountains were hiding under the just before mid-day sun. Indeed, the valley seemed to be ringed as far as she could see. As they topped a rise, they pulled up. Out in the distance there appeared to be a small town, its buildings rather spread out. She shaded her eyes and peered under her hand. As if to answer her question, William spoke.

"That will be Fairplay. Up the hill to the left will be Alma. Welcome to South Park."

"The French were the first to come here, maybe a couple hundred years ago. They called it *Bayou Salado*" interjected Clinton.

"Yes, it's beautiful. It seems to call me. This is why I must write about this place. I was able to go to Europe as a young girl, with my parents, but nothing equals this! I am enraptured, I must see more!"

By noon they had found a hotel, registered, and Clinton had taken the horses to the livery stable for a rubdown and food. William and Sarah found a nice café off Main Street, and the three were waiting for food when a tall, lanky, man in canvas pants and a denim shirt, boots and a big wide brimmed hat walked through the door. William jumped to his feet, and walked to meet him, shaking hands and clapping him on his back, jarring a bit of dust from his shoulders in the process.

"Sarah, I would like you to meet my friend, Marsh Redman. Marsh, my boss, Sarah Burns."

Marsh removed his hat quickly, his wavy auburn hair spilling out. He offered his hand to Sarah.

"I am pleased to meet you, Ma'am."

"Marsh, is it? I am happy to make your acquaintance. A friend of Mr. Wells comes highly recommended."

"Thank ya, Ma'am. And, I must say, you are not quite what I expected as his boss either. A pleasant surprise."

"Come, Marsh, join us for lunch," she caught the eye of the waitress and motioned her back to their table.

"With pleasure, Miss Burns. Breakfast was just a bit sparse this mornin' 'bout daylight. Been ridin' since." He pulled a chair from an adjoining table and slid in between Clinton and William.

William nodded at Marsh. "Marsh, this is Clinton Markam. Clint, Marsh Redman." Both men rose slightly, meeting each others eyes and shook hands.

Food came, small talk ensued, and the four leisurely acquainted themselves. William told Marsh the story of how Sarah had become his boss, and about the untimely demise of her husband. He described the luck with the mines and brought Marsh up to date with the results of their excursion so far.

With their meal over they adjourned to the hotel lobby where they were staying. Finding comfortable surroundings, they settled themselves in for a period of relaxation.

William began. "Marsh, you are probably wondering why I had you make this long ride up here, right?"

"Well, I'll admit, it has crossed my mind once or twice."

"After our discussion in Salida that evening, I couldn't help thinking that you were just not the hard rock miner sort. I have something in mind. I have discussed this to some degree with Mrs. Burns. As her business manager, I have advised her to invest in land. Then I thought of you and our discussion in Salida. I would like to start a ranch, and after all the good things I have heard and after seeing South Park and hearing it's history, I would like to find it here in this awesome high valley. What do you think?"

"Well, William, that is a fine idea. The last two days riding here, all I thought of was how this place was a rancher's paradise. Yep, that is a first class idea! But how do I figure into it?"

"Well, with Mrs. Burn's approval, I would like for you to scout out the valley and find the proper place, and kinda be in charge of getting it started. I am going to suggest that you might be considered a partner in this enterprise and the working boss of the ranch. I would kinda like an answer pretty quick, so as we can start making some plans while we are here together."

Marsh leaned back in his chair. His mind raced. This had come out of the blue! For two days he had been wondering how could he get a start ranching? No funds, no stock, no nothing. Then, suddenly, holy cow! He hadn't ever considered partners. How would that work? He really didn't know William. He had only met the attractive lady that would be his boss - or partner. But somehow he felt good about this, and he did somehow trust William. Oh well, hell, what did he have to lose?

"William, this is quite a shock, and I just am having a lot of trouble wrapping my head around all of it, but yes, *hell yes!* To be back doing what I like doing, and up here where I love, I have nothing to lose and everything to gain. Mrs. Burns, you don't know me, but I grew up with cows. If you accept me, I will treat your ranch as if it was mine, and give it my best care, and a full days labor every day!"

William turned to Sarah "Mrs. Burns?"

Sarah sat with her hands crossed. She had listened to the conversation, her mind racing wildly. William had discussed to some degree about property, and diversifying her assets. But, a ranch? *Oh my!* Her thoughts and memories had flown to her uncle's ranch in California, about her years of visiting and then living there, her rides on his horses, the freedom she felt then. But to have her own ranch, and to have the help she needed to run it! She fought to keep her face composed. She didn't dare erupt into clapping her hands and saying in a loud voice, "Oh, goody, goody!" No, she would wait until she was alone in her hotel room later to scream and jump up and down and roll on the floor. But for now, she must be an adult.

"Mr. Wells, you have been indispensible during this whole affair. Yes, I trust your judgment, and I have to admit, I am excited about this endeavor! I grew up on a ranch in California and I agree it would be much of an incentive for all if we keep this as a partnership venture. People are more apt to work for something if it is part theirs. Mr. Redman, welcome aboard! You seem to fit the type for a cattleman, and if Mr. Wells says you are the one, that is quite good enough for me. Let's get started!"

Eight o'clock the next morning found Sarah, William and Marsh seated for breakfast.

"William," says Marsh, "I will go over to the county office and check on properties. Park County is a huge part of this area. I think it is the best place to start. I know it is a bit early but how many head of cattle do you want to start with? And what kind? Also, how many hands, once we start? I have no idea what kind of funds I am looking at, so maybe you can help me out."

"Mrs. Burns, when we get back to Leadville, we will need to transfer some funds to the bank here in Fairplay. Marsh, I will have you a budget in a few days. As for cattle and hands, once you get your budget, you can make those decisions. Mrs. Burns, when are you going to be ready to head back?"

"Mr. Wells, I thought about this for several hours last evening. Indeed, much of the evening. I am not going with you, to go back and sit in that house. Just is not going to happen. I am going with Mr. Redman in search of our property, if it is alright with him. I am very excited about this prospect, and it will also give me opportunity to start my writing. What better way than to see it from the back of Bolt? You can handle the finances. My goodness, you have for the last months, and look how far we have come!"

Sarah didn't add that indeed, she had found a particular attraction to the young cowboy. And since she wanted to have a real part in this ranch and she wanted to explore this high mountain valley, and that she had always hated playing the part of a lady in society, this Mr. Redman was an added bonus.

William took his hat off and leaned back in his chair. He smiled and said "Madam, you are the boss. We are just here to do your bidding. And happy to do it. Marsh, you are to escort Mrs. Burns on a prolonged tour of the Bayou Salado!"

Marsh ducked his head and grinned, "Yes sir! And yes ma'am! It would be my honor."

He secretly was happy to have some time to get better acquainted with the young widow. He was taken a bit upon meeting her. Then after the conversations, he was deeply intrigued with her confident manner, and her general go-get-it-done attitude. He looked forward to the coming days.

William, "Well, if this is the case, I am going to the bank and set up an account and have them be ready to accept some monies. Then, I am going to head back over Mosquito Pass and start preparations. Best of luck to you two. And send me a telegram when you need to keep me advised. Marsh, I told the hotel and livery that you were in our association and we would cover your expenses. Good luck and good hunting!"

Marsh and Sarah sat a while talking about what direction to start. They were just leaving the café when William crossed the street to them. He pulled his horse up and said "Mrs. Burns, the bank said any funds that you might need they would honor in lieu of transfer, we have done some business with them in the past, they know us. Gotta be on my way now, burning daylight."

He pulled the bay around and set into a lope and quickly disappeared.

Sarah and Marsh spent the day procuring supplies. Marsh found a pack mule named Jed, and gear. He was in the process of buying the supplies at the mercantile store when she arrived. She over heard him asking for two tents. She surprised him by vetoing that idea, and proposed they share a tent. After a short discussion, he relented.

Next morning found them on the road toward Denver. They traveled all morning, only stopping to water the horses. She had never seen a place more beautiful. As they rode, Marsh told her stories of the area, and the difficulties of the early settlers. After crossing a place he called Red Hill, they turned south to camp on Tarryall Creek that night.

Hell's Kitchen

Sean Kelly sat on the bag of coal in the tiny little shack in the alley off 45th Street in downtown Manhattan Island. The rain drummed noisily on the tin roof of the little shed. He had spent the night there last night. Well, more like the wee hours of the morning. He had run for two hours, escaping the coppers. They had not gotten a good look at him, and would have to take the word of the half dozen strangers present at the card game. And he knew for a fact they were all half or more drunk. He had no intention whatsoever of killing the big man. Calling him *"little Irish Jimmy,"* and telling him if he lost his few pennies he could always work for him shining shoes or some odd job. "Come on little Jimmy," he would say, "don't ya be scared to bet your penny." Sean had kept his cool all evening. A drop of water came off the roof above him and started dripping on his trouser leg, then it turned into a stream. He shivered at the dampness of it all.

He shifted his body to get away from the leak. Outside the rain poured down and the thunder rumbled. He had started winning then, a little bit at a time. The big man laughed at first, then his sour mood started to show. His remarks toward Sean started getting more vile. Sean watched him. He knew he would have his hands full if it came to blows, but he wasn't scared. His last two cards were dealt , a Queen, high straight. The big man kept moving and turning. Suddenly he had turned to say something to one of his cronies, and forgot his hand. Sean couldn't miss it. He turned back and faced Sean,

"Well, you going to bet 2 pennies or 3 this time, Irish boy?"

Jimmy took his time. "Your Honor, I must be careful. You have so much more experience than myself."

The big man took the bait. "I tell you what, little Jimmy, I have five hundred dollars here that says I got the best hand. Now, show us how big a man you are!"

Sean replied," But, m'lord, I don't have more'n two hundred myself."

"Doesn't matter, Jimmy. I will find you a way to pay me. Now play cards!"

Sean pushed the small pile of money into the center of the table. "Alright, sir, t'is your turn."

The mustache across from him twisted and the man reached forward, pushing his pile forward.

"Now put your cards down, ye wee Irish scum!"

"You first, I will follow." The two men tossed their cards on the table face up. As the realization dawned on the big man's face that he had lost, he began to curse, and his face contorted and reddened in rage. He reached in his waist and came out with a pistol. Before he could level it at Sean, Sean fired the big Navy Colt straight into the middle of the big wide midsection. A look of disbelief came across the fat face, and he fell backwards onto the floor. Sean kept his gun levels. He scooped up the winnings and stepped through the door into the alley. As he did, he said, "Best ye not come through that door for a few minutes, lest I assume you are one of his friends, or else just a thief looking for easy money. G'nite now, a pleasant evening to ye all!" He barreled down the alley, then cut through to another street.

He ran for a good hour, changing his direction till he found this lowly hovel for the night. He pulled his coat tighter. He wished it had turned out differently last evening, but he had read the big man right. He had taken the big Colt and slipped it into the top of his boot early on. He was ready. It was his father's last gift. He had won it near the end of the Great War, while on his way home from Virginia.

"Hell's Kitchen, New York City, about the time Sean Kelly would have lived there

Sean stepped out into the misty sky and headed south, he pulled his coat collar up and his bowler hat down low, watching faces on the street. He made it to the rundown tenement in the 900 block of 39th street just as two coppers turned the corner and headed his way. He climbed the rickety steps and found his way to his room. The door was still locked. He went inside, and filled a haversack with the initials US on it. It had been his fathers as well, during the war between the states. His possessions were meager, it was not an unbearable load. He went to the outside door and peered up and down the street. No coppers in sight.

At the Grand Central Depot at 42nd and Park, the man behind the ticket window asked, "Destination, Sir?"

Sean answered "Colorado, Sir."

The young man frowned, obviously disliking the familiarity. "I can get you to Cheyenne, Wyoming, and you can get another train or stage from there. Alright?"

"Course it 'tis."

He paid the fare and found a corner to sit in. An hour later he was sitting in the lounge car of a west bound locomotive heading west out of the city.

Day two of his train ride found Sean in the broad expanses of Nebraska. He had stayed on board while stopping in Chicago. Just another city. He wanted to make sure his trail was clear. It had been a good trip so far. He spent his time sleeping or in conversation with other passengers. One gentleman that was sleeping beside him at the moment was particularly interesting. He was from Colorado, and had a small mining business, furnishing tools and equipment to the miners. He had told Sean about coming to the territory in '58 and mining as a young man. He had described the privations and hardships of the country, the dangers from Indians and grizzly bears, and the environment in general. He told of the extreme weather in the Rocky Mountains. But he also praised the state as being one of beauty and freedom. A place where the mountains touched the sky, where water babbled to the sea in crystal clear streams, and the air was so fresh and rare that it healed diseased lungs and cures the sick. Sean had listened in wonder, curious if this was an old man's delusions. His neighbor on the other side of the aisle was a mother and her daughter, a girl of about 11 or 12. Striking in her looks for one so young, the mother was an attractive women in her thirties. But she was not the beauty that her daughter promised to be. She was traveling from back east somewhere to their home in Denver. They were visiting a prestigious finishing school that the daughter was to be enrolled in in the coming fall. He had listened intently to the girl telling her mother about the things she had read about the workings of the universe; the distance the stars were from us, and our position in relationship to our sun and moon. She was quite adamant and opinionated on the subject. Sean had listened intently to animated discussions between the two women, and inwardly vowed to study the subject more at the earliest occasion. In the city where he had spent most of his life, one didn't get much of a chance to observe the sky. But he had found times to lay out on hot nights in the summer on the roofs where he could get a breeze, and those nights he studied the heavens above. He had a deep need to learn. His early life had not been well adapted for schooling. He had a quick mind. He envied those children of the well to do, going to school and having the world of academics at their fingertips. His field of study was more about how to wring a few pennies out of someone to buy food, or to afford a clean dry place to lay his head. And most times it wound up being a moderately dry place. But still, whenever he found a book, regardless of the subject, he devoured it. If he could, he would take it and read at his leisure. One thing that Sean Kelly excelled in was his ability to draw. He saw the world in pictures. He studied shadowing and lighting and perspective. He didn't truly understand it; it was just a second nature for him. When idle for a moment he would take a pencil and sketch a likeness of a person in the room or on a bench in the park. Many times he would earn his dinner in that way. A person would catch him drawing and looking at them and would become curious and stop to look over his shoulder, and would gasp at the likeness before them. He would always part with the drawing for a few pennies.

He had gotten especially appreciative of the western novels and the outlaws and mountain men in the Rocky Mountains. He would draw his concept of how they would look. How he yearned for that life of wide open living! His father told him stories of the countryside in Ireland and its beauty. He also spoke of the Texans he had fought at Kennesaw Mountain, and at Chickamauga and Atlanta, and about their fierceness and wildness. Even though he had been on the other side, he admired them. So, now he was headed that direction. His thoughts wandered ahead of him. What would it be like?

He felt the train slowing. The conductor came through, "Folks, we are coming into Cheyenne, Wyoming. Connection here for Denver, Colorado!"

He stepped from the train to the platform, his carpetbag dragging against the steel of the steps. A cold wind was blowing from the north. He pulled his collar close, and jerked his hat down over his ears. *Interesting,* he thought, *it is cold,*

*but the area has a dryness and a
freshness, even in the railroad terminal.*
He stepped into the terminal to check on
his connection to Denver.

"Sir, I am afraid we have a serious
derailment between here and Denver. We
will honor your ticket to Laramie. The
railroad is going to run stagecoaches from
Fort Collins to Laramie for a few days till
this is cleared up. If you wish, the train
leaves in 45 minutes."

Sean nodded ok and the agent handed
him a ticket to Laramie. He walked out
onto the platform and down to the end of
the ramp. He looked up at the sky.
Blimey, he had no idea there was so many
stars! He remembered the young girl and
her mother on the train. The sky was
filled! He sucked in a deep breath of air.
Aw, this was a good idea! A new life,
maybe. Yes, indeed, a new life!

Morning, and what a morning! Sean had
walked away from the railroad station and
down the street to the big hotel where the
coaches the railroad was furnishing would
arrive and depart from. The railroad agent
had given him a ticket, but it would have

been another day and a half before he could have taken a train south from Cheyenne. The derailment south of Cheyenne had messed up the scheduling. Oh well. He looked to the south and west at the snowcapped mountains. He had never seen anything quite so grand. Indeed, the gods had smiled on this place! Late March was still quite chilly, but never mind, it was worth it to just be here. Aye, but he could hardly wait to set foot up there, just to see for his-self.

He purchased his ticket and went and found himself a chair along the wall in front of the combination saloon and restaurant, and was busying himself watching the comings and goings of the street in front of him. A strange lot, not like New York at all. Cowboys on spirited horses, smaller rangier horses than he was used to seeing. Miner types leading a mule or burro, loaded with gear. Ladies and gentlemen dressed in finery, wagons, buggies, every one busy. That was typical of the city, but this was such a small city. But, he realized, surrounded by a big country. Just then, with a great clatter and a cloud of dust, the stage arrived. The team of six hauled the big stage up in front of him, with the driver hollering "Whoa! Whoa now! Dan, Bullet, whoa!" The horses came to a stop and the driver kicked the brake forward and locked it into place. Two men crossed the street and started unhooking the horses from the stage, even as the shotgun rider was sticking his rifle into the boot of the seat and swung over the side onto the sidewalk. Looking at Sean, he grunted a "Howdy!" Sean touched the brim of his hat. The six passengers stepped out on the sidewalk, shaking the dust from their clothes and stretching cramped muscles. A young mother, her baby cradled into her arms, turned and asks the shotgun, "Is there a facility inside?" The driver said, "Yes'm." She hurried inside. A lady and young boy stepped out, and a man, hurried to them from down the street. "Emma, Johnny! This way." The directions were answered by a duo of smiles. The rest of the passengers melted away. The driver peered at Sean from under his wide brimmed hat.

"You waiting for the southbound? Be 'bout half hour, soon as I get some grub under my belt and a fresh team hooked up."

Sean nodded. He leaned back, but in a minute or so, he looked up to see a tall young lady and two gentlemen emerge from the hotel down the street and walk toward them. They were talking amongst themselves and laughing. He wondered. She was striking, even at a distance. The gentlemen's dress spoke of wealth and position. He watched them as they came closer. Then he became aware of two more men, dressed in suits and bowler hats, much like his own, but they looked like a tough sort. Their demeanor held a certain furtiveness that put him ill at ease. They seem to be following the other three. They would bear watching.

About then the fresh team came across the street. They lined up two at a time, or rather they seemed to step into place themselves and stand patiently, waiting to be hitched, ready for their haul back toward the southern mountains. They eyed the people around them as the hostlers snapped leads and reins and hooked singletrees and doubletrees and traces. Finally, they were ready. As he watched they seemed almost impatient in their waiting, but so well trained they never did more than stamp a foot or whisk a fly with a tail.

He sat quietly listening to the conversation between the lady and the gentlemen. The driver and shotgun were back, mail was being loaded along with luggage in boot in back, and a large box was lifted on top and snugged with a rope.

"Miss Clausen, again, we would like to express our appreciation for your time and the pleasure of your company. It has been enlightening, and thoroughly enjoyable! Indeed, I hope we meet again. But regardless, we wish you the greatest success with your endeavors!"

"Yes, indeed, Hanne, it has been an experience I would not have missed. I will never forget, you are indeed a wise and capable person and I am sure your students will benefit greatly! So, bon voyage!"

"Gentlemen, I have so enjoyed your company! Our conversations have touched most every subject. I appreciate your wisdom and wit. I will treasure our time together, and I so appreciate your contribution to my school! My students will be constantly reminded of your generosity!"

Just then the driver called out "Ok, everyone, all aboard for Virginia Dale, Livermore, LaPorte, and Fort Collins!" The lady and the gentlemen shook hands, the men bowing and removing their hats, and the young lady stepped inside. Looking around, she sat down by Sean. He felt a tremor course up his arm as she brushed it in arranging her voluminous skirt. About that time the two men that been following the threesome climbed in and sat facing them. They glanced at Sean, but stared at the young lady sitting next to him. Yes, she was beautiful, and was probably used to men staring at her. But something in their eyes made Sean feel uneasy. Indeed, the hair on his neck seemed to stand on end. He would keep quiet for now, but he would watch them very close!

Up top he heard the driver, "Haw, out, heeeupp! Move out Bill! Gid'up Frosty!" The big stage lurched forward, and was rolling down the street and around the corner. Another block, then another left turn, then a block, then right and then the horses went into a lope and they started picking up speed. Sean could see they seemed to be heading in a south-south east direction, toward a lower lying group of hills way in the distance. They came up to a larger road running seemingly east and west. As they rushed past he picked out a pointed sign pointing east with the word *Cheyenne*, and one for the other direction labeled *Rock Springs*.

As they rolled south, the land grew flat. It was covered with a low lying brush and an even shorter grass. He glanced back at the two men. They were still eying the young lady. Sean wanted to tell them to keep their eyes to themselves, but that would just stir something up. He knew better. If you are going to have a confrontation, better it be a surprise to your opponent. Instead, he turned to the young lady. He removed his hat,

"Ma'am, I would like to present myself. I am Sean Kelly, late of New York City. I am at your service until at least Denver City, should you be in need of anything."

The young woman turned and spoke.

"Well, thank you Mr. Kelly! I appreciate your introduction. I see no immediate needs, but will keep you in mind." She smiled. "I am quite used to traveling, and try to remain prepared ahead of time. But thank you for the kind offer."

Sean was dazzled by the smile and the depth of her blue eyes. He was searching for words when again she spoke.

"I am Miss Hanne Clausen. I am from Minneapolis, Minnesota."

"I am pleased to make your acquaintance, Miss Clausen. I beg pardon for eavesdropping, but I couldn't help over hearing your conversation with the gentlemen. You say you are a schoolteacher? I must say, I hold that position with utmost respect. I have never had much opportunity for schooling, and have always envied those that did. I plan on trying to take advantage of more of it before I die. I love to read, I do it at every advantage."

"Well good for you, Mr. Kelly. We are approaching a time in our history that I believe a good education will be offered to more and more of our young people. It is a thing we should all concern ourselves with, and strive to promote it whenever and wherever we can. So, good sir, you say you are from New York City? Why have you come to the west? To seek your fortune?"

"Aye, yes ma'am. Something of the sort. I have read books about the mountains since I was but a lad. So when the opportunity availed itself to me, I seized upon it immediately, and here I am. I am headed for Denver City, and from there, I am not sure of my next step."

"Indeed, Sean, perhaps I might be able to help you. I have some contacts there."

It was mid-afternoon when they pulled into the stop at Virginia Dale. Sean stepped down from the coach and turned, offering his arm to Hanne. She smiled and took it and lowered herself gracefully. They climbed the steps to the station and was greeted by a middle aged lady wearing an apron. Her graying hair was twisted into a bun on the back of her head. She wore it a bit high, perhaps like the Germans or Nordic women did. When she opened her mouth it was proven by her greeting.

"Ja, vil yu young volks pleas to come inside! Fraulien, if you vould pass through there is a room in the back to refresh yourself. Young man, you may go thru the back door, and find a place outback." Dinner vill be ready presently."

Sean walked out through the back door. He espied the privy, with a lantern hanging inside. He stepped inside and did his business, and turned to find the two men waiting. He stepped aside and went to the pump over the big cistern and pumped some water into the pan sitting on the side. He washed his hands and face, took on of the towels hanging on the rack and dried himself. Then he tossed the water aside. Turning, he noticed that both men had gone back inside. He grinned to himself. Well, I won't be eating with those hands, anyway. Back inside, Hanne had found her a place at the long table set with food. He sat down across from her.

"Mr. Kelly, would you care for a piece of chicken? It is quite good, and the biscuits! Oh, my, they are the best! They remind me of my Aunt's in Minnesota!"

"Thank you, Miss Clausen. I believe I will. I dinna take much of a breakfast."

The older lady passed behind him and asked, "Young man, vould you like some coffee?"

Sean turned, "Would you perhaps have tea?"

"Ja, indeed, I vould. A minute please!"

Hanne raised her head. "I would take tea myself, if I may?"

"But of course, sveetheart. A tea for you, of course."

The conversation lulled as the hungry passengers finished their late lunch, or early dinner as the case might have been.

When finished, Sean and Hanne walked out of the stage stop and up the slight rise behind into the pines. They leaned against a large mossy boulder. Sean looked at her. She towered over him, but something in her manner never suggested that she made him feel inferior. Indeed, his attraction for her was different than any he had ever felt before. Almost a meeting of the minds on some level or the other. He found it difficult to explain even to himself. But now he should explain his fears to her.

"Hanne... Miss Clausen. I'm sorry, I don't wish to alarm you unduly, but the two men that are passengers with us, they have been following you from when you first left you hotel this morning. I feel inside myself, that they mean to menace you."

She glanced down. "Thank you, Sean, for noticing them. I have been aware of them. They were on the train from San Francisco that I was aboard. I spotted them last evening at the hotel, and again this morning. I am not going to allow them to catch me in a bad spot if possible. And I, as I said earlier, am prepared."

She opened her bag and partially lifted a small two barreled derringer, then let it settle back. In turn, Sean lifted his jacket aside revealing the big Colt in it's shoulder holster.

"Thank you, Sean. I feel better now."

Sean spoke, "It was nice of the railroad to make these concessions for us. The driver told me they were running these coaches special and had opened the stage stops up for our convenience. He said this one had been used back in the 1860's and was run by a famous outlaw and his wife. The fellow was named Jack Slade. I once read a nickel novel about him. Never expected to actually be here where he lived."

Hanne smiled, "This country is so full of excitement and history and, as you will find out, is still quite wild and wooly. Keep your wits about you, Mr. Kelly."

Sean nodded, "Indeed!"

Sean watched the country go by. It excited him. The sun was sliding behind the mountains to the west. A few miles south of Virginia Dale, it was getting dark when they pulled into the tiny village called Livermore. A small inn was there, called The Forks, and they were to remain there until morning. After a quick meal, Hanne excused herself to visit the out door facility. As she went out the door, the two men got up and walked out, quite innocently as if to have a smoke. Sean, seem to take no noticed, but as soon as they had closed the door, he asked the waitress if there was another door. She pointed down a hall. He quickly went down the hall to a door. He opened it slowly, looking out into the darkness. He slipped out and walked slowly around till he could see the facility behind the Inn. Hanne was obviously inside as a light was burning. As his eyes adjusted he could see the two men off to one side near some juniper bushes. He waited. The door opened and Hanne stepped outside. As she started up the slight hill to the Inn, they stepped out. One of them spoke.

"Hey Missy, c'mere. We wanna talk to ya."

Hanne answered, "I am sorry, gentlemen, but I need to get back inside."

"Aw, c'mon now. I betcha got a bit of cash for last night. We saw ya go to those guys rooms. Bet they paid real well, and maybe we would like to get some of that as well as the money."

Hanne said nothing, but hurried on by. One of the men reached for her. As he did, she spun and pointed the small derringer at him. The other started to circle to get behind her. It was then that Sean stepped behind him. He put the big barrel of his Colt against the man's neck and thumbed the hammer back. As the hammer clicked back, he spoke.

"Miss Hanne, if you will go ahead and shoot that snake, I will do the same. They are both armed. We will be justified, and the world will be a lot cleaner."

Before she could answer, a voice came out of the darkness,

"Nobody's shootin' nobody! Step away from them, we have them covered. We figured they were up to no good. They are both wanted. We have been ridin' all day from La Porte, soon as we got word they were on this stage. We thank ya for getting' the drop on them for us."

It was then that three men stepped into the light of Hanne's small lantern. They were all dressed in dusters and broad brimmed hats, and wore badges on their lapels. Sean holstered his Colt and stepped back. Hanne lowered her derringer and stepped to his side.

"I thank you, gentlemen. These two have been shadowing me since I was on the train yesterday from California, then all day today."

"You are lucky, young lady. They would have done you harm. They are wanted over in Utah. I got a wire they were headed this way yesterday."

Sean took Hanne by the elbow.

"Miss Hanne, let's go back inside. Let the lawmen take care of these wee rats, as they may."

Hanne nodded assent and they stepped back inside. People were pulling away from the windows as they entered. Some one asked what happened.

Sean answered, "Aye, well, we stepped out to take the air, and not knowing the country, we stepped onto a couple of serpents. But some kindly lawmen came along to help us out. Nothing to trouble ye, you may all relax."

Sean and Hanne walked to a corner and sat. She on a short divan, and he in an armchair near to her. Here they had a bit of privacy. Hanne glanced about to see who might be turning an ear, but finding they were quite alone, she looked intently at Sean.

"Sean, I thank you so much. That was a sticky situation you stepped into. It was quite brave of you."

"It was necessary. I had been watching those two all day. I knew they were up to no good, and the things they said about you were not very complimentary, regardless of if they were true or not. And their intentions were plainly unacceptable. They are not the only vermin I have had to deal with in me short life."

"Sean, I simply must be honest with you, and I will not feel bad at you if you pull away when I do. I don't want you endangering yourself protecting me. First of all, what they said was true. I am guilty of what they said. I fell into the lifestyle of a woman who sells herself to support herself, since I was a teenager. I do not apologize for it."

"Miss Hanne, I do not care about that. I knew you made your way in that manner first time I saw you. The average woman does not carry herself or conduct her self in the manner that you do. I have known many in my time who followed the course you follow. They were fine decent women, except for what they did with men. Not that it makes you indecent, it doesn't. You seem a kind and caring person. I am very proud to make your acquaintance. I enjoy your company and I would treasure the opportunity to have your company until at some point our trails part, if it be your will."

Hanne lowered her head, then raised her eyes to his. "I am honored, sir, to make your acquaintance. I will enjoy your company as well, until that time comes."

As they spoke, Hanne's head slowly lowered to the back of the divan, and her eyes closed. Sean waited until he knew she was asleep, then gently lowered her head onto the arm, and lifted her legs to the divan. He pulled a blanket from the back of the divan and draped over her sleeping form. Then he sat back, and slid down in his chair and propped his feet on a stool. He sat looking at the beautiful girl sleeping until his eyes closed and he drifted away. What a night, what a beginning for his first day in the wild west! It truly was a land of adventure.

Sean woke with a start. He sat upright and looked around. She was gone. Looking up, he saw Hanne was walking toward him with two steaming cups of coffee.

"Wake up, ye sleepy headed Irishman! You need to come have some breakfast, the coach leaves in about an hour."

He stretched sleepily and rubbed his eyes. "Aye, that all sounds mighty fine. But first I need to visit the facility, then comes coffee and food. So hold on to that thought, lass, and 'bide yerself here for a moment. I shall be right back."

Sean stepped out into the bracing air, found the outhouse and performed his morning obligatory's. He found the pump over the cistern and some soap and washed his face and hands, running his wet hands through his curly hair. He dried on the towel that was furnished, and turned and re-entered the Inn. As he approached the breakfast table and took a seat next to Hanne, a distinguished gentleman, lean and leathery looking, sat at the head of the table. He looked at Sean and spoke.

"You must be Mr. Kelly, the hero of last evening. Miss Clausen has been telling me of your bravery. My name is Roberts. I own this little place, and quite a bit of the land around here."

"My pleasure to make you acquaintance, Mr. Roberts. And I thank ye for your hospitality. 'Tis a small bit of paradise ye have here. I was just filling my lungs with some of your fresh air, and taking a fill of the beauty hereabouts. As for the bravery, my honored father, God rest his soul, said it was my bound duty to protect a woman from vermin whenever I found it in my power. I was most happy to assist Miss Clausen with her pest control problem."

Later, as the coach rumbled south along the hogbacks to the east, the foothills of the Rocky Mountains rose rapidly to the west. Shortly that afternoon, they were pulling into the town of LaPorte. It sat at the crossroads of the Overland Trail. The Cache De Poudre River raced by on its way to the plains to the east, and a high bluff had stood over it just prior to reaching the small town. Sean thought it was such a pretty place. He was already seeing it would be difficult finding a place to settle. Maybe he wouldn't settle right away.

He turned to Hanne, "Lass, have ye ever been here before, to this wee place here, I mean?"

"No, I haven't. I went through Fort Collins on the train once before. It is only a few miles farther on down the road. Why?"

"Ah, no reason particularly. Just kinda appeals to me. I mean, the land and everything. I suppose I will go on to Denver though, that is where I paid my ticket to."

"I was about to ask you where you were bound. We have never spoken of that. I am going to Denver as well, I have a job in a parlor there. I suppose that is where I will go. I don't really have to, though. I came into some funds recently, I do have some time."

Just then the stage came to a stop in front of a restaurant. The driver called out "Thirty minute stop folks! Just time to refresh yourselves, then on to Fort Collins train station." Everyone unloaded and sought to appease their needs. As Sean came back around to the coach, he saw the Sheriff from last night was standing beside the coach. He pulled Sean aside.

"Mr. Kelly, a few questions, please. Might you tell me about Miss Clausen? Those men made some serious allegations. What is your opinion of her?"

"Sir, I would take no account of those scum. I first saw Miss Clausen in Laramie. She was conducting herself in a responsible manner. She had dinner and went to her room. Next morning I saw her again, as we waited for the coach. I believe she is going south to open a school somewhere. I dinna get much details in conversations, but in my humble opinion, Sir, she is a fine young lady making her way in the world."

"Thank you, Mr. Kelly, I will take that and close the conversation on the matter. My regards to the lady, when you see her, and safe travels to you. We are about to give these gentlemen a ride back to Utah. Tell her they will be no more bother to her."

"Top of the day to ye sir, and thank ye kindly for being there last evening. Someone would have probably gotten shot."

As the sheriff disappeared, Hanne reappeared, a somewhat worried look on her face.

"What did he have to say?"

"He was concerned about your character, and what those vermin had to say about you."

"Oh, and you told him I was a fine lady, a Christian example to all?" she smiled.

"Nay, me poor father taught me to never bare false witness. I told him that ye was a Madam in a low class bawdy house, and that you had robbed the bank in Cheyenne and shot the mayor in his own bedroom. And the last time I saw you, you were headed for Utah to join up with a Mormon gang of outlaws," he grinned back.

A couple or so hours later they were boarding the train in Fort Collins. The stage had been packed from La Porte, and conversation had been minimal. Crying children and chiding mothers had been the sounds they had to listen to.

But now on a railroad car, they had time to plan. Both seemed reluctant to part ways.

Sean asked, "Hanne, what was the thing the gentlemen in Laramie spoke of regarding a school, that you were to be involved with?"

Hanne blushed, her face and throat becoming a bright pink that seem to highlight her eyes. She dropped her head.

"Oh, my, this is difficult, to be honest with. But come what may, I will tell you. Oh goodness, here goes. Sean, I told those two men I was going to Colorado City or somewhere down there to open a school, and that I was trying to raise money for it. We had evolved into some very provocative conversation, they knew my background, but I explained I was giving that up to do something good. To make a long story short, it was an elaborate seduction on my part, and they fell for it. That night in Laramie, they gave considerable funds and I, oh crap, I wound up rewarding them liberally for it, most of the night. That is why I was so sleepy last evening. Now do you hate me for it? I feel I must be honest with you, but now, I don't know. For some reason, I am reluctant to go back to my past profession. I keep wondering, could I do this? I have a good education. I think I must be fairly smart. I always dreamed of being a teacher. I just don't know."

"Hanne, now it is my turn. You bared your breast, so to speak, so now I will. I have been a petty criminal, a conman, a gambler. I have probably done more bad than you have ever thought of. I was born and reared in Hell's Kitchen in New York City. A few days ago I was gambling and was forced to shoot a man. I killed him. I got away clean, and that is why I am here.

I don't want to live that life anymore. This is a new place, I want to do something else. Trouble is, I don't have many talents, other than a grafter and gambler. Oh, I can draw and paint, but I have never made much money at that. I enjoy it though. So I say, hell yes, go for it! If I can be of help, I offer my services, without any strings. We have a few days to plan, let us see where it leads."

Hanne reached and took his hand. "Thank you, Sean. They always say two heads are better than one. I accept your offer. Tomorrow is a new start!"

As the train slowed and eased it's way into Denver, Sean watched in the light from the flickering gas lights. It was a new city, as cities go. Its history was short, but it was still a city. It reinforced his resolve to not remain. But where to go? His brow wrinkled.

"A penny for your thoughts, Mr. Kelly?"

"Aw, lass, me wee mind is in a quandary. As to my next step, my thoughts were to how I don't care to remain in a city, such as this."

"Sean, a wise lady told me one time that we sometimes make decisions too hard. She said we should decide where we want to be, create an image of ourselves being there, then just let it happen."

Sean thought about this. "Me dear old father used to say that you could drive a mule to water, but he would only drink when he was thirsty. So you be sayin' that we should just herd ourselves to a certain direction, and let the destination show when it's ready?"

Hanne laughed, a low tinkling laugh that lit her face and eyes. She reached and grasped Sean's hand, squeezing it. "Yes, something like that."

"Miss Hanne, I do believe you really are a teacher, and I think I am to be your first student! So, to quote a line from that writer Shakespeare fellow, lead on, McDuff!"

They made their way to the Brown Palace Hotel on Tremont Street after finding the Saint James Hotel on Curtis Street full up for the evening. This required a short carriage ride. After registering and dropping their baggage, they met down stairs in the dining room. They had a light dinner and a glass of wine. Both were plainly tired, and were soon making their way upstairs. Hanne stepped inside her room and motioned Sean inside. They took seats in two comfortable chairs opposite each other.

"Sean, since tomorrow is a new day for us both, I am tired but I just want to ask you. Since we met yesterday morning, you have been such a gentleman toward me. Last evening you made me comfortable and covered me with a blanket, not once have you ever, even knowing my history, have you ever flirted or shown any hint that you wanted to be familiar with me. I don't see that much in men. Would you care to remark upon that?"

"Miss Hanne, I will be very candid with you, just as you are to me. I find you extremely attractive. I, however, will never suggest to you that our relationship should advance. It must, if it is to go in that direction, be as natural as spring turning in summer. I am content with how we interact at the moment. I somehow believe we can learn much from each other. it is my desire to see what kind of partners we can become. But make no mistake, Lass, you do make a man's breathe come fast when ye smile."

"Sean Kelly, you are a breath of fresh air yourself! Now I must get some sleep. I will meet you downstairs for breakfast. Not early though." With that she stood and stepped to him. She put her arms about his waist and hugged herself to him. She took his hands in her own and leaned forward and kissed him softly on the cheek.

"Good night, Sean."

"Good night, Hanne."

Sean stepped across the hall to his room. He sighed and quickly undressed. He was bone dead tired, but a new feeling was inside him. It gave each beat of his heart a new surge. Like that sky full of stars he had seen the other night, his mind filled with thoughts. All new worlds to be explored! But not tonight. All the stars became shrouded in a mist that turned into darkness, not total darkness. It seemed to be a collection of scenarios that fluttered after each other, much like those machines he had seen on the streets in New York that made a picture of a woman look as if she were moving. But that was too hard of thought. The sheets were too soft, the mattress to comfortable, and he drifted away.

When Hanne woke, the morning sun was reflecting off a window across the street, sending flashes of light that highlighted the goldeness of her skin. She glanced about the room. The hotel was only a few years old. It was finely furnished, and sported bathrooms with tubs and showers. She stretched and wiggled in the silky sheets. She had slept totally nude, and felt particularly relaxed and renewed. She ran her hands over her body; it was time to try out that gorgeous bathtub. She slid from the covers and went into the bathroom were she turned the water on and was delighted to see the steam rising from the hot water. She turned a bit of cold to it, but not too much. She relieved herself on the porcelain potty, then got up and walked around the room, stopping at the window. She looked across the way at the city before her. Sean was right, just another city, with the same drama and the same traps to avoid. She turned back to her bath. After finding the array of soaps and shampoos and scented oils that were left for her pleasure, she slipped in to the water. Aw, heaven itself! She looked down the lean, well formed body just beneath the waters. Her breast rode above the surface like two golden island in a blue sea, topped with two pink nipple tips for the volcanic mountaintops. She giggled. She took the soft wash cloth and poured a bit of soap on it, and started at her feet and worked up her beautiful legs till she found the junction of them. Then she washed that spot as well, taking care to enjoy the pleasurable feelings that came along with it. Then, her belly and breasts and underarms and shoulders, and butt. She shampooed her hair, washing it carefully, trying not tangle and abuse it. Later, after toweling off, she lazily brushed her hair, drying it slowly and carefully. She frowned. *Okay, Miss Hanne, next step you were supposed to go see Miss Jennie Rogers at her House of Mirrors on Market Street.* Now that was not appealing at all. So what is next? She

still needed to find a bit of income. She
didn't want to go into the funds James and
Bill had given her. So what next? Time to
meet Sean, and put their heads together.
She smiled, she could feel his energy
about her. She wondered how long it
would take before nature took over. She
giggled as she shivered at the thought.

Laramie

Hanne Clausen was striking enough in her face alone, but due to the fact that most of her clientele had to look up to her, it gave her an Amazonian persona that had benefitted her in all the high class parlor houses she had worked in since her decision to join the ranks of soiled doves in the western frontier. At 21 years of age, the tall blonde beauty was a four year veteran of several parlor houses and high class bordellos in Montana, Wyoming and Colorado. She had been endowed with not only a figure that just drove men wild, and a face that bordered on classic beauty, but a mental fortitude for her profession. Instead of being a tool to sate men's lust, she felt them to be a tool to line her pockets, and they never touched her soul. She washed them from her beautiful body as easily as she would have washed the dust and grim from a day of pitching hay back on the farm in Minnesota!

But this day she was boarding a train for Laramie, Wyoming. She had spent the winter with a gentleman in San Francisco and had earned a half a years pay escorting him through the gambling halls of the city, distracting the other players as they went. He had won handsomely, and had rewarded her the same. As the train pulled from the station, she watched him from the window of her private compartment. He smiled, removed his top hat and bowed. She blew him a kiss. Now, for her next adventure.

A friend of hers, Alleycat Annie, had sent her word of a gold and silver strike in Colorado, in a small town named Salida. Annie praised the small town as being heaven on earth. The weather was wonderful. It was situated between two ranges of mountains along a beautiful river. A railroad ran through the town, bringing new people daily. And the men were generous. Hanne smiled at her friend's exuberance. She and Annie went back a long ways and had had many adventures together. She was sure that Annie had embellished her surroundings a bit to attract her friend. *Oh well, we will see.*

At the moment, she was aware of the two gentlemen seated across her I aisle, facing her. They had not taken their eyes from her since they had pulled from the station, and had been whispering between them. She laughed inside. She had taken in, without revealing she was looking, their dress, boots, hats, and their general manner of deportment. They were both in their late 40's, maybe one of them slightly past that, obviously educated, successful men. Their forwardness in their appraisal of her showed they were used to getting their own way. Men like them, handled properly, could prove quite lucrative to a lady. Hmmm, well it was a least almost two days to Cheyenne.

The months in San Francisco had made her extremely comfortable financially. She had groomed herself and her manners, most people would not ever suspect her vocation. All the best for her. However, she had remained quite chaste for the time. Hanne liked men. She like the physical contact of men, she liked the way they made her body feel. True, she never let the feeling of love embed itself inside her. Even with the clientele, she would, if it was the right man, allow herself the satisfaction that came with the act. That was only on occasion though. Most usually men paying were too interested in their satisfaction, that little was left for the woman. Usually her satisfaction came from a chance encounter. But even then, she would usually find a way to receive a gift in some manner.

"Madam, if I may be so bold..." It was the younger appearing gentleman. Hanne raise he eyes, then dropped her gaze not making eye contact. She answered "Yes?" her throaty soft voice displaying nothing.

"My friend and I are about to adjourn to the dining car. I wonder if we might have the honor of escorting you, and the pleasure of your company for dinner?"

Hanne smiled a polite smile. "I thank you, sir, for your kind invitation. However, I am not quite disposed to accept invitations from strange gentlemen."

"I assure you, madam, that our intentions are most honorable. We seek only your conversation, for an otherwise boring dinner."

"Well, I suppose. I am hungry. But I will pay for my own meal, I insist."

"Very well! That is wonderful! Here, may I assist you? This way, madam, please, follow me."

The second car down was the dining car. The older of the two men stood behind her chair, assisting her to seat herself, a smile playing on his lips under a well groomed mustache. When they were seated, the younger man spoke.

"If I may be allowed to introduce myself, I am William Carlson. My partner here is James Bryant. Both of us are of San Francisco, at your service."

"Mr. Carlson and Mr. Bryant, I am Hanne Clausen, originally of Minnesota, but I have spent the last several months in your faire city, visiting friends."

Bryant answered first. "Miss Clausen, it is indeed our exquisite pleasure that you would honor us with your presence this evening! We are to be away from our wives and families for a few months, it is comforting to have the female point of view in our conversations."

Carlson added, "Indeed, as my esteemed friend here what my friends speaks is true. Although we are from San Francisco, both our wives are in the east, and we are quite starved for female companionship. Pray, tell, where does your journey take you this time, and how long will we be allowed your company?"

About that time the waiter arrived, and after some discussion over the menu, decisions were made, and conversation resumed.

"Mr. Carlson, to answer you question, I am going to Cheyenne, then to Denver and Colorado Springs. Then to a small town in the mountains where I have taken a teaching position." She dropped her eyes for a moment and allowed a moment of concern to cross her face. "This is dependent, of course, on our funding. It is a school for orphans, and we are terribly short on funding. We have been advertising for gifts and grants, but with this recession we are experiencing slow returns." She hesitated, then dabbed at the corner of her eye, "But excuse me, it was not meant for me to bring my difficulties to our dinner. Please, forgive me."

Mr. Bryant, "Miss Clausen, please, it is all right. It is plain it is a concern to you. Come now, feel free to speak of it plainly. Have you always been in the teaching profession?"

Hanne dropped her eyes. She must phrase this right. Her thoughts were toward a lucrative seduction of the two men, but she must tread carefully. She sensed something in their looks and demeanor that made her think they were not quite what they seemed.

"No, Mr. Bryant, in fact, this is a new venture for me. I have experienced a difficult past that has forced me sometimes into making decisions that have not always served me well. My parents passed away when I was young and I was raised by an aunt and her husband. They did furnish me with a good education, but life was difficult with them. My Uncle Olaf was a very physical man, and sought to abuse me. As a result I ran away at just over 17 years of age, and have been forced to fend for myself since then. This school is an answer to my dreams."

Mr. Carlson said "Hanne, if I may address you so, it sometimes is the things in your past that makes you stronger and drives you to succeed. I commend you! It seems you have turned yourself into a beautiful, poised, and somewhat successful woman, judging from your style and manner of dress. After all, the end result is what counts, isn't it? The past is our education."

They chatted through dinner. Hanne was, for the most part, agreeable to their comments. She, in a most innocent way, used her expressions and her manners in as erotic a manner as was possible, without being absolutely trashy. Using her lips while eating a peach slice in a suggestive manner, and flicking her tongue across her lips without seeming to be aware of what she was doing. Taking a deep enough breath to make her bosom swell. She could see that it had its affect on the gentlemen. They were under her spell! Well, time to remove herself and make them wait for more.

Hanne removed a twenty dollar gold piece from her drawstring purse. She laid it on the table.

"Gentlemen, I have enjoyed the evening immensely, and could do with more of our conversation. But, alas, we were so late leaving the city, and it has been a long day and I am in need of rest. Thank you so much for your kind attentions and comforting words. Here is enough to pay for my meal and gratuity as well. Might I beg your leave until tomorrow?" Both men rose from their table, and bowed. Hanne turned and walked away without looking back toward the Pullman car. She allowed just the slightest roll of her hips and sway to her body to give them thoughts for their evening.

Hanne found her bunk. She stepped inside and drew the curtains. She quickly undressed and slipped in bed. As she lay quietly listening to the click-click of the wheels on the rails, feeling the slight rocking and swaying of the sleeping car, somewhere a baby cried fretfully. She could feel the labor of the train pulling the grade. They should be somewhere near the top of the mountain by now, but she would be asleep when they finally topped over and headed down into the emptiness of Nevada. She went over the conversation of the evening, remembering reactions and body language of the men. She couldn't see anything to make her think that they were dangerous. She had known many men, and had become a good judge of character. She would see where tomorrow would take her, but for now, freedom from thought.

Hanne slipped into a robe and was lucky enough to find the water closet empty and refreshed herself. Back in her bunkroom she brushed the long blonde hair and arranged it into a stylish fashion then applied her makeup artistically. She chose a dress of a dark brown with threads of red woven through. It was cut conservatively but seemed to bring out a very alluring look when she wore it. The tight sleeves and fringed cuffs brought attention to her long graceful fingers. It was not as full in the rear as many were, but allowed for the natural attractiveness of her derriere. It was cut a bit lower in front to outline and suggest her cleavage, but discreetly and slightly obscured with a filmy veil of chocolate brown. The bait was alluring. *Let us see if the fish are biting....*

Hanne had felt the car slowing and realized they were just arriving in Salt Lake City. She had always avoided this place. She bristled. The Mormons kept their women in such bondage that they were little more than breeding cattle, or worse, slaves in their own homes. She had never considered even staying over night here.

She found the dining car and about midway down, her two gentlemen friends. They were beaming as she approached.

Almost in unison "Good morning, Miss Clausen! Did you sleep well?" then laughing at their zealousness.

Hanne laughed as well. "Yes, indeed, thank you for your kindness. I am much refreshed this morning, although I look forward to leaving this horrid city."

Bryant asked "I take it you do not like Salt Lake City? Oh, here, please join us for breakfast. Here, take a seat, please. Tell me why you dislike it here? I would be most interested."

Hanne slid into a chair and managed to slide her ankle across and rub it against Bryant's leg. She pretended not to notice, keeping her eyes averted. She arranged herself, well aware of her effect on the men. They were almost secretly taking in her attractiveness.

"Well, Mr. Bryant...."

"Please, call me James."

"And you can refer to me as Bill, if you would be so kind," replied Carlson.

"Very well. If we are to be informal, then call me Hanne. To answer your question James, I have had some occasion to interact with the Mormons, and I don't appreciate how they treat their womenfolk. Their chauvinistic attitudes, so deeply woven into their religion, is appalling to me and to most other modern women. I have little regard for religion in the first place, and none for theirs."

"So you feel women should be given more freedom then, Hanne?" James asked. "Pray, tell me how would that be beneficial to society in general? And how would it effect the role in the family structure?"

"Yes," replied Bill, "If my wife got anymore liberated, I might not find a spot at home anymore!" He said laughing.

Hanne smiled warmly at Bill, looking into his eyes softly yet intently, almost as if she was wondering what kind of man is this.

"James, Bill, I can see..."

At that moment the waiter appeared. "Madam, gentlemen, we will start serving as soon as we are underway. It shouldn't be long now." The three of them nodded.

"I can see you are both men of compassion and tenderness, and I am sure that this attitude is reflected toward your families. However, this is not always the case. Many men harbor a cruel streak, and seem to point at their women with an iron rod." She could see that expression hit home. She couldn't even smile at the implication. "Women look at things in a much different light than men, and are motivated much differently. A bit of understanding with a woman, a bit of serious softness in your methods, will reap most men vast rewards. At least that is what I look for. But seldom find it."

Both men looked at each other. Bill was the first to speak.

"Hanne, I must confess, I am a bit speechless at those remarks. You are quite candid. But tell me, when the Missus and I first met, the fires of passion burned fiercely in us. But after about two or three years we fell into a routine that is more casual than romantic. How does one keep that from happening?"

James nodded his approval of the question.

"Bill, how many children did you have by the time you noticed only embers in the fire place?"

"We had two." James nodded as well, and held up three fingers.

"And when you would come home from your office for the day, what was your expectations?"

"Dinner, my newspaper, a cigar, and my easy chair." said James.

"And what was your wife doing at this time?"

"She would be straightening up the kitchen and putting the children to bed."

"Gentlemen, you are men of business. You are intelligent, probably even shrewd in your dealings, but cannot see what is happening under your noses. Look at this. Your wives are people as well as being women. They think about their lives. Firstly, the very nature that moves us all, urges them to find a mate and fall in love as soon as they reach maturity. They go with that gladly. Then they marry, and their husband goes away to work. In many cases, the drudgery that comes with maintaining a home dulls their senses, and oftimes their appetites for their husbands. Then they have a child. That is such a seriously scary time, they know full well it is something that they can die from. Childbirth is often dangerous. After a couple of children, and the time and effort that comes with it, in their mind they become little more than household servants. It is common knowledge that it is not unusual for a woman to have upwards of eight or more children during her life. That, gentlemen, is a life sentence. Which is oftimes only commuted in death. It is also here that they may not still have that sweet young freshness that they may have had before. Their conversation may take on a sharpness that causes the husband to withdraw. Now you are on that slippery slide, you may never find a method to overcome. When did you last take your wife on a date, just you and her?"

Bill and James looked at each other.

"So, I welcome your opinion, gentlemen!"

The train had left the station and was climbing out the canyon from Salt lake City when the waiter returned and took their order for breakfast and left steaming

144

cups of coffee. Breakfast was quiet. The men ate, deep in thought over Hanne's remarks, not sure of their best course of retort, indeed if there was one. And a heated argument with a lady in public, well, that was just not suitable. Indeed, this was an unusual woman. Hanne waited, realizing the impact her words had on the men. After breakfast was consumed, they adjourned for the smoking car. After being seated, the first one to speak was Carlson.

"Hanne, you gave me much to consider. I confess, I realize that my wife does carry a heavy load. We now have four children. I confess, I have just always taken it for granted it is just *quid pro quo*, you know. It is accepted lifestyle. But, our romantic life is just drab. It is not even interesting, let alone romantic and exciting. What can one do?"

Bryant sighed. "Yes, Hanne, I echo my friend Bill's remarks. I feel similar, and my wife seems to not be interested in romance with me either. I feel sometimes she resents my advances. I am embarrassed to admit, I have taken a mistress. I feel quite guilty about it. But I confess, I felt I was going mad from frustration. And she does seem so content with the children and her sewing circles and teas!"

"Gentlemen, this is what I was referring to at the outset of this conversation. And James, yours is the normal answer to that problem. I am not condemning your actions, you understand. Just, I think it is such a loss for families, and to couples, to suffer this distancing. I think it could be avoided. I have seen these scenarios play out too often."

Bryant said, "Hanne, you mention that. And with that mention, I feel I must confess something to you. You are a remarkable woman, in many ways. You are beautiful and intelligent, and quite a forward thinker. And probably a force to be reckoned with for any man that you might be meet. Forgive me for having been, let's say, less than honest since our meeting. But I saw you in San Francisco on a couple of occasions, on the arm of the gentleman you were escorting. When I saw you on the train, I related to Bill what

I knew about you. I had to get to know you, and will admit my intentions at the time were not entirely honorable. But after our conversations, I have a new perspective of you. I am indeed happy to make your acquaintance!"

Hanne leaned back and laughed softly. She smiled at James. "James, you just made a very favorable impression with me. You see, from the onset I was aware that the meeting was a bit more than casual. I was aware that the possibility of you having seen me in the city was very real. But I am pleased that you admitted to it. It is very courageous of you."

Carlson asked, "So, Miss Hanne, with this revelation I am so very curious, and hopeful, you will forgive me for asking the question; is this the way you support yourself? You seem so worldly and wise, yet your face has a look of sweet innocence. How can this be?" He looked around, nervous that someone might be listening to the conversation. Satisfied, he continued, "Are you in the pleasure business? And, if you are, why? After our conversations, it is plain to see you could be anything you wanted to be."

"Bill, you are so kind. I hardy know where to begin, or how to address that question. You are both so kind. It is not my wish to insult either of your intelligences. But, truth be known, very few men exist, or have ever existed, that truly know what thoughts and feelings dwell inside a woman. It is almost as if women have come to earth from the morning star, and men have come from another planet. They are both deposited here. They are strangers, yet are forced to work together for survival. Somehow that is what they do, and seldom try to really get to know each other. Each are driven by their basic desires, yet have much different thoughts and dreams.

"Occasionally, you will find a couple who have found a plateau of compatibility that allow them to get close enough to share that special thing together. Bill, to answer you, yes, I was in my 17th year when I became what you might call 'an upstairs girl', or what other label is forced on young ladies in that particular locality. I was starving, had no home, no place to go, no friends to help me. The future looked bleak, as I mentioned. I had been accosted a few times by my step uncle. I hated the being forced to submit, I was determined to never have to submit myself unwillingly. It started slow. I became aware even at 13 or 14 at how men looked at me, and how they treated me. I knew what they wanted. When I ran away from home, I stole some money from that vile man, enough to get me on a stage coach going south. As it were, there was a woman on that stage headed for Deadwood. She was a Madam in a bordello there. She was quite candid with me. I told her what I was doing, and she offered to help. I was mostly just young and slightly innocent at the time. I asked her what I would have to do. She told me, in no uncertain words, in graphic detail. I was appalled! I didn't think I could do it. I thanked her, but refused her offer. We arrived in some town where my ticket ran out. I got off the stage, and found work in a hotel, changing bedding and doing laundry and kitchen chores for a pittance. But at least I had a roof over my head. It turns out the lady that owned the hotel had a son. He was a handsome young man, and so gentle. He won my heart straightaway.

"Soon we were spending all our time together, both day and night. I came to love him dearly, he was one of the first people in my life that treated me good. During the course of our time together, I tried some of the horrible practices that the madam had told me about, and found that they were not so terribly unacceptable. I came to enjoy that physical contact, indeed, to want it. Then, one night two men came to the hotel. It was evident they were drinking. Morris, that was his name, Morris tried to tell them there were no more rooms available, and they became belligerent and were causing a scene. Morris told them they would have to leave. One of the men pulled a gun and shot Morris at close range. My heart died that night. I couldn't stay there any longer. I left the next morning, and went to Deadwood. The rest is history."

Carlson reached over and took her hand in his.

"Miss Hanne! I don't quite know how to react! You are most unusual, with the adversity you have faced. It is unusual to see a woman, especially one who is able to rise above situations and achieve what you have achieved. You are remarkable! But how, or I am assuming that you have, how did you break free from the world of bawdy houses? Usually a woman that does that never gets free."

"William, it took some time. It isn't an addition of the body, it is really just thoughts and a habit that makes you think that you are doomed to it. It requires one to make a firm decision and then act upon it. And to never look backward." She smiled, "In truth, it required that I started to think and act like a man. The advantage was, I was still in a woman's body. It has served me well."

At that moment the conductor approached.

"Madam, we have received word, of a very bad derailment, south of Cheyenne. It will be days before there is any traffic going to Denver from there. I would encourage you to debark at Laramie, and to secure alternate transportation to Fort Collins, and from there you can catch the train for the continuation of your journey. The railroad will pay for your hotel, and reimburse you for your inconvenience."

Hanne frowned a bit. "Thank you, sir. I shall take your offer."

"Very well, ma'am. We will be arriving at Laramie in about a half hour."

Bryant spoke up. "Well, Miss Hanne, then we are not going to be forced to say goodbye so quickly. Bill and I have some business in Laramie tomorrow. Allow us to escort you and see you to your hotel. Perhaps we can have dinner again?"

"You are so kind. I would be grateful for your assistance."

It was good to get off the train and to smell fresh air again. The cool mountain air was uplifting and just a bit bracing, but the short time that was required to gather baggage and to take the short carriage drive across town to the hotel gave Hanne time to think. She liked both the men. Firstly, she felt that they were willing to contribute to her 'school funding' and bottom line was that she had a hunger down deep inside for a male body, or maybe two. She smiled. *You wanton creature you*, she thought. She had had two threesomes in her career. One was not notable, she had been just a bit inebriated. The other was rather nice. Having sex with one man had varying degrees of good, but two men! Aw, that got ones blood going! And, who knows, it could be profitable as well!

She took time to bathe and redress. She chose a light grey skirt, and a black silky blouse that buttoned just to her cleavage. She chose a musky scent and dabbed it where it would be sure to be noted. A bit of make up, outlining her full lips, a few pieces of jewelry, and her hunting outfit and she was ready. "Tally ho!" she said to herself, looking in the mirror.

She descended the stairs, head up, making sure to use all the grace she possessed, allowing a slight roll of her hips. At the bottom step, she saw the two gentlemen at a table across the room. She smiled broadly allowing just a bit of blush to bloom on her cheeks. They had to know she was glad to see them.

James and Bill were tumbling over each other during dinner. They talked and joked, and acted much a like two school boys out on a lark. The wine livened the mood, and before long dinner was over. The restaurant was a bit crowded.

Bill nervously asked, "Miss Hanne, would it be an imposition, or would you be uncomfortable, if I enquired if you would consider adjourning to our room for a while? We would like to speak to you about assisting funding your school, and I don't feel comfortable doing it here." as he looked around the room.

"Gentlemen, I feel quite comfortable with you, yes. But I would rather you allowed me to go first. I would rather no one here was the wiser. It would not be good for a ladies reputation. Give me 30 minutes, and I will knock on your door."

"Excellent idea! Room 212. We will settle with dinner and step out and have a smoke. Thank you for your trust!"

"Indeed." She arose from her seat and in a bit louder voice, she proclaimed, "Gentlemen, thank you for your conversation and dinner. It has been a long day and I feel to retire. May the rest of your journey be pleasant."

"Miss Hanne, a good evening to you. But don't count us out yet. We will be here for breakfast tomorrow morning."

"Wonderful. I look forward to it." She turned and made her way up the stairs. Her blood hummed through her veins. *Come now, Hanne, control your-self. Take it slow*, she said to herself. In her room she removed her hat and shucked her petticoats and her skirt. She let her blonde hair tumble down over her shoulders. She unbuttoned her blouse. She pulled a dressing gown from her trunk and slipped it around her and belted it. Then she lay back across her bed, naked except for the silky outer garment. Stretching her arms and drawing her knees up as high as she could and then straightened her legs, straight up to the ceiling, causing her robe to slide down exposing the downy thighs. She was blond but her skin had a tawny color to it, and she had almost a downy fur coat over her entire body, so fine you could hardly see it, but felt silky to the touch. She brought her hands to her breasts, cupping them in her hands and lifting them. They didn't lift that much, but they were firm. Her nipples not overlarge, but hard and soft in the same breath. Her hands slipped down across her stomach and opened her robe, allowing her fingers to explore the soft moistness of herself. *Yes*, she giggled to herself, *those thoughts you have been having, have made things a bit slippery down there Miss Clausen, you should be ashamed of yourself!* But she wasn't!

She knocked twice on the door across the hall, down one from her room, hoping the men had finished their smoke. She really didn't want to be seen dressed this way in the hall.

The door opened. Bill started to speak but was instead standing with his mouth wide open. She stepped quickly through the doorway and he closed it behind her.

"I hope you gentlemen don't mind, I just had to get comfortable. You have no idea how the clothing we are supposed to wear restricts oneself and how sometimes uncomfortable."

"Not at all, Hanne. My wife has voiced the same thought many times," said James.

"And mine as well," chimed Bill. "Hanne, would you care for a drink?"

"Indeed, I would. What do you have? Oh, I would like the wine please."

Bill poured them all drinks. James raised his glass.

"To Miss Hanne, and her new school! And to friendship, one and all!"

They raised their glasses and drank a toast.

James ventured a question. "Hanne, on the subject of fashion, if you had your choice, what would you wear?"

"Hmmm, I have given this much thought. I would have to say it would be related to the activity. I would prefer to wear trousers when the activity is of an athletic nature, such as hiking, riding a horse, perhaps even many household duties that demand climbing, lifting, etc."

Bill added, "Well, in the west here it is getting more common place to seeing a woman ride astride. Hence, in many cases, wearing trousers, or a split skirt. But I do see your point. I have watched my wife in her domestic duties, and wondered."

"But never asked, huh Bill?"

Bill lowered his gaze. "No," he answered. "See, that's what I mean. Things won't change for women with out the help of their men. The men should help to suggest things to help the ladies."

James said, "I think I see what you mean. But so much is dictated by society. My wife would be scared to death for some of her friends to catch her dressed inappropriately."

Hanne lifted her second glass of wine. The glow was spreading. She scolded herself inwardly, *Slow down, Clausen, bide your time.*

"Maybe. But change needs to start somewhere. Sometime in the next 60 or 70 years, women are going to rise up. There has already been whispers of it. It will catch hold. I dare say before I am ancient or die, women will go out and search for sexual favors from men as much as men do for women." She knew this was the wine talking.

"Well, that will be great for men! I hope I live that long!" Bill laughed.

James was watching her closely, maybe sensing something in her mood.

"Would you like that Hanne? To be able to go out and pickup on men of your choice?"

"Well," she smiled, "In my past it has never been necessary. But yes to rid of the stigma that would be associated with it. But in the same breath, Bill, yes, you would hope to want to live long enough. But somewhere along the way, men are going to lose some of the control they have, and I think that is not going to come easily. There will be a heap of fighting and conjecture before it happens."

"Hanne, you are marvelous! I have never heard a young lady speak of the things you voice. I hope if you teach the thoughts in your school, the parents don't lynch you!" James smiled, "But we are on the verge of a new century. Intelligent people will expect change."

"And on that subject," Bill cleared his throat, "The purpose for our meeting. To help you get this off the ground. Now, tell me once again, how much are you trying to raise?"

"Well, Mr. Carlson, I have a couple or more contributors in Colorado that I have corresponded with. I need to raise about $5,000. Couple that with the land donations and some other efforts."

"Hanne, James and I have discussed it, and we would like to add $2,500 dollars to your funds."

"Oh my goodness! That is half what I need! Are you sure? I can never thank you enough! I never expected this! Oh, you are wonderful! I don't know what else to say!"

"Hanne, you have given us a great deal of pleasure in our short journey. The conversations we have enjoyed; they are thought provoking themselves, and quite enlightening. And frankly, we would like very much to see you succeed. Now, another glass of wine to toast your success. And here is a bank draft made out to you on our Denver bank. You may cash it at your leisure. Here's to you, Miss Hanne Clausen!"

They stood, Hanne between the men, and raised their glasses, touched them together and drank. Hanne burned inside. *Now is the time.*

"Bill, James, you are two lovely men! You are truly gentlemen. And I have talked a lot. In fact, much more than I usually do. And some of the things I have said must have seemed like, well, just like talk. But to show you I am a person of my word, another toast. This one to us and our evening and to you, gentlemen. It is my turn". They lifted their glasses and drank.

"Now, gentlemen, a hug." She reached out to both and they stepped into her arms. They both hugged her and as they stepped away, she undid her belt and slipped it from her shoulders. It fell to the floor, leaving her nude, golden body like a statue between them. She reached again, and pulled them toward her. They were like men whose brains had ceased to function. Their eyes traveled over her body, caressing, exploring, wondering, unsure of the next move. Hanne took care of the next move. Turning to her right she stepped to James, cupping his face in her hands. She leaned close and kissed him, very softly brushing his lips with her own. A touch of her tongue slide along the underside of his upper lip. She leaned away, smiling, trailing her hands down his chest and away. She then turned to Bill and repeated the same action, then leaned back and unbuttoned the two buttons on his shirt, then pulled it from his trousers and over his head. She leaned in again and traced her lips over his chest, brushing his left nipple as she did. His suspenders were off his shoulders. She unbuttoned his fly and let his trousers drop, then turning back to James. She smiled. His shirt was already off. She undid his fly as well and his trouser fell away, exposing a large lump in his drawers. It took about a moment until she had ridded him of those. She took him in her hands, and fondled him softly. He reached for her, but she pushed him back.

"Come now, James, we don't conclude the business agreement until we have consulted all the partners." He moaned something unintelligible. She turned to Bill, who was likewise exposed by now, and clearly in the same state of arousal as James. She laughed. There seemed to be no sense of embarrassment between them. They were focused entirely on her. And, well, they should be. She glowed in the lamplight, her long blond hair cascading about her shoulders. Somewhere from outside someone yelled, "She's beautiful!" They all looked at each other, then laughed. Turning, she laced her arms through the left arm of James and the right arm of Bill and walked them to the bed and placed them side by side, then crawled over the top and lay between them. She turned onto her back and lifted one golden, beautiful leg, straight to the ceiling.

"Aww, this is such a wonderful spot! I think I will just lie here and go to sleep with you two gentlemen."

She closed her eyes and feigned a snore. Both men laughed. They turned to her and Bill said, "Sleep! I think not!"

The men looked at each other and closed over the top of her each fastening his lips on a taut, hard nipple. She purred, and her hands went down along her sides and fastened on two very hard cocks, one on each side of her. She cupped her hands around them and slid her fingers up and down lightly. The sucking and licking on her nipples was mesmerizing. It was hard to focus on her hands, but she tried. Finally, she sprang up and turned facing them.

"Now, my turn!" She lowered her head to James' mid section and lowered her mouth around his cock, cupping his balls in her hand. She brought her mouth off and licked the shaft from the base out to the head looking him straight in the eye. Then she switched to Bill. As she did, James came up, in an attempted to get behind her. She turned and pushed him back on the pillow. She shook her finger in his face, and mouthed the words "You, stay." She then turned to Bill and lowered herself, taking his tool into her mouth. She looked James in the eyes as she slowly took all of the older man's cock into her mouth, sliding her lips all the way down the shaft, until she touched the very bottom, her tongue working on the lower side. She looked up at Bill. His face was in a state of bliss and amazement at the sight of his entire cock inside her mouth. James was watching her, his hand fondling his own cock as he watched her work the other man. She kept her act going until she could feel him rising in her mouth. But before he lost himself, she slid her mouth off and turned to James. As she lowered herself onto him, she felt Bill's hand slide between her legs, his fingers slipping into the moistness of her. She worked the cock in her mouth, moaning from what Bill was doing to her. Her mind was lost now in the feeling of lust and ecstasy. She no longer was going to control it any more, but was set to receive whatever the two men could give her. She rolled onto her back pulling James on top of her. His legs astride her neck, he was literal riding her mouth, thrusting and withdrawing. As he did she felt Bill's lips on her stomach, going lower and lower, until he engaged that lower set of lips that belonged to her. His tongue slipped inside her, searching, exploring. Her mind careened, lost in the feeling engulfing her body. She was climbing now, her insides growing tauter and tauter. She felt James' cock swell, and at the same time, her vision blurred. She was going over the top! Oh God! As he climaxed, James groaned and filled her throat with his seed, but they slid on down with out stopping. Bill slowed his intensity, but didn't stop. Then she felt the desire return, the need to be filled. James rolled off the top of her, and she rolled Bill over and slid down lowering her hips over his crotch. It only took a second until she felt him enter her. Then she leaned back and her hips started to move. Her vagina tightened around Bill and took a mind of its own, rocking her hips, twisting her body. She sat straight up, her head back, her eyes closed. As she rode, oblivious to anything else in the room, except that that was inside her. No man could stand that for long. Then she heard Bill start to gasp, then as his cock swelled and he spasmed up, she met him with her own self, squeezing him until seconds that seem to go on forever turned into a tumultuous upheaval that almost blacked them both out. She fell over between the two men and breathed, relaxing as a bead of sweat coursed down her cheek onto her neck.

She lay for a few moments, then said, "That was most wonderful, gentlemen! Thank you!"

The men said nothing but managed to turn to look at her and smile.

As soon as her blood returned to her body, Hanne stood up and donning her dressing gown. She turned and said, "I shall return momentarily."

She stepped across the hall into the water closet, and looked into the mirror. She smiled at the flush that still lingered in her face. "Round one!" She washed and completed her toilet and slipped back across the hall. The men were up, sitting in the chairs having a glass of wine, but still in state of undress.

She said, "Hmm, like minds," and poured herself a glass. They sat quietly, not talking, sipping their wine, the men's eyes still on her body. She, in turn, watched them, taking in their maleness. She had always loved to look at a man's body. As a girl she would find out where the boys went to skinny dip and would hide and watch them. Sometimes rubbing her self, or playing with her nipples as she watched. Now she had two nice specimens all to herself. Bill was the first to speak. He had walked to his bag on a table and taken something from his bag, a small pen knife. He did something with his fingernail, then replaced the item. Turning, he looked at Hanne and smiled.

"Earlier it was remarked that you were a most unusual and incredible young lady. And we didn't even know the half of it! You are a one in a million. The most exciting woman I have ever experienced! I will never forget you."

As he spoke he was standing behind a chaise lounge. His cock was just exposed over the top of it. It started to stand up, seeming to have a mind of its own. It was more than Hanne could stand. She arose and put down her glass and walked to him. She stepped onto the lounge on her knees and leaned in, giving him a long deep kiss. Then lowering, she kissed down his body, taking his cock into her mouth. She sucked it and massaged it with her lips and tongue, hungry again for its taste and contents. Bill was frozen in place. She became aware of hands being placed on her hips and rubbing her ass, then slipping between her buttocks and touching her. Then she felt James hard again, entering her from behind. Oh, the deliciousness of that moment! A cock in her mouth and one in her puss! She moved to both of them, in a state of bliss. She had no memory of its equal. This must have continued for maybe ten or fifteen minutes as the 3 bodies swayed together. Then, almost in unison, she felt both men reaching their pinnacle and sensed she was almost there as well. She was able to adjust the situation till, at a single moment, they all reached orgasm together and almost fell together, exhausted. Hanne on the lounge, Bill, back into a chair behind him and James onto the floor at her feet. Hanne rested a moment and went and lay down in the center of the bed. The men joined her momentarily. They looked down and both their tools for pleasure had crawled back into their dens and hibernated.

James spoke. "Hanne, I have never experience anything like this in my life! It is a fantasy, but not one I could have even dreamed up on my own. I never knew that women could experience sex as you have obviously done tonight. You must be one in a million!"

"James, I am not. My difference is I am in a position to expose my true feelings without a chance of dishonoring myself. I will probably never cross paths with you again, so I have nothing to lose. Women have been so subjected that they fear, else they be called a whore, or the man they are with feel that they are debased or even insane. Men have put us in this cage. If they want us, they need to let us out, let us be free, so that we can be true to ourselves, so we can experience our feelings. That we can allow ourselves the strength to believe in ourselves. Only then they will reap the rewards. It will not come easy, but it will be worth it."

Bill answered, "Hanne, I can believe what you are saying, but I don't believe my wife would ever come around to behaving as you have this evening."

"You are probably right. It is too late for some. But the young men your sons need to be, need to be retrained mentally to treat women differently. It is a thing for the future."

Not much more happened that evening. Cuddling, pillow talk, a bit more oral explorations. Finally, just before dawn, one more time, they each had sex with Hanne separately. More like lovemaking, signs of intimate caring. Then she vanished to her room and they prepared for the day.

Hanne met the two men at breakfast. They talked of the day. The men were headed farther east; Hanne, to meet the special stagecoach that would take her south to Fort Collins to catch her train on toward Denver. Little was spoken of the evening before, but each felt a sense of camaraderie. But it was kept suppressed, to comply with the manner of the day.

Two men, sitting to the side, watched the threesome. Quietly talking among themselves, their air of subterfuge was not noticeable to any but the most observant.

Bill and James walked Hanne to the stage stop, bid her as fond a farewell as they could for the moment, then turned and brushed by the two men from the hotel as they walked back to catch their ride back to the train.

"Bill, do you think you might find a way to write this into your memoirs?"

"Hardly, Jim, though I do wish I could shout it from the rooftops. But hell, I can't do that either. I still keep pinching myself to make sure it wasn't all a big dream!"

Jim, laughing, "I second that! It best describes my feelings as well. I hope the young lady succeeds with her plans. She has much to offer in many ways. I would treasure her as a friend, and equal, even without what we have experienced."

Hanne stepped up into the coach, seating herself beside the young man in the bowler hat, followed by the two men she had seen watching her at the hotel and even before on the train into Laramie the day before. She was used to being stared at by men, but there was a certain look about them that caused her to be immediately on her guard. They had a furtive thing about them, yet when she caught their eye, a certain hostility showed. She had developed a bit a sixth sense over the years, a gut feeling, especially about men, that was seldom wrong. She hadn't mentioned the men to Bill and James, lest the might decide to take matters in their own hands. She had seen the men board in Salt Lake City. Perhaps it was something else, but she would make sure to not let herself be caught unawares.

The young man beside her turned and "Ma'am, I would like to introduce myself. I am Sean Kelly, late of New York City. I am at your Service until Denver City, if ye have need of anything."

Hanne thanked the man and assured him that she was quite used to travel, but appreciated his chivalry. The next hours were spent bumping up the road through the remainder of Wyoming and into Colorado, stopping for a bit at the Virginia Dale station, which had been temporarily reopened for a few days. Then off to the Forks Inn at Livermore in Colorado. Sean had spoken to her about the two men that were their fellow passengers, and expressed his feelings of mistrust. He also showed her that he was armed. Then, at The Forks, she had went to the facility and, upon leaving it to return to the Inn, was jumped by the two men. She had pulled her gun and was quite prepared to use it, but men had her surrounded and it would have been difficult to shoot both of them. But at that moment Sean stepped from the shadows and placed his big Colt against the back of one of the men's head. Just moments later, a Sheriff and a couple of his men appeared out of the darkness and took the two men into custody. Turned out they were wanted men.

Hanne realized she was quite taken by her young Irish knight. He was intelligent, mannerly and courteous, and, it seemed, quite brave. Moreover, something down deep inside her was starting to feel an attraction to him. Still, she wasn't sure she quite wanted that.

They reached Fort Collins after a short stop in the little town of La Porte. Then they boarded the southbound train to Denver. They both realized they were not quite ready to part ways, and found themselves in a hotel in Denver, mind you separate rooms though.

Denver

Sean had been out early this morning, walking about Denver's downtown streets. The spring morning had just a touch of chill yet, the huge mountains towering to the west, still covered in snow. He watched the men on the street. He liked the way they dressed, especially the boots for riding. Seemed as if everyone in this world rode a horse. He looked at his reflection in the window of the store. Nay, was time to change his appearance to meet his new life. An hour later he stepped into the street with new boots, a Stetson hat - flat brimmed turned slightly down in the front and back, a new set of trousers made of a bit courser material than his fancy pants. He kept his jacket for now. It covered his shoulder holster quite well. He made his way back to the hotel, going directly to the dining room and taking a table near the window so that he might enjoy the traffic on the street.

Half an hour later, the lithe blonde form of Hanne entered the room, causing all heads to turn. She smiled as she caught his eye, causing his heart to flutter. She walked directly to him. He rose and assisted her with her chair. He had to admit to himself, it was flattering to see the looks on the other faces as she chose to join him. He hoped he would be able to become accustomed to those looks of envy.

"Good morning, Sean. Did you sleep well?"

"Aye, lass, th' saints preserve us. If I had not awoke when I did, you may well have been attending a wake, for I surely slept like the dead! T'was the first time I have been able to stretch out for what seems an eternity. And to able to take such a grand bath! I feel entirely like a new man!"

"Looks as if you went shopping as well. New hat, new boots, new whatever else...." she smiled at the 'whatever else'.

"Aye, I plan on starting a new life here. And changing from your old ways is a part of a new start. Change doesn't usually happen unless one changes with it. The hat and boots are just a start."

Hanne laughed her soft, throaty laugh that rose at the end to a tiny tinkle. "Sean Kelly, you have such a wisdom! I declare, I find myself more in wonder of you each hour I know you. Yes indeed, and I most heartily agree! And today is the day we must start! I awoke this morning and as I dressed, I realized that my plans originally had been to go visit Miss Jennie Rogers this morning. But now, I realize that is simply not the path I wish to follow any more. So, do you intend to have a breakfast? Or is that tiny cup of tea your only intake for the morning?"

"No, lass, I was waiting for your fair presence to have my morning meal. To bask in your radiance as I partake of eggs and toast with bacon. And pray tell, who is Miss Jennie Rogers?"

"Oh, she runs Denver's most high class bordello. The famed House of Mirrors."

"Oh, I see. I think."

Sean raised his hand for the waiter, who nodded. Finishing his immediate task, he turned and headed to them.

After a breakfast of eggs with bacon, some cheese, a few pieces of toasted bread, more tea, with a small glass of orange juice and marmalade butter on the toast, the two of them seemed ready to face the day. Sean had found a small hotel farther down Market Street. It was clean and well furnished, but half the price of the one they were in. So they packed their baggage and took a buggy to the new residence. After checking into two adjoining rooms, they decided to explore the city.

The first day was a bit short, so they followed the streets looking at the fashions in the windows and watching the variety of people. As they passed a shop displaying women's gowns, a loud gaggle of voices erupted from within. A shrill falsetto voice cried out.

"You foolish girl! That is much too large a size for me! What do you think I am, a cow? Take it back!"

A softer voice, "But madam, you insisted on that color! Please, let us just try it. We can size it later."

"TAKE IT AWAY!"

"Very well."

Hanne turned to Sean, "Wait here a moment." She stepped inside the door. The sales lady started by her, with the rejected gown.

"Wait, ma'am, if you please. That is a beautiful fabric! And oh my Goodness! The color! Could I please try it? I know I am a bit tall, but maybe your seamstresses might be able to do something?"

The older lady, a bit on the matronly side, was quick to take notice. Her shrill voice erupted again, "Madam, do you really like that?"

"Oh, indeed yes! I have just come from Chicago, and nowhere in that city did I find a gown so beautiful!" Hanne's smile, her glowing face, was working magic on the older lady. She went on. "My goodness! I would hate to take your gown! Especially since the color brings out your beautiful green eyes! And I can just see your hair done up in a certain style would be embellished with the cut of the neckline! Oh, yes, it was made for you! Maybe they have two? I will ask."

The older lady replies, "Maybe I was a bit hasty. I just don't feel well today, my patience a bit worn." Looking at Hanne, "You should not worry, my dear. You can wear anything and still be attractive. Come, girl, let us go to a changing room and see if it can fit me."

Hanne, "Oh, thank you ma'am, for your compliment! And I know you are just going to love it!"

The older lady was lead away by the staff, and a lady walked up to Hanne. She smiled and offered her hand.

"I am Mrs. Brenda Hamilton. Thank you, young lady. That was very well done! I don't suppose you are looking for a position as a sales person, are you?"

"Hanne Clausen, madam. And yes, I am. I have just relocated to Denver from San Francisco. I sold women's clothes there for a time."

"Would you available to start next Monday, say about noon? I am away until then."

Clothing store, Denver, CO

"Yes, that would give me time to get settled. Yes, Monday at noon will be wonderful. Good evening, madam!"

That evening after a light dinner, the two returned to their rooms and opened their adjoining door. They settled down to a glass of wine.

"Well, Miss Hanne, that did not take long! And I will admit and praise your technique, indeed ye are Mistress of the occasion! Now 'tis up to me. I have a bit of funds saved, could last me for several weeks, even living in a hotel. But I shan't await no longer than I must. A gentleman told me today that Denver suffered a serious financial depression due to some legislation about silver thereabouts three or four years ago. He said that it is still being felt today. So I best be looking to the future."

"Yes, but don't think you have to rush out and grab the first thing. Select something that will give you opportunity for contacts of the right sort, and time to plan your next move. I will have the eyes and ears of countless ladies of society in my position. They will show me the next step."

"Hanne, tis a rare combination that ye reflect! Brains and beauty are a rare combination. Thank ye for allowing me to be your friend and partner. It truly is a new life for me. I can hardly wait for tomorrow, to see what it will bring!"

"Well, tomorrow," Hanne smiled her most vixen-ist smile, "Tomorrow we are going to Elitch Gardens, Mr. Kelly, if you would be so kind as to escort me."

"Aye, Madam Clausen! T'would be an honor to my lowly self, to see ye to ye whatever ye said garden..... wherever on God's green earth that might be."

"Do you ride, Sean? I mean, ride a horse?"

"But of course, Hanne. When but a lad, I worked in the stables in the city for the carriage horses. I both learned to ride and to drive as well. Indeed, I was quite interested to maybe be a jockey. But I never quite picked up on the opportunity. But I trained and exercised horses for a bit. Why?"

"Well, the hotel clerk said that a stable nearby gave a good price for people staying here. Many business men and contractors stay here. He has made a deal with stables."

"A fine idea, lass. Would love to take a ride around our surroundings."

Riding through the streets of Denver the next morning seemed surreal to Sean. For one thing, it was just a much different city than the one he was brought up in back east. And two, never had he even dreamed of having a riding companion such as Hanne. Riding just to the right of her, and just slightly behind, her profile against the scene behind her was pleasing to the eye. She sat her horse well. She had complained about the sidesaddle. She said as a girl she had mostly ridden astride. Sean told her in gentile society she would be expected to ride sidesaddle. She smiled and submitted.

She sat straight on the pony, her arms slightly lifted, her body moved with the movement of the horse, she was dressed in a light green gown with matching hat. It was designed as a ladies riding habit, she wore a pair of short black gloves. He watched her as she rode as they climbed out of the Platte River Valley that was Denver, Colorado. As they crossed over 38th Street and Federal, Sean was able to see the mountains to the west. The majesty just seemed to take his breathe away. He studied them as he rode, scarcely aware of the rows of houses and small businesses that had sprung up as the city continued to grow. He looked at what seemed to be a canyon just ahead, but several miles away. He just had to get closer to those mountains! They seem to draw him. He had never experienced anything quite so beautiful. When the man beside him spoke, he just about jumped out of his skin.

"Huh, what?"

"I said, you new to these parts?" The question was directed to him by a man riding a black horse, dressed in a dark suit and black flat brimmed hat. He had a bedroll tied behind his saddle wrapped in a slicker. A Winchester carbine protruded from the saddle boot, and a large revolver hung at his hip. He wore high boots with pull tabs that dangled over their tops.

Sean, totally caught unawares, finally regained his composure.

"Yes sir. Ye fairly well judged me right. I have only just arrived. And, I must confess, was way up there on that mountain when ye spoke to me. Fair scared the wits out of me, ye did."

Hanne had reined her horse back and was now beside Sean.

"Kind sir, I am Sean Kelly, late of New York. I would like to present Miss Hanne Clausen, late of Minnesota."

The gentleman nodded his head and touched the brim of his hat. "Pleased to make your acquaintance, Mr. Kelly, Miss Clausen. I am William Wells. I am manager of a mining operation up in the California Gulch area, better known as Leadville. I am at your service. You two young folks out enjoying the day?"

"Indeed, Mr. Wells. Miss Clausen is escorting me to a fine park in the vicinity called Elitch Gardens, I believe. How about you, Mr. Wells? You seem to be going a bit farther, judging by your rig."

"And it's your turn to make a correct observation, Mr. Kelly. I am headed back to Leadville. Had to make a trip down here for business reasons. I will probably make it to Idaho Springs tonight."

"What's it like up there, Mr. Wells? I mean, is it as beautiful as it seems from here?" Sean asked.

"Even more so, Sean! But I think you will be finding out for yourself. 'Pears to me you have been bitten by the Rocky Mountain bug." William gave a big grin.

"Huh, what is the "Rocky Mountain bug, sir?"

"Well, folks, there is something about that high country that has been getting into people's systems for as long as anybody remembers. The old fur trappers 50 or 60 years ago called it the *high shining*. If it gets you, you are hooked. You will never want to leave. I confess, my first time up, it got me. I left and went back to Mississippi, then went to Texas for a spell, but I just kept remembering. Pretty soon I found my self headed this-away."

It was it was just then they arrived at an intersection, the sign on the street corner pointed to Elitch Gardens. Sean was sorry to see it so soon. He could have talked to the older man for hours at least, if not a day.

"Mr. Wells, I am afraid we must leave you here. I must apologize. Your words about up there" nodding toward the mountains to the west, "fills me with a yearning to explore, I confess. I feel drawn to a place I have never been."

"Well, when you come up, come to see me in Leadville. I would be honored to continue the conversation."

Hanne was silent until now. "Mr. Wells, it is my desire to start a school. What opportunities would be available where you live?"

"Miss Hanne, I must confess, that is out of my field. I do know Leadville has schools, that is about all I know. However, if there is a way to get word to you, I will inquire, and send you anything I might find out."

"Mr. Wells, I have position at *My Ladies Boutique*, on Market Street. If you might find anything, I would be so grateful."

"Then I hope to correspond soon. I must be away, I am burning daylight, and it comes soon in the shadow of the mountains. It has been my pleasure!"

With that he removed his hat and bowed low in the saddle, saying, "Come, Bolt!" He spun the big black around and galloped away.

Hanne and Sean looked at each other. Hanne spoke first. "What a nice gentleman."

"Yes ma'am, he is." Sean replied as he watched the figure getting smaller as he rode away.

Both turned to the right, heading north toward their visit to the park.

Sean stood on the corner of Larimer Street looking down the street. A couple of taverns showed lights thru their windows.

He strolled slowly down Market street. Hanne would be closing the shop in an hour and a half. He would be there to walk her back to the hotel. He walked to the saloon door and stepped inside. A tinkle from a piano tickled his ear, and immediately the smells of alcohol, tobacco smoke, and the dozens of other smells that emanate from almost ever tavern assaulted his sense of smell. The gaming tables were busy. No one seemed to take notice of him. Almost no one, that is. He walked to bar. and ordered whiskey. Shortly it was set in front of him. He took a drink, reminded himself to be more specific next time as to what he ordered.

He turned and leaned his back on the bar, kicking his heel up on the foot rail at the bottom. He picked out about three types of games being played. He spotted four different professional gamblers, and a couple of town drunks. And two others, sitting under the second floor stairs to his left, talking in low voices between each other. They were the only two that sent warning shivers up his neck.

"My good sir, you appear to be the type of gentlemen that would have rather tasted a better grade of drink than was put before him."

Sean turned to see a man, probably in his 50's, maybe early 60's, in a dark suit and hat sitting back on his head.

"Aye, sir. Ya read that right. Not what one would call sipping whiskey."

The man laughed. "Here ya go, son. Let me share a draft or two with you. My name is John Vermillion from Virginia." He poured Sean's glass about quarter way full. "Try that."

"Thank ye, sir. Allow me to introduce myself. I'm Sean Kelly, late of New York City. I was just taking in the sights."

"Young man, ye should been here twenty years ago! That was the time to see the sights, back when me an 'Ol Soapy Smith was wheelin' and dealin! Well, yeah, but I s'pect those days are gone for sure now. But it sure is good to come back to Denver and see the place agin. I'm boardin' th' east bound for Virginny early in the morning."

"So, who is Soapy Smith? Is he here?"

"Naw. They tell me he is up in Skagway, Alaska. But you can betcha socks he is doin' big thangs up there!"

"Sounds like an interesting fellow."

"Yessiree! He got his name by standing on the corner here in Denver and selling packages of soap. Now ya might say that's not a very lucrative job, right? But Soapy, he told everybody that in one of his packages of soap he put a $50 dollar gold piece! Everybody said they need a little soap anyway, so here they came! Sometime during the evening he would have one of his cronies - and he had a few - pop up in a saloon and start hollerin' *Hey I opened this soap, there is a whole wad of cash in it!*' And he would buy a round and, well, business boomed!"

Sean smiled. "Sounds kinda slick to me."

"Yeah, that weren't all either. He started messin' in politics and manupulatin' people runnin' for office. He left town pretty quick. Went up to Creed. I heerd he was up to his ol' tricks up there. Then next thing, he's up in Alaska. You been up in the high country son?"

"No sir. Had a gentleman ask us to come up though. So I imagine we will."

"We? Are they two of ya?"

"Ye'sir. My friend, Miss Hanne Clausen. We are travelin together."

"I see. Well, you two be sure you do just that. Denver is just another city, just as mean and nasty as any other one. There is lots of opportunity up there. There is land, and money to be made. I was lucky here in town, back then. I allas told ol' Soapy that he should have been really happy that the Earp boys and Doc Holliday weren't lawmen here. His life wouldn't have been so free and easy."

"You knew the Earps, and Doc?"

"Yessir, I did. I'm proud to say. When the war was over, I just couldn't stay down south. Had too much stew rumbling round in my gullet. They was too much Union soldiers down there, and no money. So I drifted west. Wound up in some of them cow towns where the drovers were bringin' up herds from Texas. Then down to Arizona. Son, there was a might lot of rebel soldiers out here then, and yankee too. It's too hard to live through something like that, and then just quit."

"So, you were in the War? My father was too."

"Yessir, I served with Wheeler and Forrest both. There was a lot of killin' done, those days. It weren't right those, shouldn't ever happened. Just greedy men."

Sean looked at his watch.

"Well, Mr. Vermillion, I have certainly enjoyed your remarks. An' I swear, I could stand here and listen all night. But Miss Hanne is probably ready to come home about now. So, with that, I will bid you a good evening, and safe journey to your home."

"The pleasure has been mine, lad. Best wishes to you and your young lady. And you listen to what I have to say about going up high. I am about ready to turn in myself."

The men shook hands. Sean left the tavern and hurried to meet Hanne. As they walked to the hotel, he told her of his evening.

As they were reaching the door, he said, "He said his name was John Vermillion."

Hanne stopped in her tracks.

"Sean! *YOU* met Texas Jack Vermillion? He is a legend! I didn't know he was alive! Oh my goodness! You are a lucky man, Sean Kelly!"

The final snow of the winter came on May 5th, filling the streets with drifts and slowing traffic for a few days. Sean found the snow different than in New York, and even Minnesota girl that Hanne was, said she liked it better. They went for walks and skated at a frozen pond near Cherry Creek. It wasn't big, but it was nice. As Sean watched Hanne glide in circles, he thought to himself, *Beauty and grace. And brains.* All in a nearly six foot tall package.

Sean had found a niche in Denver. He gained a reputation for architectural drawing, and he painted signs for businesses. He finally rented a small shop that had previously been a carriage house, just off 6th. It had a small acreage behind it, and a lean-to on the south side. Within about two weeks he had sign business by day, and drew plans in the evening until Hanne got off work. Then the two of them would walk to a local café or dining room and have a leisurely dinner and talk of the day. Coming from as different a backgrounds as they did, they were amazed at the things in common they shared. The goals they both wanted , the things in everyday life that they both enjoyed. By the end of May they had accumulated some wealth, and Hanne had heard of a school up in South Park that the teacher was leaving at the end of the school season. They spoke of maybe visiting the area as soon as the weather settled for spring.

Sean bought two horses. Actually he took two horses in trade for some work he did. One, a black bay mustang gelding about three years old, the other, a sometimes grey, sometimes roanish mare of undetermined breed. Both were saddle wise, sound of feet, bodies and teeth. Finally it was decided. Fourth of July weekend they would take the ride, making preparations to be gone a week or more.

Monday was to be the 4th, so they selected to leave Thursday evening. Sean was elated. He had waited for months now to see that country where the snowcapped peaks were. He dreamed of it. The ride started uphill from the very start. Up through Turkey Creek, through the foothills. Just before Bailey, he came out of the valley and there to his right was Mount Evans. Snow was still covering the peak. It looked as if he could reach out and take it. At Bailey they followed the South Platte River. Higher and higher, the aspens had just gotten their spring leaves, and were busy fluttering them for all to see. The Platte sped by them in a hurry to reach the plains, it had a hundred things to do. Deer were everywhere. Sean had fitted a rifle scabbard on the little mustang, and bought a .44-.40 Winchester to fit into it. His Colt hung in a holster on his right hip. They had spent their first night in Bailey. Now, mid afternoon, they were climbing above the timber on

Kenosha Pass. As they crossed over its broad top, there before them was South Park, looking much as if someone had arranged it neatly and landscaped it to their perfection. They sat and looked at it.

"Sean, it is so big! I wonder where Fairplay is?"

"I am not sure, a bit farther I believe. But look at it, isn't it grand! It makes one think it was touched by the gods! I cannot see a single imperfection. Ah, Hanne, I could spend the rest of me days here!"

Hanne looked at him. It was pleasant to see the young Irishman with a smile on his face and looking happy. Life must have been hard for him in New York. Such a brilliant, talented, courteous gentleman! She felt her heart rate rise a bit. She had not encouraged any intimacy with him, although she could tell he was attracted to her. Several evenings, while home, she would dress quite casually, sometimes probably a bit to casual, but never once had he been suggestive. She was jarred from her musings by Sean speaking.

"Hanne, the town of Jefferson lies just around that curve of mountain. Shall we go there and have dinner and spend the night? Two days in the saddle I am not quite settled to yet, and I wager you might feel the same."

"That is fine with me. I am far better than I would have been if I had been forced to ride a side saddle, though. But yes, perhaps even a bath, if one is available."

Well, a bath wasn't available in Jefferson, but rooms were cheap and the beds were soft. Much better than the bedrolls had been in Bailey the night before. Still, Sean had enjoyed the sleeping under the stars.

The next day as they rode over Red Hill Pass, Sean was still taken by the country around him.

"Hanne, where was the town that the school was in, that you were to go see?"

"The lady said it was a little mining town called Whitehorn. She didn't say where it was, except it was in a place called South Park. If it is anything like this, I think I would like it. I bet the winters up here would be ferocious though."

"I can only imagine. The men in Denver have told me of the snows in the high country, how deep they get."

"We can probably find out when we get to Fairplay."

"Aye, for sure."

"No sir, we have no rooms available, sir. Everyone is in town for Fourth of July celebration. I am very sorry."

"We had no idea there would be this many people here."

"Yes ma'am. Even more than usual this year, because of the war."

"Sir, a thought for ye. Is there perhaps a lady Miss Hanne could share a space with? Me self, I can get by."

"Hmmmm. That is a thought Mr. ...er, ah...."

"Kelly, sir. Sean Kelly. At your service, sir."

"If you would check with me in a while, perhaps maybe we could arrange something."

"Thank ye, sir. You're too kind."

Hanne and Sean elbowed their way through the crowd and found the local café and had a late lunch. As they were finishing, Hanne remarked, "Sean, that was quite gallant of you. You know, the offer at the hotel. I thank you for that, you are so very kind to me. I am not used to that kind of treatment."

"Hanne, it is my pleasure. I enjoy your company. We in so many ways think alike. 'Tis a small sacrifice. Anyway, I like the outdoors. I 'ner thought of it so much in New York. I would sleep on the roofs in the summer, to catch the breezes, but here it is almost pleasurable."

"Why, Mr. Kelly, I do believe you are going to turn into a mountain man on me!" Hanne laughed.

"Mr. Kelly!" It was the hotel clerk. "Good news! We have a couple who are traveling through. The young lady has consented to sharing with Miss Clausen, and her traveling companion is willing to share with you as well. The rooms are adjoining."

"Ah, thank ye sir! you're a saint!"

Hanne and Sean were shown to their rooms and met their roommates, Tom Handy and Maryanne Grey, soon to be Mr. and Mrs. Tom Handy.

"So, Sean, what is your business?"

"I suppose, sir, you might label me a jack of all trades, and maybe master of none. But of late, I have been drawing building designs and plans and doing signs for businesses in Denver. I have a shop there. And you, sir? Or may I call ye Tom?"

"Indeed you may. Well, I am on my way to Leadville. I have been offered a position by a mining company there in their assay office. I trained in California, and came here and was accepted. That is, when I sent for Maryanne. She has been living in Santé Fe with her uncles. We are getting married on July Fourth in Leadville. So in essence, Sean, you and Miss Hanne are our chaperones for the evening. In case wagging tongues were to start. We are taking the stage out tomorrow and have some kin there to stay with tomorrow evening before our wedding."

"That is capitol, Tom! Our congratulations on your new life, Miss Maryanne! Congratulations, and best wishes to ye both."

"Indeed!" Hanne added, "And you are going to live in Leadville, I suppose?"

Maryanne said, "Yes we are. Tom has already secured us a house in the city. He is going to work for a mining company that is owned by a lady, a Mrs. Burns, I believe. He was hired by a Mr. Wells who runs her business interests."

"A Mr. William Wells, by any chance?"

"Why yes, that is his name. Do you know him?"

"We met him a few months ago. He actually invited us up here, although he isn't our reason for being here. He seems a nice man."

"I liked him. He is very straight forward. He is a Southern man, very courteous. He offered me an excellent position at a mine that I understand is not far from here."

The couples talked through the afternoon and evening. As the day was drawing to a close, Maryanne suggested, "Why don't you come to Leadville? Since this place is so crowded, and come to our wedding and be our witnesses? We would be so honored."

Sean and Hanne looked at each other, then both smiled and replied "Sure, why not? We would love too. Thank you for inviting us."

Sean and Hanne excused themselves to go take some air. As they walked through the quiet streets of the town Hanne said,

"Sean, I hope you don't mind this side trip."

"No, of course not. I rather wanted to see Leadville anyway. I have heard so much about it."

"Good, because I need time to talk to this girl. She is nineteen. She is a virgin, and she knows nothing about sex and she is scared to death of her wedding night. This is my first lesson to teach. I am going to try to show her it is not to be feared and can be looked forward to. Oh, by the way, they think we are married. I didn't tell her any difference. Are you okay with that?"

"Sure. It isn't necessary for them to know that right away. Maybe later."

Hanne turned and faced Sean, placing her hands on his arms.

"Anyway, Mr. Kelly, if I was to feel free to marry someone, I think you would be the first on the list. You are a fine man, and a best friend! Right, partner?"

She took both his hands and kissed the backs of them. Sean reached his hand beside her face, then leaned up and kissed her a quick kiss on the lips, answering, "My sentiments exactly, Miss Hanne. My sentiments exactly."

Sean and Hanne were mounted and ready when the stage departed Fairplay next morning. They had to ride at a canter to keep up with the stage for the first few miles, but once they started up over Mosquito Pass the stage slowed to a crawl. The couple welcomed this, as they could ride alongside the coach and talk to Tom and Maryanne. As the trip progressed, they climbed high and higher. Soon they were above the timber. The trail was rutted and rocky, and the heavy coach lurched aback and forth. Maryanne's face began to take on a pale look.

"Maryanne, are you alright?"

"I am not certain, Hanne. I am having difficulty breathing," she wheezed.

"Tom," said Hanne, "loosen her corset, quickly. She needs free breathing. We are reaching a very high altitude and she is not used to it."

It was just then the driver called *whoa* to rest the horses.

Hanne asked, "Driver, can I trade places with Mr. Handy? Miss Grey is having some difficulties, and could use some female help!"

"Yes ma'am, you go right ahead and help the little lady. This is a rugged trail up over the hill here."

While Tom and Hanne switched places, Sean was looking around in awe. Snow patches were everywhere, little miniature glaciers that looked as if they had always been here. And the view! The view was unimaginable! To the west and south huge spines of rock and earth toped with layers of ice and snow stabbed at the blue sky, as if trying to make way for a higher reach. The air was so thin that he was glad he was on a good horse and not on foot. To the north lay miles of forest. He could see at least three or four different kinds of trees. A medium sized rat creature ran across the dirt road, and down between two rocks.

"What in the name of the saints was that?" Sean asked the driver.

"That be a marmot," returned the driver, as he spat a wad of tobacco juice off the side of the coach's high seat. "Little creatures are all over up here."

"Hit-up there, Bessie, Tim, Rounder, Rusty!"

And once again they were in motion. Hanne and Maryanne were talking to each other. Maryanne's color had returned to her face, and she appeared much more comfortable. Within a couple of hours, after another breather for the horses, they lurched to a stop.

The driver called out. "Folks, jump out and stretch your legs! We need to check our equipment for the downhill side. Watch your activity, and I don't advise any alcohol. This is something over 13,000 feet up here and the air is mighty thin. If ya have some snacks, now would be a good time to eat them. We'll be ready in about a half hour."

"Oh, look Sean!" whispered Hanne.

Sean turned to see about a dozen snow white goats, with thick long fur, standing on a stack of boulders.

"Aw, saints alive! Those are Rocky Mountain Goats! I saw a picture of one, I never dreamed of seeing one close up. They are magnificent!"

"They are beautiful," Hanne whispered.

Tom and Maryanne huddled close as they watched the goats. Maryanne spoke.

"Sean, that is wonderful! You are an artist! That is such a good sketch. The goat is simply appearing as I watch, and the mountain, just rising up on your paper! How remarkable!"

"Thank you, Maryanne. I will sketch it now and later perhaps I will either paint or detail it more. This is such an incredible place! I want to capture every detail."

"A'wright folks! All aboard! We are going to do the downhill side now!"

The sun was almost down as they came out of the mountains. The huge range of mountains in the background seemed to serve as a gigantic picture frame for the town below and in front of them. A few lights were starting to show as the stage braked to a stop. Tom and Maryanne were soon mobbed by family and friends. Laughter and tears were the order of the evening. Sean and Hanne stepped to the side and watched the proceedings. Tom broke away, and joined them.

"Hanne, Sean, would you consider continuing your chaperoning for one more evening? We would love to have you. We have grown quite fond of your company!"

Sean looked at Hanne. Hanne replied, "Of course, Tom, it would be our honor. I quite enjoy the time with you fiancé. But tonight it is women's time, no men allowed!"

"Very well, Hanne. After dinner we will give you your space, and Sean and I shall go have a drink together as I spend my last evening as a carefree bachelor!"

After dinner Tom and Sean headed for the Silver Dollar Saloon on Harrison Street. They bellied up to the bar and ordered a pint. The bartender quickly granted their wish. As they drank, they begin to relax and tongues became looser.

"Sean, my friend, I want you to know, I am a bit nervous about tomorrow evening. Maryanne, is, well, she is not acquainted with the relations of a physical nature between men and women. I have, let's say, a bit more, but not with an inexperienced lady as she is. I am not quite sure as how to proceed."

"Tom, I would not fret. It is plain to see that the two of you have a great feeling for each other. I, myself, am not an exceptionally experienced man. So, I would just take things slowly, and let nature take its course."

"But, your Miss Hanne, she is a beautiful woman! Surely you, well, you know..."

Sean smiled, and thought for a moment. "Tom, Miss Hanne and I do not share a bed. We are partners, and have pooled our efforts to further our fortunes. We protect each other, and are the best of friends. But our relationship has not proceeded beyond that."

"Well, I'll be damned! I would have never guessed! You two make a fine couple, and we are proud to call you friends. So be it. Let's drink to it!" They raised their mugs, and clicked them....

Hanne and Maryanne had undressed and dressed for bed. They were sitting cross-legged in the middle of the big four-poster bed.

"Hanne, will it hurt much? None of my friends or none else will speak of it. I really don't know what to expect!"

"Anne, may I call you Anne? Much of how it hurts will have to do with how much you are relaxed, and how much you are stimulated, and the passion you feel toward your mate. You and Tom are both young and healthy, and obviously very much in love. If you in the moment relax, and raise your spirits toward the act of love, you will not find the pain unpleasant for long. Can we speak candidly? Will it embarrass you?"

Maryanne perked up. "Of course. I want to know, I want Tom to be pleased with me. I want him to be happy with me!"

"Anne, the key to Tom being happy is for you to be happy and satisfied in your relationship. For years women have been suppressed, made to feel that the marriage bed was their duty and the act was to conceive children only. And women would respond that way. Then the men would decide that their wives were just cold and uncaring, and they would go find mistresses or prostitutes. That does not need to happen."

"Yes, I can see that"

"Tomorrow evening, when you are alone, you need to tell Tom that you want to be his lover as well as his wife. That you have no experience, but if you will try together, that you will be all he ever wants. Don't be afraid to show your body, and don't be afraid to see his. Learn to explore each other. I advise you to go take a bath first, preferably together. Kiss each other and let your bodies touch each other in the tub. Believe me, you will like it! Let your hands wander, touch and feel each other."

Maryanne, blushing, "Oh, Miss Hanne! I don't know! I don't want him to think me some kind of strumpet!"

"If you make it plain to him this is all new to you, that this is your first time, even to see a man's body, that you simply want to know how it all works, then he shouldn't feel that you are a, well, a 'strumpet'. Be honest with him. Express how much you love him, how you want it to be perfect."

Anne sighed, her head down. She toyed with the folds of her dress.

"I just want it to be good. I do love him so much! When we hug or kiss, I feel the warmth that he emits. I feel the strength of his body, and it excites me! I know that our union can be a bond. And I want it so much! I just have no idea what I will be feeling. I am afraid of the fear of surrender, and the fear of possible pain. I have just heard so many horror stories."

"Anne, I know this is a bit personal, and maybe embarrassing, but…. have you ever - and it is a natural thing, and many, if not most, women do it - have you ever fondled yourself, in your privates?"

"Oh my God! Hanne! Such a question! How could you ask such a thing? And expect a reply!"

"Well, have you?"

Maryanne looked hard at Hanne. Her face flaming, wondering, *where did this tall blonde woman come from, that she could speak with such ease?*

Finally she answered, meekly. "Yes. But not often. And I always felt so guilty afterward."

"But you admit it was pleasurable, right?"

Anne dropped her head and starred at her lap, her face still reddening.

"Yes."

"Then what you are to experience tomorrow evening can be a dozen times more pleasurable. Because it will also be a sharing thing. And it will inspire a passion between you that will add to the experience. So just seek to make it as good for Tom as you can, and relax. With an open mind, you will be fine."

"Oh, Hanne, I hope so! But you said to make it good for Tom, what can I do? I know so little!"

Hanne laughed. She reached forward and put her arms around Maryanne and hugged her.

"You are so brave, my dear! I have shocked you so much this evening, and here you are, still asking for more! Okay, here you go. First of all, don't be modest with your body. Share its sight and feelings liberally. Your body alone will give him great pleasure just to see it and touch it, even before the act itself. If it feels right to you, and if he seems relaxed, touch his penis. Hold it in your hand, move your hand around it, up and down it, watch it grow from its flaccid state until it becomes hard and stiff. If you become bold enough, and he doesn't seem to object, lean forward and kiss his chest, lightly, several places, just tracing your lips over his torso. Then work your way down, kissing, lightly, over his stomach, and when you get that far, kiss his penis, all around it. Then take it in your lips, and maybe into your mouth, but only slightly. These things are things that you grow into over time. Soon they will give you pleasure too. I can't explain how. But they do. I can see by your face you are about to swoon, so I will stop with this."

"Hanne Clausen, how do you even know about these things? Oh my Goodness! Whew! It is just really hot in here, where is my fan? Oh, my. I don't even know what to say!"

"Say nothing, my sweet. It is a new world to you. Take only those things I have mentioned when you feel comfortable. I had this one chance to speak with you, and I know that much of what I said is more than you can deal with. But think about them, and you two just grow together and love each other. Now, any more questions?"

"Only, how do you know so much? You seem far to young to have so much experience."

Hanne smiled. She couldn't tell her that she had been a prostitute. So for now, perhaps a bit of a lie would make the lesson easier to swallow.

"Well, I had an aunt who was brought up in a very free society, where women were allowed to be as assertive as men, choosing their own mates, running the community they were in. She taught me. I had a man for a while, I did what she said, and it worked. We were very happy together, but he was killed. So I know this to be true, and I know that it is the only way I will ever be happy in a relationship. I must have a man who treats me as an equal in all things."

"But, Mr. Sean... aren't you and he... I mean, don't you... rather, aren't you, well, you know?"

"Sean and I are business partners. We are not lovers yet, although I hope and I believe that we will be, maybe soon. But I must be sure. He is kind and respectful, and gallant. And talented. I truly do love him even now, but I can't make a mistake."

"Hanne, I am still speechless. But thank you. You have given me confidence, and I hope for you that Mr. Kelly is the one for you. I agree, he is a really nice man. Ooh, I need to sleep now! Tomorrow is to be a long day! I am so glad I found you as a friend! Whatever happens after tomorrow, I want you to remain my friend and I want for us to be able to talk often! Oh, my head is so full it is spinning! Goodnight, sweet Hanne!"

"Sweet dreams, Anne."

Hanne lay awake for sometime, dreaming. She almost envied Maryanne her love affair, and her innocence. But she knew that would be or her, She thought of Sean, about what he would be like with her. She wished she could find out, but without commitment. But, no, that would not be fair to either of them. Her thoughts gave rise to a hunger down low in her body. Her hand automatically drifted down to the junction of her legs. *No! No cheating! Get serious Hanne Clausen, you have a new life now.*

South Park

As the fire burned down, Marsh notice Sarah's head jerk a bit, her eyes closing.

"Sarah, you need to wake up before you fall in the fire. It's time to turn in. Early day tomorrow. You go first, and get bedded down. I will check on the horses, and be there shortly."

"Oh, thanks Marsh. Yes, I was dozing. I'm on my way." She got up and disappeared into the tent.

Marsh watched her go then got up and walked out to where the horses were grazing. He petted The Buckskin, and whispered some 'pretty boy' and 'goodboy's' in his ear. Then he walked over to Sarah's horse and did the same to him. He looked up at the stars. *My God, who would be able to make a big dome and paint it inside to come close to resembling the splendor of the night sky!* He had spent countless nights looking at that sky during his cowboy days, but nothing compared to the sky over South Park. It was a wonder to behold. He sighed.

Returning inside he found his bunk without a light and, dropping his trousers and his heavy shirt, he crawled in and spread his blanket over him. He slid down and as quiet spread over him, he could hear Sarah's steady breathing nearby. Out in the distance a coyote yipped, then another from the opposite direction. The whoosh of a big night bird flashed overhead. Probably an owl, he thought to himself. But his thoughts were wandering by now.....

"Sarah, time to rise and shine!" Marsh had rebuilt the fire and had water boiling for coffee. He had taken out bacon and some beans, had stirred up some biscuit fixin's. The sun was just coming over the mountains to the east, breaking a bright red. The rolling hills of South Park were lighting up. Heavy clouds had not started to build over the Continental Divide as of yet.

He wanted to head a bit south yet along these foothills before turning west toward Guffey. He had ridden this route several years before, and his cowman's eye picked up on the fact that this was great ranch country. It would be another day's ride toward the town of Balfour, down almost out of the Park. He had never been there but knew about where it was.

"I'm ready Marsh. I will finish the breakfast if you want to catch up the horses."

"I've got it started, at least the coffee. I'll be back shortly."

Marsh headed out toward the sound of The Buckskin's bell, which he tied on every night. He had heard it moments before. He walked up out of a gully and there in front of him was a young man, dressed in sloppy pants and shirt, with a round hat on his head, slipping up on The Buckskin. Or trying to. Whenever he got close The Buckskin would move away. Marsh watched for a moment, then spoke.

"Mister, you may not know it, but you can be shot for stealing a man's horse."

The little man spun so quickly he tripped, and then fell. He scrambled to his feet.

"No! No! No! No steelee! Borrow horse, find help! Chan much hungry, need food, need ride horse for help. Please, Chan just need help!"

"Well, Mr. Chan, where did you come from? How did you get way up here?"

"Chan work for mine, way north," pointing in the general direction of north. "Bad man Boss, he beat Chan. Beat all Chinee man. He bad man, get drunk all time. Chan run away."

"Well, Mr. Chan, where are you trying to get to, after borrowing my horse?"

"Chan go look for job. Chan very good cook. Chan make good dinners, Chan work hard."

Marsh walked over to The Buckskin and slipped his bridle on, then led him over to Sarah's horse, and bridled him as well. He knew something of the bad treatment the Chinese workers got. It wasn't good. Many of them had gotten 'shanghaied' to California, some had come of their own accord. Most of them got a raw deal.

"C'mon Chan, lead this horse back to camp, and we will talk about this." Turning, he took Sarah's hose and started ahead. He wasn't worried about the young man stealing The Buckskin. The mustang took offence to anyone but Marsh riding him. But Chan obediently followed Marsh.

Sarah looked up as the two and the horse popped up out of the gully.

"Who is this?"

"Calls himself Chan. Was going to borrow The Buckskin to go look for a job, he said."

Chan took one look at Sarah about to put food on the fire and jumped to her side so quickly that Sarah jumped back.

"No, no, pretty lady! Let Chan cook for you! Chan make velly good food for you and Mister. Please, pretty lady, go sit while Chan cook."

"Okay, Chan, you go right ahead."

Chan pulled a bag from a cord hanging around his neck. He spread it on a big rock. Next he reached into another unobvious pocket and came out with four nameless eggs and began his preparations.

Marsh and Sarah stepped back and watched as a meal began to take shape. Dough was made, and the magic bag seemed to have all kinds of ingredients in it. Soon a delicious smell emanated from the fire.

"What are we going to do with him, Marsh?"

"Reckon we'll just wait and see. We can help him get to Balfour, maybe help him find a place."

It was just then that Chan said "You come, eat! Breakfast ready!" The couple looked to see two plates set with cups of coffee steaming beside them.

Marsh said "Where is yours Chan?"

Chan said, "Chan no eat your food!"

Sarah said "Chan, you fill you a plate or bowl, and eat with us."

"Thank you, pretty lady. Chan hungry!"

Halfway thru the meal Marsh looked at Sarah. She nodded and smiled.

"Chan, we are starting a ranch up here. If you would like, we will hire you to be our cook. If you really want a job."

"OH! Master Marsh make Chan very happy to be cook for you and pretty lady! Yes! I will work for you! When start?"

Sarah laughed, "You already have!"

Marsh and Sarah stood just under the porch over the forge at Quinn's Livery and Blacksmith establishment in Balfour. The owner was evidently well schooled in horse trading. They had been negotiating for over an hour for a 14 hand paint gelding. Marsh knew and so did the owner, that the little paint was just a bit small for the average user. But he was just the right size for the wiry little Chinaman. Finally a price was agreed upon, with a saddle and tack.

"Marsh, you sure you want to head out, now? That rain sure gets cold, and I believe I saw snow or hail in some of it."

Marsh laughed. "No doubt about it. Seldom see rain up this high that you don't get those little pellets. Mind you now, an hour from now, the sun will be shining. But anyhow, time to go ever to the mercantile and pick up some bedroll and gear for Chan maybe even a coat. And take him to shop for more supplies. I sure like his cooking."

"Good. C'mon Chan, time to go shopping!"

45 minutes later......

"You were sure right, Marsh. It's beautiful, everything is so green, the air is almost to good too breathe! Something smell like butterscotch!"

Marsh pulled up and slid off his horse, dropping the reins to the ground.

"C'mere, Sarah. Come stick your nose between the cracks on this tree."

As he talked he walked over to a large pine tree Sarah dismounted and followed. She stuck her nose up to the tree and looked at Marsh.

"Well, I never! What kind of tree? Come here, Chan, smell this. I know not all pine trees don't smell this way."

Chan leaned into the tree. He stepped back and made a face and said something in Chinese that ended in a high note.

"It's a Ponderosa Pine. Really smells good, huh? Ok, we are burning daylight. But thought you might like that."

Marsh watched as Chan wiped the paint pony down and talked to it in a low voice. The green hills behind him were accented with the white trunks of aspen trees. The darkness behind the small forest might have looked ominous except for the last rays of sunshine piercing it.

They would be a day later than he planned getting to Guffey, but that didn't matter. They had lost a day but gained a cook. He was surprised to see the Chinaman so seemingly proficient with horses. Seemed to like them, too. Guess maybe his worldly education was a bit lacking in that area.

Sarah came walking around the trees. She had gone to the small creek to bathe; a few days on the trail made even the cold mountain water acceptable. She was toweling her hair and had a bit of glow to her cheeks. She headed directly to the fire.

"You feel better now Miss Boss lady?"

"Yes I do, Mr. Ranch Foreman. But that water does take some getting used to. But I will sleep better tonight."

"Miss Boss Lady, Chan think you boss. Mr. Marsh, thought pretty lady your wife. Chan not understand."

Marsh looked up to see the Chinaman's look of perplexion.

"No, Chan, I work for Miss Sarah. We are looking for a ranch to buy, and I will be the boss of the ranch."

"Oh. Chan never work for lady boss before. But no matter, do good job anyway."

Sarah looked at Chan. "I know you will Chan."

Days went by. Marsh and Sarah explored valleys and mountains along the east side of South Park. They rode west one afternoon, As they dipped into Badger Creek, they turned downstream about a quarter mile. There the small stream trickled down a narrow bed, then, just before rounding a bend to the right, it started getting bigger and bigger.

Sarah exclaimed, "Marsh! The creek is getting bigger!"

"Yep, these are all springs. Water flow pretty much triples right here."

The three rode up over a small rise and there before them was a beautiful waterfall with little rivers of water pouring between huge boulders. Big, flat rocks glistened in the sun, surrounded by pools of clear water. All this housed in a narrow canyon with towering walls, high on each side. The larger creek now flowing from the waterfalls was much nosier, but pleasantly so. They dismounted and led the horses down to the creek. Chan was acting like a rabbit going down the creek, jumping from rock to rock. He stopped, and called back.

"Hey Boss! Chan go wash horse stink off and look for dinner."

Marsh nodded. The sun was dropping over the mountain to their right. It would be dark soon. Marsh found a bunch of downed timber on the other side of the creek, and carried it in for firewood and built a fire. He carried the tent over the creek and in a small clearing where he set it up. When he returned, Sarah was still sitting looking at the water.

"Marsh, as soon as it gets dark I am going to bathe. You and Chan are just going to have to make yourself scarce."

Marsh laughed. "That's fine, but have you checked the temperature of that water? It is mighty cold, it is all spring fed."

"I don't care. It was hot today, and like Chan said, I smell like a horse now. Mind you, I love my horse, but I don't want to smell like him. Besides, it can't be much worse than these little streams we have bathed in before."

"We will make way. You can have all the privacy except from those."

"Those what?"

Marsh pointed up across the creek. Up high silhouetted against the evening sky was a bighorn ram and about 6 ewes, staring at them from their lofty perch.

"Them."

"Oh, how beautiful! They are magnificent! Oh, Marsh, if only I could paint! I write about these places we visit, and try to describe what I see. But to be able to capture that, oh, my!"

After dinner they sat around the fire. Marsh told them stories about the area, and how this creek had been one that Kit Carson had trapped on back in the 40's. Then he had to explain to Chan who

Carson was. By the time he was finished, Chan took his bedroll and said he was going up on the ridge to sleep where he could see the stars.

Marsh looked at Sarah. "Ok, Missy, I will build the fire up and go to my tent. Luckily, it is a warm evening by South Park standards, and there is no wind. The falls are yours."

Marsh picked up his canteen and went to the tent. He went inside and rolled his bed out. It was about then he realized Sarah's towel was laying on her bedroll. He picked it up and stepped out and walked to the ledge, looking down. He was too late. She had already undressed and was standing almost hip deep in the pool.

Marsh started to pull back, hoping she hadn't seen him, but something stopped him. She was beautiful. A slender form that the flickering fire highlighted. Her breasts stood high, her hair hung half down her back. She had nice hips, not as slender as her body was, but shapely. A small patch of short tightly curved hairs set at her pelvic mound. Her arms were lifted, as she eased her way into the water.

Marsh was frozen where he stood. As she turned, her beautiful butt was turned toward him. Oh God! He should not be seeing this, but he could not pull away. *Jeezus.* But finally he did. He returned to the tent and crawled under his blanket. It was only minutes, till he heard her outside.

"Marsh, if you are still awake, please turn away, I forgot my towel."

"Okey doke. C'mon in."

He heard her come in and grab the towel. He could hear her shivering. She got dry and got into her bed, but the shivering continued. He could hear her teeth chattering.

"Sarah, I think you are dangerously chilled. I was concerned about that. I am coming over and lay with you to help warm you. We don't want you getting sick out here."

Marsh grabbed his bedroll and pulled it next to her he threw his blanket over her, and then crawled under both. As he settled next to her he realized she was still nude, and he was still wearing his drawers. He reached around her, and drew her next to him. She was shivering uncontrollably. He pulled the blankets closer and leaned over her pressing his body onto hers so as to transfer as much of his body heat around her as he could. He wrapped his arms around her, and pulled her to him. Lowering his head, he blew his warm breath slowly onto her breasts and chest and neck. He held her tight for what seemed like half an hour. Slowly the shivering subsided, and she started to relax. They lay quietly.

He loosened his arms, and started to move away.

"No, Marsh, don't let me go yet, please."

Marsh chuckled, "Okay, you're the boss."

"Damn you, Marsh!" she laughed.

They stayed close for another few minutes. Then Sarah turned in his arms and faced him. Her breast brushed his bare chest, the nipples still hard. As she put her arms around his neck and pressed herself tightly against his body, she pulled her head back and kissed him fully on the lips, at first softly, then more eagerly. She leaned back and looked at him fully into his eyes. She smiled.

"Marsh, stay close to me tonight. I don't think I realized how much I needed to be held. A person forgets, sometimes, that need." Sarah rolled him back onto his side facing her. She lay looking at him.

"Marsh, I really like you. I realize we are in an unconventional relationship. I don't want this to go any farther tonight, but I still want you close to me, if it is alright with you. If you can be comfortable with it."

Marsh hesitated. What was he supposed to say? He was never so confused in his life! He liked his pretty young boss, but how would that work? He was quite attracted to her, especially after tonight. He thought it was something to be talked about, something to proceed slowly with. Take it a day at a time.

"Very well, Sarah. I am here, go to sleep. We need to keep you warm tonight."

The next morning the trio saddled up and rode the next two or three miles to Whitehorn. The early morning sun highlighted them as they sat on the ridge above the little town nestled into the small park. The smoke from the hotel restaurant below gave promise to a breakfast of bacon, eggs and biscuits.

After breakfast the two walked across the town and down to school house in the south corner of the city limits. Children were playing; one little boy with about a three foot hoop and a stick was rolling it as fast as he could. A little girl with blonde curly hair and a white dress with little flowers stood to one side, watching. A young lady in her twenties wearing a dark dress was standing by the tiny school house door, watching her charges. High over head an eagle screamed. Marsh looked up, just in time to see the big bird dropping out the sky, headed directly for the little girl. He reacted quickly. As the eagle struck the girl, Marsh grabbed the raptor, causing it to break it's hold. He released it as soon as released it's grip on the child.

The little girl was screaming. She was terrified. The boys had abandoned the hoop and were running back to her. Sarah quickly folded the little girl into her arms.

"Shhhh, shhhhhh sweetie. You are ok now. The bad bird is gone. Mr. Marsh ran him off, nothing is going to hurt you now. Quickly, now, let's look at your scratches."

The child was still crying. She had a deep gash in her arm, and another in her shoulder and back where the powerful talons had caught her. Marsh picked her up out of Sarah's arms and turning to the schoolmistress, who was just reaching them asked "Ma'am, where is the doctor?"

The mistress pointed, "That building just to the right of the mercantile." Marsh started in at a run, with Sarah close on his heels. As he reached the door he shouldered his way inside. A slight built young man in his late thirties, wearing small glasses that sat down on his nose looked up from his desk.

"What's wrong with the child?"

Sarah answered, "An eagle almost got her."

"Oh my. Put her on the table, let's have a look. She isn't your child, is she? Of course not, she is pretty Patricia. Hello, Patricia. Her Dad is the telegraph operator. Could you run to the post office and let him know? Missus, would you stay with me, please? I think she would feel better"

Whitehorn Stage Stop, aka known as US Post Office and probably telegraph office

"Of Course," Marsh wheeled to the door.

Later, after Patricia's parents arrived, they continued their walk. They went up on the north side of Whitehorn and into a canyon that eventually widened into a meadow full of aspen. They turned and headed east along a ridge that took them to meadow on the north side of the town. Looking down at the town site, they passed miners digging along the way, stopping occasionally to speak to someone Marsh knew. They stopped on the ridge and sat on some big flat boulders under the aspen. Far to the east you could see the hazy outline of the front range of the Rockies. On a clear day you could see Pikes Peak.

Sarah sat down hard on the big rock.

"Phew, that was bit of a climb!"

"It's the rarefied air makes it seem more so than it really is."

Sarah smiled.

"Sarah, have you ever thought about having children? I mean, if you ever get married again?"

"Of course, in due time. I love children. And, by the way Marsh, that was quick thinking back there."

"Scared me. I knew about an eight year old boy that an eagle carried off and killed over in Mississippi. Back in the 70's I think. A friend of the family, I think. Sure didn't intend for her to wind up that way."

"Marsh..." Sarah lay down on the flat boulder Marsh had lain back on.

"Marsh, about last night. I know you were only trying to protect me, but it made me realize that I, in my own little conservative way, have been quite attracted to you. And I had a good relationship with my husband, a good physical relationship is what I am speaking of. We were quite affectionate with each other. I miss that. I don't want to jump in over our heads, I treasure the partnership we are working on, and I don't want to endanger it. But, can we court? I mean, could you court me, as we work together?"

"Sarah, I think we can. I pride myself as being a cautious person. You seem to be a disciplined woman. I would be honored to call on you, ma'am, when we are at leisure. I, however, would like to encourage total honesty between us. If at anytime you feel uncomfortable, you are to tell me. I give you my word, it will be put at ease. You are giving me a chance to have a ranch and spread to care for, I don't want to jeopardize it for either of us. And in the spirit of honesty, I must confess, I saw you last night as you were starting to bathe. It was not my desire to spy on you. I found your towel, and was going to bring it to you, but you were already undressed. I was spellbound for a moment, but finally gained control of my sense and returned to the tent. My intentions later was but to get you warm, and nothing else."

"I believe you, Marsh. And that says much for your character, to not try to take advantage of my vulnerability of the moment. You could have, with little effort. I admire you more for it."

Sarah rolled over and leaned above Marsh. She touched his face with her hand and straightened his hair over his ear. Then she leaned down and kissed him, running her lips softly along his, then rubbing her nose to his.

"Sarah, I am only human, so keep that in mind. And understand, I am attracted to you as well."

"Ok. Let's go exploring again, sir!" She jumped up and extended her hand to help him arise.

He took her hand and pulled himself to his feet

Whitehorn, Colorado looking a bit NE. at the bottom of Cameron Mountain. In the background rises Black Mountain, about 15 miles away. Circa 1901

"This way, ma'am." A few minutes and at least three claims being worked later, they reached Marsh's old cabin and claim. No one was home at the tiny cabin, so they turned their paths back to town and were soon having lunch at the Whitehorn cafe, when Chan appeared. Marsh motioned him to sit and eat. He smiled.

After the three ate, they went outside and sat on the porch of the hotel. They were enjoying the last rays of sunshine before it sunk below the continental divide, when Arne and Jon Johanson appeared.

"Mr. Redman!"

"Oh, hello, Arne, Jon. I would like you to meet Miss Sarah Burns, and this is Chan."

The men nodded, both Sarah and Chan acknowledged the greetings.

"Mr. Marsh, we have the papers for the claim, if you would sign them."

"Of course I will. Here, put them on the table. Sarah, do you have a pen? How is it working out for you?"

"We have not hit anything big yet. It has paid for itself and bought our supplies. The assays are good, we have hopes."

"Well, I am glad. Good for you."

"Ja, we are not worried. We are both carpenters. When we are not mining, we are building. We just finished a building in Salida. We also have some experience as bricklaying. There is plenty of work here."

"Boys, that is good to know. Miss Burns is looking to build a ranch. When we find the right place, we will need some carpenters. If you are available."

"Ja, Mr. Marsh. We will make ourselves available when you are ready."

As the afternoon faded into evening, the sun dropped, spreading shadows across Whitehorn, lighting the buildings and the timbered hill behind it. As twilight settled, it seemed that time stood still, that motion had ceased. Even the town seemed to have become deserted, and held a ghostly appearance. The couple sat on the ridge that lay on the northwest side of the small park. Sarah leaned to Marsh.

"Marsh I am afraid to speak. The moment is full of magic. The town, the mountains, the dying sun, the lighting, the stillness; my heart almost seems to want to hesitate, to wait for a moment. That something totally un-explainable will happen that we will be witness to, something marvelous. I am so happy. I don't think I have ever felt this way." She slid her fingers into his hand, locking her fingers into his and clasping them tight. Far up on the hill across the way, a pack of coyotes started making plans for the evening hunt.

Marsh, Sarah, and Chan sat on their horses. The late July sun beat down relentlessly. Where is struck bare skin, it felt like tiny needles piercing. Yet, a slight breeze off the Continental Divide kept it comfortably cool. Behind them Cameron Mountain, just a few feet short of 11,000

feet, seemed dwarfed when compared with the display before them. The long chain of the Rockies filled a panorama starting to their right, and as their gaze swept to left, Mount Princeton, Shavano, and Antero pierced the blue summer sky. Then, as their gaze traveled to the south and east, the Sangre de Cristos rose into the sky, tracing a pathway to the south.

"Chan took a breath. "Aww, velly plitty. Have no ever seen so big mountains since Chan small boy. When little, he lived near big mountains west of China. So long ago!"

"Chan, you are so right. This whole place is so beautiful!" Sarah answered.

"I have been taken with it for some time. I first visited these parts in '84 after a trail drive up to Cheyenne. Never quite happy with Texas afterward. Mind you, Texas has some pretty places."

Coming up the hill in front of them were a couple of riders, a man and a woman. As the couple broke out of the aspens, when suddenly a bear came loping down the hillside past them. That was just too much for her mount. It squealed and bolted. The rider sitting in a side saddle was quickly unhorsed and tumbled into the short brush. Like a flash, Chan was in pursuit of the runaway horse, heading it off. Within a couple of hundred yards he was alongside and had its reins, pulling it into a circle and stopping it. Sarah and Marsh hurried to the lady and her companion. Sarah dismounted and ran to the woman's side. She knelt over her and cradled her head in her lap. The young lady moaned, then slowly set up, apparently not injured to any great degree.

"Careful, now. Let's check you over, make sure you are alright."

The girl laughed lightly, "I am alright, just greatly embarrassed that I wasn't able to control my horse. But that bear just came out of nowhere! Thank you so very kindly. I am Rose Bennett. My husband, Adam Bennett." She motioned.

"I am pleased to make you acquaintance. I am Sarah Burns, this is my ranch foreman and business partner, Marsh Redman, and Chan, our cook."

"Miss Burns," Adam spoke, "Did I understand Mr. Redman is your foreman? Do you have a ranch in these parts? I thought I knew most of the ranchers hereabouts."

"You heard right, Mr. Bennett. Miss Burns is looking to buy a place and start a ranch." Marsh answered.

"And where did you prefer for it to be?"

"Mr. Bennett, we all really like the southern Park County and northern Fremont or east Chaffee Counties area."

"Well Mrs. Burns, fate, and that damn bear, may have brought us together! Rose and I are here to sell my father's place. He came here in the 60's. I was born and reared up here. His ranch is on the west side of the Park, near Trout Creek Pass. Maybe 40 miles or so from here."

"How many acres?"

"Neighborhood of 5,000."

Fairplay

Sean was looking for Hanne. The wedding was over and the bride and groom had been whisked away. Hanne had spent the entire day with Maryanne, assisting her in all preparations. Sean had consoled the nervous groom until that moment when the couple stood together before the minister and made their pledges to their life together. Sean himself listened to the pledges, and then caught the eye of Hanne and saw a mistiness and a look that he had not seen before. He smiled, and received a smile in return. Gone was the almost tough confident bearing he normally saw. Instead, a sweetness, a vulnerability, a touch femininity that left him a bit breathless.

But where was she now?

"Mr. Kelly, I believe." The soft southern baritone voice hailed him. He turned to see William Wells approaching him.

"Mr. Wells! A pleasure, sir, we meet again."

"I wasn't aware that you and Miss Clausen, I believe was her name, were friends of young Tom and his new bride?"

"It is a recent acquaintance, sir. But one that quickly grew into a friendship. We met them in Fairplay, and had the honor of chaperoning them until the wedding. They are a fine young couple sir. We are proud to know them."

"Ah yes, I am sure. Tom is going to work in one of our company assay offices. He came highly recommended. I will confess, I had not time to be allowed an introduction to his new wife, but they seemed quite happy today, despite the drama of a wedding."

"Yes sir. They are quite taken with each other."

"So, are you and your companion here on business or just taking a holiday?"

"Some of both, sir. We both wanted to see what the high mountain world was like. I have started a business in Denver. Miss Clausen wants to start a school. We thought maybe up here would offer an opportunity. And again, sir, you encouraged us, do you remember?"

"Aye yes, I do remember. What type of business do you have Mr. Kelly?"

"I do landscape and architectural drawings. And we also do signage."

"Splendid. Ah! Here is the young lady now."

Sean turned as Hanne approached and took his arm.

"Miss Hanne, so good to see you again!"

"And you as well, Mr. Wells. Did you see the wedding?"

"I did. I was just telling Mr. Kelly that young Tom is to work for our company. Are you enjoying Leadville during your stay?"

Hanne laughed. "I am afraid that I have not seen much of it. And I am not sure how long we are to be able to stay."

"Well, I am going to try to detain you. If I may, I am going to offer you lodging for a few days in order to entice you to stay a few days. I must go to Fairplay tomorrow, I will be back in a few days. I have a venture that you might be interested in. Could I offer the two of you dinner tonight? What say you? I will explain a bit more then."

Hanne and Sean looked at each other Sean answered, "Sure, we will do that. I will send a message to my foreman in Denver that we are delayed."

Sean and Hanne slept late. The dinner last evening with Mr. Wells had been intriguing. Mr. Wells' southern manner was easy and relaxed. During dinner the conversation ranged from history items in the old south to Sean' life in the big city of New York to Hanne's life and Minnesota, a place Mr. Wells said he knew nothing about. But his natural curiosity touched every aspect of the state - industry, weather, natural resources. He said that after the great war he started to see how the massive rebuilding would affect everyone. Fortunes would be made. It would be a time for expansion, a time for exploring our great country. He closed by admitting he wished he had found Colorado a bit sooner.

"Hanne!" Knock knock. "Are ye living dear?"

"Yes, yes. Well, mostly. I believe that last glass of wine was a bit much. Ok, be there in a minute!"

"Take your time. I will be in the restaurant."

"Mumble, mumble….."

Sean joined William Wells at his table.

"Good morning, Mr. Wells."

"And you as well, Mr. Kelly. Is Miss Clausen to join us this morning?"

"Aye, sir. Shortly, I believe."

"Ah, well, let's us have a cup of coffee while she waits Where is that waiter?"

"If you don't mind, sir, tea for me."

"Tea it is."

"There is our Miss Clausen now! Lovely, as usual. Did you sleep well, my dear?"

"I did, Mr. Wells, thank you."

"While we are waiting for the waiter, I have a proposal. My employer, Mrs. Burns, has given me leave to invest her profits from her mining interests. One of the things we are to do is build a couple of hotels. After our talk last evening, and viewing some of your drawings, I would like for you to go to Salida. I will give you an address. I would like for you to design me a building. I will pay you for your time, and your board and travel expenses will be on me. I like you both. Miss Hanne, I feel this will be a joint venture for you both. You show great taste in your manners and dress, you possess and project a great confidence. If you are schooled to be a teacher, I feel those same talents will be of use to me. Every business needs a woman's touch. If and when we build these hotels, I will need someone to decorate and someone to train staff. Do you see where I am coming from?"

Hanne and Sean both nodded. They were both a bit stunned by the offer. Still, both could see the advantages to it. The portfolio that could emerge would be several steps up their success ladders.

"Mr. Wells, you are most kind, sir. Without speaking to each other, I am in favor of the arrangement. Hanne?"

"Yes, I can see advantage of a course such as this. You are taking a huge gamble, Mr. Wells. You don't know either of us well, but if you are willing, I agree with Sean. Yes."

"Very well. I must leave this morning for Fairplay. Come to the office today, and I will have vouchers and letters of introduction ready for you. Actually, they are already ready. I took the liberty of assuming that you would be in favor." He smiled, "Go by way of Buena Vista, and go look for the hotel at Cottonwood Hot

Springs. It is a small resort and sanatorium. I like its basic design, but it isn't quite as fancy as I would like. Do me some sketches, both landscape and floor plan, and mail them to my office.
I can't tell you how happy this makes me. I am looking forward to you meeting Mrs. Burns and Mr. Redman, her ranch foreman. They are presently wandering all over South Park. Maybe they will be in Salida at some point. Now, if you would excuse me, I must catch my train. I look forward to hearing from you soon."

Sean remarked as they shook hands all around, "You are a busy man, Mr. Wells."

"And, as you well know Mr. Kelly, your world never changes until you start walking. Good day Miss Clausen."

Hotel at Cottonwood Hot Springs, near Buena Vista, Colorado

Sean and Hanne had been at Cottonwood Hot Springs two days when Sam, one of the staff, told Sean, "If you and your lady would like to share a hot spring experience privately, I can show you where to go." Turns out, above the resort a couple of hundred yards a spring came out and ran into the creek. By building a little dam to divert some of the water, you could make the temperature cool enough for bathing. In most places it was too hot.

"So, here I am Mr. Kelly. I have a lot of trust in you. You are leading me down a wilderness path in the middle of the night, dressed in a robe, and carrying only a lantern and a towel. This had better be good."

"Ah, Hanne, I think ye will be pleased, from what I saw this afternoon. Here, we are almost there."

"Sean, it's beautiful! The pool, the rocks and trees around us. The steam on the water!"

"Here, Hanne, I will turn my back. You get in. No, wait, you turn your back, and I will make sure the temp is right. Ah, yeah, a bit hot, but that is the purpose. If you don't like it, I will cool it some."

Sean turned and listened for Hanne to enter the pool. The flickering lanterns cast shadows that played on the rocks, reflecting from the pool to the aspen leaves above them. He heard her say "Oh, my!" He turned slowly. She was submerged to her waist, her breasts floating on the hot water she was like a golden goddess. The light from the lanterns lit her hair and golden skin.

"Hanne, saint's preserve us! You are so beautiful lass. I have never seen anyone like you. I expected you to be totally underwater, but here you are like one of those portraits of the goddesses in the books at the New York Library. Oh, my, I shall try not to stare!"

Hanne leaned back on a rock and slid down into the water, her blonde hair floating around her, just her nipples sticking above the surface. She closed her eyes, her head back. She lay that way for minutes. Then she lifted her head, and looked at Sean. Her eyes held a strange look, a warmth, and something else he didn't recognize. But it excited him.

"Sean, we have been together for months now. You have become my confidant, my companion, my very best friend ever. Our lives just seem to grow together in every way. For sometime now, I have been thinking that, well..." she set up and moved across the pool to him putting her arms around his neck and pulling him close, "…well, I want you. My body wants you, and I am tired of saying no. I think, no, I do love you, Sean."

She pressed her body to his, her lips meeting his, kissing him hungrily. Her breasts against his chest, her belly flattening against his as she brought her legs around and wrapped then 'round his hips. He could feel himself erect, hard, and as her pelvic met his, he slipped inside her. They stood in water above their waists, wrapped in each other, almost motionless. Arms wrapped tightly, mouths tasting mouths, he had dreamed of this. Not often, mind you. He couldn't allow himself. But now, the wonder was answered. They started to move, hips thrusting to hips. It wasn't long before the mutual hunger took them to their pinnacle. Hanne moaned aloud, Sean gasped at his release.

They stood, arms locked, still kissing. Softly, sweetly, their faces smiling, their eyes spoke of the joy they felt. They drifted over to the little sandy beach and lay together. They were still joined together, reluctant to pull apart.

"Sean, that was so wonderful! I knew it was right, I care so much for you!"

"Hanne, this was so unexpected! I scarce know what to think, but what I know is, is I have been given an incredible gift, and will treasure it and honor it's giver as long as ye will have me."

Adam and Rose followed Marsh and Sarah to Salida that afternoon. The evening was spent discussing the properties in question. Was it watered properly? How did the land lay? They were able to reach Salida in time to procure maps from the courthouse, although the property lay in a different county.

Adam described the hills, the backdrops to the mountains, the vegetation available for grazing. It lay northwest of Salida, and a bit west of Hartsel. The decision was made to gather supplies and head up that way the following morning.

Daybreak found the five riders following the Arkansas River upstream. As the morning progressed, they left the river following a canyon that took them past the town of Turret, then north along a long ridge covered in aspen for what seemed miles. It was late morning on the second day when they topped a hill and looked into a valley.

Adam said "That is it. It runs all the way along that valley, then back to the west to the base of the mountains. Then north to that gap, up there. A lot of it is in timber back there, but even there, there are meadows for grazing and shelter for winter. Badger Creek gets its start somewhere up there."

Sarah sighed, "It's beautiful, so serene! Almost looks as if time stands still here."

Rose said "Adam's father would say, on occasion, that it was where God would come to spend an afternoon of rest."

"Miss Burns, and where would you like your house to be built?" Marsh smiled.

The look of rapture filling Sarah's face made him feel good inside. Himself, he could never have expected to find a place like this. The long meadow of grass, the rocky crags that seem to be reaching for the sky. Until you looked past them to behold the mighty behemoths that truly could be home for the sky Gods. Yeah, it would do.

"Well, I just don't know Mr. Redman, seeing has how I have been here for a whole three minutes. I just haven't planned that far enough ahead, so it seems." she laughed.

Marsh smiled as the others laughed heartily at the exchange.

Adam said "Marsh, let us head off down that valley. Around that corner of that ridge is the remains of the old cabin dad built. It burned in a brush fire a few years back, but the corrals and some out buildings are still there. We can unload the pack horses and go for a bit more ride."

"You lead out, Adam. We will follow you."

Riding beside Sarah, he leaned over, "So, what do you think?"

"I think yes! But I would like to see more before I say yes."

"Smart lady, my boss!" he grinned.

After a cold lunch and unpacking the pack horses, the two men and the women left Chan to set up his camp. They headed out into the hills and rode in a semi-circle for about three and a half hours. They came across two different running streams, one of which they decided was Badger Creek. They were nearing the old ranch site when a rider came tearing across the flat at a dead run. It was Chan. He was saddle-less and bridle-less, just using the little horses halter to guide her. He saw them and turned and rode to them, pulling his horse up short. It was plain to see something was wrong. He was talking a mixture of English and something Chinese, but mostly, undefinable.

"Chan, slow down, please! Speak slowly, what is wrong?"

"Bear, Mr. Marsh! Big, big, bear! got horse, tried get Chan! Chan run away velly fast."

"Oh crap!" Marsh pulled his saddle gun from it's boot, "All of you stay back, and watch around you! I am going to ride ahead. Maybe I will get a shot at him. It hast to be Ol' Mose, he is 'bout the only grizzly left, and it must be a grizzly to have attacked the horses. Now keep your eyes open!"

He eased The Buckskin out ahead. By the time he reached the corrals, he could see it was too late. Both horses were dead. One had been fed from, the other just killed. He rode a circle around the kills. There, in the soft dirt was the rear track with the missing toe, and it was headed east, back toward Black Mountain, miles away. He kicked the Buckskin into a lope. After a mile, the track never varied. He was going home.

He rode back to the corrals. Rose was aghast at the slaughter. Sarah seemed concerned, but show no particular emotion.

"What do you think, Marsh?"

"I think he is headed home. Look, I don't want to stay here though, with a fresh kill next to us. Lets throw the gear in that building, and ride for Hartsel. It will be late, but the hotel is nice, and everyone will be safe for sure. But we better get moving, it's a long ride over there."

"Adam, you and Rose will be our guests tonight. Let's ride."

It was about an hour after dark when the riders pulled up at the livery behind the hotel. Everyone was tired, hungry and still excited about the days events. The kitchen was closing, but was happy to oblige the late guests.

Sarah spoke. "Well, Adam, Marsh and I have had scarce time to talk, but we want the ranch. The price is right. It is where we would like to build. So if you will, I would like to shake hands on the deal."

"Thank you, Miss Burns. I was afraid after that episode this afternoon, you would find it a bit too wild. I am happy to shake your hand, and Marsh's as well!"

Marsh said, "Adam, pleasure to take your hand. That old bear is a dangerous one. He is needing to be taken down pretty soon. He is the last of his kind around here. He has killed lots of cattle and sheep and horses, and a few men up here. Chan had a really close call today. Good job getting away, Chan!"

Chan nodded, "Yes, Boss Marsh. Chan not like big bear."

When their dinners were served, Marsh turned to Chan.

"Chan, I have been meaning to ask this, but the time never seemed quite right. But now, tell me, are Chinamen all as good a horsemen as you are? You, on occasion, have made me think you might be half Comanche!"

"What Comanche, Boss?"

Everyone laughed.

"Well the Comanche's were a tribe of Indians that were down in Texas. Actually, they came up here too. They were great horsemen and warriors. So, how about it? How do you know so much about horses for a Chinaman?"

Chan looked down at his plate, "Boss, don't be mad, will tell whole story. Chan not from China. Come from much farther away. A place that looks like this place. Chan not right name. Name is Chagan. Chagan is a Mongol. Chagan grew up with horses, would sleep in the herds of horses on the plains, could ride when almost a baby. Chagan loves horses, so sad when bear killed horses. They should have been buried, Boss. Boss, don't be mad."

Marsh reached across and lay his hand on the man's shoulder.

"Chagan, we are not mad. You are welcome with us. Tell us about you came to be here."

"Chagan was very young man. He was caught by Chinese bandits and sold in Shanghai as a slave. He came to America on a boat. Very hard, very sad. Never see home again. Was force to work on railroads, then in mines. Ran away 3 times and was sent back. That is when Chagan found you and pretty boss lady."

"Well Chagan," Marsh put his hand on the man's shoulder, "We hope you get to call this home now."

"Thank you, Boss! Chagan feels better here."

"Marsh, when can we get started with the building? When can we go live at our ranch? And what are we going to call it? Have you thought about that?"

Sarah's face was all aglow. She had stepped into Marsh's room, everyone else had turned in for the night. It was alright, Marsh was just as excited as she was. She had walked right up to him, and was looking up at him. He just couldn't help himself. It could have been the desire he had felt for the last weeks, or the excitement, or just the attraction. But he reached out and pulled her to him, and kissed her very tenderly, lingering on her delicious lips for what seemed like hours but were really seconds. He relaxed his grip slightly, but still held her in an embrace. He looked down at the wonderment in her face that had softened. She was holding him as well, just as securely.

"Miss Burns, you really need to quit asking me three questions at once without pausing to breathe. If I try to answer you, I might just pass out from lack of oxygen in this rarified air up here."

"Mr. Redman, I didn't hear you breathe in that 15 minute kiss, that you just presented me with just now, so I don't believe it will be a problem. Would you like to answer now, or practice holding your breathe again?"

"Miss Burns, I don't want to ever fail you in any of my endeavors as foreman of your ranch. Those were very long complicated questions, and just maybe I should practice my breathing again, to make sure I got it right!"

"I hoped you would say something like that. Actually, I have been hoping for weeks."

She stepped closer and lifted her face to his, sliding her hand up behind his neck and holding her mouth to his. She was so delicious. He felt like he could do this for days.

Hartsel Hotel

It was getting close to midnight when the two lovers finally lay back on their pillows, hands still entwined together.

"Marsh, oh you have no idea how long I have dreamed of this! I am so happy right now, I just want to jump up and run down the hall shouting!"

"Well, I am pretty excited too, but we really probably should get dressed, or they might not let us ever stay in Hartsel, Colorado again."

"Oh, if they only had a bathtub here, it would be perfect."

"Oh, really? You would like a bath? Here, slip your boots on and wrap a blanket around you and come with me."

"Oh, really? A bath? Here, oh well, lead on!"

They quickly donned their blankets and boots, and they slipped out down the deserted hallway and out of the Inn, whispering and giggling like two children. Across the road and down the trail to the Platte River, across the foot bridge and down to the spring. They tossed their blankets up on some bushes, and hoping the hour was too late for intrusions, they walked into the water.

"Oh my!" exclaimed Sarah, "Oh my, this is hot! How... how wonderful! Oh, my goodness! There are little hot bubbles running up my legs!"

She lowered herself into the water and turned to Marsh.

"How did you know it was here? This so extraordinary, so soothing, so beautiful!" Suddenly she burst into tears. "Oh, Marsh, I am so happy! I love this place! I mean, not only this place, but all of these mountains, our ranch. I love my life now! I didn't know I could ever feel so free. But most of all, I love you, my beautiful cowboy!"

"There you go again, asking question and just filling my mind up till I'm speechless. I think I spent too long following cows around, Sarah. But to answer your question I found it the day before I met you on the ride up. And yes, you can say it better. Your words come so easy, but I found this place years ago, and it is the only place I have ever wanted to be since then. And now, my dream has more than come true because of you. I would never have dreamed of finding a woman like you that would want to be my partner, and then you just came along and handed it all to me, and now you are offering yourself as well. I love you, too, and I pledge, on my honor, to always support you and be by your side, as long as you want me."

Sarah reached and embraced Marsh again.

"Marsh, make love to me again, right here, right now."

It was nearer two a.m. before they crept into Sarah's room. Marsh hugged her and kissed her again.

"Sarah, I am going to go to my room. I don't want to put your reputation in jeopardy. Sleep tight."

"Oh, I suppose. But I really don't want you to go. We will need to work on this situation."

"I know. I don't want to go either. And we will. Good night, dear Sarah."

"Sarah, did you not sleep well, my dear? Your eyes seem heavy." Rose was busy checking her silver ware and plates.

Sarah smiled. "I was a bit restless, what with all the excitement, and didn't really doze off until quite late. But I am in fine spirits this morning. How about you, Mr. Redman, are you rested?"

Marsh smiled. The nerve of that girl, to tease him first thing in the morning, and in front of people! Well, his face was too burned by the sun and wind to blush.

"Oh yes, Miss Burns, I'm right tolerable this morning. I have been tossing around that question you put to me last evening, and never gave me time to answer." Right back at her, he smiled.

"You asked, about when we could build and when we could get started, and what to call it."

"And......?"

"Well, we can start immediately gathering materials and supplies and shipping them up there. We won't be able to build. It is too late, I'm afraid, but we should have everything there to start in the spring. And for a name, how about *High Country Dreams*? I have an idea for a brand. We will have to find us an architect to design it, I am afraid that is out of my league. What do you think?"

"High Country Dreams, hmmmm, yes. Cause that is what it is, isn't it? I suppose you are right, about not being able to get started any quicker. But there is a lot to do, I must be patient. But we can spend time there, can't we, till snow flies?"

"Yes ma'am, we shorly will."

Three days later, Marsh and Sarah and Chagan rode down F Street toward the river, unaware of the two people watching from the hotel above.

"You know, of course, I was a, an upstairs girl."

Hanne, was lying on her bed flat on her back, holding her long legs straight up over her head, looking at her toes. It was a lazy summer day in Salida. A cool breeze came in the window, and caused the lacy curtains to blow a bit.

"Aye, yes, I do know that."

Sean had pulled the hinge pins from the closet door, taken the door and put it across another table and an upright chair, taking care to not scratch anything. He needed room for the sketches of the mountains around Salida, particularly the little mountain that rose right at the edge of the town across the railroad at the end of F Street. Pages of mountain landscapes, drawings of buildings, detailed outlines of architecture were everywhere. He reached quickly as a gust picked up a sheet of paper and threatened to whisk it away.

He looked out the window. The sky was darkening behind Shavano Mountain.

"Methinks we are to get some rain. Yes, Hanne, I know that. What is your thought, in bringing it up?"

"Well, you have never questioned me, regarding it. Like..... why did I do it? Or will I do it again? Actually, I do not really know why I brought it up."

"Well, my dear, that life you did was before I met you. You were living under different circumstances. It is not my place to question anything that you did then. I have had opportunity to observe your intelligence, your talents, your personal resolve, and your general nature. All those things are impressive to me, and deserve my admiration and respect. This is the moment we live in, not your past. Our common goals are our future. That is where my thoughts lie."

Hanne rolled over on her stomach and looked through the framework of the iron bedstead. She studied him for a moment. "You know, sir, it was the best thing I ever did, to team up with you, after we met. I am the most satisfied with my life that I have ever been. And I still believe there is a great adventure awaiting us! Wish I could see the future!"

She had gotten up from the bed and walked to the window and was sitting on a stool with her elbows propped on the sill.

"Hmmm, those are interesting looking people. I wonder where they have been?"

Sean turned to see three riders. A man, a cowboy type, a lady, somewhat fashionable but riding astride a big horse, and small man, obviously oriental, following and leading a pack horse.

"Indeed" said Sean.

"Well, my wild Irish rogue, I have caught myself thinking of late of how that person feels so foreign to me. I don't ever want to do that again. I can't see myself in that life anymore."

"Hanne, every day of our life changes us. And as my father always said, puts us on a different path. It is how we traverse those paths, what we glean from them, and when another path lies before us, the decisions we make about remaining or taking another course. My congratulations to you for re-inventing yourself. Aye, I myself, see our paths continuing up the mountain of progress, and it is fair exciting. And, if I may be so personal, it is much better sharing it with you than it would ever have been by myself."

Hanne spread the red and white checkered table cloth under the shade of the big Cottonwood tree along the bank of the Arkansas River. The river was running a bit higher this morning than normal. The thunderstorms of last evening they had watched from their hotel window had grown dark and lightening had flashed up on the peaks of Shavano and Antero. Indeed, all the way back to Princeton. Not a lot of rain had fallen, but the late July morning was just a bit cooler than normal, even with the hot sun. She set up the small card table and threw a towel over the big stump next to it and set out the wicker baskets of the small appetizer sandwiches and the fried chicken that the hotel kitchen had prepared for her.

Sean had been here for over two hours, his easel set up near the bank of the

River. He faced upstream, and directly above the river in the distance, Mount Princeton raised it magnificent head. He had stopped several times to let the oils dry before continuing, but already one could see the mastery of colors and shades and shadows, coupled with the brilliance of snow patches that lingered this late in the season.

She took a small sandwich and a slice of pickled cucumber and walked slowly over to look over his shoulder. She was lost in his painting and didn't see the couple walk up until a voice spoke.

"Hello, are you Hanne Clausen and Sean Kelly?" It was the couple from last evening that had ridden into Salida just before the storm.

The lady spoke, "I am Sarah Burns. This is Marsh Redman. William Wells said to look for you here in town."

"Good morning Miss Burns. Yes, I am Hanne, so pleased to make your acquaintance. This is Sean, busy at his painting."

"Aye, good day to ye, Mistress Burns and Mr. Redman. Let me wipe my hands here, and I would be happy to shake ye hand. Mr. Wells has spoken so highly of you."

As they spoke Sarah walked around till she was in front of Sean's painting.

"Oh my word, Mr. Kelly! What a wonderful talent you have! I am so very impressed, no finer work could be found in the galleries of San Francisco!"

Hanne stood by her. "Indeed, Miss Burns, I have watched him for several months. His drawings and sketches are equally impressive. Yet it is a new born talent, though.... not really, no. The talent was always his, but the outlet for it is new, and he is like a waterfall just gushing forth impressive works in a seemingly never ending stream!"

"I suppose, we should get this over with. First all, I would prefer to be called Sarah, and the cowboy prefers Marsh. Mr. Wells wants to bring you into our partnership, and I trust his judgement. If it is good with you."

"Mr. Wells also spoke to us on that subject. Yes, I, or we, Hanne and I, would like to join with you. But only if you refer to us as Sean and Hanne."

"Sean, it is my pleasure. Hanne, happy to meet you." Marsh nodded and touched the brim of his hat.

"Well then, come and share our picnic! We have sandwiches, fried chicken, potato salad, and some very good beans. And these little loafs of bread with good butter. I am afraid we will be limited to some iced tea and water to drink."

It only took a couple of days of discussion regarding the ranch till Sean, especially, was champing at the bit to go and see the spot. His excuse, he wanted to be able to design a ranch house and draw it all up so as to be ready for an early spring start on building. So a day was picked, goods for a week on the trail was put together, and a wagon was rented from a local rancher, a Mr. Everett. The weather was starting to turn; a wagon would give them a place to hold up if needed. It took about 3 days drive to the far west central side of the Bayou Salado by wagon. It was messy the last part of the trip. It was a half day out of Whitehorn when the rain started.

It had started off cold, as the four headed out of Whitehorn. The early August morning held a somberness. The clouds hung low, appearing as a fog bank in some spots as they headed north west along the stage coach trail, then lifting to hang over their heads. The heavy wagon had come up from Salida by a team of six. The long pull up over Cameron Mountain was difficult in places, 18 miles and 2300 feet in elevation gain.

The cargo had come from all over. Big cooking stoves and ovens, two wood stoves, other odds and ends of household goods that couldn't be obtained locally. One treasure in particular was boxed and stowed away. They had decided to get a head start on spring. They could take this wagon load up and be that far ahead. But, like most good things, it didn't come easily. Currently, Hanne was sitting on that particular box, and Sarah was lounging on box two of this combination. Sean had climbed up in the front and pulled the end closure a little tighter as the wind picked up and the rain got harder.

Sarah and Marsh had discussed the mechanism contained in the two boxes for weeks before deciding to buy. Something new, a new invention only ten years old. In '88 a guy named Brush back east had developed a windmill that powered an electric generator. With luck, they would have lights in the new ranch house! But first, they had to get to the ranch. And the rain was not getting lighter.

Sarah remarked, "It is so very cold up here when it rains!" She snuggled into her jacket.

"Yes. And Sarah, I am glad though it doesn't rain like in Minnesota. Here you seem to get some sun every day."

"Be glad ye are not a horse. The poor dears are standing with their tails to it and their heads down. Least we found a couple of trees to put them under. In the city, when I was growing up, it would be so grey sometimes I would stay inside and read the whole day."

Marsh chuckled. "I was just thinking about one evening up on the Red River, near Doan's Store. Sometime in the early eighties, I recollect, I was just a shirt-tail kid on my first drive to market. It had been an early spring anyhow, and just rained all the time. Every river we came to, we had to swim the herd. Wet all time, chaffing in the saddles. First thing, the horses started getting tender-footed from the water, their hooves softened up. Then the cattle did the same. But anyway, the Red was on a tear. We were beat and hungry, cause we couldn't even build a fire to cook with that night. Not a real happy bunch. But we were semi dry for the moment. Had put up some wagon sheets over two wagons, making a dry spot between them. 'Bout that time, this feller just slid in under the tarp and squatted right next to me. He was dressed in a suit and bowler hat, boots, right fancy he was for the spot and the conditions. Well, he turned to face me, and I realized he was an Indian. Took me a bit by surprise. You know, growing up where I did and when I did, the word Indian sometimes meant serious consequences. They killed a lot o' our neighbors, and some of our kin, in them early days.

"He looked at me, then asked, 'May I share your shelter?'

"I reckon, I answered. Who are ya?

"My name is Quanah Parker, he replied.

"Well, I set way back. Everyone knew who Quanah Parker was, and he was sitting here not a foot from me!

"Well, Mr. Quanah Parker, I told him, I am sorry we don't have a cup of coffee to share with you. But everything is pretty wet, and that God damned rain just won't stop for nothing. Anyway, my handle is Marsh.

"Pleasure to meet you, Mr. Marsh. Now you come with me. Bring him too.' pointing at my friend Rowdy.

"We stood up and pulled on our slickers and went out in the pouring rain. The Indian took us out into the mesquite brush and pointed out to us dead limbs to pull off trees, where to find dry wood. He found rotten wood and would pull the rotten hearts. He found dry grass growing in a shelter. We went back to the wagons, and soon had a warm fire going, enough to make coffee and a bit of food the cook could do. We were lucky. The herd stayed quite that night and didn't run. It would have been hell trying to turn them.

"Next morning Parker woke and said to me, 'Thank you, Mr. Marsh, for sharing your shelter with me. Because you have done this, you will find shelter from storms when you need them. Do not lose your way in the white man's thinking. If you do, you will miss many things in your life. The white man complains if it rains, not understanding that this was the plan for the earth, water to refresh it. He complains, if the sun shines too hot, and says he wants it to be cloudy, or rain, not understanding that all these things must happen in their on time. We must have the sun to give energy to all things. Without it we would all perish.

'Learn to be happy when it rains. Feel the freshness, take time in your life to stop and rest. Enjoy the sun. If the day is too hot to travel, find a shady place and reflect on your life, and the things around you. The world was made to continue itself. Man is not a part of it. Man is only a guest, sometimes an unwelcome guest. But if man becomes too unwelcome, the earth will shake him off like the great shaggy buffalo would do to mud from a wallow. He tries to subdue the earth, not live on it. Look how he has killed the buffalo, wantonly, and without regard. Have a good life, Mr. Marsh.'

"With that, he turned and was gone. I never saw him again. But his words have stuck with me to this day."

"Wow, what a great story Marsh! Quanah Parker! How amazing!" Sarah whispered.

Hanne asked, "Who is Quanah Parker?"

Sean answered, "I will tell you of him. I have read of him and his mother. It is an interesting story."

It was at that moment the clouds lifted, and the Rocky Mountain sun showed its face.

"Another time." Marsh said, "If we hurry, we will have just enough time to reach the ranch by dark or almost." As he spoke, Marsh crawled out the back opening and dropped to the ground. Streams of golden sunlight flooded the big wagon.

Old Spanish Trail

The two couples enjoyed the days getting acquainted. They quickly relaxed and became good friends. Coming from such varied backgrounds seem to leave a cohesiveness that leant to stimulating conversations, and perked new ideas. Sean and Hanne had been quick to accept the invitation to join in the challenge of building a new ranch, and although the event would be challenging physically, they were young and looked forward to it. Plans were made to buy Hanne and Sean new mounts, as they had disposed of theirs at Fairplay weeks back. Marsh wasn't happy with anything he found in Salida, so the couples took a trip down into the San Louis Valley to Marsh's friend, Señor Trujillo.

They arrived at Señor Trujillo's hacienda outside a small village north of Alamosa just before sundown. They were met at the gate by two of his heavily armed vaqueros who wanted, in no uncertain terms, to know their business and who they were. As soon as Marsh identified himself, the party was immediately welcomed and the one man who spoke quite good english explained that he was sorry for their rudeness and inhospitality, but tensions were high in that part of the country. The white ranchers were challenging the Mexican's rights to be there, sometimes bordering on outright violence.

It was just dark when Señor Pedro Trujillo strode into the large living room of his log cabin hacienda. Pedro was a man of the future. His father, of the old school, was more interested in sheep than in cattle, and had brought down on the family all the hate and disrespect of the Anglo cattle ranchers. Pedro was a cattle rancher, and instead of doing a traditional adobe house, he built a rather large, two story log cabin, after the Anglo tradition. He bred and raised excellent horses.

The two couples were welcomed to his home and spent almost a week, observing a working ranch at its best. It was harvest time. The men worked in the fields bringing in hay and picking the fruits of their gardens and orchards. The women took care of the houses, canned and dried the food, and somehow in the midst of it all managed to remain beautiful and cheerful. Truly they lived in a paradise. Sean spent hours sketching the snowless peaks in late fall of the majestic Sangre de Cristos. He questioned everyone about how it looked when the snows of winter lingered there. Finally, one afternoon one of Pedro' nieces approached Sean shyly. Her English was limited and halting. She was somewhere in her 16th year, but already a beautiful girl. She clutched in her hand some good sized heavy pieces of paper.

"Señor Kelly, por favor. You like mountains, si?"

Sean looked at her. "Si, I like the pretty mountains."

"Mi Madre tell me to show you…." she handed the pieces of paper to Sean. He turned them to face him and stood them against the wall he had been leaning against. One look and he was aghast! They were beautiful! And the colors! They were not oils, but something she had prepared herself, maybe dyes, he didn't know. But whatever, they portrayed a setting sun lighting the snowy peaks, casting lights of various tints and hues. The young girl had a talent, a magnificent talent! But she was still young, she needed a bit of help with perspective and depth of field. But, still, she could be a world class artist.

"Angel, those are beautiful! They inspire me. What did you use for colors? Miss Burns, would you come here for a moment, and look at these?"

As Sarah was walking towards them, Angel related that she didn't know how to explain the colors, partly with words and with her hands. Sean understood, and patted her shoulder.

But for the next few days the two artists were inseparable. Sean showed her what few oils he had in his case, and how to use them. And he had such a willing pupil. Sarah bought the young lady's art, but instead of paying her money, promised as soon as they were back in Salida she would buy brushes and canvases and oils and have them sent to her. Angel was overjoyed. By the time the party was ready to head back north, huge improvements were noted in the young artist's techniques and work. Marsh and Sarah spent hours out riding with Pedro, looking at cattle and horses. They outlined their plans for the ranch, and told him of its location. Agreements were made for cattle to be purchased and moved in the spring to the new ranch.

It took a while but four new horses were selected and purchased. They had been trained beautifully. All four had worked cattle. A sorrel gelding for Sean, a blue roan mare for Hanne, and two extras, a bay and a painted pony. Hanne laughed and said she had two redheads now.

The last evening a fiesta was called at Pedro's home and a steer was put on a spit over a pit of hot coals.

Pedro and Marsh sat sipping coffee in a small ramada at the rear of the house. "Señor Marsh, I am so happy for the life you have found. You have always been such a good friend to me and my family."

"Gracias, Pedro. You have always been courteous to me from the very first time I wandered through these parts."

"Now, Señor Marsh, it is even better. We can do business together, and it will be a very beneficial arrangement."

They were joined by Sarah.

"Señor Trujillo, I thank you from the bottom of my heart for the hospitality you have shown to us. I love your beautiful valley, and your wonderful family. It has brought back sweet memories of my youth in California. I hope we can afford you the same at our ranch in the future."

"I will look forward to that Señorita Burns. I am grateful to you already for taking such great care of my friend Señor Marsh. I think of him as *mi hermano*, and you are showing him much happiness!"

"Marsh, do you see..." It was Sean approaching from the corner of the house.

"Yes, I see." Marsh had been watching the ten riders coming in slow. They were fanned out wide as if they intended to cover the whole group at the hacienda.

"I will gather my vaqueros." Pedro said.

"No, compadre. If they mean ill, your men will just fan the flame. Let me give it a shot." Marsh quickly stepped inside the door and grabbed his sidearm and buckled it on.

"I am going with you, Marsh." It was Sean. He pulled his big colt and checked it, and holstered it again.

"Ok, but be calm. We don't really want to start anything with all these people around."

The two walked out the path to the corral and stood about 10 feet apart, waiting as the riders approached.

"Afternoon, gentlemen. Did you hear of our party and decide to attend? If so, you are welcome. But you will need to leave your weapons on your horses."

The leader, a blondish man with a medium beard, also blonde, answered rather harshly.

"Who the hell are you to be telling me what I need to do with my guns?"

"Well, I am Marsh Redman. This here is Sean Kelly. We are friends and business acquaintances of the Trujillo family."

"You soun' like a Texan. Didn't know Texans liked greasers."

"Well, it obvious you don't know much about Texans. And with that kinda name calling, I think you need to just turn around and head out of here."

With that the blonde man went for his gun. But before it had cleared its holster, Marsh's big colt was staring him in the eye.

"You got ten seconds or a bunch of you are going to die. Now, get outta here! Now!"

With a nasty oathe, the man spun his horse and the group galloped away.

Sun up the next morning found the four fed, mounted and hearts full of goodbyes from their friends. Marsh turned his horse eastward and they headed out toward the

Sangre de Cristos Mountains. The sun had climbed slowly over the towering peaks bringing light to the valley and its inhabitants. After a couple of hours riding, Marsh raised up and turned in his saddle. Far to the west, the San Juan Mountains loomed high and formidable. Stories had come out of those mountains about hardship and about the early travelers who sometimes barely survived trying to cross them near winter.

"I thought I would show you something a lot of people don't know about. When we come up over this little rise, be prepared."

They had reached the foot of the mountains a few minutes before and had ridden along the base. A few minutes later, they topped a rise and laid about before them was a picture straight out of the mighty Sahara Desert. Great sand dunes rippled across the plain and hills in front of them, shaped by the wind and weather. Sarah was the first to find her tongue.

"This beautiful place we have chosen to call our home never ceases to amaze me! Just when I think I have reached the bounds of its beauty and resources, it surprises me again!"

Sean was next, "Marsh, could we take some time so that I may sketch this marvel? I believe this may be the only place in this country where you will find this phenomenon."

"Yep, take yer time, Sean. We only have a short ride till where we are going to camp tonight. I believe somebody told me once that they had some dunes down in the southern part of California, where the Colorado River cuts through into Mexico. Never seen 'em though. Found these on my second ride down through these parts in the late 80's."

The next couple of hours were spent exploring the dunes, climbing to the tops of the tallest, discussing the layers that looked like ocean waves suspended in time, seemingly frozen by some great unseen blizzard that affected them only.

When Sean finished his drawing, the group mounted once again, and a short ride later found a place where a stream of hot water traced down the side of the

Sangre de Cristos, forming steaming pools. When night fell and they had eaten, it being a dark night, they gathered at the lower pool, undressed and entered the chest deep water. As they relaxed, Marsh spoke.

"After passing through these parts, and discovering more about all the great things goin' on, I wanted to know more." Marsh continued his narrative, "My education had mostly been gained lookin' at the back of a horses head. I didn't have much want to go back east. Never really liked cities, still don't. So I decided to educate myself about the west.

"After spending some time around Santa Fe, I rode on down and followed the Rio Grande down thru Albuquerque and finally to El Paso in Texas. I followed that old river down where it goes in the big bend country, then cut across toward Austin. Took me two months with all the dawdling around. It was early winter time when I got home. But I was young, it didn't matter. I caught another drive going north next spring, and rode back though the mountains again. This time was when I met the Trujillos."

Hanne asked, "How did you meet them?"

"Well, I almost didn't get to meet 'em. I was riding this half broke mustang bronc, and I guess I was I was sittin' too comfortable and lookin' at the pretty mountains when a rattler sounded off, just as we got up on him. The horse shied away. I didn't lose him there, though, but it upset him a bit, and he decided to buck. And I didn't have my seat proper. He tossed me kinda head first onto the only boulder in a hundred yards. I hit my head and my back, and broke some ribs, and I don't know what all. I laid there the rest of the day and all night. No water, but I was out most of the time anyway. Next morning I opened my eyes to this sheep staring down at me. It was one of the Trujillo boys. They slung a blanket on two poles and loaded me on it, and took me to the hacienda. I was down for over two weeks. I hung around that winter and worked for them to pay them back for saving my life. I made some good friends. I taught them what I knew about Texas cow business, and how we worked them. I'll never forget them, I owe them."

"That is why you stepped out to help them yesterday?"

"Yep. How about you, Sean? We know nothing about you."

Sean smiled, "What would like to know, Marsh? I can tell you that I grew up in one of those big cities you don't like. And yes, you have reason to not like them. I never knew that I didn't like them until a few months ago, when I came out here. They were just a fact of life. I was born there, and I learned to live there. As soon as I got old enough to read, I started reading stories about the west. Marsh, can you imagine what it would be like to never be able to see a horizon? Just buildings all around you. Once, my father took me to the seashore and I was able to look out over the sea. I was astounded! As a child, I thought that the whole world was all buildings. And when he told me there were forests and mountains as well, I right then wanted to see.

"Growing up was hard for a young man on the streets of New York. Out here you have lions and wolves and bears. There we had different kind of predators. They were thieves and muggers and bullies and murderers. I had to grow up quick. I learned to use my wits. As you see, I am not a large man, so I had to resort to other strengths. Like you, my father fought in that Great War. He came home, though. Well, at least physically. He lost his left arm, and had shrapnel still in him when he died. He would have terrible dreams at night, and scream and thrash about. He always had a haunted look about him, as though the war had followed him home. He taught me how to shoot and how to fight. He spent his life sitting at a desk keeping books for a shipping company, writing strings of numbers on long sheets of paper. At least that is what it looked like to a young boy. I would accompany him to work some days, and set on bales or bags and look out the windows and draw pictures of the ships at the dock. The reason I left was I was playing cards, gambling, with a big man. He was trying to cheat me. I called him on it, he pulled a gun. I shot him first. I am not proud of it, but he was not a nice man either. I left the city the next day. I've told all this to Miss Hanne. I thought you and Miss Burns should know as well if we are to work together. And, oh yes, I gave up gambling. I don't need it!"

Sarah, "I appreciate your honesty, Sean, and I admire your gentle spirit. And I am sure that after watching you yesterday with Marsh, your valor can never be questioned. Since we are having such a wonderful evening, Hanne, would you like to share anything?"

"Miss Burns... Sarah... I, like Sean, had to grow up fast. But unlike Sean, and being a woman, there were not as many doors open to me. I grew up on a farm. I learned to ride and to work, and milk cows and take care of animals. I confess, though, I never became a good cook. Then I found myself thrown out into the world. I found myself forced to use the wiles of women to support myself. I will not bow my head to this, and act ashamed. It was not a chosen profession, but it educated me. I had always wanted to be a teacher. I still do. In fact, as Sean will tell you, I have funds set aside for a school. I have learned many talents in my life. I never expected to find myself in the position, that I am in now, but fate doesn't always warn you in advance of what it has in mind for you, or what might be good for you. I find myself pleasantly surprised at my present situation. I am growing quite fond of all of you, and I am willing to do what is asked to contribute to our goal."

Sarah sighed, "I feel so blessed, with what has happened to me in the last months. Hanne, you are such a beautiful lady, both in body and in spirit. You are a lady. Sean and Marsh, both of you are our knights in shining armor. Marsh knows that I was brought up in California on a small ranch. And that is where I would have preferred to have stayed. I married a good man, and we had started our life together, but last spring he was killed. Actually, Sean, by another gambler. I am so glad your story was different than his. But, strange as it may seem, he had won some mining holdings that at about that very moment were turning into riches. Riches that I intend for all of us to share. You are my family now.

"But if I don't get out of this pool, you are going to have to get a dipper and dip me out of it!" Everyone laughed and agreed. So as fast as modesty allowed, the pool was emptied and the four travelers gathered around their fire and consumed their dinner. Marsh looked around at the night sky. The loneliness of the place made him mindful of his company. He had traveled through here himself alone before, not seeing anyone for days. It reminded him of another man.

The fire had burned down after dinner. Marsh reached for another piece of knotted pine, and placed it on top of the glowing coals. The wood caught immediately, and flared into a flame, illuminating the aspen grove around them. He thought for a minute about the wildness of the country side around them, and how it had been for those early settlers in South Park. The savage winters that lasted from October 'till June. He leaned back against the mossy chunk of granite that had been his repose during dinner. Sarah was lying lazily back against her saddle. Sean and Hanne were cuddled on a blanket with their jackets thrown over them for comfort's sake against the coolness of the September air. Hanne was tracing her fingers through Sean's curls over his left ear.

Marsh cleared his throat and remarked, seemingly to himself, as he stared into the mesmerizing flames. "There was an old preacher up here at one time." His brow wrinkled in thought. "He came here in the early '60's... '61 I believe, just as the war between the states was breaking out. I've heard stories about him almost everywhere I've been. Dyer, I think his name was. John Dyer. He walked all over South Park, preaching wherever he could find anyone that would listen. Mostly ten or fifteen miners, or maybe some Mexicans, if he could find any that spoke English. Seldom would get more than a few dollars for his subsistence. Fact of the matter was, he walked all the way from Wisconsin to Denver, then up the canyons and gulches to about where Breckenridge is and then over to 'bout Fairplay." He heard Hanne gasp as she lost focus on Sean's curls,

"Oh my God, he walked all that way?"

Marsh nodded. "He had 2 dollars left when he got to Denver." He chuckled, "Matter of fact, most of his life he was a poor man. But he was just about unstoppable. Sarah, you've been over Mosquito pass between Leadville and Fairplay. He packed the mail over that for several years on his back, wearing either snowshoes, which he made himself, or nine foot long ski's. Some of the stories 'bout him are almost miracles. But he survived. But he did he froze his feet 'til he lost 'most his toes. Wasn't all he did, either. He went all the way to Las Cruces, New Mexico, preachin'. He got married up here. He had been married before, back in Wisconsin. Had some kids, one of his sons became a judge over in Granite. He was killed, shot dead in his courtroom, during the range wars over there."

Sean spoke, "Marsh, that was a fine story and all, but what made you think of that?"

"I dunno. It just popped in my head. I think maybe just looking around at this place, thinkin' of its wildness. Then I remembered 'ol man Dyer. Sean, you haven't wintered here yet. It can be a fearsome place, but all the while, ya can't look around without seeing the beauty of it."

"I have no doubt. I still remember my first look at it," remarked Sean, to a chorus of murmurs from the women. Sean snuggled back into Hanne's arms. The two had fallen in love almost at first sight, and were now inseparable.

Marsh slid down into his blankets next to Sarah and pillowed his head on his saddle.

"Gonna be a long day tomorrow if we make it to the Salida by dark." The sky was darkening as the flames died. The Milky Way stood out like a white river in the mid heavens, flowing to the south over the Sangre de Cristos Mountains. The only sounds were the muffled snorts of the horses grazing nearby. The little camp slept.

Turrett

Sean knocked twice on the door of Marsh and Sarah's room.

They had sat up late last evening playing chess and making ranch plans. He was fascinated with all the little details for the project. He had been toying with the elevation drawing for the house when he, too, had a knock at his door. It was the lad from the telegraph office. He knocked again. There was shuffling sounds within. The door opened and Marsh, sleepy faced, peered out the crack in the door. His eyes were slits, like cracks in a worn saddle. His face was just as leathery.

"Mornin' Sean. Come in."

"Thank ye, Master Marsh. 'Tis not necessary. Here is a telegram from Mr. Wells. Seems he has a chore for us. Hanne and I will be ready and meet you at the restaurant for breakfast. I will let the stable know to have the horses ready."

"Thanks Sean, we will be there directly."

Shortly afterward the four were having breakfast. Chagan had appeared before they were finished and tied the horses out front. His horse was in the bunch. "You joining us today Chagan? Better come get some victuals before we go."

Chagan snorted, "You eat too late. Chagan ate before sun came up." He smiled, "Soon be time for lunch. Chagan brought food for trail."

It was not long before the five riders had ascended the crooked creek bed and were climbing into brushy foothills. By the time they made the turn off the stage road to Whitehorn onto the road to Turret, spots of yellow and gold were starting to appear wherever patches of aspen grew. The September air was fresh, but it was almost October now. Soon the little trips would become more difficult and more dangerous. The Colorado high country could be a beast, hidden by beauty.

"So, Marsh, William said he was going to meet us at Turret. I didn't really have time to read the message."

"Yes, Sarah. That man really works for you. He is a good friend, and a great partner. He said something about a mine he wanted to buy, but this time he wants your opinion."

"Well, that is mighty nice of him. But I would think he might know a lot more than I would know about that."

"He is taking the train to Buena Vista, and riding up to Turret. Should maybe be there by the time we are. We are supposed to meet a Mr. Keyes, one of the owners. The mine is called the Jasper Mine. He say's it shows some promise."

As they topped a ridge just short of the little town of Turrett, Sean whistled. There, to the north, lay a mountain that appeared to be afire for as far north as the eye could see. A mountain almost totally of aspen trees, dressed in their fall splendor.

"The Saints be praised! I have never beheld anything near that kind of splendor! So many colors! One would

316

think all the gold in Colorado had been dug up and spread out there in the sun. The streets of Heaven would scarce compare! I must get closer, Marsh. I must try to capture some of that."

"Let's go see Mr. Keys first. And, well, I suppose we could stay another day and ride up. Don't see why not."

There was and echo, of *yeses* from the ladies.

William Wells stood in front of the tiny mercantile store slash tavern on the main street of Turrett. He was watching the five riders approaching him. As they reined up he stepped to the side of his boss's horse and as she swung off, he caught her arm, to steady her.

Marsh answered, "Chagan, this is Mr. William Wells. He is another partner. William, this is Chagan. He forced himself on us, said he is going to be our cook, once we get to the ranch. But I think maybe he might be something else as well. He is one of the finest horsemen as I have ever come across. And actually, he has become a friend as well."

"Well, Mr. Chagan, I am very pleased to meet you. I am looking forward to one of your meals."

"Chagan happy to meet Mr. Wells. Chagan would fix a fancy dinner for him." He bowed, and went and gathered the horses and tied them to the hitching post.

Wells and the four partners crowded into a small café down the street from the mercantile where they had coffee and a bowl of stew. Shortly, three men entered and approached. Marsh and Sean and William stood.

"Afternoon folks. I am Frank Keyes. These are my partners Charles Klisinger and Emil Becker. Welcome to Turrett."

"A pleasure to meet you Mr. Keys. Gentlemen, would you join us for a quick lunch? This is Miss Sarah Burns. She is the owner of this outfit. I am William Wells, I run her mining interests. This gentleman is Marsh Redman, a partner, and head of her ranch, and our two remaining members, Miss Hanne Clausen and Mr. Sean Kelly."

The men seated themselves and decided on just coffee, and the discussion was opened. Frank pulled a sizeable piece of ore from his jacket pocket. The hard granite was laced with quartz and several threads of metal that had to be gold, surrounded by black spots of another metal.

"This is high grade ore, Mr. Wells. I want you to see that your investment into the Jasper Mine would be a safe one. It is going to be a big venture here soon."

William frowned. "Mr. Keys, our plans was to buy the mine, not invest in it."

"I am sorry, Mr. Wells, we were not interested in selling it. We believe it is going to produce millions of dollars."

"I understand, sir, but do you have the capitol to develop it? It is going to take thousands of dollars to get through this granite. You are going to need steam engines and all manner of equipment, plus manpower to do the work."

"Yes sir, we know all that. That is why, we put out that advertisement for investors."

"Mr. Keyes, I would like to see the mine, and then make you an offer. Then you gentlemen can deliberate on it and give us an answer on the 'morrow, if you please."

"Mr. Wells, folks, we would be pleased to show you our mine. But I reiterate we are not selling. But come ahead."

Marsh, Sarah, and William stepped outside.

William said "I am going with these men. I will return later this evening and tell you what their answer is to be."

"Alright, William. We are going to ride up to that ridge so Sean can get a closer look at the trees. He wants to paint them."

"Very well, then. Until later..."

It was almost midafternoon when the foursome climbed to Aspen Ridge. Following an elk path through the gold was almost surreal. Winding through the white trees, with wrinkled bark, they seemed almost like eyes, watching carefully that thieves might steal their precious gold. In some spots, a slight breeze would stir the leaves and glimpses of red would flicker, as if the gold was catching fire. Finally, Sean reined his horse up and slid out of the saddle. He untied his palette and easel, and set them up. He next unwrapped a medium sized canvas from its oil cloth bag and placed it on the easel.

The others dismounted. Marsh walked over the ridge. Sarah and Hanne found a spot in the sun shielded from the north west wind. They untied their blanket rolls and spread them out and lay down on them. The warm sun was mesmerizing after a day of riding.

It was Hanne that spoke first.

"Sarah, I really do thank you for your acceptance for one such as myself and my background. You have treated me like a sister from the very first time we met." She pulled a stem of grass from its shaft and stuck it between her full lips. Her long blonde hair fell over her shoulders, her blue eyes were soft.

"I just want you to know, I appreciate it. And I am very excited about our project. I want to be a big part of it, I can hardly wait for spring!"

"Hanne, dear, I really don't believe a person - especially a young person such as yourself - should be judged. I see so many good traits in you. You may have been what you say, but it doesn't show in your attitude. It doesn't really seem to be in your thoughts. And watching you with Sean, you look at him so tenderly, so much love! And you know what, Hanne? I always wanted a sister, and now I have one! For that is the way I think of you!"

With that, she rolled over and put her arms around Hanne and hugged her and gave her a kiss on the cheek. Hanne returned the kiss and hugged Sarah back. She sniffed just a bit.

"See, you made me blubber! I always wanted a sister, too."

It was almost an hour before Marsh appeared.

"Sean, you 'bout done? We got a dark cloud startin' to form over Princeton there. We might need to start back to Turret."

"I'm ready Marsh. Let me get this gear tied back on, and cinch up a bit tighter."

"So, Marsh, where did you get off to?" Sarah asked "We were afraid 'Ol Mose might have got you. But Hanne said he wouldn't dare, you would tear him limb from limb!"

Marsh grinned. "Well, thank ya kindly, Miss Hanne, for the vote of confidence. More than likely I would have choked him to death with heel dust getting away. But I think I might have found a better trail from Salida to the ranch than going by way of Whitehorn."

Quarters were crowded in Turret that evening. The little saloon smelled of unwashed bodies, tobacco smoke and whiskey, among other things. But still, the foursome enjoyed the evening listening to the tall stories told by the miners. Sarah sat smiling with her pencil and pad, making notes, copying stories she was able to hear. Two men sat talking nearby, one wearing a Union soldiers keppe. As the whiskey took hold, their voices got louder and louder.

"Yeah, but if ol' man Rosecrans hadn't just got totally outta his mind, we woulda whipped you Rebs at Chicamauga! Ya wouldn'a had a chance!"

"Now, dang it, Bob! Ya know that ain't true! We had you boys licked frum the get-go. We had ya out manned an' everthin'! Your troops when that Rebel Yell wuz raised would jus' turn tail and run. Like fur instance that Friday night Ol' Pat Cleburne and his boys hit that line there in th trees at the edge of the Winfrey field. Yer boys just crumpled. Iffen he hadna been called back, we would have wound up in Rosecrans' hedquarters that evenin.' "

It was plain to see the anger was rising. William Wells stepped up and leaned over the table and whispered something undiscernible to the two men. Both nodded, and then reached across and shook each others hands, then shook hands with William.

"What did you say to them, Mr. Wells?" asked Sarah.

"I just reminded them the war had been over for forty years, and that we had signed a pledge of loyalty to the United States and that we should let those men who died rest in peace."

"That is well said," exclaimed Marsh.

That December turned out to be pretty mild at first. Marsh had excused himself to ride to the ranch for a day to take some measurements, and to scout some logs for the building. He would only be gone a couple of days, three at the most. Sarah wanted to go, but Marsh said it was a bit too cold. He would be able to take care of himself, but worried about having to be responsible for her. But he asked if they wished to meet him in Turret, and they would ride down to Buena Vista from there.

Everything went as planned. He selected some trees for cutting, drew some plans for the cabin foundation, leaving out the layout as the women would want control of that. On his way back he rode through a huge aspen forest. He was just 10 miles above Turret when the first shot rang out.

The little Buckskin had always been such a good horse. Marsh patted his shoulder and arranged his mane down the side of his neck. The aspen leaves fluttered all gold with tinges of red. They stood out sharply against the new snow that cushioned the ground up the ridge.

Marsh sighed. A tear formed in his eye. He brushed it away quickly. He was just a horse. He had owned many horses before. Still, that hollow knot in his chest and stomach prevailed. He was sad. So many good rides, so many memories of the trail from behind the sharp ears of the ever alert animal. Then there was that gait that covered miles. Even longer-legged horses couldn't maintain keeping up with him. Marsh would miss those low nickers every morning when he appeared with oats and hay. He would miss the horse smell as he brushed out his coat. The mustang was a horse among horses. He leaned down and placed his head against that beautiful head, and put his arm around the animal's neck. He kissed him on his muzzle, and lay the head back down. This time the tears came, and he didn't try to hold them back. He cried unashamedly.

When he regained his composure he stood up, and looked at the two men on the ground, their life blood staining the white snow. It looked as if the aspens had shed their brightest leaves around their bodies. What had happened puzzled him. Why the ambush? Why here, of all places? He wasn't carrying money. The north end of Aspen Ridge certainly wasn't a major thoroughfare. It had not been much more than elk trail till a week or so ago. Well, he might never know. He rolled them over. He didn't recognize either one. He would let the sheriff in Salida know. He could recover the bodies, if ol' Mose didn't find them first. It was then that he realized he had been shot. He pulled his shirt-tail out. A bullet had passed through just above his hip-bone, and out, clean through. It hard hardly even bled, but now it was starting to hurt some. He took a clean hand-kerchief out of his saddlebag and folded and placed it on the two holes, he tucked his shirt around it to hold it into place. Damn, he didn't need this. He shook his head. Best get on down to Turret, the others would be waiting. He unsaddled the Buckskin and pulled the saddle free with some effort. He carried it to one of the other rider's horses. He picked the best looking one, a leggy sorrel that had a spark in his eye. He dumped the other saddle and replaced it with his own. He looked back at The Buckskin, remembering at the sound of the first gunshot the game little mustang had wheeled. The second bullet caught him in his neck, severing his spine, and he had dropped like a sack of rocks, spilling Marsh. There had been a third shot that must have been the one that had got him. The horse had probably saved his life, losing his own. Marsh had rolled as he fell, drawing his Colt and had fired two shots, hitting one man in the head, the other mid chest. Marsh wondered which one had killed his horse. Best he didn't know. He would come back tomorrow and bury his horse. He turned south, midst the fall splendor that now had no joy. The sun would be low when he reached the little mining town.

Sarah was sitting on a split log bench in front of the little mercantile store on the main drag of Turret. At first she didn't recognize the lone rider on the sorrel coming down the street. He was slouched a bit to the right in the saddle, his head down.

Then suddenly, "Oh my God! Marsh!"

She jumped from her seat and ran to him, spooking the sorrel till it shied sideways. It was then she saw the blood on his shirt.

"Oh, Marsh! Are you alright? My love, here, let me help you!"

"I'm okay, Sarah. Bullet went through, didn't hit anything serious. Just a bit sore is all."

"What happened? Why are you riding this horse? Where is The Buckskin?"

"The Buckskin is dead. He took a bullet meant for me. I took one of the ambusher's horses."

By that time the street was full of people. Sean took the reins of the sorrel. A man came through the crowd.

"Mr. Redman, I'm Bill Cox, town marshall. What happened?"

"Couple of riders ambushed me about five miles back toward Aspen Ridge. Shot my horse, and me too, I guess. I killed them both, and left them there. Somebody needs to go get them. The animals will get to them eventually."

Marshall Cox glanced at the setting sun and remarked, "Come first light I will take a couple of men and head up. Let's get you over to the doc's. You need a bit of patchin' up it appears."

The doctor had Marsh undress and cleaned around the bullet holes. He took a long pair of slender forceps, with a bit of cotton gauze on it and held it up.

"This may hurt a bit, Mr. Redman, but we need to clean the wound inside."

"Go ahead, Doc. Do what you must do."

As the doctor swabbed the wound Marsh groaned. But it was over quick enough. When he was dressed and on his feet again it didn't feel real bad at all. He was lucky. He and Sarah walked down the street to the café where Hanne and Sean waited.

"Marsh, who were these men and why did they attack you?"

"I wish I knew Sarah. As far as I know, I don't really have any enemies up here. Yet, I don't think it was robbery. I just plain don't know."

As they entered the café Hanne and Sean rose from their chairs. Hanne was the first to speak.

"Marsh, are you alright? We were so worried!"

"I will be fine, Hanne. A few days from now I will be as good as new, thanks for your concern."

"I unsaddled the sorrel and put him in the stable for you. I am so sorry about the Buckskin, I know you really cared for him. I hope he didn't suffer."

"I appreciate that, Sean. No, he went down fast. I am not sure he felt anything. I am grateful for that, he was more than a horse. He was a reliable and loyal companion. They don't happen by that often."

The next morning Marsh was up getting dressed to go with Marshall Cox. Sarah put her foot down.

"Marsh Redman, this might turn out to be our first fight, but you are not going!"

"Sarah, I need to go bury my horse. He deserves that. I can't let him get torn apart by critters."

"No, I will hire three or four men to go take care of that. Marshall Cox can see it gets taken care of properly."

Sean spoke. "I will go and oversee it Marsh. I will take a piece of canvas up to cover him with and we will pile stones on it, just don't you worry. I will make sure it is done right. You stay here and heal up. We are going to need you."

"Ok. Thank you, Sean. I owe you. And thanks, my dear, but you worry too much though."

Sara laughed slightly. "Says a man who just had a horse shot from under him, then was shot himself."

It was late afternoon when Marshall Cox returned with the bodies of the two assailants.

"Marsh, these boys are from down in the San Luis Valley. One of my men that went up said they were in town yesterday and were asking about you. Said they were looking for work, heard you were starting a ranch."

"Ok, now I understand. I had a run-in with some cowboys recently down there. They were meaning to do some mischief to Señor Trujillo's family. This won't be the end to this. I will need to watch my back."

Marsh and Sarah, along with Sean and Hanne, took the train to Fairplay just before Christmas 1898 to meet with William Wells and celebrate Christmas.

While waiting for William at a restaurant in Fairplay, Marsh became aware of an older gentleman sitting outside on a bench. It was quite cold that day. Marsh arose and walked out to him.

"Sir, could I help you find a warmer spot? It is a cold morning."

The old man glanced up. "Thank ye, lad. But I am fine. I think I was a mite lost in the past. You see, I first came here in 1861, and I suppose I was just living the times back then. Lord, how it has changed! It is all grown up now."

"Sir, I am Marsh Redman. We are about to establish a ranch a bit southwest of here."

The old man slowly stood. "Mr. Redman, sir, I am the Reverend John Lewis Dyer. This is probably my last trip up here. I will be turning this beautiful part of God's creation over to you young folks."

Marsh's heart jumped in his breast. "Reverend Dyer! Might I convince you to join us inside? There is a lady who is with me that is trying to capture the history of this place, and I am sure she would be delighted to speak with you!"

"Mr. Redman, it would be my honor." Marsh helped the old man inside and introduced him to the other three of the party. For the next two and one half hours they sat as history unfolded before them, as related by one who was a part of that history and had watched as it happened about him.

Stories of Indian raids and blizzards, outlaws, hardships and rewards. But through it all lay a thread of a life bent with difficulty. As they listened and tried to imagine the happenings, Sarah wrote and took notes, and on the other side of the table Sean sketched. First of Mr. Dyer, then of the scenarios he spoke of, or at least his vision of them.

This would be a Christmas they would remember.

Later they stood outside as the snowflakes began to swirl about them. Marsh helped Rev. Dyer into the stagecoach. He turned and raised his hand and smiled. As the coach lurched into motion, he leaned out the window and shouted,

"Merry Christmas and God Bless You, One and All!"

And then he vanished in swirls of snowflakes, like a specter from the past come to remind them of days of Christmas Past.

The four looked at each other, visibly moved. Tears glistened in the cold on their cheeks.

They smiled. They had been honored with their very own Christmas Carol.

Winter was intense that year. Heavy snow fell all around Salida. All the passes were snowbound for almost three months. Salida held true to the story people spoke of, saying that there was a hole in the sky over the town. Because of the way the mountain ranges around it lay, it just didn't get the snow that the rest of the valley got. Marsh and Sean picked a sunny day in mid February and tried a ride up to Whitehorn. They made it just over Cameron Mountain before the snow got too deep for the horses to break through. Whitehorn had 10 feet of standing snow in the middle of the valley. They turned back and barely made it back to Salida before dark. Exhausted horses, and two cold men. It was March before they tried again.

Everyone was anxious to get started with the ranch. It burned in their minds. Sean went wild. Sunny days would find him on the hotel roof, painting mountain vistas, or along the Arkansas River capturing the beauty of ice and snow, stone and water. Sarah spent days, visiting the newspaper, searching old editions for stories of the area. She visited old pioneers and wrote down their stories of bad weather, hardships, Indian raids and bandits, and all the lore she could find of the past days of valley of the Arkansas and the mountains that surrounded it. Hanne came in one morning and announced she had taken a winter position at the local school in Salida, to start training herself in the teaching profession.

Marsh received a letter from his mother on Christmas Eve. She and his stepfather were thinking of selling their place outside Elgin, Texas. She said they were getting on up in years, and the hot summers were starting to drain them to much. And she was wondering if Marsh thought that she would be happy in Colorado. Marsh was elated. He had been concerned with their welfare for sometime. He wrote her back that he thought she would, but not until spring when the weather was more accommodating, as the change would be difficult enough to adjust to.

On January 1st, 1899 Marsh Redman proposed to Miss Sarah Burns. She accepted his proposal, and a wedding date was set for early April.

The evening of the first, laying in bed, Sean turned to Hanne.

"Hanne, would you consider making that a double wedding?"

"Is that a proposal?"

"Well, not really. I would prefer to get on my knee in a humble manner, and beseech ye to become my wife. But being a practical man, I thought first to lay the ground work. But since we are on the subject...."

Sean dropped to his knee before Hanne, and pulling a ring from his vest pocket, he looked up into her blue eyes already swimming with tears. Her lip quivered, and her hands trembled.

Sean cleared his throat.

"Miss Hanne Clausen, from the first moment I set eyes on ye, I felt how special a person you are. As the months have passed, I have come to love thee from the depths of my being. I would ask you now on bended knee, and a promise that I will always love you and stand with you against whatever might be before us. Would you consent to marry me and be my wife?"

Hanne slowly melted, her legs seemingly not able to hold her until her face was inches from Sean's. She looked into his green eyes. She raised her hand to his auburn locks, then slid both arms around his shoulders.

"Sean Kelly, I have been blessed! You are such a giant of a man! If I can share your life, regardless of where or whatever it leads, I would need little else. Yes, my darling! Yes, I will marry you! You are my hearts desire! I want to live with you until we grow old together. I would love for us to pass from this earth, locked in each others arms!"

Their lips met and the world seemed to take on a glow. They sat for minutes on the floor on their knees facing each other their arms locked tightly around each other.

Marsh's horse wandered a bit to the right of the trail. As he did, Marsh caught sight of Sean raising himself in his stirrups and rubbing his behind. Marsh smiled, thinking that after all these years how at home in a saddle he was, as much as he would have been in an easy chair back at the ranch. Maybe more so. Still, they had been riding upwards of seven hours now. Maybe they should bear a bit to the left at Badger Creek and stop a bit at Whitehorn for a late lunch. There would still be time to make Salida by dark, if they didn't tarry too long.

"Sean, do ya think your backside can handle another hour?"

"Maybe so, Marsh. I believe I have only just lost one layer of skin, an th' good Lord knows it will grow back. But perhaps ye might tell me what type of leather they made *your* arse from? Ye just sit there like ya are part of that horse. I swear, when you step off from him, ye both look naked!"

Marsh laughed. "Sean, I have been sitting on one or another horse's back since I was about eight, maybe nine year old. I guess like ya say, I kinda feel like I am part of the horse. Sometimes I feel like I can feel what he is thinking, and sometimes I just think about something and he does it. Down in Texas, where I grew up, after the Civil War it was necessary for a boy to learn to ride, and ride well. The Comanche were still raiding the ranchers back then. We had a place down on the Nueces River, about fifty miles north of Uvalde. The Indians would swoop down out of them hills and run off our horses, and even kill the cattle. Would sometimes wipe out whole families. Twice, as a young boy, I had to just plain outride them. Once even my horse got an arrow in his butt, but he still ran real fast!"

"That seems a bit exciting, but not nearly enough to make me want to do it. In the city growing up, I had to learn to get away, too. But mostly from just the gangs and those my age that thought to kick a young Irishman's ass. Was a real

343

treat. Still, though, not too many were out to kill me.

"So, ye have been riding most your whole life? Have to admit, you fit the description of a real cowboy to a tee. Is that what ye have done your whole life? A cowboy, I mean?"

"Pretty much. When I was about 16 I had already herded cows all over Texas. But that was the year I first headed up the trail. Over the next several years, I went most every year, sometimes taking time off every other year. I did work some other jobs, but most of them were cattle related. I guess the first time would have been about '81. We spent 12 or so hours a day in the saddle, everyday, plus night herding. And that was when things went well. We had lots of stampedes, which sometimes would keep you in the saddle a couple of days plumb steady. Sometimes I would find myself asleep, just riding around the herd. Yeah, and that got me in trouble, too. Then we had to swim them big herds, sometimes a couple of thousand steers and a hundred or so horses, across swollen rivers. We would spend mostly three months in the saddle, sometimes more if we took some of the western trails to Wyoming or Montana. Then leave the cattle and ride home. Once, we took a herd all the way to Idaho. I really liked it. It was really hard, and real dangerous. That is the way I found Colorado, though, coming back from a trail drive.

"Whoa, Sandy! Sean, it is becoming a bit disagreeable as the sun drops. Let's go down to Whitehorn and have some grub."

As Marsh had finished telling his story, they had ridden up a little valley of aspen and up to the edge of a high ridge. With the afternoon sun at their backs, they looked down on the little town nestled in the little park below them.

Sean remarked, "Ah, tis a fair village. I would never have expected to see it there. I Marsh, I want you to know, I am grateful for this life. It was near a year ago that this adventure started for me. I was musing about this as we rode. If ye hear a complaint, it is but my back side doing it. The rest of me is happy. In a few days I am going to marry a remarkable woman, beautiful beyond what I deserve. So thank ye for listening to me palaver."

Marsh turned in the saddle.

"Sean, that just about sums up my thoughts actually." A quick March breeze passed over them. Marsh turned his collar up and they headed down into the little town of Whitehorn.

"Marsh, has anyone ever told you that you are bowlegged?"

"No. Has anyone ever told you are a brash young lady, and perhaps if you are so full of humor, maybe you should spend some time laughing?"

With that Marsh, grabbed her around the waist and pulled her to him, tickling her in her ribs and under her arms. Sarah shrieked and laughed, which just inspired Marsh to tickle more. They fell off the chair and into the floor, knocking the table over with a loud thump. Sarah, with a loud scream, jumped up and ran around the divan. Marsh was instantly on his feet.

At that moment the door crashed open and a large body sprang through, grabbing Marsh and spinning him around. The large man was speaking some foreign language as he swung at Marsh. Marsh ducked, and jabbed his opponent full in the face. The man grabbed Marsh in a tight bear hug. Just then, a bottle broke over the big man's head, and he went limp and slumped to the floor.

"Oh my God! Marsh, did I kill him?"

"No, he is just knocked out. Looks like he might have a nasty cut though. Here, grab a towel and wrap it around his head. Anyone you know?"

"No, never. What language was he speaking? German, maybe?"

"Naw. Some of my neighbors in Texas were German, pretty sure it wasn't that."

The stranger groaned and started to sit up, then fell back.

Marsh spoke, "Whoa, partner. You better stay down there for a minute. And maybe explain why you broke into our room."

The man burped loudly, emitting a strong smell of alcohol.

"Whew! Well, maybe that might explain part of it!"

The couple looked at each other, then at their assailant, who mumbled something unintelligible.

"You need to speak English if you can."

"What hit Olek?"

Marsh smiled. "I believe Miss Sarah wasted a bottle of wine over your head. Why did you break in?"

"Olek hear woman scream. Thought she was being hurt. Come inside, see woman getting off floor, man chasing."

"Oh my! Marsh, he was coming to my aid, and I almost killed him!"

"You say your name is Olek?"

"Da, Olek Andruko."

"Marsh, he is Russian!"

"Da, am Russky."

"Well, Mr. Olek, let me help you up on the divan here. C,mon, let's look at that head, and maybe the nose, too. I got a pretty good punch, before you went all grizzly on me."

Marsh and Sarah moved the man to the divan, cleaned his head wound and bandaged him. He was basically ok, but they figured he would have a headache most of the day.

"Olek, what are you doing here? In Salida, I mean?" inquired Sarah.

"I come here for work. To make fortune digging gold."

"How is that working out?" Marsh asked, rubbing his knuckles and wishing he had chosen his punch better. Nothing broken, but the hand will be sore tomorrow.

"Naw, not so very good. Olek not so wise as miner. Spent all his rubles on claim that other miners say has no minerals. Olek been cleaning stables to make money to eat."

Sarah said, "I am sorry to hear that. But mining is risky anyway."

"Aw, thank ya, Miss. It not so bad. Olek like horses better than people anyway. In old country, I ride before I can walk, and father make me train my first horse. Not give me one from herd. I had to catch and train. It was good, my horse was my friend. We eat together, we sleep together, we never apart, till....." His voice dropped. He dropped his head, and one could see tears in his eyes. "Anyway, we were friends for many years."

"Are you a good horse trainer?" Marsh asked.

"Olek good with horses. Won't let anyone mistreat horses in his presence."

Marsh looked at Sarah. She smiled at his thought, and nodded.

Marsh squatted in front of the sad face. "So, if someone gave you a job, at good wages, room and board to train horses, what would you say?"

Olek raised his head. "I would be very happy! But who would do such a grand thing for strange man in strange country?"

"Well, I think I know someone who is starting up a ranch this spring, and will need a wrangler."

"Where would Olek find this person, and what is wrangler?"

"A wrangler is a person who trains and is responsible for horses on a ranch. And she is standing right there behind you. The woman you were trying to save."

"Oh, yes! Missy, Olek do whatever wrangler is supposed to do for you! When do I start?"

It had fallen dark. The March wind would have been unbearable out in the open. But just south of Hartsel aways, smoke rising from a rocky outcropping caught Marsh's attention. Sean and Marsh had left Whitehorn a bit later than they had planned, and the two mules loaded with gear had slowed them considerably. They made their way to the small hill as the sun cast its last beams on the icy patches of snow. What they found was a surprise.

Under the rocky outcropping facing the southeast were two walls forming a ten foot room. Two people rose as they approached.

"Could we join your camp? We are about frozen!"

"You are welcome. Come sit by the fire. We have coffee made."

When the light from the fire flared, a face weathered by the high country air and sun smiled at them. The face was framed by dark hair, with just a touch of silver, braided and falling down on wide shoulders covered by lined leather jacket. Just behind him was a woman wrapped in a blanket, probably in her thirties. Her long black hair fell over her face as she nursed the infant at her breast. When Marsh stepped forward, she looked directly at him, her eyes expressionless. Marsh nodded to her, then looked back at the man.

"My name is Marsh Redman. This is Sean Kelly, my friend. Thank you for your shelter. We do not come empty handed. We have some bacon and beans, and we can make biscuits to feed us all, if that would be acceptable."

"I am happy to meet you, Marsh Redman and Sean Kelly. Welcome to our fire. We would be grateful for your gifts. Hunting has not been good today."

"Sean, grab that bag off the mule there and I will get some hardware."

In under an hour food was made and being eaten by the travelers. Marsh had cut out some bacon and opened 3 cans of beans. The Indian woman had stirred the biscuits together and put everything on the fire, still having not spoken a word. Sean had taken the horses and mules to a tiny creek close by and broken the ice to let them drink. They pulled the loads off the packhorses and piled them up, and tied the horses and mules on a sheltered side of the rocks. Marsh threw a tarp over the pile in case it snowed during the night. Finally, the tall Indian man spoke.

"My name is Parso. It is what my father called me. This is my wife. You would probably have trouble with her Sioux name, but in English it means Spotted Fawn. And this is our son."

"And what be the lad's name, sir?" asked Sean.

Parso looked at Sean. "We will not name him until he has seen two summers."

"I see."

Marsh asked, "Are you Sioux? Parso does not have the sound of a Sioux word."

"No, Marsh, I am Ute. I was captured by the Sioux as a small boy. It is told that I am the son of a great chief, his name was Ouray."

"You are the son of Ouray? I am honored to meet you! He was a great man, and a great chief. I was a shirttail boy when he died. It was the first time I went up the trail with a herd. I was making my way back down the front of the mountains when I got to Ignacio. They were having a funeral, and I asked who it was. Someone said Chief Ouray."

"Then you would know where his bones lie, Marsh?"

"Not exactly. But wouldn't be hard to find. He had friends there."

Parso leaned back against a robe and looked at the fire.

"The Great Spirit lead you to my camp, Marsh Redman."

"Yes, maybe so."

"I have been told my father walked these mountains and hunted and trapped here."

"That is probably so. His name is well known here."

"And what is your business, Marsh and Kelly?"

"Well, we are starting up a ranch west of here, near the mountains. This is one of our first loads of supplies for building a house."

Parso smiled. He looked into the fire. "The land is changing. The world is changing. The white man has tamed the earth, he has changed the seasons. When he finds a place of land, he digs a hole and puts something in it. Or he takes something out. He builds a fence around it. That piece of land is never free again. It is tamed like the horse the white man rides or the cows he raises to eat. He takes that place away from the Great Spirit and keeps it for himself. When the Indian comes on a piece of land, he stops and puts his blanket down and sets up his house. The grass still grows, the streams still run, it belongs to the Great Spirit. And when he needs to go, he takes his blanket, and his house and follows the buffalo, and the Great Spirit still has the land." He paused, and poked the fire. "Where the white man builds his cities like Denver and Cheyenne, if he left the Great Spirit would spit on that land, and send a great prairie fire to cleanse it. But he would never look on its filth again. But even with this, the red man must change and be like the white man, or he will cease to be."

"All you say is true, Parso. No argument from me. When I first came through almost 20 years ago, it was a much purer place. More game. It will never be the same."

As they talked, Sean sat and sketched the figures in the firelight, drawing there likenesses outlined in their shadows on the rock walls behind them. Their words sank deep in his heart, awakening stories of the Irish his father had related to him. Stories about how the clans had fought and died for Ireland. The tribes were all gone now. Ireland was just a country. These native tribesmen, what was left of them, would soon almost be extinct, so mixed with the white races one would not be able to look at their faces and see their history, or hear their stories spoken in their native tongue. Was this the future? Was there anyone left to conquer? He slid down into his blanket, his head resting on his saddle, and the shadows on the rock walls covered him with darkness.

It was about 9 in the evening when the train pulled into Salida. Late March had cold days and warm days; this had been one of the latter. Marsh and Sarah stood backed into the doorway of the railway station. After the sun had dropped behind Mt. Shavano the warmth departed quickly. The engine chugged by them, then a couple of freight cars and three passenger cars slowed to a stop at the platform. The couple watched the people departing, and others waiting. Then a man in his early 60's appeared, stepping down then turning to lend a hand to a lady. She was small, slender and bowed somewhat from years of work. She looked around, her head erect, eyes searching. Grey curls were held down by her bonnet tied tightly under her chin. Marsh said softly, with a choke in his voice, "There they are."

He stepped forward out of the shadows, hurrying to meet them.

"Ma, Pa! Welcome to Colorado!"

The older lady quickly closed the distance and just fell into Marsh's arms. Her voice was choked with emotion, tears fell down her cheeks.

"Oh, son! I am so glad to see you! You look so good! Come here to the light, let me look at you!"

The man stuck his hand forward and Marsh reached and took it and pumped it.

"Hello Pa! I am glad to see you both! I'm really happy to see you, you are going to like it here."

Marsh's mother was the first to spot Sarah standing a bit to the side.

"Well, who is this lovely creature?"

"Ma, Pa, this is Sarah Burns. But we are changing her name in a few days."

"Hello Sarah. I am Martha Hargis. I am so happy to meet you! Marsh has spoken so highly of you. You know, I have always wanted a daughter, I would have imagined her to look just like you! So, you just call me Ma from now on, alright?"

"Oh, I would be thrilled to do that Mother Hargis! Or Ma…. Your coming to Colorado has made Marsh a happy man."

"Excuse me, young lady, I am Josh Hargis. And you can call me Pa, too. And from what I understand, you have had something to do with making Marsh a happy man, too. For that, we are ever in your debt. We were starting to think he would just marry a horse and continue to ride the rest of his days. Just *joshing*!" Josh winked.

"Pa, knock off that nonsense. You will talk her out of it before we get the knot tied." But Marsh smiled.

"Not on your life, Marsh Redman! That knot is tied! We just haven't branded you yet!"

"Ouch, Marsh." Josh joked.

"Well, let's get you two out of the night air and settled in. Tomorrow is another day and time to talk. We have taken a house on D Street for you. Get in the carriage and I will throw a robe for you, till we get you luggage."

"Yes, sir. No problem there. It is a mite chilly here, isn't it?"

"Yes, Pa, winter is not quite over up here."

The short carriage ride took them to a medium size two story home, somewhat Victorian in design, with a gable corner facing the east. As they entered, Sean trotted out to the carriage to help Marsh and Josh with the few bags the couple had with them. As they all doffed their coats and heavy apparel, Hanne entered with coffee and some small cakes and cookies.

An atmosphere of family settled over the house in the 300 block of D Street. It was felt by all, and each member felt conscious of the things to come this New Year as soon as the snows lifted, and spring would arrive in the Colorado High Country.

It was a warm day for April. The park along the river was set with tables donated from the various churches. A magnificent arch had been erected for the ceremonies from willows from along the riverbank. By noon the tables began creak under the loads of food heaped up on them. It seemed the whole town turned out. Marsh had made many friends, and when they heard he had found a bride, well, it was time to celebrate. The morning stage had brought many of the Trujillo family from the San Luis Valley. Riders from Whitehorn poured down to the Arkansas. Pits had been dug and filled with coals and elk quarters sizzled, giving off fragrances to cause the saliva to form in the mouths of many.

At 1 o'clock afternoon the band struck up *Here Comes the Bride*, and a grand carriage pull up at the foot of F Street and the two couples stepped down, resplendent in their wedding gowns and tuxedos. Sarah wore a beautiful gown of a baby blue. It was accented in a darker blue, including her hat and veil.

Hanne's dress matched Sarah's in design but was of a rose color, complete with a matching accent. The grooms were well adorned in tuxedos, with dark jackets and striped trousers. They both wore tophats.

Both were just a bit self-conscious, being more used to work-a-day clothing. They took their respective brides arms, and assisted them from the carriage. Señor Trujillo came and took Hanne's arm and led her to one side. William Wells did the same for Sarah, smiling warmly at his charming boss. Marsh and Sean walked to the arch, now occupied by a local minister.

Now the wedding march was resumed and the brides were lead forth by their escorts. When they were replaced beside the grooms, the minister raised his head.

"It is indeed a beautiful morning. It is our charge that it will be remembered for decades to come. A beautiful spring morning bespeaks of a new beginning. And indeed, that is the occurrence of which we are here to celebrate. These fine folks have joined our community. They have become successful in their lives, successful enough that they could have chosen anywhere to live. But they chose here in our region. We are thankful of that. Their love for each other has brought them here to share their vows with you as witness. The affection between them made them want to share this moment with each other. So, with no further adieu, who gives the women....?"

Both William and Señor Trujillo responded in unison, "I do."

"Dearly beloved, we gather here in the eyes of God, and before these witnesses..."

The ceremony was conducted in silence, each eye on the two couples. Marsh's mother dabbed at her eyes. His Pa swallowed and shifted in his seat. Marsh wasn't his blood, but he was his son, and his pride in who he had become would have been the same if he was blood.

"Is there any here that see reason why these couples should not be joined, speak now or forever hold your peace."

He hesitated momentarily and raised his eyes.

"Then I now pronounce the both of you Husband and Wife, and may God's blessings be on you. You gentlemen may kiss your brides."

A rousing hurrah went up, scattering the birds from their perches.,

"Th' grub's ready! Git yourselves a plate!"

The two couples spent the next couple of hours being congratulated and receiving best wishes.

Hanne very delicately wiped tears from her eyes, careful to not damage her eye make-up. She glanced up at Marsh's smile.

"I just am a bit overwhelmed! I never expected people to make this much of a 'to-do' over this. I am very touched. I doubt my own home town would have turned out this way."

"I think the people in these mountains are perhaps a bit more giving, maybe a little more conscious of their lives and the lives of people around them." returned Sarah.

"Remember, you are in a pioneering community still with lots of room to grow.

They are aware they have need of neighbors." added Marsh.

"I remember. When but a wee lad, I remember my sainted mother and her friends, our neighbor ladies, coming together and cooking meals together for us all because no one was able to buy all the necessities. So, they would join together." replied Sean.

Marsh's mother wiped a tear from her eye. "Thank you, Sean. It touches my heart to hear you tell of that. Those poor Yankee women probably learned that from the great war. Down in Texas th' womenfolk had to learn to do that same thing. It was usually on a Sunday we would all go to church and after church was over we would spread out food together. Lordy, those meals were so good! We had to depend on each other. Those darned Indians were always raiding, we needed each other!"

"Thank you, Ma," answered Sarah. "I had not thought of that. Those must have been trying times, with all the men gone. It would have been a hard life."

"Mr. Redman."

"Yes sir?"

The man in the grey suit was carrying a box and a tripod. He was breathing hard and mopping his brow with a large red 'kerchief.

"I am Ronald Jones, sir. I am a photographer."

Pointing his finger at the sharp, steep little peak that lay just across the river on the far side of the tracks behind the railway depot, he continued, "I had a carriage take me up to the tall little hill, or mountain, such as the case may be. I wanted to get a picture of this quaint little town, especially with the crowd and the gathering along this beautiful river. I then realized it was a wedding. So I took the liberty of taking several pictures during the ceremony. If I may be so bold, I would like to inquire if you and your party would care for some copies."

Before Marsh was able to open his mouth to answer, Sarah intervened.

"Yes sir! We would like several copies! And if you have the time, we would like some close-ups of us as well. I had tried to hire a photographer for our wedding, but was unable to do it. Would you be able to honor my request?"

"Indeed, I would, ma'am. I would be more than happy to capture your moments. Here, let's move away from the crowds. Perhaps using the cottonwoods as a background? And, yes, we will take a couple of you under the arch as well. Come, let's hurry to catch the light. Those clouds are starting to drift over from the mountains to the west."

Salida, CO circa 1900
Taken from the top of Tenderfoot Mountain

Soon a late afternoon shower brought the festivities to a halt. The newlyweds and Marsh's parents returned home by carriage. As they got inside, Marsh's mother looked back out the window where a whirl of snowflakes covered the lawn and shrubs with a glistening blanket. It was still snowing when darkness obscured the view from the turret window. Marsh's Pa closed the curtain and backed up to the warm fire burning in the fireplace.

"This is right purty country, up here. Kinda hard to wrap my head around it snowing like this, this late in the year. And another thing… I thought the first few days I would never catch another full breath the rest of my days! But that past. Anyway, I still probably ain't gonna run no footraces."

Marsh answered, "But, ya think yuh might learn to like it?"

"Yes sir, I do. I am getting quite anxious to saddle up a horse and go exploring."

"Did you sell your horses before you came up Pa?"

"Well, yes and no. They were getting on up in years, like me. I gave my old saddle horse to Mr. Jolly, over near Austin. He said he could just run loose with his remuda for the rest of his days. I 'spect he deserved that, he had worked hard his whole life." The older man wiped his nose, and kinda dropped his head, remembering. "The team, they were a bit younger. Old Uncle Bob and Aunt Minnie, that colored couple that live over a few miles east of us, you remember them? I gave the team to them. I knew they would care for them, and would never be worked too hard again."

"Yes, indeed, I do remember Bob and Aunt Minnie. How are they getting on?"

"Oh, tolerable, I suppose. They are still active, just move a bit slower these days. Bob helped me so much the last few months. I tried to pay him, but he would never take anything. Just said he was being neighborly." he laughed, "The only way I got him to take the team and old wagon was I told him I wanted him to take care of them, in case I needed to come back for anything."

"That sounds a lot like Bob. Salt of the earth, a fine man."

"Yep. Anyhows, they got a passel of children and grandchildren around them now. They are quite happy. And with that,

I am going to trot off upstairs and see if that old woman has the bed warm yet. Me feet are still cold."

"Alright, Pa. Goodnight."

"Goodnight sir. A good rest for ye," added Sean.

As Josh left, Sara and Hanne joined the two men.

"What a day!" said Sarah.

"One of my favorites!" replied Hanne.

Sean grinned. "One I hope to tell me young grand lad and lasses about one day."

"Oh," exclaimed Hanne, "We hadn't discussed that, have we?"

"Nay, lass, but it had crossed me mind to go upstairs and perhaps bring it up to ye."

Hanne looked at Marsh and Sarah.

"It seems my randy little Irishman is going to misbehave this evening. So perhaps I should take him to his room, where he can't embarrass refined folk."

Marsh and Sarah burst into laughter.

"Refined folk! So that is what you think of us?" laughed Marsh. "So, very well then, you young folk go to bed now and leave us refined folk here to our own diverses."

Sarah waved good evening.

"Hanne and Sean, you have a wonderful evening. See you tomorrow."

Sarah came and sat on the arm of the divan, then fell backwards across Marsh's lap, putting her arms around his neck. She batted her eyes and with a sexy look asked, "So, how many children are we going to have, Mr. Redman?"

"Oh, at least 15 to 18, Mrs. Redman."

"Um, that sounds so nice. I love being called Mrs. Redman. Hmmm, when would you like to start?"

"Either right now, or we can go upstairs."

"I love you, Marsh."

The end of April arrived. The snow was melting and the Arkansas was on a real tear. It got plum out of banks in Salida, damned near getting up in the hotel near the railroad station. Everyone thought the bridge was going to go for sure. But by May 5th the river had dropped in town and the bridge was still there. On the 10th of May three wagons loaded heavy with tools, various building material, supplies, tents, and whatever one might think one might need to build a ranch house and out buildings headed across the bridge and up the road out of Salida.

Marsh and Sarah sat up high on the seat of the first wagon, followed by Josh and Martha Hargis in wagon number two. Sean and Hanne followed with a buggy filled with suitcases and trunks in the rear seats. Wagon number three was driven by Olek, while Chagan herded the small remuda of riding stock. It was slow going, loaded the way they were. The sharp ups and downs near Turret were especially bad. They camped that first night near Turret on a small stream. The horses and mules were hobbled. They probably didn't need it though, they were fair worn out. Sunrise next morning found them moving northeast again. After reaching about midway of Aspen Ridge, it got a bit easier, but they still had to spend one more night on the trail. By noon the third day they topped the small rise, overlooking the site of the old ranch used by the previous owners. In its run down condition it had little use other than firewood. It was Josh that broke the silence other than the breathing of horses, and the rattle of harness as the animals took the time to shake off the strain of pulling the wagons.

"By God, Marsh, you weren't just talking when you said this place was paradise! It is just beautiful, I swear. I ain't never saw its equal."

"Josh Hargis, you quit your takin' the Lord's name in vain! I think maybe he just might be nearby, we are so high up here."

"Oh, shush woman. I think he might tend to overlook that when I am praising his creation."

"Pa, the people we bought from remarked that her father would say that this is where God came to spend his off time. So I reckon you might be close to right."

Marsh turned and called to Olek and Chagan. "You two! Get the stock secured, and we will get on down there and get unhooked. We need to get some kind of a camp set up before evening."

Chagan started his small band of horses out ahead of them. As he passed Marsh, he turned in the saddle.

"Chagan hope big bear long gone."

"Me too, Chagan."

Josh looked at Marsh. "What's that about a bear?"

"Pa, we have a big ol' rogue grizzly up here. He is called Ol' Mose. He is responsible for a lot of destruction. He killed a couple of horses the first time we came up."

"Humph!"

"Yeah, keep your eyes open, always. We got big cat, too. Maybe a few wolves. Country up here is still pretty raw."

"Reckon I should get my ol' hogleg out again? I had wrapped it up and packed it away, I thought for good. Maybe not, huh?"

"Yessir, I would."

"This place is a breath of fresh air, though! Makes an ol' man's blood get up and race again. I thank ye, son, for this opportunity."

"Aw, ya don't have to thank me. You can thank Mrs. Redman here."

"Uh, who, what....?" Sarah had been engrossed in staring at what would be her new home and had missed most of the conversation.

"Marsh, let's get on down. I can't wait to get started."

"Yes ma'am!"

By mid-afternoon tents had been set up near what had been a fire pit from years ago. Stones had been set in a circle, and two large iron rods had been set in the ground and a large rod place on top to hang pots and such from. The smaller of the three wagons had been backed up a few feet away. It contained all the food supplies and the cooking tools, pots, pans, kettle, dutch ovens, etc. Chagan had finished helping Olek pen the stock up, now he was ready to fix his first meal. He carried on his work of setting up his kitchen while carrying on a conversation in his native language to himself, causing Martha to remark "Sakes alive! It sounds like he is singing some pretty song! Wish I knew what he was saying."

Chagan stopped. He bowed to the older lady.

"Missy, Boss Man Mother... Chagan talk to ancestors, ask them to keep away bad spirits from Chagan's new friends. Ask them to make new home a happy place. Ask them to help Chagan cook good food. But most of all, to keep Mr. Mose Bear far,

far away, from here. Chagan sing his prayer to ancestors so that it is pretty sound to make them listen."

"Well, I'll swan!"

By dusk the camp was set and animals fed. Beds were set up in empty wagons. Chagan and Olek had found one of the out buildings in good repair and had taken possession of it for their quarters. A box of steaks had been acquired at Turret and packed in ice, and they were now on the fire cooking, along with various dishes being prepared by the Mongol cook. Martha had to restrain herself from wanting to get into the act herself, after long years of habit being the chief cook for her family.

Sean came into the camp circle and found a block to sit on.

"Sarah, I have staked out the cabin plan, but I think we might want to adjust it some from what we spoke about. From the lay of the land, and then from walking around, I am not sure the kitchen or the living space is quite large enough."

"Sounds good. I am so excited, I can't wait until tomorrow!"

A large table had been hauled up from Salida, complete with eight chairs. It had been set up in the open near the campfire for the evening. That night, those eight chairs were filled by eight people from the four corners of the country and, indeed, from halfway around the earth. They were all here to start new lives, to pool their energies, their talents, their thoughts and dreams. The table was lit by two lanterns. The air was chill, the stars shone down on smiling faces, and the forest around them teamed with life unseen. The Milky Way blazed a wagon road across the sky above in the Bayou Salado, the land of the 190-degree horizon.

A week later, Arnie and Jon Johannson had moved over from Whitehorn, and a foundation of granite and mortar was being laid. As each day passed by progress was evident to the beholder.

The sun was really intense. It burned with tiny needles into his face, but not nearly as severe as his bare chest and naked arms. But wait, why was he not wearing a shirt? He had always dressed thoroughly before going out. Well, regardless, he was burning. Just fairly cooking, actually. Most of the fire felt as if it was going through the hole in the upper part of his chest on the right side. Strange, he didn't remember a hole, either. But maybe something had happened while he was sleeping. But he didn't sleep in daylight, and never in the bright sun.

He opened his eyes. His dad was sitting on the rock next to him.

"Don't worry yourself, son. I haven't come to get you yet, you will be ok. Some folks 'bout here, they'll fix you up."

Marsh opened his mouth and tried to speak, but words didn't come out. Didn't matter though. His father was still wearing Confederate Gray. There was a bad stain right over his heart, and a hole in his shirt.

His dad caught him looking. "Oh, don't worry 'bout that. It's just what your mind remembers 'bout me, what was told. When you leave the world, you will be happy to lay that body down. It's pretty useless. Well, I gotta go. Them folks are here. You just relax. Oh, yeah, you have growed into a really good man. I am right proud of you. See ya down the trail, son." Then he was gone.

Marsh tried to rise, but he couldn't do it. Kinda like none of his muscles worked no more. Then he heard the scramble of hoof beats, and someone that smelled like Sarah was leaning over him, cradling his head.

"Oh my God! Marsh, what happened? Please, talk to me! Open your eyes!"

It was then when he realized he really wasn't conscious. He was dreaming. No, wait, the pain was real.

"He has lost a lot of blood, we have to get a doctor. Sean, ride for Whitehorn. Tell them we are coming in. If the doctor can meet us, tell him to do it. Chang, go cut a couple of poles, we'll make a travois. Marsh, you hang on. Now we got you."

Marsh thought he smiled at her, but he could hear her sobs and feel her tears as she knelt above his face. He thought he could smell that wonderful fragrance that came from her. He opened his eyes. There was an old Indian man in buckskins with a feather in his hair behind her. He smiled at Marsh and raised his hand, palm out to him, then brought his hand across his body. He turned and walked away and turned into a mist that spread up into the blue sky.

"Oh God, Marsh! Please! Open your eyes, my darling! Let me know you hear me, please!"

He felt hands lifting him and carrying, then laying him in a hammock. No, not a hammock, something softer than the ground. Someone trickled some water into his mouth or on his lips. He felt it slide into his throat. It was nice, but he was so tired, and now the hammock was moving and the sun wasn't burning him any more. Except for the hole, it still burned plenty.

Hmm wonder if it had something to do with the two men he had met that morning? Yes, it had to be.... Yes, now it had to be. Marsh remembered he had met the two on the upper part of Badger creek where it came down off the mountain. They mumbled as they passed, not meeting his eye. He turned in the saddle, just in time to see the red bearded one pull a pistol. He might have heard it go off, or it might have been his own. But then he was falling, his horse racing away. Yeah, that's what happened. He had been shot. So tired. The hammock was rocking him to sleep. He would think about it later, after some rest.

His horse walked to the front porch of the white frame house. There were plants growing everywhere. Yellow roses interlaced themselves on the wooden arches leading to the vegetable garden, which seemed past its season. But it was late September, but this wasn't South Park. It couldn't be, but it was. His mom walked out of the door. She wore a grey prairie dress, her hair in a bun. She carried a bonnet in her hand. She looked right through him. How could she? Then she faded into a picture that kept rolling by him, as if on some kind of conveyer belt. *I can't be dead* he thought. But obviously I am not in Texas either. Down at the end of the trail, or street or whatever it was, was a bright light shining from above, like maybe through a hole in the sky or ceiling. He glanced down at himself. He felt really young and fit. He felt strong. He did not want to go to that light though, just something inside him said, no, not this time. But there was something really familiar about it, almost as if he had seen that before. No, need to go somewhere else.

He opened his eyes. The window was open. There was a familiar smell of pine, and a bit of dust and maybe wet earth somewhere. Outside it was dark but, the forest stood silent, almost as if time stood still. Then, off a bit to the right, the clear squeal of a trumpeting bull elk. Now, to the left, just a bit higher up, another, a bit more mature. Then another, and another. He turned his head from the window. Sarah sat beside him, her arms folded, her eyes closed. She looked so tired.

There was another person. Yes, in the corner, squatted against the wall. It was Chagan. He saw Marsh looking at him. His eyes brightened, and a smile lit his face as he stood up still against the wall. Sarah stirred. She turned to him, she blinked.

"Oh my darling! you are awake! Lay still, you have been so very ill."

"Sarah, where am I? I heard the elk bugling."

"You were dreaming, I think, my love It is spring, do the elk bugle now? You were shot, the bullet passed through a part of your lung. But the doctor says you will heal. It narrowly missed your spine. It hit a couple of ribs. Do you know who the two men were? The Deputy will be by later. You have been out for about 3 days. Oh, Marsh, I am so glad to hear you speak!"

Marsh tried to smile, but even that hurt. He took a deep breathe, but that hurt worse.

"No, Sarah, I don't know who they were. Did they catch them?" He lay back against his pillow. That was exhausting, trying to breathe.

"They are both dead, you shot them."

"Hmmmm. I don't remember much."

"You hit your head on a rock when you fell, as well as getting shot. That worried the doctor almost as much as the bullet wound."

"Bet you're beginning to wonder about a guy that's allays getting' shot."

"I will take the bad with the good, Marsh Redman. You always stand for good. I know that will always make you a target for some."

"We are going to move you down to the hospital in Salida for a few days until you can gain some strength back. The altitude is a bit lower and you will breathe easier. But that is tomorrow morning. Are you hungry?"

"Maybe. Not sure. Feels like I have been gone somewhere for a while. Just tired."

"Chagan has gone to get some of his chicken soup. He says it should have you back on a horse in 24 hours," Sarah laughed.

"Then bring it here. I need to get back to work. This ranch is not going to build itself."

"Now, hold on young man, you have a lot of healing to do. You must bide your time. The work goes on. You laid things out, people are doing their jobs you allotted them. It will all get done."

The next morning Chagan and Sean appeared with a team and a nice carriage with leaf spring support. It was a long built frame and should ride quite nice. Marsh was carried out on a stretcher and placed cross the seats with room for Sarah to ride beside him. The canopy was brought forward to cover the couple, and the long ride to Salida began.

It was late afternoon before they pulled up in front of the Denver-Rio Grande Hospital on First Street in Salida. Marsh was placed on a rolling table and transported to his room on the second floor, over looking the Arkansas River. Here he would spend the next week.

The window beside his bed revealed a splendid view of the sharp, pointed little hill that rose above the town of Salida. His eyes, out of habit, searched the gulches and ravines on the hill side across the river. He moved his right arm to stretch it above his head and was rewarded by a sharp stabbing pain that seemed to come from somewhere deep inside behind his should blade. He grunted.

"That didn't feel very good, did it?"

He glanced to his left. Sarah was sitting in a large chair with her feet drawn up under her, an Indian blanket of sorts was thrown over her lap and legs.

"Have you been here all night?"

She smiled. "No, I went back to the house last evening. Didn't have much luck sleeping, so I came back a couple of hours ago. I slipped in and dozed here. I just felt better, being here."

"You are right, that smarted a bit when I lifted my arm. But I couldn't have done that yesterday. So it shows some improvement."

She giggled. "Yeah, but you don't start teaching dancing until a day after tomorrow."

Marsh smiled "My dear, you have a smart mouth. If you would come over here, I would kiss it and make it all better."

"If you think you are up to the chore, I will give it a try!" She slid out of her chair and gently lowered her lips to his, tasting his mouth, gently tugging at his lip with her teeth, then settling her lips to his in a deep soulful kiss. When she raised her head, tears were running down her cheeks.

"Marsh, I was so scared. I love you so much, I don't know what I would have done if, if.......never mind. You are going to be well, and I, well, I just am so happy with you! Oh, yes, you had a visitor last evening. A pretty lady. Said she was a friend and had heard you had been shot. She said she would return. Her name was Laura Evans, I believe."

"Oh." Marsh could feel the color rise in his face. He had never mentioned her to Sarah. Well, now is the time.

"Sarah, Miss Laura is the local Madam. She runs those working girls down on Sackett Street in the cribs. I have known her for a couple of years. She is a good person, regardless of her profession."

Sarah never batted an eye, but answered, "She certainly seemed pleasant to me."

Just then, William Wells and the local sheriff entered the room.

"Marsh, how are you this morning?" William walked to Marsh's bedside, affectionately laying his hand on Marsh's shoulder. "You know Sheriff Charles Ankele, I believe?"

Marsh nodded. "Sheriff."

Sheriff Ankele said, "Marsh, good morning. Thought you might want to know, we identified those two that bushwhacked you. Seems they were part of that group from down in the San Luis Valley that you stirred up by siding with Señor Trujillo."

"It doesn't surprise me, Sheriff. That is a bad bunch."

"Well, I spoke with the Sheriff down that aways, in Saguache County. We are going to go have a visit with them in a few days. This ain't the wild west anymore, and we ain't going to condone that kinda activity anymore."

D&RG Hospital, Salida, CO.

Marsh leaned against the slender aspen tree. His recovery was a bit slower than expected. Still, he was still alive. The breeze rustled through the trees, ruffling the few early leaves just reaching out to see a sunny blue sky. He wrinkled his brow. So much work to do, he had to get to it. Summers were short up here. He was suddenly warmed by the softness of two arms and soft breasts that leaned against his back. He smiled inside. *Just when I feel sorry for myself, there she is.*

Sarah spoke, "A penny for your thoughts, Mr. Redman."

"Ma'am, to be honest with you, it would take a whole wagon load of them to be a fair transaction for a penny value."

"And where is my Marsh Redman, sir? What did you do with my beloved husband and companion?"

Marsh turned and put his arms around her. He reached up and slid his hat back on the back of his head and kissed her on the forehead. He smiled and stroked her hair back from her face,

"Right here, Mrs. Redman. At your service. I believe the one reason that I am so partial to you is you never leave me alone in a quandary for two whole minutes without popping up. And when you do, it just suddenly becomes a sunny day, and a man's life is just all planned out. Thank you, ma'am."

"So, will you give me any idea what had your brow so furrowed a moment ago?"

Marsh couldn't help smiling at her. She could just look into his soul somehow. He had resolved himself that his thoughts would never be just his alone anymore, but.... that was ok.

"Well, with the war with Spain being so short-lived, and ending in February, I see nothing but a bright future for the country. However, I was not pleased with President McKinley's handling of those affairs. He seems to be much more akin to the rich manufacturers than he does the common man. Pa says he fought in the Civil War, but he was a Yankee Commissary Officer, so I guess he comes by it naturally. Now, I know for sure we need the rest of the world for trade, I am not too backward to understand that. But when the rich just get richer, and working man lives by th' skin of his teeth, then somethin' is just not right."

"Did you vote for McKinley in '96?"

"I did not. At the time I was kinda in between Texas and Colorado. Mostly here, but hadn't put my mind to politics too much. I have read the papers considerable. As of late it has become apparent that there is a bit of difference of opinions about what is good for us and what is not."

"At least you get to have a say in it. As a woman, our opinions seem not to matter very much."

"That is a fault of which we as a country suffers. I think in the not to distant future we will see that corrected. Already there are protests and such. Leastways, that is my hope. Women contribute too much to life to not have a say in which way it goes."

Sarah giggled. "And that is why I am a bit partial to you! You are such a smart man!"

"Shucks, ma'am, I just don't want to get my boss riled up at me." Marsh smiled and reached his arm around her shoulder and hugged her to him.

"By the way, the day the doctor released me to come home, and the Hutchison boys Joe and Art came by to see me. Joe says they have some calves they would like for me to look at. Some Angus stock they acquired. But while we were talking, I mentioned to them that you were interested in writing about the country around here. Well, Art pipes up and says he would love to set down with you as he has written some stories about the Indians and early settlers, including his family, that he would be happy to share with you."

"My goodness Marsh, how exciting!"

"Yes, his Pa came here about 1868."

"Oh my!'

As the late spring sun dropped lower in the sky, the shadows reached pointy fingers across the valley as if it was their job and theirs alone to darken the land to make it habitable for the creatures of the night to begin their day. As the shadows below the ridge turned to night over the young couple, they dreamed about their future in the Bayou Salado.

Sean leaned down and picked up a shard of ceramic ware alongside the tracks at Buena Vista. He stood up turning it over in his fingers.

"The Kitchen staff tosses all the broken dinner ware out when the train stops at depots," Hanne remarked, as if reading his mind.

"Aye," Sean agreed. "There must be considerable breakage with all the jostling and jolting."

Hanne added, "A gentleman that I conversed with in San Francisco worked in a high level position for Pullman. He said that because of the expense, it made profits possible with only a maximum amount of careful management."

"I understand that he has built a village near his works for his people to live in."

"Yes, that is true. He was a model employer until a few yeas ago, when the country went into recession. Because of his profits dropping, he cut wages severely, but he didn't cut his rents. His workers went on strike, aided and spurred on by the Anarchists and their movement."

"Aye, though I fail to see what good their need for violence will do."

Hanne smiled and hugged Sean. "My lovely young Irishman, you are the most gentle of your kind. There are few things that are changed except by battle, few things acquired without a fight. Many of these things will require blood to flow before being accomplished. The simple fact is that there are many who simply won't change their mind except by force."

"Hanne, my darling, the blood of the Vikings does yet flow in those lovely veins of yourself. I still hold that there should not be battle until all else fails."

Hanne just smiled.

"So many young women are stepping out of their traditional roles with this movement though, such as Emma

Goldman, it gives me hope. Most movements start with a jerk, and a headlong plunge, and a kick and a snarl. Then mellow into a navigable stream and flow on down to the sea. I have hope this will do the same. I believe it is time that men start giving women their rightful place in the world, such as voting."

"So, me lovely shield-maiden, who would you vote for in this coming election? Mr. McKinley?"

"No, I don't think so. I do like some of his ideas, and manners, but he is still on the side of the rich and nothing can be gained of that."

"You don't think that by the United States adding Hawaii and Guam and Puerto Rico, an' the entire Philippine Islands, as well as liberating Cuba, is a good idea?"

"It remains to be seen, Sean. That is spreading ourselves very thin. We will have to police a lot of country already. The people are having trouble in China.

A group of radicals called the Boxers are fighting back, and we aren't even trying to occupy China."

"Aye, Lass, I like the way you think."

"All Aboard!"

"C'mon, lass, we need to get ourselves to Leadville. Mr. Wells sounded a bit in a hurry for us to get there."

"Sean, I think the Monte Cristo would be a good choice for the night. They have a place for the horses, and we will be right there when the train arrives tomorrow morning. I want to get those heifers started early, try to make it at least halfway back to the ranch by dark."

"Sounds good to me, Marsh. Yeah, how come you didn't let them ride the train all the way around to Trout Creek and take them into the valley that way?"

"Thought about it. But they would be on the train another day, maybe more. Just think they would be happier moving on their all four and maybe grazin' some."

"Aye, I can see that. Probably feel that way myself."

The two men rode down through Smelter Town and forded the Arkansas, then turned along the south side of the river, heading for Salida. Night was getting close, and they had been riding all day. A good steak and a place to stretch out would feel mighty fine. As they turned down F Street, a crowd of people filled the street in front of the small saloon on the south side of the street. They reined up and dismounted and tied their mounts to the hitching rail and walked to the crowd to see what was going on. Marsh recognized a man and asked.

"Hey, Bill, what's all the commotion?"

"Howdy, Marsh. Well, couple them cowboys from over in Villa Grove had a

403

run-in with that Mexican rancher and his two sons. It came to gunplay, and one of the cowboys bit the dust. One of the Mexican boys got shot in the arm. They took him to the doctor's office. The crowd is getting kinda worked up over it. One of the cowboys were sayin' it was unfair."

"Who was the Mexican rancher, Bill?"

"Feller name of Trujillo."

"Oh Shit! I know him! He is a fine man. Sean, keep an eye on my back. I am going to see if I can get close."

Sean followed Marsh thru the crowd. They entered saloon, and as they walked through they could hear the remarks of *"Damned Mexicans, otta string 'em up!"* and *"They better be outta town 'fore nightfall!"* were just some of the comments.

As they entered, they spotted the Sheriff and Señor Trujillo and a younger Mexican man near the bar.

"Señor Redman, so good to see you my friend!"

"Good to see you Juan, as well. What happened?"

"Hello Marsh. What brings you to Salida? Let me explain. As far as I can tell, a couple of those rowdies that work at that big ranch over near Saguache kept on trying to pick a fight until they succeeded. My problem now is trying to get them out of town safe. Crowd is pretty nasty."

"Yeah, we noticed. We are picking up a load of heifers off the train tomorrow morning, but whatever you need, to keep my friend safe, you got it."

"Marsh, could I offer the services of myself and my sons to help you run your cattle tomorrow? We were headed to Fairplay, it would be our pleasure."

"That would be fine, Juan. You can spend the night with us at the Monte Cristo. We can back you up, and we will head right up river when the train comes in. How does that sound Sheriff?"

"Sounds like a plan. Now we just got to get them up there, and get this crowd simmered down. I will put three deputies up at the hotel tonight, and they can hang around till you get underway in the morning."

"The ladies will be meeting us at Whitehorn with a chuck wagon and another couple of hands. Sean, step out back and see if the way is clear. We will go out back and let the Sheriff go out and distract the crowd."

"Thanks, Marsh. Hope I don't get shot. It is a good plan though."

"Marsh, the alley is clear. I will go down to the river and keep an eye out."

"Good. Ok, Juan, c'mon. Let's see if we can pull this off."

Marsh stepped into the alley. It was clear. He was trailed by the Mexican men, and as they made their way down the darkening alley, just as they were about to turn along the river, two men stepped out of the shadows from the rear of a building.

"Just where do you think you are going with them thieving Mexicans?"

"Well, sir, myself and Señor Trujillo are on our way over to the hotel to have a steak and settle in for the evening. Then tomorrow we are going to drive some cattle. Would you and your friend care to join us? I might consider buying you a drink."

"I don't drink with no dirty greasers."

"Well, now that ain't real polite. So I am going withdraw my offer of a drink, and ask you to step aside. Right now."

The stranger standing in the dark, uttered an expletive and reached for his gun. He and Marsh fired at the same time, his bullet grazing Marsh's shoulder. Marsh's aim was a bit better, striking the right side of the man's chest. The other man didn't get his draw completed. Sean's big Colt cracked across his head, laying the man flat in the alley.

"C'mon, Señor Trujillo, let's get you two safe. I will send help to them."

The four headed for the hotel in a hurry. Minutes later they were in a third floor room.

One of the deputies had met them at the door and had secured an un-divulged room for them. Marsh told him of the altercation in the alley. The deputy sent another man to tell the Sheriff and get medical help for the two downed men.

"Well, Juan, guess we will hole up here tonight. Maybe things will simmer down a bit by morning. The kitchen is going to send up some food for us, so figure out what ya want and we will get our orders in. By the way, Sean, thanks for the help. Bet that guy is gonna have a whale of a headache come morning."

"Well, he can say a couple *Our Fathers* in gratitude that he is still alive. I could have shot him."

"That you could."

After eating dinner the men settled in and sat till midnight. The conversation was varied.

Marsh inquired as to Juan's thoughts about the recent war between the U.S. and Spain. Juan's answer came as no surprise. Juan was an American, had always been.

"Marsh, my heritage goes back to Spain, but is also goes back to *los Indios* - the native people. We have been here since the Anglo Americans were wearing animal skins in Europe, that goes for the Spanish as well. We have been here for thousands of years. It is why I refuse to let the gringo's in the valley try to push me out. I apologize for the gringo word, I do not think of you and Señor Sean as such. You have shown your selves as our brothers, *mi hermanos*. I owe you much, amigo."

"And I, as well, Juan. You 'bout saved my life down there that time. You are my brother."

Around 4 in the morning, Marsh woke to the sound of the steam engine and it's whistle coming up the canyon along the river.

"Ok, cowboys, let's saddle up! We got cattle to drive."

By daylight the small herd was headed northwest along the north side of the Arkansas River, heading up toward the little creek bottom that wound it's way up alongside the wagon road that headed toward Turret. The men bedded down outside Turret that evening. The next day they topped the rise that looked down on the ranch, where workmen could be seen building a house. Juan Trujillo rode up beside Marsh.

"Ah, Marsh! This is a beautiful spot! You have a fine place. You will prosper, amigo. I know you will."

"Gracias, Juan. Let's head 'em on down. I want off this horse, my back is hurting today. Hope this thing gets better before winter."

"I really wanted to have a white Christmas, but this about ridiculous."

Sean turned from the window. It faced south toward Aspen Ridge. But you couldn't see anywhere near that at the moment. The heavy snow had been coming down for nigh on thirty hours, with no let up in sight. The wind howled and the snow swirled and drifted. A warm fire was burning in both fireplaces, and the rooms themselves were quite comfortable. The high vaulted ceiling left air space. At 9,400 feet altitude, oxygen was scarce and sometimes a fire burned up too much of it. He walked back to the corner by the east window and sat down before his canvas, resuming his painting.

Chores that morning had been difficult. The small herd had been sheltered in a box ravine about a quarter mile away, and a load of hay was hauled with difficulty and tossed over to them. The horses, wading in belly deep drifts, were glad to return to their stables when the job was done.

Olek had shouted at one point that this was Russian snow. It reminded him of home.

Still, it came down. By the next morning it was piling deep. Sean had designed the porch roof in such a way that the drifts never quite reached the door. Still, a few feet away it was over waist deep. In some places it was seven or eight feet deep.

"I think we will wait on chores for a few hours and see if this abates a bit. The cows can stand it, and Olek and the boys are close enough to the stables to take care of the horses." Marsh said with a sigh. "I believe this is the biggest snow I have ever seen up here."

The next morning, December 31st, 1899, dawned bright and sunny. The snow had let up in the afternoon of the previous day, but the day had remained dark and windy.

Everyone donned their heavy coats and walked out. The air was awash with a sea of crystals, so light you could hardly feel them against your face. But the sun reflected through them in a myriad of colors. Reds, blues, oranges, like a rainbow all broken up and floating before them. A slight breeze would stir them and send sparkling streams flying through the air.

"Oh, my! I have never seen anything like this! It is breathtaking!" Sarah whispered.

"Sarah, it may also be the air that is breathtaking. The thermometer says it is 35 degrees below zero. Try not to breath with your mouth open, you might frostbite your lungs." Sean advised.

"So, here we are in this magic wonderland. Almost 10,000 feet up in the sky, isolated and cut off from civilization on the last day of the century. It causes one to wonder what the New Year will bring," mused Hanne.

"Whatever it brings, I daresay it will bring happiness. Already I am surrounded by people I love and trust, people who bring hope in my life. Each of you is so different that, coupled with the variety of your talents, the difference your minds bring to our lives, it makes me believe that together, we can achieve wonderful things!"

"Hear! Hear!" responded Sean.

Marsh clapped his hands together. "Well, I like all of you a lot, but time has come to get them cows some hay and shovel some paths to the barn and see if the boys can get out of the bunkhouse. All of them are gonna need water, including the horses. So let's go, cowboys!"

"Yes sir, boss!" in unison came the reply.

It turned out the door to the bunk house was snowed in. But as cowboys would, they had escaped through a window and were in the barn, taking care of the horses when the four got to them. It was almost noon by the time hay was distributed. A path to the well was shoveled, horses were saddled, and a path made to the stream by riding the horses back and forth and breaking down the drifts. The ice was broken and the cows were turned out. They made their way down to the creek and drank heartedly.

As they returned to the barn Marsh announced, "All of you, slick yur hair back and wash your dirty paws and come to the ranch house! Chagan has dinner ready for everyone! Thanks for your help, we didn't lose a single cow. It has been a great day to end the year, and a good way to start a new century!"

After everyone had finished their last piece of elk roast and their last potato, and sopped up their last drop of gravy with the last morsel of fresh bread straight from Chagan's oven, did chairs start to be pushed back and murmers of "Boy, I'm stuffed!" and "Can't eat 'nother bite!" or "Don't stick me with a pin, I'll 'splode!"

All the men stepped outside onto the sunny porch to take their tobacco. Marsh and Sean joined them, though neither smoked.

Young Tim Madison spoke. "Mr. Kelly, I was admiring your paintings inside a moment ago. Where did you learn to do that, if I may ask?"

"Well Tim, I would find it more comfortable if you addressed me as Sean. We are not that far in age. But to answer your question, it didn't come all at once. As a wee lad I was brought up in New York City. I was more or less jerked up by the seat of me trousers. I, at an early age, found I could sketch out somewhat recognizable pictures. As I grew up, I would draw pictures of people and sometimes they would pay me a penny or two. That just fueled the fire, so I had a desire to do better. I would go to the parks on Sunday and watch the artists paint. I learned a lot watching them. As I got older I would go to the library and get books on art and spend whole days reading books on light and perspective, shading and color, and I just kept on and on. It has become my passion. Did that help any?"

Billy Madison piped up. "Tim can draw! Rite good, too! Leastwise, horses and cows and animals and such. He's not quite as good with people."

Tim turned and frowned at Billy. "Thanks, brother." Turning back to Sean. "I din't mean to be nosy, but I do love to draw. I allas wondered if it was something that was taught to them that was good, or if they just allas had it in their head. You are 'bout the only real artist I've ever known, and I do rightly admire what you do."

"I do thank you for that, Tim. I truly do. And if I can ever be of help to you, feel free to ask. I have had the help of many, and I am ready to pass those favors on. And, oh yeah, I have some great books I would be happy to loan you."

Just then Chagan stepped to the door. "All you, come inside. Chagan has made two cakes for everybody. One chocolate and one banana cake with coconut frosting. Come eat!"

Winter passed. For the most part, to the casual glance, life didn't change much. But for the members of Paradise Ranch - for that was what they had selected to call it - life was advancing every day. New advances in technology were exploding across the country. A new invention across the country was itself taking the country forward. With it came the need for fuel, and oil. And with that came the battery technology. Windmills now could be erected and connected to generators that would supply lights to homes and businesses. The surplus energy the windmills created could be stored in batteries.

Those who were able were taking advantage of these improvements.

"Hanne, where are you lass?" Sean tossed his hat onto a hat stand to the right of the front door and made for the kitchen. "Hanne!"

"I'm here with Sarah and Chagan. What's wrong? Are you ok?"

"Aye, lass, I am fine. Nothing wrong. I have news, that is all. Do ya remember the settlement at the small crossroads a few miles east of us?"

"Yes, the one we rode by a couple of weeks ago?"

"Aye, indeed. Well, I was talking to a family there called Trump, and they want to build a school there. They have several children. The mother says she has about reached a point till the children - mostly girls - are smarter than she is. She says there are about three or four other families near abouts, and they want to build something of a school. I took the liberty of informing them that I knew of a fine lady teacher that could probably be convinced to assist them. They were quite excited by that."

Sarah replied, "I would be happy to contribute to that endeavor. We will talk to Marsh when he returns."

Sean turned to Sarah. "That won't be till late. He and the Madison boys are headed up toward the salt ponds to talk with a woman whose husband has died, and perhaps buy their small herd. Fellow told us about it earlier today. He sent me back to let ya know."

"Well, what do ya think Hanne? Ye nay have spoken a word."

"Oh, I am quite stunned! I had almost given up hope. Remember, I still have some funds to add to it, too. Fact is, I had already started to create a curriculum in my mind. So much has happened since I first set this goal, so many new experiences which have given me ideas on things to teach."

"Ah, lass, I am quiet sure ye will be a grand teacher. You have such a head on ye pretty shoulders, I can scarce wait meself to see it happen!"

Marsh dismounted while his step dad, Josh, was climbing down from the heavy wagon of logs. They had hauled the pine logs from the mountains west of the ranch house to the building site for the new school house. Construction was already underway. Josh unhooked the team and led them away to an empty wagon for the return trip to the logging site. The men walked over to a table set up with food and a bucket of cold water. Each drank liberally from the wooden dipper.

"Marsh, I do believe this is some of the finest drinking water I have ever tasted!"

"Yeah, Pa, it is. It always seems to be cold. It has a clean taste, maybe just a bit of a mineral, but not enough to really notice. This valley is just a very healthy place for the most part."

"Yep, just wish it had a bit more air to breathe. It's better than when we first come up, but I still ain't gonna sign up for no footraces."

"It is fairly noticeable, even for the horses."

"Marsh, if we have a minute, I would like to sit a spell and talk to you about something."

"Sure, Pa. Let's drag us a seat over by the wagon here and lite for spell."

The older man found a block of pine log, rolled it over and set it up on end and placed himself on it.

"Marsh, I want to talk to you about your real dad. It has been on my mind for a spell. Actually, for years. Your dad and I grew up nigh to one another, but didn't really know each other more than a nod of the head till during the war. It was there we became the best of friends. He would get letters from yore Ma, and just brag about how purty she was and what a fine woman she was. I had only seen yore ma once or twice, but it was easy for me to agree with him. He took off once. We were down in Mississippi, had fought some pretty bad battles, and he had fallen quiet for some time. I had seen soldiers that way before. I was a bit concerned, then he just up and disappeared. He caught back up with us a couple of months later. Made up some kind of story about being ill and getting lost. Didn't get punished for desertion or nothin'.

"Shucks, all the officers knew how brave he was and all that. In a couple of days I asked him, 'Hey, Jess, what really happened?' He kinda gave me a sidelong glance and smiled just a bit, but didn't answer. Later that night, after the horses were cared for and we had had our mess, we were sitting off from the fire enjoying a bit of tobacco. He turned and said, 'Josh, this ain't for no body else but you. I went home to see Martha. I knew it would be dangerous, but I had to do it. I had to see her one more time and tell her of my feelings to her face. Ya see Josh, I had a dream. I ain't gonna survive this war. I know that very well.

And Josh, I want you to take care of her for me, if you make it. I told her about you, and how you were one of the finest men I ever met and a good friend. I didn't tell her about the dream, but I wanted her to know who you are. It is gonna be hard in the South, especially in Texas, when it's all over. And I don't 'spect us to win. Will you do that for me Josh? It would set my mind at ease.'

"Well, I started to tell him that it was just in his mind, and he would be alright. But I looked into his eyes and decided that was not what I should say. So I just looked him in the eye, and said, 'Jess, 'iffen that is what you wish, here is my hand on it.' And we shook hands on it. It was never mentioned again.

"Well, it weren' too long till he got a letter from yur Ma saying she was with child. 'Spect that was you. Then, later we were headed out to North Carolina to try to stop Sherman's from his rampage up the coast. And he found out about you. Lordy, he was so proud! Well, that young man's chest just fairly stuck out! It's a wonder he didn't jump up on a post and crow. He talked about you to everbody. Now he now had a son.

"Then, in the last day or so of Bentonville, we was headed up this narrow road out there in the swamps. We ran headlong into a bunch of Yankee Cavalry. They were about as surprised as we were, and a gunfight started. Well, your Pa was wheeling that big bay he was riding and shooting left and right, and whenever he shot, a Yankee would fall. They were just turning tail and a bullet fairly tore my pistol from my hand, and it was then I saw your Pa jus' kinda straighten up in the saddle and get a funny look on his face, kinda perplexed like. Then I saw blood on his jacket. That big bay seemed to know and he just took off the way we had come and I took off after him. My shootin' iron was gone anyway. I caught up about a hundred yards or so back down the road. The horse was just standin' there, the reins on the ground. Your dad was kinda sitting with his head on his chest, his gun still in his hand. I rode up and put my arm around his shoulder. He looked up, and said 'Josh, remember your promise, and be good to my son. There is a letter to them in my saddle bag to Martha and Marshall. Take it home and give it to her.' And he just smiled and closed his eyes and died, in the saddle.

"Marsh, I have his gun. I wanted to tell you this story before I gave it to you. Now I have, and it is yours." Josh unwrapped a Dragoon Colt from the oil cloth and handed it to Marsh.

"Pa..... I don't know what to say. Except thank you for the story." Marsh blowed his nose and wiped his eyes. "Thanks for keeping your word, and thanks for being the father you have always been. Right now that is about all I can get out of me. Maybe we need to ride for a while and let me digest all this."

Marsh and Sarah had ridden about an hour when they topped a hill deep in the forest above Turret. The country was rough. A few strays of their small herd had become missing and Olek had ridden out before daylight. It was now late afternoon. He should have returned by now.

Down below them, sounds of a struggle emerged through the downed timber on the north side of the small ridge.

"Sarah, come this way! We have to go around this mess. We will lose a horses leg trying to go down. Let's take the east side."

A few minutes later they topped over a slight rise and looked down at a scene of carnage. Three dead cattle lay in the small spot of grass, torn to shreds. But worse, was Olek on his scrappy little mustang, circling a huge bear! Olek held under his arm a long pole, probably aspen. Whenever the bear attempted to charge, Olek would give him a sharp rap on the muzzle and the bear would rear and swipe at the would-be lance, but to no avail. The Cossack man sat square and straight on his brave mount. He would dash away a few yards and the bear would rise to give chase, and then

Olek would face him again. But it looked as if he couldn't get free to actually run. Marsh had to do something quick.

Olek tussling with Ol' Mose,

"Sarah, it's Mose. Ride back up a few hundred yards where you can watch. If this goes bad, get out of here. Ride to the ranch and get more men with rifles. I have to slow this bear down so Olek can get away."

Sarah turned and rode away, calling over her shoulder, "Marsh, please be careful!"

Marsh pulled his Winchester 44-40 from the saddle boot. He levered a shell into the chamber, then took deliberate aim and fired at the bear as he stood, hitting his foot. The bear spun and clawed at his foot. Marsh fired again, hitting the bear's other leg.

"Get out of there Olek!"

Olek took his opportunity and spurred the little mustang up out of the gulch he was trapped in. As he turned, Marsh could see blood dripping from the man's leg and the horse's flank.

Oh shit, thought Marsh.

He turned his attention back to the bear, to try to get a kill shot, but the old bruin was too smart. He realized he was hurt and his quarry had gotten away. He had turned down the steep hillside at a gallop and was heading away. Marsh lowered his gun.

"You ok, Olek?" he questioned.

"Da, Boss. We ok. Need some patching, but not serious."

"What in the name of God were you doing jousting with that monster for? You out of your mind?"

Olek laughed. "We have bears in Russia too, Boss. We hunt them with lances. Even as young boys, a lance is better than a gun. This lance, it had no blade. Bear surprised Olek while he looked at dead cows. Almost got us both. Small tree was dead nearby. Olek grabbed it and used it to keep bear out of reach. Glad you and Missus came by. Game was getting old with big bear, he might have won."

It was just after dark when the trio rode into the corral near the barn at the ranch. Chagan had heard them and was holding Olek's horse and making unintelligible sounds to the horse. The horse's flank and rump had four deep gashes. He was already favoring it.

Almost by the time Olek had lit, Chang had the saddle off and was headed to the barn.

"Olek, let Chagan take care of the pony. You come in the house."

"Ok, Boss." Olek started to limp toward the bright window a few yards away, but he staggered and grabbed the top rail of the corral.

"Here, let me help." Marsh put his arm around the man from the right side and held him up. They continued toward the house. Once inside Marsh guided him to a divan where he proceeded to lay down on his right side. Marsh could see the deep lacerations from his side down his thigh. Sarah appeared from the kitchen with a basin of hot water.

"Get you pants off, Olek," she ordered. "And shirt, as well. Marsh, let's move him to the kitchen table. There is more light there."

Olek looked at Marsh questioningly.

"You better do as she says. Remember, she is the boss," Marsh grinned and said. By the time they reached the big table in the dining room, he was down to his long johns. Sarah stretched him out on his right side and put a pillow under his head.

She took a pair of scissors and cut away the left side of his long johns from armpit to knee and pulled back the material. The bear had gotten a single swipe at Olek, catching him just above the belt and raking him almost to his knee. The two outer claws had done little damage, but the two inner ones had cut deeply from hip almost to the knee. It would need be cleaned and stitched.

"Marsh, get one of the boys to ride to the settlement and get Mrs. Trump to come. She worked in the Confederate hospital in Richmond during the War. She should be able to do this. The nearest doctor would be at Fairplay or Whitehorn. I will clean it, but I am not good at stitching."

"Ok, I am also going to go check on Chagan and the horse. Get the man some whiskey, may help with the pain."

He looked at Olek. The man's face was a mask, but his eyes gave away the discomfort he felt.

Out side he found Chagan working on the young mare. She rivaled Olek's cuts. Chagan had washed and cleaned her injuries, and had sewed the cuts together and closed the wound. He had an odd mixture of a yellow salve that smelled to high heaven, and he smeared it from one end of the wounds to the other.

"Chagan, will she be ok?"

"Chagan think so, Boss. Bad cuts, but no tendons. Just muscle. She be lame for a while. Chagan stay with her tonight, make sure she not lay down. She lay down, she might not ever get up again."

"Damned bear."

"Same bear, Boss?"

"Yep, same bear."

After a good breakfast, Mrs. Trump was taken home. She had arrived late, and had spent hours stitching Olek back together. She found time to sleep a few hours, ate breakfast and praised Chagan's cooking. Said he should open a restaurant at the crossroads where their settlement was located. She climbed aboard the buckboard and waved goodbye, and was whisked away.

Olek slept most of the day, sipping a bit of whiskey when he awoke. By evening he seemed to be much better. Marsh sat down to visit.

"Olek, how are you feeling?"

"Feel better, Boss. Ready to go back to work tomorrow."

"Naw, that won't be necessary. I appreciate your dedication, but we don't want those stitches ripped out and have to be done over. Mrs. Trump did a good job."

"Da, she fine woman. Remind me of Russian lady that lived with my family in Ukraine."

"That was some mighty tall riding you were doing. Scrappin' with big ol' bear, usin' that little pole."

"Da. Cossaks learn to use lance as little boys. Not unusual to kill bears with lance."

"Olek, that bear is a killer. He has killed several men, and tons of cows and sheep around these parts."

"Da, he big bear. Olek was a bit worried. Afraid little horse was going to go down. Bear got one good lick in. I was lucky to find pole. How is little horse? Is horse going to live?"

"Yep. Chagan sewed her up. She is going to be ok, will just need some corral time. But she will make it just fine. These little mustangs are tough little horses."

"They tough like Russian horses. Glad it ok."

"So, tell me, when did you start riding?"

"Ha! Olek always ride. Don't remember first time. Maybe 3 years old. Cossacks, always warriors. Start young, learn to fight from horse. Live with horse, sleep with horse. Horse is greatest friend."

"Yeah, always felt that way 'bout horses myself."

"Horses reason Olek come to America. Big Ruskie, noble, wanted to come to America to go hunting. Olek and five others were chosen to go with party. In Russia, Cossack had freedom so long as he served government as soldier. We lived in communities to ourselves, but history always had a way of disruption. Now there is a people who are fighting to gain power. They want to over throw the Czars. Olek thinks it will happen. So when time came to go back to Russia, Olek just kinda got lost. They had to leave without me. Olek liked what he saw in America. Want to stay here."

"Well, you are welcome here. If you wish, I will have Sarah inquire to find out how to get you started to full citizenship. Now, you rest easy for a week, maybe more. We'll see then. You are a good man, Olek. Welcome to America!"

"Thank you, Mr. Marsh!"

"Hanne, if you don't stop flitting around, the students at the school will all be grown up and parents themselves before they have a single class."

"I am so nervous Sean! I thought I was all ready, but my thoughts are so scattered. I am just a mess! Help me find that brown folder with the leather tie. It has all my notes on scheduling classes and curriculum. Please, I know I had it just a short time ago..."

"You mean this one on your bag?"

"Oh, yes, you are such a dear! What would I do without you? Maybe you should come to class?"

"Ah, me lovely, ye will do fine. Gather yourself up, we don't want to be late the first day, do we? Here, I will load this into the buckboard. Come along now, me love."

Mid-August in South Park was not the favorite time of the year, but the school was built, and should be put to use. In a short time the winter winds would start to blow, and school would be difficult to do. Now was a time to get it off the ground. The hour and a half commute from the range was not a problem now, but could get that way in the coming months.

Sean helped Hanne unload her materials and arrange the room to her satisfaction. Shortly before 9 in the morning the first small face appeared through the door. With it came another, and another, until 12 children had gathered, shuffling about at the rear of the room, nervously glancing at the tall blond lady who was to be their teacher.

Hanne finally glanced up and acknowledged the students.

"Welcome, young gentlemen and ladies. Come forward and take a seat. We are about to get started this morning."

"Good morning. I am Mrs. Hanne Clausen-Kelly. You may call me Ms. Kelly. This is my husband, Sean Kelly. He will be around from time to time. I am to be your teacher. Now, I would like your names and ages, and if you have been schooled, and what was the last class you finished. Start over here with the front row and stand and introduce yourself."

"Good morning, Mrs. Kelly! I am Melissa Gilbert. I have studied through 8th grade. I am 14 years old."

"Thank you, Miss Gilbert."

"Good morning! I am Rebecca Smith. I am 12, and I went to 6th grade. Didn't finish though."

By the time she had gone through the roll she found she had seven boys and five girls ranging from 14 to 6 years of age.

The ride from Canon City had been warm, even at the 9,500-foot elevation, but it was beautiful. Waugh Mountain had outlined their journey all day, and Marsh and Sarah and Hanne and Sean were looking forward to an evening in Whitehorn before continuing on to the ranch. They had spent the night before at a ranch northeast of the Arkansas River. Marsh had wanted to see the country along the range of mountains that followed the north bank of the Arkansas River.

They had just passed the Stirrup Ranch when Sarah commented, "Marsh, let's take Hanne and Sean to that wonderful little waterfall where I almost froze that night after bathing in the creek."

"Sounds fine with me. It might be a bit shorter to cut across, rather than follow the road." He reined his horse to the left a bit as they approached a hill directly in front of them. The wagon road continued to the right, over much smoother land.

About a half hour later, they were nosing down a rather steep hillside toward the bottom of the little canyon that contained the water of Badger Creek, which at this point was barely a trickle. Across the canyon, a herd of bighorn stared at them, blankly, wondering why these humans had to invade their grazing territory. Back to the right, a dozen elk loped off to the north. The couples rode alongside the trickle, which within yards turned into a torrent. They rode up over a slight hill as they did. Below, as the canyon narrowed, the water fell through boulders and ran across rocky beds, as it danced its way down the canyon. In its path, at the base of the falls, several pools shimmered in the afternoon sun.

Hanne exclaimed, "Oh, my goodness, you boys need to ride a bit down the canyon. Sarah and I are going to take a bit of time to wash off some dust and horse smell. Right, Sarah?"

"Sure, fine with me, but I will tell you for sure, that water is cold. Do you guys mind, it is lady time."

"C,mon Sean, there is another pool down below here where we can wash up. It's less than an hour to Whitehorn."

When the men had barely gotten around the bend in the canyon, Hanne was already out of her riding outfit, and Sarah wasn't far behind her. They walked with each other, jumping from rock to rock, until they reached the deepest pool. The waterfall in the back fell from about 4 feet. Hanne waded into the pool, letting out a squeal, "Oh! That is cold."

"I told you."

"I don't care. Two days in the saddle and my lady parts need water."

Sarah giggled, "Hanne, your directness of language is quite colorful sometimes."

Hanne laughed, "I suppose so. I didn't have to watch myself in my previous life. Sean says I have a bit of a potty mouth."

Hanne smiled as she floated in the cold water, her nipples swelling like ripe grapes from the cold water. She washed herself hurriedly. Indeed, both of the ladies attended to their toilet in a bit of haste. Hanne backed herself into the waterfall and let the cold water pour over her head. She squealed again. Sarah, obviously, was not going to let the younger woman outdo her, so she backed into the waterfall and gasped as the cold torrent took her breath away.

Then both women raced for shore. They climbed on a flat boulder that sat barely out of the water and had been warmed by the sun. They lay down, side by side, toweling themselves. Hanne said hesitantly, "Sarah, I, uh, can't or…

couldn't help noticing, you seem to be a bit heavier about the waist, er, uh ..."

"Yes, I am expecting. This will be my last ride, for a while, but I had to do it."

"Does Marsh know?"

"No, and please don't say anything. I will tell him as soon as we get home."

"When is it due?"

"I calculate sometime in January."

"Oh Sarah, I am so excited. You have been like a sister to me! Whatever you need, I am here. Please, let me help where I can."

"Of course I will. Thank you so much for offering. I so enjoy having you with us."

"Oh Sarah, thank you!" Hanne rolled to her side and put her arms around Sarah and hugged her to her. "This is wonderful! When can I tell Sean?"

Sarah smiled, "Not until we get home."

About then, a horse squealed back up stream from the falls. Sarah's horse, Bolt, turned his head and answered. "Hanne, someone is coming. We need to dress. Hurry." They barely got dressed in time. Sarah stepped to Bolt's side and pulled the Henry from its saddle boot. She stood with the horse blocking her from view as two riders topped the rise above the falls. Both men were coarsely dressed, their hats worn and soiled with sweat.

"Wal, looky here! Two fine young ladies taking a bath. Too bad we were late, huh Lefty. I cudda stood a bath too. Maybe they wudda scrubbed my back."

"Aw c'mon, Sarge, leave them be. We need to get down the canyon."

"Aw, Im jus trying to be friendly. That blonde one shore is purty. Hey blondy, wanna take a swim with me?"

Hanne looked up and smiled, "Why sure, cowboy, c'mon down. We got time for a swim, don't we, Sarah?"

Sarah stammered, "Well maybe." She wasn't sure where Hanne was headed but decided to follow her lead. "But we will have to hurry."

The big guy, the one wearing the blue shirt who had done all the talking, swung off his horse and headed for Hanne. She waited until he was on the rock across from her with about 3 feet of water between them. As he started to step across, she reached inside her boot and came out with a little double-barreled derringer, pointing it right at the man's middle. He braked to a stop and stood swaying.

Hanne smiled at him, "Mister, this is not going to go the way you intended. Now, you jump over to that other rock and with your left hand unbuckle your gun belt and let it drop. Do it. Now! Or I will just shoot you where you stand."

"Lefty, shoot the bitch!"

"I couldn't do that if I wanted, Sarge. The other lady has a rifle pointed right at me."

"Sarge, I told you, unbuckle that belt, now!" The man did as he was told. "Now, Mister Sarge, kick off those boots next, and then the trousers, and wade over to those falls. You still aren't out of danger yet."

"I'm gonna kill ye, ye sorry whore."

"Well, not right now. Now, you do as I say." In a few minutes, Sarge was standing in chest-deep water under the waterfall, shaking and turning a bit blue.

The other man spoke, "Ma'am, I am real sorry about this. He got all lickered up, and he don't hold it no wise."

"Okay, but just to make sure, I want you to unload your handgun, and your rifle, and then his rifle, and tie up the ammo in your kerchief and put it in the saddlebag of the bay. Then, back up that hill a ways, and we will excuse ourselves."

When the man had done as told, the girls mounted up and rode down the canyon in the direction that Sean and

Marsh had gone. Marsh and Sean had washed and dressed when the girls appeared. Sean asked, "Are ye ladies a bit more comfortable at last?"

"Indeed we are. And we have a bit of an adventure story to relate as well," said Sarah.

Marsh's brow furrowed, "I hope it wasn't that old bear. I thought of that as we left, and it was of some concern to me."

"No, it wasn't a bear. We had finished bathing and were drying ourselves on the rocks when we heard a horse. We quickly dressed, and just in time, 'cause two riders appeared above the falls. I stepped to Bolt and pulled my rifle and stood behind him where they couldn't see. They came up and one of them was drunk and being very rude and belligerent. Hanne threw him off guard by appearing to be ready to bathe with him, but when he approached her, she pulled this tiny little gun out of her boot and confronted him. Next, she made him undress and get into the cold water. We disarmed the men, took their ammunition, and left them."

"Saints preserve us, Marsh! We need to go back and give those two a whupping such as they have never seen."

"No gentlemen, let's ride on to Whitehorn and have our dinner. I believe they learned their lesson."

An hour later found the four riders descending from the hill on the south side of Whitehorn. After a hearty dinner, they took themselves outside and sat on the porch in front of the hotel. As the sun set over the mountains to the west, the evening shadows spread over the little mining town like fingers from a dark world that was waiting to wake up the creatures of the forest. Off to the side, a coyote barked and was answered by another one's howl from the aspen ridge to the east. From somewhere deep in the forest, a bull elk whistled. A few weeks from now, the rut would start, and the forest would be alive with their bugling. Up on the ridge to the west of town, a few hundred feet above them, a sow cinnamon bear crawled out of a shallow cave and rolled a log over, searching for tasty grubs.

Time stood still once again, in the little valley cradled in the south end of South Park.

"Hanne..."

"Yes, Sarah?"

"Back at the waterfall, I couldn't help but marvel at a side of you I had never seen before. You were very cool and collected. You really seemed as if you were ready to get in the water with that man. You must have had a lot of experience to teach you that."

"I suppose experience has lot to do with it. But when you live in a world where men are dominating you and using you like you're nothing but a tool for their gratification, if you wish to survive, you have to learn to rely on your wits. Believe me, if a woman tells a man she is ready to be... well, "frisky" with him, and smiles, and maybe shows a bit of cleavage or leg, he is in no state of mind to think of anything else. That little man in his pants takes over his thinking and only has one goal."

"Still, it was a marvel to behold, I really didn't know where you were headed, but I thought it best to follow your lead. Do you always carry a gun in your boot?"

Hanne smiled, "Usually, but I also have one in my bag." She pulled her bag around and reached carefully in and pulled out another tiny derringer. "You have to get very close for these to be accurate and efficient. That is why I told him to come ahead and let him see a bit of leg as I was reaching for my boot. He never saw anything else."

"My dear, you are marvelous. I am so glad you've come into my life. I am so glad to have you at a friend."

"Sarah, thank you. You have given me a life I always dreamed of, and with Sean, I am just in a bit of heaven here in the mountains." The girls kicked their horses and caught up with the men, who had been riding ahead of them.

Hanne said, "Sean, I would like to stop at the school for a moment. There's a book I need to acquire for this week's lessons."

"Of course, me love. We can let the horses breathe a moment before going on home."

Marsh sat across the huge aspen log that was bleached a stark white from the high country sun. They would never have cut it, but when spring had come, it refused to put forth its leaves. They had waited, thinking perhaps it was just late, but, no, this tree had served its time on the mountain, it roots linked to thousands of others of its kind. It had released its hold on the big root system to make way for others. Marsh had said that we could all take a lesson from that and not try to hold on to something that was not supposed to be.

Sarah let a single tear fall down her pretty cheek, and it rolled down the leather lapel of her jacket. It was true. Without her husband's passing, she may never have found this wonderful life that had befallen her. Now was the time to tell him, but... what if he wasn't ready? It had been only slightly over a year since they'd met. Still, winter was coming, and plans would have to be made. She looked down and touched Marsh's shoulder. He had punched holes in the apron of the big saddle he rode and laced leather thongs through them to add some strapping. He was always inventing something.

He glanced up from his work, and seeing her seriousness, his brow furrowed. "What's wrong?" Seeing his concern, Sarah said, "Oh no, nothing is wrong. On the contrary, everything is right. Here, turn around and face me for a second." Marsh complied. Sarah took his hand in hers and brought them to her belly.

"My love, it is only just over a year since we met. It seems as if it were only days. So much has happened, so many gifts, so many wonderful experiences, so many new friends... and now, you have given me another gift, an unexpected gift, but one that brings such joy to my heart."

"Sarah, I am so happy you are satisfied with our life, but a new gift? What is it? Where?"

Sarah whispered, "Darling, it is beneath your hands right now."

Marsh looked down at his hands, searching Sarah's own for something. Then, almost as if a light started to grow in him, he said, "You mean?"

"Yes, we are to have a child. Sometime after the first of the New Year."

"Oh, my!"

As Sarah watched, the tough cowboy's face seemed to melt. His eyes softened, and tears appeared. He slowly lowered himself to his knees, slipped his hands from Sarah's hands, put his arms around her hips, and hugged his face to her abdomen. There was just the lightest trace of a sob, and then the expelling of breath.

"Ma will be so excited. We must get word to her. We need to tell Sean and Hanne. We probably need to spend the winter in Salida where a doctor is more available. Are you alright? I mean…. do I need to do, well…. whatever I need to do?"

Sarah smiled, "Hanne already knows. Yes, we need to invite your parents up here. No, we don't need to leave now. No, there is nothing you need to do but be happy. And, Marsh, I love you so very much."

December 31, 1900, 11:45 p.m. The entire length of F Street, for about three blocks, was lined with revelers who were shouting and dancing in the street. The girls from the cribs along 1st Street had come out in all their finery. Miners, cowboys, smelter workers, business people, people from over in the San Luis Valley, from Whitehorn and Turret, from down the river at Howard, and all around gathered for this momentous occasion.

The last one had started with war in 1812. Then, mid-century the young nation had been torn asunder. As it was once again united, the beloved President had been shot and killed by an assassin, the first to suffer that injustice. But because of the programs he had put in place, America became a world power. By the end of the war, the Union had the largest Navy on the planet. The practice of connecting the world via telegraph had begun.

Like a giant blacksmith, the nation's leaders took a raw piece of iron and melted and fashioned it into a working thing that would grow and become a beacon to which people around the world could aspire to, becoming a part of its purpose. With the Great War came inventions and industry. With the westward expansion, both before and after that refiner's fire of destruction, the westward movement filled new lands from sea to shining sea. From mountain to desert, from prairie to primeval forest, everyone did their part to expand the nation. America was moving into a new era. Wise men made predictions and ordinary men dreamed dreams, but in about "one minute," the new century was to begin.

From the hotel balcony above the street, Marsh and Sarah watched and waited. Sarah leaned against Marsh to support herself. Her time was near. A bell tolled, then another, and then all the bells from all the churches started to ring. A sliver of fire left the top of the sharp, cone-shaped mountain at the end of the street, then another, and another, as the rockets lit the sky and burst into a myriad of bursting lights. *Happy New Year!* echoed up and down the street and from the bars and rooms.

"Marsh, you need to find the doctor. My water just broke; you're going to be a father."

Marsh paced the floor outside Sarah's room, saying a silent prayer, "Please, God, don't let anything happen to Sarah." He remembered when he was in his teens and a woman and her husband who lived down the road were having a baby. He had stood outside their cabin and listened to her screams, and then the screams had stopped. She had been in labor for hours, and when the husband came out of the house, Marsh knew that woman and the baby had perished.

"Mr. Redman, you can come in now." Marsh raced for the door. Sarah was sitting up against two big pillows, in her arms was a blanket. She was staring down at it as if she had found a vein of gold, a rapt expression on her face. She turned her head and looked at Marsh. The softest, sweetest smile lighted her face.

"Marsh, it's a little boy! And Marsh, he is so beautiful! Come look!"

As Marsh hurried to her side, she pulled the blanket back, and there in her arms was their little boy. He had dark hair like his mother, but who cares about that - they were both healthy and happy. Just then, Marsh's Ma and Pa came into the room. His mother tiptoed to the bedside.

"Aw, Marsh, he looks just like you did all those years ago. I would that your father had lived to be able to see this day. He would have been so proud." She sat down and began to weep softly. As she put her finger in the hand of the infant, who grasped it readily, bringing a smile to the elderly woman's face, she said, "Oh, look at that."

His Pa put his arm around Marsh's shoulder, "You will be a good father, Marsh." "I had a good father for an example, Pa!" Marsh smiled at the older man.

"Oh, look Sean! Your baby is beautiful, Sarah." Sean and Hanne had slipped quietly into the room and had reached Sarah and the new babe.

"Aw, it's a wee lad! Congratulations, my friend. What did ye name the wee lad?"

Sarah answered, "We named him Joshua Theodore Redman, after his Pa and Theodore Roosevelt."

Josh shook hands with Marsh and said, "You honor me, son! And imagine having my name linked with that of the brave man who is sure to be our President sometime in the future. He is a good, brave man. Well, thank you!" Marsh squeezed Josh's hand and smiled.

"Sarah, are you well?" Hanne placed her hand on Sarah's shoulder, "Is there anything we can get for you to make you more comfortable?"

"No, thank you, Hanne, dear. I am fine, I am happy, and oh, so very tired."

Martha said, "Josh, let us get out of here and let this poor darling get some rest. Come now, Sarah, just you rest now, and take care of that sweet little boy. We will return this evening or tomorrow when you have had time to recover."

"Thank you, Mother Hargis. I suppose I should say *Grandmother Hargis*. Thank you for coming. You need to spend time with your new grandson. And, oh yes, Happy New Year," Sarah smiled.

After the grandparents had left the room, Hanne looked at Sean and smiled. "Marsh, Sarah, we have some news for you as well."

"What is it, Hanne?" asked Marsh.

"Well, we are going to be parents as well!"

Sarah exclaimed, "Oh, how exciting! When?"

"Well, as near as I can tell, late July or August, I believe."

Marsh turned to Sean and grabbed him by the hand, "Congratulations, Sean! I am pretty new to this fatherhood stuff, but it is pretty exciting."

"Thank you, Marsh. After seeing your little boy, I am more excited than ever."

"Hanne, I think it is so wonderful. I will be able to help you as you have helped me, and that will make me happy. You have been so good, even with your teaching, I don't know how I would have done without you."

"Sarah, I am so glad I was here to do what I could. And what a wonderful place for our children to grow up," she sighed, "And what a beginning for our new century!"

"Aye," said Sean, "In this past century, we took the railroads from sea to sea, and we have carriages that run around without horses. Who knows? In time, we may even go to the moon."

Everyone laughed.

Chagan carried young Josh around in his arms, singing some oriental lullaby. He would stop at the front window and talk to the baby in his native tongue, then walk to the kitchen to stir the large pot that was simmering on the big kitchen range. Finally, he walked slowly to the big wooden rocker cradle that Olek had built even before Josh was born. It had carved horse heads at the corner posts and a carved cossack in full gallop on the headboard. Chagan had told everyone that the child would be a boy, and he had gloated for days when his prophesy came true. Marsh said the boy had more uncles than a child in a Mormon family. All the ranch hands checked in frequently to see if the "boss lady" needed anything.

By now, Hanne's once-girlish figure had become difficult to see. It was the first of June. In South Park, the aspens were putting forth their leaves. Days were becoming warmer, and hummingbirds dashed from flower to flower, performing their aerial maneuvers. The mines were holding out, the ranch was growing, and all was well. Life was good.

The country seemed to be taking on new life in this, the beginning of the century. It seemed as though a flame had taken over. With the winning of the war with Spain, we now had new territories, the Philippine Islands and Guam. Hawaii had taken on a whole new importance. Trade with China was becoming a competition among all of the world powers.

Hanne and Sean made the decision to return to Salida to live until their baby arrived. On July 2, they caught the stage at Hartsell and took it to Salida, spending one night in Whitehorn. As the afternoon sun disappeared behind the western hills and finger-like shadows crawled toward the hotel in the tiny park, the lights in Whitehorn came on. Hanne and Sean sat on the porch of the hotel.

Sean said, "My love, did ye fare well with the ride today? It got a bit rough on the hill just before we forded Badger Creek."

"I suppose so. There aren't many times that I am truly comfortable these days." She scooted up in her chair and wriggled a bit to find a good position. "Sean, this is such a unique place. Do you think this town will grow and become a place where people live?"

"They live here now, my dear."

"No, that's not what I mean. Will it ever grow into a city like Denver, or even Salida?"

"Time will tell, my love. But nay, I dinna think so. Its livelihood is based on digging silver and gold out of the ground. I don't think it will grow into a city because it sits up here on a mountain where it's too hard to live in the winter. But we will see."

"I want our child to be able to enjoy places like this though. They are more personal than the big cities. When we come here, people are so nice to us."

As they hesitated in their conversation, a female voice raised itself in a hymn. They turned to the sound, which seemed to emanate from near the water plant at the top of the park near the livery. As they listened and looked, a negro woman, probably in her early 40s, emerged from a building and came walking up the boardwalk sidewalk, singing *Amazing Grace*. Her powerful voice seemed to fill the entire valley with sound. She sang as she walked by Sean and Hanne, breaking her song just long enough to say, "G'evenin' Missy and Mister, a pleasant evenin' to yuh!" Then she returned to her song. She had an almost simple look on her face, but when singing, she fairly glowed. As she faded into the growing darkness, her song faded with her.

The couple looked at each other. Sean said, "I think I know what you mean."

Hanne looked up from her sewing. She was trying to make a little nightshirt for the baby. Friends and neighbors, all ladies of Salida, had given her a baby shower, and for the most part she had no want for anything, but she felt she should contribute something for the first of her offspring. She had never excelled in sewing, but she understood fashion and design. Anyway, it was a way to pass the long days and nights, waiting.

July in Salida was nice. Her windows were open, and a breeze off the mountains to the west kept the room cool and comfortable. Most afternoons, a quick rain shower would wet the town down and refresh the already fresh air even more. It was a pleasant place to be. She and Sean had taken rooms in a house on the first block of E Street. She could look out her window and see the Arkansas River as it rushed by, as if it were a serpent trying to flee the mountains where it was born.

Each day, Sean would take her by the arm, and they would walk along the river and turn up F Street to admire the wares in the shop windows. They would slowly round the block, and by the time they reached their house, she would be ready to sit again. She looked at Sean. He was so attentive, so helpful; if he caught her reaching for the slightest thing, he was immediately there. She smiled. He was such a good man.

He had become well known among many of the businessmen of the town and county. He designed buildings and consulted in the mining industry. He had been involved in the creating of a new smelter across the river and upstream from Salida. He was respected far and wide for his drawings and his art. Some of his paintings could be found in galleries in Colorado Springs and Denver. He had made his mark very quickly. Now, at the moment, he was lost behind a stack of books that was big enough to almost obscure Hanne from him. He always said that he believed art should be useful, and the evidence was in that art.

"Sean, that is a lot of books, you have. Do you care to share?" He slowly pulled his attention from his reading, rubbed his eyes, and shook himself back to reality. "Aye, me love, they are much about the minerals and ores of the region, the types of stone they are found in, and what it takes to break them down so that they can be extracted. I have been looking into the mills that are presently used. Many of the machines are not as efficient as they should be. I thought perhaps that I might be able to advance some improvement on them. Mr. Wells has already put some of my ideas to use. It's a new challenge for me."

He leaned back in his chair and hooked his thumbs into his suspenders. "Lass, I have to laugh occasionally about how I thought my education was complete as a lad. Nay, it had only begun. I am glad that I did, at that time, learn how to learn and how to look for answers. My education has been multiplied at least twenty-fold in the last two years or so. Coming to Colorado was the best possible thing I could have done in my life, for multiple reasons."

Sean got up from his chair and stood by Hanne. He laid his arm on her shoulder and bowed to kiss her sweetly on the forehead. "The best reason of all has been meeting you, the joy of my life." He patted her swollen belly lightly and added, "Now a part of each of us is to join us even closer. I can scarce wait for that marvelous event."

Hanne teased, "Yes, I confess that I will be happy to get back to that activity that created that marvelous event. I miss my man and the pleasure he gives." She reached to run her hand softly up the inside of his leg and rubbed over the slight bulge above.

"Careful, Lass, you nay should get something started you canna finish," he laughed.

"Oh, I could finish, believe me," she laughed back at him.

"Aye, but I believe that it would be more special if we both could be a part of the business."

"Fuddy duddy! If you wish, but don't say I didn't offer."

"Aye, Lass. That ye did, and that makes it even more special."

August 3, 1901. "Oh, Hanne," said Sarah, when she first saw the new baby. "He is beautiful. His hair is like spun gold, and he looks like some young Adonis. Have you named him yet?"

Hanne nodded, "Oh yes, his father took one look at him and pronounced his name to be Michael Finn Kelly. When I asked him why, he said (imitating an Irish accent) "Ah lass, ye take but one look at him and ye can see he is but a wee angel, so I must name him for the first angel,

Michael, but with parents such as he has, I will call him Finn as well. Finn was an outlaw, so it's a name befitting a strong lad to grow up with in these mountains."

Sarah laughed. She turned young Josh around on her lap and said to him, "Josh, this is Michael. You and he will have many adventures and grow up being best friends, just you wait and see."

Christmas of 1900 was unusually warm and dry; no snow had yet fallen in South Park. It had been a good year for growth in Whitehorn. The town boasted a population of just over a thousand souls, maybe a few more. The citizens were catching the Christmas spirit a bit early. The managers of the hotels and the owner of the mercantile started talking about a Christmas celebration, and it caught on.

On Christmas Eve the children would gather around a decorated tree in the middle of town near the Post Office and

Santa Claus would come riding down out of the forest that was on the south side of the town. The steep hill would be an ideal setting for torches to be lit to guide his entrance into town. Tables of food would be set out, musicians would perform, and carols would be sung. Ah, it was a great plan -- if only it would snow!

Marsh and Sarah caught wind of the plans during the week before Christmas and decided right away that they wanted young Josh to attend his first Christmas party. Sean and Hanne were living in Salida, and Marsh and Sarah were at the ranch. Marsh had a telegram sent to Sean, and it was decided that they would meet in Whitehorn and celebrate the holiday together.

The Christmas celebration was all the talk for the week before. People from Whitehorn's sister city, Turret, made plans to travel over the mountain and add to the Christmas cheer. But, still, it wouldn't snow. What would they do about the sleigh for old Andy Olsen? Andy was a jolly man and looked the part of Saint Nick most every day. He was short and a bit rounded, but he was as spry as a man 30 years his junior. He had long white hair and a full long white beard. He even wore a pair of those little half glasses that perched on the end of his nose. Even better, he, Andy, loved children, and his accent was of a Norwegian dialect. The town had its Santa Claus, and they had a sleigh from Mr. Everett's ranch. They had a team of white horses to pull the sleigh, sans reindeer, but they still did not have snow. Still they came, and they planned.

By noon on Christmas Day the wagons came over the hill from all directions, most of them were covered. Whitehorn had a couple of hotels, but there were never enough rooms. Most everyone knew that, so they brought their bedrooms with them. The wagons circled around the Post Office/Stage Stop, and tents were set up all over the meadow. The cloudless sky was blue and clear, and the air was still. The temperature sat just above freezing. Winter had gotten lost this year, but spirits were high.

"Merry Christmas, my friend Marsh! And good afternoon to you, Mrs. Redman!

And who is this young man, dressed like an Eskimo?" It was George Alexander, the telegraph operator in Whitehorn. "Marsh, a couple of messages for you here. They came in about noon, but I had not seen you until now."

"Thank you, George, we only arrived about an hour ago. A buggy wheel came loose and we had to makeshift it together. Barely made it too; it was loose again upon arrival. Oh, yes, George, this is Josh. He is close to a year old now, and he's being groomed as the new ranch foreman."

"Yes, indeed. I took the stage up to Guffy a few days ago, and that stretch just past the north side of Badger Creek is hard on wheels, and passengers too," he laughed. "And I am happy to meet you, Josh. I know you will be a good foreman, and your Pa will be proud of you!"

"Indeed it is. Thank you, George. Sarah, Ma and Pa, and Sean and Hanne have hired a carriage large enough for all and will be here before dark. It will be good to be together for Christmas."

Just as the sun started to drop over the mountains to the west of Whitehorn, a dark grey rim of clouds made an appearance. The afternoon sun sunk into them like a pumpkin into a down pillow, and darkness began to sink over the valley. By now, poles had been erected and lanterns hung around the tables, giving a festive look to the tables laden with turkey, ham, loaves of bread, and bowls of various dishes, representing all the various cultures that made up this community: German, Irish, Norwegian, Hispanic, Indian, those of English descent, and a sprinkling of nation representations that missed mentioning. Some had ancestors that had been in America since the 1500s, and some had only been off the boat for a few months. But tonight was Christmas, and there was lots of food and drink and merriment to satisfy everyone's taste.

A band of sorts, with guitars, banjos, violins, and other instruments, was busy playing Christmas carols. After dinner was eaten, and preparations were being made for the entrance of St. Nick, quite suddenly, with no warning, large, white, fluffy snowflakes began to fall. First came just one or two, then two or more, then half a dozen, and then a full-on snowfall. The lanterns lit the upturned face of young and old, highlighting the smiles and little dances of joy. It was a magical moment in a land above the clouds.

Marsh turned to Hanne and the two boys, "Where is Sean?"

Hanne replied, "He was just here." The three of them looked around to locate him. But then, as they did, a violin started a slow, almost lullaby-like note, and clear nighttime mountain air gave forth. A lilting Irish tenor started low on the scale; his voice lifting as the song came forth,

Silent night, holy night,
All is calm, all is bright,
Round yon virgin, mother and child,
Holy infant so tender and mild,
Sleep . . .

It was the voice of an angel. No one had known, not even Hanne, that Sean could sing. Not like that, anyway. Every face turned, and every ear was tuned, listening.

> *Radiant beams, from thy holy face,*
> *With the dawn of redeeming grace,*
> *Jesus, Lord, at Thy birth,*
> *Jesus, Lord, at Thy birth.*

The rich tenor highlighted on 'redeeming grace', then lowered to a reverent, 'Jesus, Lord, at thy birth'. The words faded until they seemed to be but a whispered prayer. The crowd stood speechless.

Then was heard the sound of hooves and sleigh bells. Sean straightened himself, waved his arms toward the hillside, and broke into, *Dashing through the snow, in a one-horse open sleigh . . .* when suddenly Santa's sleigh burst through between the buildings from the hillside above and slid to a stop below the makeshift stage. A little, round man in a red suit, with white whiskers, jumped from the sleigh, turned to the crowd, raised his hands, and said, "Merry, Merry Christmas, Ho, Ho, Ho. Gather round everyone."

He mounted the stage with a huge bag on his shoulders, and one by one, he had all the children come round and receive a present of something or other. The snow swirled around as flickering lanterns cast shadows and light on the crowd. Men shook hands and smiled, and women gathered children close. Yes, indeed, Christmas 1900 was all anyone could have wished for in a little mining town situated 9,100 feet in the Rocky Mountains, in a place that was known as South Park.

It was a winter of little snow. Marsh feared the coming summer; the native grasses depended on the high country blankets of white. Most years it snowed all winter. If travel was necessary, narrow trails were what one followed. The stage trails were plowed with huge arrowhead devices that left maybe somewhat passable roads. The plows were manned by hardy men as it was backbreaking work, oft-times in severely cold weather. But not this year, nope. Not until April 12th.

It had been an extremely warm day. The cowboys had taken the herds out, even the yearlings, and spread them out to graze in a little valley just to the northwest of the ranch house. They decided to leave them there for a day. Sean and Hanne had ridden in a day or so early to spend some time in the mountains with their friends.

Hanne and Sarah sat on the veranda, in the huge swing, watching their baby boys. Hanne said, "Sarah, you seem so suited for being a mother. It has been a bit of a struggle for me. Don't get me wrong; I love that little man with all my heart, but my whole life has been one big drive to further myself. I never spent much time thinking of having a family."

Sarah sat quietly for a moment. Then, she lifted her eyes from the notebook that was before her in her lap and raised her gaze to meet Hanne's. "Yes, Hanne dear, I can understand that, especially in your early years. I confess, though, that you are a most unusual woman, and one to be admired. You are so beautiful, in such a classic way. I can only imagine, and probably with little accuracy, how you have managed. Yet, you have, and in such a magnificent way. Anything you attempt seems to be accomplished with the greatest of ease and grace. I marvel at you. I am so proud to have you as my friend."

Sarah picked up Hanne's hand, and wrapping the long, slender fingers around her own, she raised the hand to her lips, and kissed it softly, looking in Hanne's eyes as she did. She watched Hanne's eyes flicker, then soften and become moist. "You are a special lady."

Hanne sat quiet for a moment, as if thinking how to respond. She sighed and then raised her hand to caress Sarah's face, leaning forward and kissing her full on the lips, softly, just for a moment.

"Sarah, you are the special lady. I'm sure I would have done quite well had I not met you, but I probably wouldn't have found this incredible family that I feel a part of now. I love you, Mrs. Sarah Redman. You have made so much possible with your acceptance, your grace, and your charitable ways. This still all seems like a miracle to me. Sometimes I wake up and pinch myself to see if it is real. It is peculiar how life directs you sometimes. Because of a train accident, I met a young Irishman who just seemed to have been planted their by fate's fortune, and when I take him for a ride, we meet a Southern Mississippi gentleman on a black horse, and that event set me on a path to a great adventure. It makes one feel as if this is a magical place in a magical time."

"It is a magical place and a magical time. So magical, in fact, that weeks ago I thought to write it as a story. I have written all I know of you and Sean, and Marsh, but would you tell me in more detail about you and the days leading up to your first meeting with Sean?

"I have written a lot about Marsh," she giggled, "but, it is like pulling teeth to get that cowboy to open up. I think this whole thing will make a wonderful story somewhere down the road. It will be my first novel, and I am a bit nervous about it, rather like when you kissed me. I was a bit nervous about that too, but I confess it was quite pleasant. I hope you will share with me to make this story about you as well."

Hanne smiled, "Of course I will. I am honored you asked me. Pray tell, what is the name of your novel?"

"That has been difficult in choosing, but I think I want to name it after this high beautiful land. Marsh said something to me once about how high we were here, so I am going to call it *A 190-Degree Horizon.*"

"That is an unusual title, but living up here, it is easy to understand. Last night, we stopped up in Whitehorn. It was such a warm evening, we walked up to the ridge on the north side of town to that little aspen meadow; you know the one. Marsh and you took us up there one afternoon. We reclined on those big, flat granite boulders and put our little man between us while we watched the stars. The Milky Way seemed like it was a deep river across the sky, and then there was this shooting star that seemed to start out of the north, flame across the sky and over the town, and disappear beyond the hills to the southeast. It seemed so close, and up there it does seem that you can look down on everything. It was so beautiful."

"Yes, Hanne, we are very lucky people." Sarah shivered. She looked up to see that the sun had disappeared behind a dark cloud that had appeared unnoticed from out of the northwest. "My goodness, where did that come from? We had better bring the boys inside where it's warmer. Come in, Josh. You will catch your death of cold out here."

The cloud seemed to move quickly. Marsh stuck his head inside and informed them he was going to get the boys to drive the cows back in because it looked like snow was coming. Sean got up from the table where he had been writing and volunteered to bring in some more firewood. By the time he had filled the wood box and placed several larger logs on the porch, convenient to the door, it had gotten much darker, and gusts of wind were whipping small blankets of snow around the grove of aspen outside. Sean said, "Sarah, Hanne, methinks I might need to go and see if I can be of assistance to Marsh and the boys. It is snowing harder."

Sarah frowned, "Sean, that might have been a good idea a half hour ago, but I think perhaps, it might be too dangerous now. You could get seriously lost out there. Marsh and the boys would have started the cows in by now, and you might miss them in this and go too far. Stay here, and if they need help with the penning, then you go out, please."

"Yes ma'am, if ye think that best."

"I do. I think we need to get food and coffee started. They're going to be frozen when they come in. Chagan!"

"Yes, Missee boss?"

"Get some food and coffee started."

"Yes Ma'am, right away."

Minutes dragged by, then a half hour, then about an hour before the sound of cows bawling came faintly through the howling wind. Minutes later, Marsh and two of the cowboys appeared on the porch carrying a third man. It was Billy Madison, one of the boys that Marsh had trailed with in Texas.

"Sarah, get blankets. Sean, help us get him on this daybed here. He is hurt pretty bad and half frozen. Get Chagan in here. He will know what to do. I have got to go back out to help get those cows in, and I hope we didn't lose too many. It is a full-blown blizzard."

Chagan answered, "I am here boss, need to get wet clothes off and boots, and get blankets. Missee Hanne, go to kitchen, get two jars, fill with hot water to put under blankets." As the young man was undressed to his long johns, Chagan said, "Hmm, leg broken, shoulder joint out place, head banged. But he be alright Chagan thinks."

About 20 minutes later Marsh and three other riders appeared in the doorway. Marsh looked down at Billy, "How is he?"

"He be okey dokey, boss. Be down for a while, leg broken."

"Thank God. I thought he was a goner for sure."

Sarah asked, "What happened, Marsh?"

"Billy was just a bit ahead of me. We were coming down off the big hill back there in blinding snow. Suddenly, his horse went down over a boulder. It looked like the horse rolled right over top of him, and then was sliding downhill, dragging him. Billy finally came loose. I picked him up, threw him over my saddle, and led my horse the rest of the way down." Marsh turned to Chagan, "Has he come to yet?"

"Just little bit, boss, but I set him leg and popped shoulder back, and he pass out again. Just keep him warm now."

With everyone fed and the children confined to their beds, the fire was built up and as its flames illuminated the sturdy ranch house. The storm screamed outside. Soon the drifts were reaching window level, and still the snow came down. Tim Madison sat by his brother, and helped him with a bowl of Chagan's beef tips and noodles, washed down with a sweet but at the same time rather tart tea, with faint herbal undertones.

Tim took a sip from his brother's cup, wrinkled his nose, and said, "Whoosh, I think this tea would just about cure snakebite."

"You likee Mr. Tim? Chagan get you a cup."

"That would be real nice, Chagan. Thanks, I will."

Hanne turned to Chagan, "I was just about to ask, would you care to reveal the ingredients of this tea? It reminds me of something my aunt made when I was a little girl." Chagan frowned, "Yes, Missee Hanne, would be happy to, but Chagan not sure of names in English. Maybe we look in Missee Sarah's books we can find names. My mother made the tea for cold days and nights on the steppes. She said it make the blood run hot and keep the body warm."

"It surely does that," remarked Sean.

"Tim, do you think we got most of the calves? I am a bit worried. I'm not sure they can survive a storm this bad."

"I think so, Marsh. I tried to keep a runnin' tally as we drove. I never saw any break away, seemed to be following that ol' brindle cow and she made straight for the corrals."

"Yeah, well, I'm anxious for morning. Maybe if this wind lets up, we can get out and check on them."

"Maybe so. Anyways, Olek said he would be out at first light. He had all the horses in the barn, rubbing them down, and told me to head on in to see about Billy. He said he'd take care of the horses, and those other two riders had the corral closed as I left. All we can do is wait, Marsh."

"Yessir, anyway, I wanna thank all you boys for the help. I didn't expect a storm like this."

"Aw shucks, Marsh, it's just all a part of cowboyin'. You 'member that last herd of cows we pushed up the trail for Mr. Mahan, in '88 I think it was? We got hit at every stream, flooding all the way from the Nueces to the Brazos. Anyhow, we got up to the Red at that ford nearby Doan's store and we built that raft to put the chuck wagon on and run them ropes across to the other side. All us boys stripped off butt naked - 'scuse me, lady folks - then we headed them cattle across. Then that danged chuck wagon got a rope tangled, tipped, and slid off the back of the raft. We lost all our salt. Jimmy Besome and Hoss Hatcher got dislocated from their hosses, and Jose Gonzales roped Jimmy and drug him to the bank and on the way snagged Hoss and pulled him in as well. After that, Jose said them was two of the beegest feeshes he afra caught, but they smelled too bad to cook."

Everyone had a good laugh.

Sarah said, "Thanks, Tim, for that wonderful story. I am going to call you and Marsh in and have you tell me cowboy stories one day when the weather doesn't permit outdoor chores. I want to write them down, and keep them."

"It would be my pleasure Miss Sarah, but you might otta know, some of them stories ain't decent for a lady to hear."

"Well, I would be the judge of that, would I not?"

"Marsh, did you not spend any winters up here, when you first came up to the Park, or at Whitehorn."

"No, not really. I found work down in Salida. Mostly, there is something funny about Salida. It seems like there is a hole in the sky above it because it can be storming and snowing and blowing 20 miles any direction from Salida and be downright balmy down there. Now I weren't ignorant of the fact that we got heavy snows, just never really experienced any of these whiteouts. One time, I got caught in a dust storm over by Odessa, Texas, but I don't think it was this bad."

"Well, I guess we can all learn from it," said Sean.

"Yep. Come outdoor weather, we are going to make some weather breaks back in the canyon. We can even store some hay back there for emergencies like this."

Daylight came slowly out of the east, only a grayish dimness that was obscured for moments by waves of snow blowing through it. By noon, one could see the drifts in some places reaching the lower limbs of the pines along the ridge, and snow was stacked halfway up the north and west walls of the ranch house and other buildings. Then almost as if there was a handle on the storm, the winds died, and the snow slowed to a halt.

Then, as if a blanket had been removed, the bright spring sun broke through, revealing a wonderland of unbroken snow, standing level at about 4 inches below the tops of the 6-foot fence posts, making one think of tiny markers that bordered a strange land of tiny people. Drifts, where they were blocked, went up as high as the roof edges at about 8 feet or so along all the buildings. Marsh stood almost waist deep on the porch of the ranch house.

"Well, I suppose we need to man some shovels and see if we can find the barn. Let's get after it."

"Sarah."

"Yes, Sean."

"I have an idea, and with it, a suggestion."

"Well, come, let us hear it."

Sean looked around the table, every eye on him. "Just after the first of the year, I submitted a painting to the Pan American Exposition that is being held in Buffalo, New York, this year. Well, in fact, it started in May. I have only just been notified of the acceptance of my painting. It is to be displayed in the Art Building at the Expo."

A chorus of *Splendid! Well Done! Extraordinary!* and other bits of congratulations echoed back at him.

"I propose that we will go and attend the Expo at some point. It runs till November."

In the same voice, Hanne and Sarah chimed, "Oh, yes." Hanne added, "It would bring a world of new material to my students that I could not find elsewhere."

Sarah replied, "I find the idea just exciting, Marsh. What do you say?"

"Hmm, I have never in my whole life been east of the Mississippi, nor had any inclination to do so. But I've been reading about all the things on display, including engines to drive almost anything. And I am interested in the new electricity inventions. I vote yes, but I would prefer making the trip at the first of September. By then, I will be caught up on the ranch work, and the weather will be more pleasant for traveling."

"Oh, how exciting! Hanne, this gives us time to prepare."

"Indeed, what a wonderful opportunity! Sean, I am so proud of you! I had no idea. Why did you keep it a secret?"

"Aww, indeed I had nay idea they would even look at it, much less display it."

"What is the painting about?"

"Tis a painting of Mt. Princeton from the middle of the railroad bridge over the Arkansas River, in midwinter snow. The day I painted it was bright and sunny, with the peak of the mountain shining bright and wind blowing a stream of snow from the very top. It was a bonny sight."

Picture of Mt Princeton, Collegiate Range, Continental Divide, Colorado. Taken from mid-bridge over the Arkansas River, downtown Salida, Colorado. The image that Sean Kelly would have used for his award winning painting

Buffalo

The summer of 1901 was one of work and growth. New buildings were built, and new calves were born in the spring. Every day brought a new addition. A limited garden was added by Chagan, mostly herbs he delighted in for flavoring his dinners and a few vegetables that were able to produce in the short growing season of South Park. Walls of stone and split rail with a gate completed the garden. The gate was made of three pine logs, stripped and stained, two standing with a third lying across the top of the standing ones. One of the hands who was handy at carving, carved "High Country" on the top log, and so the name High Country Ranch came to be.

Before long, it was the last week of August. It had been decided that the little boys were too young to make such a long trip, so they would stay with Grampa Josh and Grandma Martha. One of Señor Trujillo's granddaughters, Marie, was to come up and stay in the house at Salida and help out with the two children. The other granddaughter, Angel, a budding artist in her own right, was to accompany the four on the trip.

Angel was about 18 now and had developed into a beautiful young lady. Her art was becoming well known in the valley. She had already filled several commissions and was fast becoming self-sufficient. She took art classes from Sean and was instructed in being a proper lady by Hanne. Indeed, the couple laughed, at times, about having this older daughter, but it was plain to see they loved the young lady and admired the zeal in her efforts.

Hanne took Angel shopping in the last week or so before the trip and had her outfitted properly in the latest fashions. Now as Angel walked from the depot to the waiting train car, heads turned, and people were overheard wondering, "Who could that be?"

The next morning, as the train chugged its way east from Cheyenne, Marsh sat by a window, looking south over the high plains. Sarah could see that his mind was somewhere far away.

"A penny for your thoughts, my love."

Marsh lifted his head and grinned, "I guess I was back a few years, looking at things from behind two horse's ears. Back in the '80s we drove some big herds up through here. The going got plenty tough at times, 'specially near the end of the drive. The danger from Indians was still very real back then, and grass supply would get short, and so would water. I was just thinkin' about those times. You know, I never say much about our life, but I am so damned beholden to you and so madly in love with you, I am never sure which way comes first."

"Well, you know what? You can just get that 'beholden' part out of your system because none of this could have happened without you. I will just be satisfied with the love part." Marsh grinned and ducked his head, "And now you take me on this other great adventure that I doubt would ever have happened without you, right?"

"Makes no difference. You realize that this will be our honeymoon, and that there is a tradition going to be set. After us, everyone is going to want to go to Niagara Falls for their honeymoon. Because we did, or will, or are."

"Niagara Falls? I thought we were going to an exposition in Buffalo."

"We are, but we are going to stop by Niagara Falls first. It is only 25 miles from Buffalo and right on the way. I figured do it first and not miss it. We will probably be exhausted after the Expo."

"Oh, OK, that's fine with me."

At dinner, Angel smiled as Marsh and Sarah seated themselves. "Oh, thank you, Señor Marsh and Señora Redman. I have never seen places like this. It almost seems as if there is no end to the earth. At home, we have the mountains all around us to keep us safe. And here, there is nothing to guide you, no point to refer to. Señor Kelly, he say that people that live in the mountains, they all come here in huge trains of wagons. I don't understand why they did not get lost."

Marsh laughed, "Sometimes they did, Angel. Those greenhorns from the east got lost plenty of times, and they sometimes ran out of water and didn't know how to find more. And then there were the Indians. Many of those easterners didn't make it to your mountains."

Angel looked sad, "I feel so, so *simpático* to them. They were so brave to leave their homes and journey out here."

"Angel, your people had it just as difficult. Part of them who had originally come from Spain came up here all the way from Mexico. It took years before they found their way to where your home is now, and they had to defend it from all kinds of predators. You should maybe feel a bit sad for them, too."

"Oh, I do. My grandfather has told me so many stories about how we came to be. It seems almost like a miracle that we have survived."

"Angel," said Hanne, "That has been the story of what America has been about. Almost from the 1600's, when Europeans first landed in America, there has been a push to the west. And now we have reached it. Now, what will be exciting is to see what we do with it in this new generation. That is why we are making this trip and why we wanted you to go. It will be a huge part of your education to take back home to your family, your cousins, and your neighbors. You will see things you would not have believed are possible."

It was a pleasant fall morning in upper New York, and the five westerners sat at a bench looking up at the great falls of the Niagara. Marsh was the first to break the silence. "I guess the west doesn't hold all the beauty of this country."

Hanne added, "Marsh, it's simply breathtaking. My Aunt Ruthie tried to describe it to me once, years ago, but I must say, she didn't do it justice. It is one of those things that I don't believe even a great artist, such as Sean, can capture. It is much more than that. There is the roar of the water and the mist that is almost as dense as a heavy rain. And there is more than I can even describe. It is a wonder."

"Senora, I agree with you. I would not try to paint all of it, but only small parts, like that faraway rivulet that seeks to escape from the rest of the raging torrent, and perhaps one of the swirling whirlpools that circle under the falls." Her brow furrowed in thought, "At least that is what I intend to do. I purchased some small prints at the little shop over there. I will take them to support my memories when it comes time to make sketches. *Madre de Dios*, it is so beautiful! I wish *Abuelo* could see it. He talks sometimes of his regrets about not traveling, but he said they were so poor that it would have been difficult."

"Your grandfather is a great man, and a smart one. It was kind of him to help you to make this trip. I am sure your family will benefit from it. He is *un buen hombre*."

"Thank you, Señor Marsh. He always speaks highly of you, as well."

Sean asked, "Marsh, do you see the building tucked under and to the side of the falls, with the wires running from it? That is the generator that is supplying the electricity for the Exposition. I read about it. It seems that they have lit the place up with light bulbs. Indeed, they have a tower that is covered with light bulbs. It will be a sight to see."

"Yeah, Sean, I also read of it in the papers. One paper said that before too many years go by, every home in America will be lighted by such as that. I find that hard to believe, but wonders never cease."

"Aye, and this electricity is AC, or alternating current, whereas the lights from the windmill at the ranch operate on DC, or direct current."

"Yep, that's my understanding, as well," said Marsh.

Hanne said, "I understand that clothing factories are trying to develop electric machines that will sew clothing. A lady in Salida said her uncle in Baltimore owns one of those facilities. He claims that sewing machines will double their production rate, and they will need fewer workers."

"But Hanne, how will those factory workers earn a living if they can't get a job? One would think you should be careful of that, else half the country will become unemployed."

"I don't know, I had not thought of it in that light. But you are right, I suppose."

Sean added, "I believe this new century will be one of considerable change, such as we have never seen before in history. I have already read of men trying to make machines that fly. It will be something to watch."

Looking around, Marsh sighed, "I, for one, will be content to sit on my mountain and watch it all happen. There are just too many people back here. One can scarcely turn around without rubbing elbows with someone."

Sarah burst into laughter, "Well, as we travel, we must all gather around Marsh and protect his elbows."

Marsh looked at Sarah, feigning a frown, and grunted, "Funny lady."

The rather stout man, dressed in a brown jacket and a top hat, was stationed at the gate of the Pan American Pavilion, loudly proclaiming the virtues that those who were entering were about to enjoy. As their party approached, he waved his hand excitedly at Sean, "My Good Sir! This spectacle sits on a parcel of land that contains 343 acres of land. Can you imagine, young man, that huge amount of land anywhere in the world dedicated to a single purpose?"

"Aye, I can. Mrs. Redman's ranch in the mountains of Colorado contains 5,000 acres. And she didn't even buy the whole valley!" Sean laughed.

"Hrumph, well, that is quite marvelous. Mrs. Redman, you have traveled quite a distance to behold this extravaganza, have you not? We welcome you. Enter here and enjoy the most modern things of our time and behold the proposals of our future. And, by the way, keep your purses tight about you. Our security has not quite purged all the criminal elements from our midst. Now, I bid a good day to you all."

Hanne turned to Sean and Marsh, "I propose that we split up for now and meet in an hour at the Tower of Lights. I would like to go to the women's building. I am curious what they may have on display there that might affect our future. I am hoping for new visions of life and family and education for the ladies that may be ahead of us. Sarah and Angel, would you care to accompany me?"

Sarah replied, "That sounds like a good idea. Marsh, it might give you an opportunity to peruse some of the engineering innovations that you've read about. Let's say we meet at the tower about 11 o'clock."

"Eleven it is. Enjoy yourself ladies. C'mon, Sean."

Sean and Marsh headed for the agricultural section of the Expo, and as they walked, they passed dozens of plows and tools for tilling the soil. When they came to the Louden Company's display of haying equipment, Marsh absorbed himself in the latest rakes, pulleys, and ropes for handling hay after cutting. They spent about half of their hour of time there and Marsh took business cards from the men manning the display and promised to write them in the near future. He remarked to Sean, "As our herd grows, the thought of keeping them fed in some of the long winters keeps me awake at night."

They stopped and took pamphlets and flyers from the F. E. Myers and Bros. Company about more haying tools and pumps of all types, and they found many more interesting items. One of the most intriguing to Marsh was the display of gasoline engines by the Otto Gas Engine Works of Philadelphia. "Sean, do you realize the importance of these engines? There are so many ways we could use them. I simply must have one. Do you remember the outcropping of granite high on the hill above Turret? We rode by there once."

"Aye, I do remember."

"Well, I was conversing with Mr. Wells, and William and I believe that granite is to be the next great export from the Rocky Mountains because many of the eastern cities favor it for their building purposes. With a couple of these engines and some cable and winches, we could handle the weight of that stone much easier."

"Aye, I can see that. Even an architect friend of mine in Denver has spoken of using the granite. Yes, I can see a future in a project such as that." Sean pulled his watch from his vest, and peered at it. "I do believe though, we are late for the ladies."

Marsh said, "Oh my, you're right. We better mount up and get movin'."

As they approached the Tower of Lights, they could see the girls gathered around a gentleman who seemed to be cornered by the three of them. They hurried their stride.

"What's going on, Sarah?" asked Marsh.

"This 'gentleman' was being a bit too familiar with Angel until Hanne and I arrived. We had just started to inquire as to his intentions. Perhaps, he can explain to you."

The man was quick to respond, "Señores, I meant the young lady no insult, or inconvenience. I saw at once that she was of my heritage and wished to introduce myself. Please, allow me. I am Jorge Bustemonte Raphael Hernandez Castillo, and I'm representing my country and city of Bueños Aries, Argentina, in South America. Allow me to apologize to the lady and to you. In my haste, I am afraid I lost my manners. I am afraid I am quite overwhelmed by this spectacle here in Buffalo, USA."

"Please Señor Marsh, he was not being rude. It is as he said. He was introducing himself, and I had offered my hand. Just as he took it, Señora Redman and Señora Hanne caught sight of us. Por favor, don't be angry!"

Sarah answered, "Perhaps I was a bit forward Señor Castillo. We have taken Angel as our charge on this a long trip away from home to a strange place, and we feel quite protective toward her. Her family trusts us to keep her safe."

"Señora Redman, your apologies are not necessary. It is with gratitude that I accept your sense of responsibility. I honor that. This can be a somewhat rude place. Please excuse my forwardness."

Marsh said, "Señor Castillo, would you like to join us? We are headed for the Art Building. Sean here has a painting on display there, and it is one of our main purposes for attending the Expo."

"I would be honored Señor Redman! And congratulations, Señor . . . uh, Sean. I also have a painting on display there.

511

Perhaps after we have the opportunity of admiring your work, you would honor me with a look at my efforts."

Angel exclaimed, "You are an artist, too?"

"Si, Señorita."

"How interesting! I am an artist as well. I would love to see your painting!"

"Mia gracias, Señorita. Por favor."

As they entered the great hall, all eyes were overcome with the variance of art laid out before them. Hanne worried, "How will we ever find yours, Sean? There must be hundreds!"

"I nay have no idea. Perhaps we will ask that gentleman. He is wearing some sort of a badge on his coat. You, sir, is there a directory for the art displays?"

"Yes, here let me get you one." He turned to a table and returned with a folder of about three or four pages. "Here, the exhibits are numbered by artists' names and a color code. You will find your display by the colored banners. Perhaps you would do me the honor of assisting? What is the name of the artist, please?"

"Sean Kelly. I am the artist, sir."

"Ah, well, come with me, Mr. Kelly. I believe you are right over here. Yes, yes, there we are. I say, Mr. Kelly, what a magnificent effort and what a beautiful place. Does it exist in reality?"

"It does, sir. It is a mountain on the Continental Divide called Mt. Princeton. It is over 14,000 feet high. I was within the city limits of a town called Salida, Colorado, when I painted it, which is over 40 miles away."

"It is an inspiring scene, sir. Let me offer you my heartiest congratulations on your rendering, and my best wishes in the competition. Now, I must be off. I see others with questions as well. Good day to you, sir."

Looking at the painting, Hanne said, "Oh, Sean, I remember it now! It was always my favorite mountain. We talked of it one day when we were living in the hotel of F Street."

"Aye, I can scarce look up without my eyes turning to it. I must climb it one day."

Angel said, "Señor Sean, it is inspiring. I so appreciate your talent. You have been so kind in directing me in my study of art that I think you should open an art school. It would be of such a value. I know there are many who would value your help."

Jorge added, "I agree with Angel, Señor Kelly. What a masterpiece! You can see the snow blowing from the tops of the peaks. It reminds me of the Andes in my home country. It's plain to me that you have a deep love for that beautiful spot. You say that it's in Colorado. I would love to visit there someday." Angel's eyes softened, and she turned to the young man as he made that assertion. He did not notice her reaction.

Marsh said, "Sean, I am very grateful that we have become friends and that we are exposed to your efforts. I believe we all become better people for it."

"Marsh, I thank you for allowing us to be a part of your life and for our home. It is such a beautiful place where we live."

"Sean, I remember you were painting this on the first day we met, there at the Arkansas River," recalled Sarah. "I was taken with it then, even though it was not yet complete, and I have always admired your talent. You and Hanne make our home complete. It would not be the same without you."

"Ah, ye words do warm the cockles of me heart, Sarah, but enough of this patter. I would like to gaze upon Jorge's work. Another artist, especially one so young, will be much more enjoyable. Lead on, Jorge."

"Ah, very well. It is in the red section this way. It isn't far. I will value your critiques. Here it is. It was inspired by a favorite place on the Pampas of Argentina and shows a group of my family's gauchos at work."

There on a large canvas was a panorama
of cattle grazing at the end of day, a
stream with both horses and cattle
drinking, and the gauchos washing off the
day's dust. A campfire is burning, and
kettles and pots are hung above it. One
gaucho reclines against a tree, his guitar
before him, his fingers plucking notes
from the box. High in the background is a
towering mountain range. It appeared to
be the end of a day, and it was perfectly
captured. The five stood silently.

Finally, it was Sean who broke the
silence. "Jorge, it is my honor to meet you,
this is so very brilliant! You have
captured these men so perfectly. Their
surroundings, magnificent in themselves,
seem to accent the men's lives. I
congratulate you! May I shake your
hand?"

"It would be my pleasure, Señor Kelly!"

Angel spoke, "Oh, Jorge, if my abuelo
could see this, he would shed tears of joy!
Much as I am doing now, I am afraid. I so
wish he could see it. He has worked his

ranch all his life, and his father before him, and his father before him. We live in a place similar to this, called the San Luis Valley. It is so beautiful."

"Thank you, Señorita. It is my desire that I someday will be able to see your paintings and return that praise."

Marsh interrupted, "Jorge, this is just one of the best things I have seen. You see, for most of my young life, I followed the cattle trails from South Texas to almost the border with Canada, driving big herds of cattle, sleeping under the stars, and living with a group of men. This is what I remember most, when day is done. I side with Sean. I would like to shake your hand."

"Mucho gracias, Señor Redman, you honor me."

Sarah said, "Well, Señor Castillo, I hope you will forgive Hanne and I for the attack on your person. I am sincerely sorry for the affront. Your ability to capture such beauty shows the depth of your soul. I will enjoy the days we have here together and hope you will share your time with us."

Admiring the painting, Hanne added, "And I second that. This is wonderful, Jorge."

"Señoras, you did exactly what mi madre and mi tias would have done under the same situation. You did the right thing. I am quite alone here and would savor your friendship and company. Muy gracias."

Next morning was a busy one for the travelers. They decided to take a carriage and tour the city of Buffalo. About 10 o'clock the carriage arrived and the grand tour began. Buffalo was the eighth largest city in the nation, with a population of 350,000 souls. Angel, of course, having only experienced the City of Salida and a quick trip to Canon City with Hanne once, was aghast at the vastness of the city. The taller structures amazed her. Her escort, Jorge, who was a bit more worldly, was nonetheless appreciative of the industry that was apparent.

The riverfront was bustling on this Thursday morning. After about an hour and a half, the travelers were delivered to the gate of the Exposition. Upon their arrival, suddenly from out of nowhere, around the corner came this cracking, sputtering, contrivance of a vehicle, with a man sitting in the front seat, holding a stick between his knees. The carriage horses were alarmed and started to rear and buck.

In an instant, Marsh was out of the carriage on one side and was at the side of the lead horse, holding it, talking to it, and calming it. Jorge was just as quick to jump from the other side. Between them, the horses settled down quickly. And as the disturbance had passed, all was well. The driver thanked the men.

Sean assisted the ladies as they stepped down from the carriage in their long skirts and, once again, the day was passed attending the exhibits. Marsh continued to look for things to better their lives at home. Later, they were drawn to a gathering crowd. Sean said, "Seems to be something of an attraction here."

A stranger turned, "President McKinley is speaking."

Sarah took Marsh's arm and said, "Oh, let's get closer." They pressed forward into the crowd, and when they reached hearing distance and were able to see the President, they stood in the midst of the crowd and listened to his speech. Sarah looked around her at the faces, so many races evident, so many different kinds of Americans, wondering, "Is this what makes the United States so different, so special? Perhaps the different blood lines and the blending of philosophies. If a leader in Italy was to stand and speak to the people, his listeners would be almost exclusively of one blood, of one philosophy, of one culture. The same would be said of France, maybe even England for the most part, and certainly in the Asian cultures, even more so."

Expositions of this nature seem to be born in this country, furthering that need to expand, in size, in knowledge, and in advancement. Sarah's thoughts went to her son, a thousand miles away. What will it all look like by the time he is full grown? Will we still be growing? Will it be peaceful?

The Spanish-American War had just ended, and it had changed the geography of the world. Entire countries had been taken over by the United States, countries that were thousands of miles away. It was all a bit staggering. The advances in science that they had witnessed in the last 2 days at the Expo were astounding. Would they continue? Who would push them? Who would finance them?

Then, as Sarah regained her attention, President McKinley remarked, "Expositions are the timekeepers of progress. They record the world's advancement. They stimulate the energy, enterprise, and intellect of the people, and quicken human genius. They go into the home. They broaden and brighten the daily life of the people. They open mighty storehouses of information to the student."

Sarah thought, *That is true, that is what we came to see.* She looked at Marsh, whose weathered face was focused on the man on the steps, a man known to be the leader of this continent. The President held no apparent beauty; he could have been any one of the men they had mixed with here. Sarah acknowledged that because he had that position, he stood above them, but she wondered did he really influence the aspects of this great spectacle. What does he influence, really?

She was jarred back to reality. A man had quite briskly pushed himself between Sean and Hanne, and Sean grabbed him by the shoulder. "Lad, you should perhaps learn some manners, else someone may take affront to your antics and give ye a proper thrashing!" The stranger turned confront Sean, when Marsh stepped to Sean's side, saying, "I agree with you, Mr. Kelly. That was plumb rude." The stranger mumbled something, then turned and vanished into the crowd.

Sean said, "It would be well to keep your eyes open to the likes of him. I fear he is up to no good." Marsh nodded in agreement. Sarah asked, "Could we go find a place to sit and have some food? I would like to talk about some thoughts I have had while here."

The first place they found was tearoom, of sorts. It was shaded, and they served little cups of tea and small plates of food that seemed strange, but tasted quite good. They determined that the culture wasn't Japanese or Chinese, but some other Asian culture. Hanne said, "Chagan would think he had died and gone to heaven here."

Sarah added, "He is going to think that anyway. I have become familiar with many of his spices, and I found a little shop yesterday where I purchased a bag of almost everything they had, and I took their business card. They said they would ship their goods. Marsh, it's a good thing that they don't charge us for the weight of our baggage, else we would be in trouble on the way back."

"Sarah, if I had purchased all that I saw that I wanted, we would have been forced to hire another train!"

"You have found that much?"

"Oh, yes ma'am."

Sarah began, "As I was listening to the President's speech, I started looking at all the people around me. I began to realize that the difference in Americans, what you don't see anywhere else in the world, is the diversity. As I read the papers, I see that even in our bad times, we are still the most affluent society in the world. I believe that is because of our diversity."

Sarah continued, "Right here at this table, we have, well, I am mostly English, except my mother's family who was German; Marsh is Scotch-Irish, or so his mother says; Sean is Irish to the core; Hanne is Norwegian, with a little something else, Finnish, yes Finnish; and Angel is of Mexican and Spanish heritage. Sorry, Jorge, we love you, but you're not a citizen so we can't include you in this comparison. Anyway, the point is our backgrounds are so different, yet our goals bring us together. It becomes more so every year. Talent from the four corners of the world comes together to create a great society. It must be that diversity that makes the difference."

Sean responded, "Speaking as an immigrant, which my father surely was, it has not been easy for new people coming here. The Irish were treated like dogs, still are in the bigger cities. My father, immediately upon landing, was left little option to put bread on his table. He had to join the Union Army. He told me years later that they told him he was going south to fight the Confederates, but it took him weeks to find out what Confederates were. Then, after finding that out, it was still very vague as to why they were fighting. Coming to America was sometimes the only option, the only route open, but it was not necessarily a good one. Oh, by the way, both my parents told me that there was Viking blood in my veins as well."

"Sean, you never told me that. Could it be that we are related?" laughed Hanne.

Sean smiled, "Don't worry ye wee head lass. I don't believe it would be close enough to conflict."

Marsh commented, "I think what Sarah and the President both seem to be saying is that we come here and we find the things that we can take home with us and raise our level of living." Gesturing to the west, he added, "Eighty years ago, reaching those mountains out there was only a dream for most. It took years to prepare to try to reach them, and some never did. The path west was a trackless wasteland full of savage men who didn't want you there. But here, in the lifespan of a man, the mountains of the West are only a train ride away. I wouldn't be much surprised, by what I have seen here, that someday maybe in the next 80 years, the journey will take only hours. It is a reasonable thought."

The Pan American Expo had been an astounding success, and the families from South Park were filled with new ideas. Friday was to be the last day, and it was well spent. Marsh led Sarah through the agricultural section, directing her attention to the various haying equipment, absorbing new techniques in the school of feeding livestock and blending of grains, and the equipment needed for the tasks.

In the section for industrial equipment, they viewed engines, transmissions, and all the new tools for moving large objects. They spent time studying engineering techniques and gathered informative material. Marsh had prepared a bag for all the pamphlets and printed materials he was taking home with him.

"Sarah, upon our return, I would like to make a trip to Leadville and have a conversation with William. So many ideas have been created in my head for new businesses, from being here, that it seems as if it will for sure burst. There are businesses that our area needs. For instance, I need to talk to Señor Trujillo about the area in the south of the San Luis Valley. It may be ripe for growing certain vegetables that could be consumed locally, or state wide, and perhaps shipped even farther away. And here we've learned about the companies that have the equipment to make that happen. I would like to perhaps partner with Señor Trujillo, and there are so many more ideas." He patted his bag, "And they are all in here."

Sarah smiled, "Yes, all that makes so much sense, and it could be accomplished. Mr. Wells has said often that the mines won't last forever. It would be smart to diversify." We will make a trip to see him in a few days, but let's soak up all that we can today."

Marsh responded, "Yes, we will do that. The very last thing, about 4 o'clock this afternoon, the President is going to speak at the Temple of Music. I would like hear him again. I never cared for the man, but I confess, I liked what he had to say yesterday."

Sarah said, "I think maybe we should gather everyone, as it will be so late. We can see him and then go directly to the hotel from there." Marsh asked, "Where are they, do you know?" "Yes, they were going to the art exhibits again. After being here, and after much encouragement from Angel and Jorge, Sean is talking to people about opening art schools. It seems this Expo has inspired people from all over the country. Sean has met another artist from Colorado Springs, and they are considering joining together."

Marsh nodded, "Well, I suppose we can wander over that way. I'm thinking that Angel and Jorge are going to have a difficult time saying goodbye. They seem to be quite taken with each other."

"I think so, too. When she looks at him, she looks as if she is going to melt. It looks like a case of young love. It is somewhat sad that they come from so far away from each other, but that has not stopped people in love before."

Marsh took Sarah's arm and smiled at her, "You are right, but then you are such a smart lady."

"Smart enough to grab a certain handsome cowboy when I saw him," she said, taking the crook of his arm as they walked away.

Their last afternoon at the Expo was spent at the midway. Angel and Jorge wanted to ride every ride available. Also at the midway were representatives of different villages from all over the world. The contrasting cultures ignited thoughts as to how those sometimes more primitive-appearing people might think, how their cultures perceived life and its cycle. Then, it was time to see the President, and just maybe to be lucky enough to shake his hand.

They studied the approach to the Temple of Music, so as to politely locate themselves at the most advantageous location. And when the doors opened, they were right. The line moved forward slowly. President McKinley was taking each person's hand and then clasping their hand with his other. Marsh said it was to keep people from squeezing his hand too hard. They inched forward.

The first in their line was Angel. She smiled and curtsied; the President returned her smile and bowed, ever so slightly. Then Jorge greeted the President and cited his country. Then Sean shook the President's hand and introduced his wife, Hanne. Sarah was next. She also shook hands with the President and thanked him for his inspiring words. Then, it was Marsh's turn. As the two men shook hands, the President remarked, "Sir, I take you for a westerner. Your look reminds me of the men who helped build our great country." Marsh responded, "Yes, sir. A Texan who now ranches in the tops of the Rocky Mountains. Marsh Redman at your service, sir."

They moved on, and they had but gone a dozen steps when Sean yelled, "Look out! That man has a gun." Marsh spun around in time to see a medium-sized man with dark complexion and dark hair. His right hand, which was bandaged, was outstretched to President McKinley. The President evidently perceived the man's right hand to be injured and reached out to shake the man's left hand. Then, two shots blasted the stillness. McKinley staggered to the right, almost falling, and the two men on each side of him grabbed him, supporting him. Marsh and Sean both lunged at the man with the gun but were too late. He had been tackled and downed by soldiers and policemen and was being beaten severely. McKinley called out, "Stop that!"

At that moment, one of the policemen slugged the would-be assassin, knocking him out. People were screaming and running, fearing for their lives. There was nothing more that could be done. The President was surrounded by his guard. Our party exited the building and walked away toward the exit to the pavilion, stunned by the events of that last hour, hopeful, even prayerful for the injured leader.

Their evening at the hotel was quiet and introspective. The edition of a local paper stated the President was still alive and was undergoing surgery. The assailant was identified as Leon Czolgosz, a member of the local Polish community. He was identified as a member of a group known as **anarchists**. The group had been known to be involved in other mischief and unlawful activities. The hotel atmosphere was subdued, the dining room almost empty.

Sean said, "Marsh, that man who shot the President was the same man that we had the altercation with in the crowd yesterday. I am sure of it."

"Yes, Sean, I believe you are right. He had the gun hidden in a towel or something today, and he had planned this, I believe. He was probably making an attempt yesterday, and the incident with us probably scared him off."

"Aye, it was not a big gun. Not like a .44 or a .45. It had a sharper crack. Do you think the President will be alright?"

"I don't know. Time will tell."

Angel interrupted, "Señor Marsh, Jorge and I wish to take a walk through the park across the street before time to retire. Would that be alright?"

Marsh said, "Yes, of course."

Sarah added, "Angel dear, don't be too late. We must all be packed tonight. Our train leaves at six tomorrow morning."

Angel promised, "Yes, Señora, we won't be late. We have so much to talk about."

As the young couple walked away, Hanne remarked, "I think in this short time they have fallen in love. It will be hard for them to say goodbye."

Sean said, "I think perhaps, that is what they are doing tonight."

Marsh changed the subject, "Sean, how about your painting? What will become of it?"

"Ah, I was saving that news till now. I sold my painting for $250."

Hanne exclaimed, "That is wonderful! Who bought it?"

Sean said, "A lady from Virginia. Her husband went west to mine in Colorado, and she said that he wrote her glowing letters about the mountains and how he loved them. She was about to join him when she received notice that he was killed in an accident. But, she said the painting reminded her of his letters, and she had to have it. She said she will leave it on display until the end of the Expo so that others can enjoy it. It made me quite proud, you know, for it to go to someone like that."

Sarah dabbed at her eye momentarily, "What a beautiful story, at the end of such a sad day. We should all say a prayer for Mrs. McKinley this evening." All of them responded, "Yes, indeed."

Saturday morning, at 6 a.m., the steam engine puffed lazily almost as if it was resting for the day's work ahead. Baggage was loaded into the baggage car, and personal luggage taken by the porters to the sleeping cars. The band of travelers stood on the platform, savoring one last few moments of terra firma, before the jostle of the train ride began.

Angel kept looking back at the hotel, as if somehow she could get one last look at the young man she had met. Then the whistle blew, and everyone began to board. At that moment, Jorge appeared. He ran quickly to Angel, swept her into his arms, embracing her tightly. Her arms went around his neck and their lips met in a kiss that lasted for a moment, then two. Then he sat her back on her feet and bowed low to her. She smiled, and turned and stepped aboard the train as it started to move.

Marsh called out, "It was a pleasure, Jorge. You must come and visit!"

"Señor Redman, it is my intention to do just that. Vaya con dios, Señor."

The next three days of traveling, changing trains, and reliving their experiences were long and tiring. So much had transpired. Then, on the eve of the third day, the mountains slowly came into view. First was Pike's Peak, and then the ranges came into view. That night they slept in Colorado Springs. Home was just over the hill. The mothers were anxious to see their sons.

Salida roundhouse

The next day the little train puffed up the canyon from Canon City. Even the Arkansas River seemed to greet them as it rush by on its way to the plains. Marsh and Sarah stood on the platform outside the train car, breathing the fresh air.

"Marsh, this coming home thing is even better when you have a home like this to come home to."

"Sarah, that is the way I felt all those years cowboying, until I finally came here to stay. I once rode this little gray mustang all the way up this canyon. Every time I heard a train, I had to find a gully to ride up in a hurry, or else she would try to unload me. It was a two-day ride, I camped somewhere near about here, damned near got bit by a rattler that night. Yes, I really do love this place."

That afternoon as they pulled into Salida, the news was that the President's health was improving, and it was thought he would recover. Perhaps all was not lost. The assassination attempt had failed.

Grandparents and grandchildren were on hand at the station. Señor Trujillo and family were there as well. He shook Marsh's hand warmly and thanked him for giving his granddaughter such an opportunity. Marsh said it was his pleasure, but decided he would not speak of Jorge for the moment. There was plenty of time for that.

By dinnertime, everyone had settled at the house in Salida, and the boys were playing with new toys. Grampa Josh said,

"Marsh, what do you know about President McKinley?"

"Pa, we were only just feet away from him when he was shot. We had all just had the opportunity to shake hands with him. We listened to him speak a couple of times, and I was impressed with him. He seemed to really care about the people and the country."

"You were there?"

"Yessir. We saw the whole thing."

Martha exclaimed, "My heavens, son, how horrible! They got that man didn't they?"

"Yes, ma'am, they did. And they were beating the tar out of him until the President called out for them to stop."

"God willing, he will be alright?"

"Yes, Ma'am, that is what we hope."

Josh turned to Marsh, "Well, son, tell us all about the Exposition. It was in all the newspapers. How was it?"

"Well, sir, it was mind-boggling, to say the least. What struck me most were the advancements in industry and agriculture. I could have spent a week just talking to the representatives from the companies that were present. I soaked up a ton of information and brought home a case of documents. I am going to order some stuff as soon as I have a meeting with William Wells. Sarah and I are going to take the train up there to Leadville before we go back to the ranch."

Marsh continued, "With open ranges shrinking and more people moving in, we need to rethink our winter stock-feeding habits. You have raised cattle all your life, so I want to get your opinions. Also, I am going to buy a couple of gasoline motors. They have so many uses, and they're much easier to use than steam engines. I need to thin some timber on the back side of the ranch, and we have some dead standing spruce and lodge pole that would make good lumber. If we set up a saw mill, we could cut it and ship it directly, instead of hauling logs. I have so many new ideas. It will take me a week to relate them all. For instance, automobiles, or horseless carriages, are going to become popular, and they will require fuel. There will need to be places for their owners to buy fuel. I think we should prepare for that, be on the ground floor, so to speak. I saw one of the first filling station pumps at the Expo."

Martha turned to Sarah, "Dearie, what did you do with our Marsh, and where did you find this man?"

Sarah laughed, "Ma, we all feel that way. It was such an eye-opening experience! My little bit of 'eye-opening' was about people. How there are so many in America, from so many places, and how all of the different cultures and philosophies serve to make this country grow and develop faster than most others. I have already started writing about these thoughts, and I will probably publish some of them in *The Mountain Mail* very soon. Yes, the Expo has us all fired up. Everyone, including Hanne and Sean, wants to start a new business. We want to bring home the seeds of ideas we discovered at the Expo, plant them, and see if they will grow."

"My lands," said Martha, "I can see you are both just plumb worn out! But you have such a shine to your eyes. I am so proud of you!"

Home

On September 14th, Marsh and Sarah disembarked from the train at the Leadville Station. It was a beautiful fall day; the mountains around Leadville, viewed during their train ride, were a blaze of gold, with some touches of red, set into backgrounds of dark green. Some of the surrounding peaks wore small caps of white where a passing storm had left an early snow. It was a day to start a new beginning in the high Rockies. The couple was brimming with ideas and excited with a new energy.

As they stepped from the train, a newspaper caught Marsh's eye. The headlines read

PRESIDENT MCKINLEY DEAD!
Great Grief Prevails!

"Aw, Sarah, he didn't make it."

"My goodness, Marsh, they said he was doing so well. I wonder what happened?"
'

Looking at the newspaper, Marsh said, "It says here says it was blood poisoning inside him. It took him fast at the end. Our new President is Theodore Roosevelt. I drove some cattle up there to his area once in the '80s. Old Rough and Ready, they call him."

Sarah said, "This is just terrible. This is the third president to be killed in office in 26 years - Lincoln, Garfield, and now McKinley. What are we coming to?"

Marsh let them in the door to Mr. Wells' office. His secretary, James, was seated in William's chair.

"Oh, good morning, Mr. and Mrs. Redman! I was just about to dash a telegram off to you."

Sarah said, "Good morning, James. Is William about?"

James answered, "No ma'am. That was what the telegram was to be about. He is in the hospital. He took ill yesterday. He fainted away here in his chair. We revived him and took him to the hospital, but he was not doing well about an hour ago when I went by to see him."

Marsh stood to leave, "Sarah, we should get right over there." Sarah turned to James, "Yes, we will. Thank you. James, would you get us a hotel room, please?"

"Yes ma'am. You go. I will take care of it."

"Thank you."

Sarah stood at the window in the hospital room, looking out. She couldn't help thinking back to the day that she had stood looking at the same scene as she said good bye to her husband. Now, the man who had opened her eyes to the dream she was now living seemed to be fading away.

William Wells' voice seemed weak and faltering, a far cry from the normal strong, positive, upbeat deliverance they had all grown used to hearing. He said, "Marsh, how was your trip? You know, in all my days I never once went that far to the east. There was one morning that I thought I might. We were surrounded by Yankee troops, and the old man said we were going to surrender, but old Sarge Broom said, 'Suh, maybe you will let them Yankee devils take you, but I am going back tuh Geoga'.' So, we just got up and followed the Sarge. Most of the regiment was captured that day. We found out later that they all went to some prison camp back east. Not many came home. I was lucky, to only serve the last few months of the war." He coughed and wiped his mouth.

He looked at Sarah, "Ma'am, I just want you to know, it has been a pleasure working for you. I call it a fit way to end my days."

"Oh, shush, William, you have got a while yet. We will get you well, and you can take time to heal."

"Well, that's mighty kind of you, but I have spent several years in this body and know how it works, and I hear what it's telling me. I am much obliged for your kind words and your encouragement, but I can feel my heart, and I feel tolerable sure that with every beat it skips and every time it slows down that it's tellin' me that I should get my affairs in order."

William continued, "It's probably my Cherokee blood that tells me that. My gramma was full blood, named Betsy Walker. Her Indian name was Aquatake. I was just a youngster when she died. I saw her only one time, and I dreamed about her last night. She said she wanted me to come home and hunt with her. I reckon I am ready. But first, my advice is to put James and Tom Handy in charge of the mines; their advice to me has always been top notch. About the investments, James can give whoever you chose the papers on that, and I am sure you can handle it. All is well with your business."

He was obviously tired, but William wasn't finished speaking. "I wish I could stick around and see how your boy grows up. Marsh, I am so glad you two saw each other for what you were. I think that is one of my greatest satisfactions. I would like you to send my very best wishes to Sean and Hanne. I might suggest that Sean take charge of your investments. He has a good head on his shoulders, and his pretty wife is as shrewd as he is. I am so glad you came to see me. I am very tired now; I think it is time to rest. Come shake hands with me."

Marsh and Sarah gathered to his bed, one on each side, and he took each by the hand. He looked at them and smiled. The pain in his face faded, and for a moment or two, he looked almost young. He sighed, took a breath, and closed his eyes, for the last time.

Marsh said, "Well, I guess Aquatake was waiting for him."

Sarah sobbed, "Oh Marsh, I am going to miss him! He means so much to me. I never realized how much I loved him."

"Yeah," whispered Marsh, "Me too."

The minister stood at the head of the grave, his monotone reflective of the somberness of the occasion. He looked back over the crowd of people that had gathered to pay homage to a relatively new member of their community. Only three years had passed since he had first come to California Gulch, or the City of Leadville, if you wish. But he had made his mark, as do all those who wish to pay back for the blessings they receive.

"Brother William was a man of faith. He believed, as the Good Book says, that we should love our neighbor. He frequented our little church as much as his busy life allowed, but although his physical presence was not always there, he supported his community with his monies and with his great influence. He told me frequently how much he missed his family back in his native Mississippi. He said they had, for the most part, all passed on to their rewards, except for some cousins and maybe a niece or two. But he spoke lovingly of them and his desire to meet them again in the hereafter. He spoke highly of his employer and business partners, here with us today. He said their association had brought more joy to him than any venture of his life."

The minister continued, "Mr. Wells, our dear William, was a soldier in the great Civil War. He fought on the side of the Confederacy. He mentioned to me just the other day that he did not do so because he believed in slavery. He said that scourge had no place in our great country, and he was happy when President Lincoln set the slaves free. William remarked that he was never in favor of secession of the states. He said that he never denied that all through the war, even though his belief sometimes brought him personal grief.

"He said that when the war came to an end, his feelings were mixed and confused. He said he had joined the Rebel army to protect his family who lived in the path of the Union forces that set their goal to overpower the South. He said that when the war ended, he felt sorrow for his brothers in arms who had fallen around him, and that to this day some of them bear the scars of war, both internally and outwardly on their bodies, yet inside him came the joy that the country was once again united, and that he could once again be a citizen of the United States of America.

"So we gather here to say goodbye to William, our friend. It is our loss, Brother William. We have profited so very much from having known you, from being comforted by your steady hand, inspired by your ever busy mind, and calmed by your great spirit. Now go, fly away to those spirits that have awaited you all these years. It's time to cross over the river and rejoin them in the shade of the trees. Brother Smith, would you close with a prayer?"

Hanne and Sean had arrived just the evening before the funeral, and they were shocked, as all were, at William's unexpected passing. As the funeral ended and the crowd broke up and people started to melt away to their respective homes, some approached Marsh and Sarah with their condolences. They shook hands and then went on their way with words like, "We'll shore miss him," or "He was a fine man." One even said, "He won't be easily replaced." That comment struck both Marsh and Sarah with more impact than any of the others. William had been their rock, their anchor. Now would come the need for decision making that would, no doubt, put a few grey hairs on their heads.

Both of the children had been taken to the ranch from Salida, and were being attended by Josh, Martha, and Maria, so the couples decided to take their horses and ride back to the ranch. It was a long day or perhaps two-day trip over the pass and down the west side of the valley, but it would give them time to think, to plan, and to try to find a way to fill this huge hole that was left in their midst. Before heading south, they made a small camp in a grove of aspen trees along side a small creak at the bottom of the pass. Dinner was a small affair because none of them felt like eating.

"I will nay forget that man," said Sean. "I still have the memory of our first meeting etched inside me. Hanne and I had only been together a few days. She was taking me for a ride out to the west side of Denver. We had topped a rise, and there before me was the splendor of the Rocky Mountains. I was all aghast, like a wee lad with me mouth open catchin' flies, when, with a clatter of hooves, came this man on a black horse, dressed as a real westerner with a big black hat and gun at his side. He greeted me, and we talked for a moment. Then, he kicked his horse and vanished into those mountains that I yearned to see."

Sarah said, "He first appeared to me on the day of my husband's burial in the same cemetery we were in yesterday. He came as a guardian angel. Most all of this that we enjoy we owe to him, even our friendship itself."

Sean walked away and stood looking at the boulders in the stream. Nodding at Sean, Sarah asked, "Marsh, is it okay, what William wanted?"

Marsh smiled and said, "Yes." Hanne looked up as Sean was mentioned. Sarah stood and walked to Sean's side. She said,

"Sean, do you remember the big boots and hat that William wore?"

Sean turned to face her with a puzzled look on his face. "Aye, I do."

"Do you think you might be able to fill them?"

"Aww, Sarah, what do ya mean? He was, aw, do you mean . . .? Aww, Miss Sarah, I dunno what to say."

"It was his wish, Sean, it was what William wanted."

"Aw, the Saints preserve us!"

Sean turned away, and pulling his handkerchief from his pocket, he stood for a moment and then wiped his eyes and blew his nose. "If that great man believed in me that much, I couldn't betray that honor he gave me by saying no. Yes, I will, I will give it my very best. But ye must promise me, if at any time ye feel I am lost, ye must tell me!"

"I promise, Sean. And you must promise to never let it keep you from your family, from Hanne and your son. If you need help, we hire more people. William said to allow James and Tom Hardy the responsibility of the mine work, and you handle the business and the investments."

"I thank thee, Sarah and Marsh. I will not let ye down."

Marsh said, "Sarah and I know that, Sean. Congratulations. I want to add, don't let it take away your aspirations with your art either. It is just as important."

"Thank ye, Marsh, I appreciate that."

The year 1901 had been a year of change, and it had been a year of growth and stability for the High Country Ranch. The couples were no longer focused on a single goal of building the ranch; they were now pulled in many directions. Sean found himself traveling much of the time - - to Leadville, Denver, Salida, and

Colorado Springs. When it was possible, his family traveled with him, and sometimes just Hanne accompanied.

Smelter Town

Hanne became active in the Women's Suffrage Movement. She was active in forming chapters in Leadville and Canon City, and she spoke at meetings often, even in Salida. Her firm beliefs about the role of women had given her the drive to raise herself from humble beginnings, and her broad intellect had given her the drive and ability to master any task she tackled.

Marsh partnered with Señor Trujillo and one of his sons, Joachem. Joachem had been growing vegetables for families in the San Luis Valley for several years. He had mastered the short seasons and understood the soil types. With his experience, he had become a successful farmer, but he lacked the funds and the equipment to do the job on a scale that would be profitable. Instead, he had been doing it the old way, by hand with human labor, assisted at times by a horse or a mule.

Marsh ordered equipment shipped in to turn the soil, and he bought pumps to irrigate where necessary. He bought harvesting equipment; the labor to operate it was already there. The effort would lead to advancement in the economy of that isolated region, and 1902 would be their first harvest.

Sarah was writing. Her mind had been filled by the myriad of faces at the Expo in Buffalo. She made trips to Denver and searched records in the courthouses and libraries. She gathered oral histories from the old pioneers still living. She compiled and wrote for her novel, *A 190- Degree Horizon*, and also published articles in the local newspapers, constantly reminding the new families what had transpired in the past century. Soon, she was being called to speak at various functions and at the schools.

Young Josh was growing like a weed and was soon to approach his second birthday. Just before Christmas, he was playing near the wide porch of the ranch house. Sarah was inside, but she could see him from the window. He was a good boy. He never strayed from her sight. She noticed him standing, looking at something, just out of her line of vision. It was a look of fascination. Josh stood, with his thumb in his mouth, almost frozen in his attention.

Sarah moved to the door, and opened it to see what the child was looking at. The sight instantly brought terror to her heart. About 50 yards away stood a giant grizzly bear, staring at the boy, almost as if it, too, was experiencing something strange, as if it had never seen a human so small.

Sarah called out, "Chagan! Grab a gun and go out the backdoor! There's a big bear, be careful! Josh, would you come inside? Mommy needs you. C'mon, now!"

The little boy didn't move, the sight was so overpowering. Sarah spoke a bit louder, "Josh!" The bear snorted and growled. "Josh, come here, now!" The boy turned and headed for his mother. The bear started walking toward him in a fast shuffle.

Sarah reached out and grabbed Josh, pulling him in the door. At that moment, there was a loud bang, then another, and the bear turned and charged in that direction. Then they heard the sound of the backdoor banging, then a crashing sound, then a bang from inside the house, and a roar. Sarah grabbed a big Colt revolver from a peg near the door and started toward the kitchen.

There she met Chagan. He had blood running down his arm and a nasty scratch on his forehead. In his hand was another Colt revolver. "Pistol empty, Missee Sarah."

Then from outside came several gunshots, the sound of horses, men shouting, and an animal growling.

Marsh came crashing through the front door. "Are yuh alright, Sarah? And Josh, where is he? Chagan, are you hurt bad?"

"No, boss man. Bear almost missed, only scratched Chagan."

Sarah said, "We are all alright, Marsh. Or will be, as soon as my heart returns to my chest. Are you and the boys okay?"

"Yeah. One of the boys, that bear killed his horse right under him, then Olek charged the bear with a long pole. The bear seemed more afraid of that pole than being shot. The animal must have been hit several times. Tim Madison lost his favorite horse though. That bear was Ol' Mose, no doubt about it. We didn't have anything 'cept six-shooters. My rifle jammed. Ol' Mose must have a hundred lives. Right now, he's headed back toward Black Mountain again."

Marsh tossed his hat to one side and collapsed into his chair. "Somebody needs to kill that infernal bear."

Sarah said, "You said several have tried."

"Yeah, but nobody has done it yet. When we first saw him, he was just watching Josh. Oh God, come here, Josh! Set on your Pa's lap." Josh toddled over and climbed up on Marsh and lay back on Marsh's chest and in the crook of his arm. Marsh patted his head and hugged him.

Just then Tim Madison appeared at the door, hat in hand. "Boss, would you happen to have something to drink?" His hand was visibly shaking as he held his hat.

"Sarah, would you please give Tim a shot of whiskey? No, on the second thought, give him a double, and I will have a taste myself."

Sipping his whiskey, Tim said, "Marsh, that bear must be over 10 feet tall. I was sitting in the saddle looking up at him. He damned near took poor old Spot's head off with one swipe. Jeezus, I thought I was a goner for sure. Then here comes that crazy Russian with that pole. I never seen nothing like it in all my born days!"

Marsh said, "Yeah, tell Olek to come settle his nerves if he has a need to."

"Yessir, I will pass that on. Well, I gotta go bury my horse. Couple of the boys said they would help." Marsh nodded as Tim left.

"Sheriff, I ain't one to declare war on any animal, but we need to find a way to kill that bear before he kills someone."

"Marsh, I agree. You do know he has killed several fellows that we know of. Somebody even found a few human bones in a cave up above Whitehorn a couple of years ago. They believed it was Ol' Mose that did it. Poor fellow, we'll never know who he was. People disappear in this country all the time, always have. There's no telling how many Ol' Mose has taken to a lair."

"I'm sure you're right. I propose we hire some professional hunters to come in and take him out. He came close to getting my boy a few days ago and killed one of our horses. Not to mention scaring the bejesus out of the hand that was riding the horse at the time. I will contribute to a fund."

The Sheriff nodded, "Alright, I will bring it up at the next county meeting."

Marsh and Sean had just met with a rancher up in the pass over the San Luis Valley. A bear had gotten one of his cows that morning, and the settler who was new to the valley was much shaken. Marsh and Sean had just happened along as the man was relating his story. Fifty years before, big bears had roamed the park areas and fed at will. The Indians had dealt with them. They respected the grizzly and considered him 'big medicine'.

But as it does everywhere, time is like an acid that washes away the old fabric of life and lays bare a palette for a new painting. That new palette interrupted the bears' mode of living. Game became scarcer, and the country became more crowded with people. And the two did not mesh very well. Mankind could best be described as "the great disrupter". It has been their pattern since they came down from the trees, with their opposable thumbs and their bigger brains.

Marsh said, "Sean, we should collect some of the big ranchers and put up a big reward for that bear's hide."

"Aye, I will make inquiries for professional hunters tomorrow in The Springs."

"Good. What time does your train leave?"

"Fair quick, I believe. I should go on down to the depot now. Is there anything else I can do while on the Front Range?"

Marsh pondered the question a moment, "Nothing comes to mind, right now. Are you staying at the regular place?"

"Nay, I am not sure. Hanne is meeting me at the station and taking me to someone's private home for dinner.

Someone she said she wanted me to meet. But I dunno where we are staying. If you are going to your Pa's, I will send a message there."

Marsh laughed, "That will be fine for now, but I am going to rent a space and hire a person to work full-time. We need an office here in Salida, a place where we can coordinate our work. At least for a while. I have freight on that train you are meeting, and I don't even know where to put it until the Trujillos can get over to pick it up."

"Aye, that is a good plan. The man at the livery on H Street has been nice to me about storage. He has some space in the empty lot back of the stable."

"Thanks, Sean. I will ride over and see him before I go to the depot."

Marsh added, "Christmas in less than a week. Do we want to spend it at the ranch or here at the house in town?"

Sean said, "I say the town. We will scarce be back by then."

"Town it is then. I will get Sarah down here, and let Pa and Ma know. Have a good ride down the canyon, my friend."

"Thank you, Marsh, stay well yourself."

"Land's sakes, Sarah, I'll swear that boy grows an inch ever time I see him! C'mere, little Josh, let granny see yuh!"

Josh ran to his granny's open arms and Martha picked him up to hug him.

"Goodness, fore long you will hafta carry me, little boy."

"I can't carry you gramma! You're too big."

"Oh, really? Well, we shall see. Look here, would you like one of granny's sugar cookies?"

Sarah said, "What do you say Josh?"

"Thank you, gramma!"

"You are welcome, sweetheart. Come here, Sarah, I need a hug from you too. Was it a cold trip from the ranch? Have you had any snow? I declare, this is the strangest country. It will snow on one side of a hill, and the sun will shine on the other."

Sarah took the questions in order, "Well, I always need one of your hugs, Mother Hargis. Yes, it was a bit brisk, but we had plenty of warm things around us. And the only snow we've seen, other than a couple weeks ago, was coming over Cameron Mountain a bit earlier. It started snowing those big flakes and was quite beautiful. The sun was shining over the Divide, and everything had turned golden. The aspens were red and gold, yet here were those big white flakes falling. And you are right. This is strange country, different than anyplace I have ever seen. But it is so very beautiful. Have you seen my husband today? And by the way, I brought Chagan to help in the kitchen. His feelings would have been hurt otherwise."

"Marsh should be here any minute, and Sean and Hanne should be here soon as well. They sent notice earlier. Oh, and I thank you for bringing Chagan. I just love that Chinaman! He is so funny and so quick to do everything, and his food is always so good. In the morning he can start Christmas dinner anytime he pleases!"

Sarah said, "Well, he brought two big baskets that he would not let anyone touch all the way here. I imagine he is ahead of the game as usual."

By the time darkness had fallen in Salida, Colorado, on December 24, 1901, the family had gathered, and the old house on E Street was filled with children laughing, happy conversations, and great expectations for the yearly visit from Santa Claus. It had been a good year.

The door opened and in came Marsh, carrying young Michael, with Hanne and Sean following, laden down with bags and boxes and parcels galore.

"Hey, Joshy! Look who I found! Your buddy Michael, he was asking after you." As soon as Marsh put the youngster down on the floor, he promptly headed for Josh and his toy horses.

Marsh then turned to his mother, "Merry Christmas, Ma! Where's Pa? Hmmmm, Sarah, I suppose you want a hug too?" Sarah smiled and gave Marsh a quick hug, then punched her finger into his ribs, "Don't forget your son."

"He can't see me right now. Mikie is here. I will get him later."

"Marsh, your Pa is feelin' poorly. You should go upstairs and say hello to him. He wanted to lay down and rest a spell before everyone came."

Marsh sprinted up the stairs. His parents' bedroom was the first on the left. He looked in and found Josh lying on his back, propped up on his pillows, looking out the window to the west. "Hey Pa, how are you?" he said softly.

"Oh, I'm tol'able, just had a bit trouble getting my breath, today. That's all. Thought I would take it easy so as to have strength to play with the kids this evenin'. How about yourself? You been down in the valley for a couple of days, right?"

"Yes sir, we got a bunch of new equipment in, plows and cultivators, and got them all assembled. We actually hooked them up to a team and worked them a bit to get the bugs outta them. I am surely lookin' forward to spring."

Josh glanced out the window. "From th' looks of things that might be a spell. Down home, you would be turning earth by first of March, maybe earlier."

It was snowing lightly outside. The sun was down, and the picture outside the window was fitting for the season. Josh said, "Well, let me get out of bed here and slip my slippers on. I want to get down and see my boys. I swear, Marsh, I just about think of that Michael as a grandson too. He is such a good baby."

"It looks like they are going to grow up as close as brothers."

"Yeah, it does."

When Josh and Marsh went downstairs, they heard Hanne saying, "Sean and I couldn't hardly get Michael away from old Duke down at the depot when we arrived. That old dog just loves him. He wags his tail and rolls over on his back and lets Michael climb on him. You would think sometimes he is going to purr. He washes Michael's face while the kid giggles and screams. Sean and I talk about getting him a dog sometime, but right now we are on the go too much. It would be a disservice to the poor animal."

Duke

Marsh said, "I think, sometimes, that is why Duke takes his passenger greeting to the point that he does. His owner, Charlie Catlan, is so busy all the time at the depot that Duke just took up his job as a pastime. Duke is a really good dog, though. I heard tell of a breed of dog in Australia that is being developed as a herding dog for cattle. They call them Hall's Heelers because of their unique way of moving cows. They are bred out of some collie stock. I met a guy at the Expo who promised to send me some pictures, and he said he would ship me a couple of the dogs if I wished. We could use them at the ranch, on those rough wooded hillsides. I told him I would wire him in the spring. I wouldn't want to bring un-adapted dogs into a South Park winter."

Sarah exclaimed, "Oh, Marsh, you never told me that. I would love having a dog up there. I would feel safer for Josh. I am totally in favor."

"Well maybe I will send him a wire then. They would be pups, and we would have to care for them till they get their brains."

"Oh do! I would so love that. Did you hear that Josh? We are going to get a puppy!"

"When? Hey, Mikey, you can come to the ranch and play with my puppy?"

"Name puppy Duke."

"Okey."

Sarah laughed, "Well they took that really well."

Everyone laughed. The boys looked around as if the adults were having an invisible joke. Adults did that sometimes.

After dinner, the boys went upstairs with Grampa Josh, and lay on his bed with him. They were asleep in minutes.

"Pa doesn't seem to be hisself." Marsh said.

His mother said, "No, Marsh, he isn't. He complains that his shoulders and arm hurt, and he often rubs his throat. The other night he had a bad dream, and he was talking to some of his war buddies. They seem so real to him when he dreams. He shouts, and cries, and struggles. I feel so sorry for him. He won't talk about it when he is awake though. I just lay and listen to him. I've done it for years and gotten to know a man who only exists in those dreams. He doesn't do it as much these days, unless he is feelin' poorly.

"Mr. Wells came by a couple of weeks before he passed away, and he and Josh sat there in the yard for most of an afternoon and talked about the war. They evidently had been in some of the same battles. They talked until I would come and bring them a glass of iced tea or lemonade, then they would be quiet, and as soon as I walked away their conversation would go on again. I guess they figured an old woman wouldn't want to hear that. Yes, I worry about him. He seems lonely and morose, except when those boys are around. He is so glad we moved here. He says over and over how it is so beautiful and comfortable here, and he loves having his grandsons near."

Sean said, "'Tis a fair thing, too. My own father would have been content with the same arrangement. And, Mrs. Hargis, I canna count the nights I would lay in my bed and listen to him fight the battles over and over again, much as you have described. The horrors must have been indescribable. I quickly learned to not remark about it. He didn't wish to speak of it. He was embarrassed that he dreamed and talked in his dreams, but still he would not ask what he said, or discuss it.

Sean continued, "My father came from the west of Ireland, along the coast. They were the hardest hit by the blight of the potatoes. They starved from the time he was a small child. They were so starved that they ate, excuse me for saying this, and I wouldn't speak of it in front of the children, but they ate rats, and clams from the seashore, and sea grass and even dogs. He said their clothes literally fell off of them. They had no strength to make clothing, or to work.

Sean went on, "He met a young maid not long before he came to America. They wanted to marry, but there were no priests there. A protestant preacher had come to the region and was trying to convert people to his religion, but people would not do it. They would rather starve. Finally, when the maid had fallen ill and was weakening, he told this preacher that if he would feed her, they would join his church. So they did, and she was given one bowl of soup per day. But it was too little, too late. She died, God rest her soul. Father mourned her for a year, even after he met me own good mother. Sometimes, he would say her name. Me mother never seemed to mind. She had gone through that hell in the old country as well, so she understood, she did. It's why I am so grateful these days, Mrs. Hargis, for your son and his blessed wife, and for my own beautiful Hanne, and for our life and our home. I pray to the Blessed Virgin nightly that our family will never have to face such troubling times."

"Bless you, Sean. I thank you for that sweet story. Josh and I have come to regard you and Hanne and young Michael as our children, too, you know."

"I thank ye ma'am, I truly do. It is especially appreciated this time of year to be with family."

On the 29th day of December in the year of 1901, Josh Hargis left this valley of the mountains, and went to meet all his old soldier friends. Marsh met the loss with all his strength. He had loved his stepfather as he did his natural father. They buried Josh in the cemetery outside of town, on a beautiful mesa. He had spent most of his life in Texas, but had to come to love his new home. Martha

Hargis was a strong woman. Saying goodbye to her husband, she placed a flower on his casket, kissed her hand, and then touched her fingers on the casket near where his forehead might have been.

She said, "Old Man, you told me not to mourn for you. You told me that you and Marsh's father would be waiting for me across the river, and we would just spend the rest of eternity together as the best of friends. You told me to go and be social and find friends and live the rest of my days in this beautiful place, and love these children and grandchildren, and be a blessing to them. You told me to not shed any tear for you. Well, I can do all the other things, but I ain't gonna promise you that. I will shed a tear every time I think of one of your hugs, ever time I remember one of our conversations, every time I think of you, but they won't be tears of sorrow. They will be tears of happiness for having the blessing of knowing you and living with you all these years. So, goodbye for now, you old scoundrel. Say hello to all my family and friends. And don't walk too fast. I will catch up with you in the by and by. I love you, Josh."

She turned on her heel, and with Marsh beside her, walked back to the carriage. Hanne strolled ahead of Sean and Sarah, with a little boy's hand in each of hers.

Watching Marsh's mother walk to the carriage, Sarah said, "Sean, you know, that is a brave woman. I so admire her. It is easy to see where Marsh gets his resilience, but she was only partly right. Josh has been dictating his stories to me for months, especially about the war and his and Martha's early years together. He said he wanted the grandchildren to know about those days. He told me everything he could remember about his friend who was Marsh's father so that little Josh would know more. I am going to publish it into a book for the family. But don't tell anyone yet. I would rather it be a surprise."

Sean said, "Your secret is safe with me, Sarah. That will be a wonderful gift. You know, you're a special person. My own father said there were people in Ireland who kept the stories of the people. They passed them down for years and years, orally. They were called *seanechai's*. Sarah Burns Redman you are a true seanechai. Your heart is into keeping those stories alive. Bless ye for it. For that, and so many other things."

Within a few days, 1902 was ushered into reality. The ranch in the high country prospered and grew. Marsh and Sarah and Sean and Hanne involved themselves in many ventures. Some failed, as is natural, but others went on to become successes. South Park grew in population. Colorado became renowned for its beauty.

It was the 24th of May, a cold, windy day. Marsh and Sean had taken the big freight wagon and two of the riders from the ranch to pick up a load of freight in Salida. They were just coming into Whitehorn when smoke appeared. Sean said, "Marsh, something is burning, and it's big." The riders hurried. As they broke out of the trees, they could see two of the buildings were fully involved. A string of men, passing buckets, could be seen throwing water on the buildings.

Sean and Marsh and their men hurried to the line and jumped in to help, but they were too far from the water source down where Willow Creek came into the park that was the town site. Before long, half the town's buildings were gone, totally destroyed. The residents and the firefighters sat down on the bank of the creek. Mr. Witting, owner of one of the mercantile stores and hotel, was seriously burned. Mrs. Lampe was inconsolable and in critical condition; she had lost her home and everything.

Marsh and Sean and the boys mounted up and headed north. As they reached the ridge at the edge of town, Marsh reined up. He looked back, "Sean, that's probably the end of Whitehorn. I doubt they will ever rebuild."

"Aw, sure they will, Marsh."

"I'm not so sure. They have had so much trouble getting backing to operate. We will see, but something inside me says that it will never be what it was, or what it could have become. Anyhow, c'mon, we have other fish to fry, so to speak. *Hea-yup!* Horses, move out!"

The End........ *for now!*

Epilogue

Marsh was right. Whitehorn never rebuilt. It had a good year, it is said, in 1904. Some investment money had come into Turret and helped Whitehorn's economy somewhat, but it began to slump again.

It never came back. Different ventures were put forth, but at 9500 feet, your options in the late 19th and early 20th century were limited. It slowly, like an old ghost, disappeared. Many of the buildings were hauled away. Its business's slowly died. Those 17 graves on the mesa, southeast of town, slowly faded away. In 2012 we finally found the sight of the graveyard. There were no markers were left, only a few pieces of lumber and some depressions in the ground. We found it by looking at a very old photo and lining up the landmarks. Those spirits lay in silence, except for the sounds of the tribe of coyotes that inhabit the area, and the bugling of the bull elk in the fall. The wind through the aspen trees continues the conversation of the little green leaves, and makes the big pines moan as it passes through.

Time takes back the marks of man. A piece of glass here, a broken piece of mining equipment, a rundown log cabin. But the memories are still there, the asperations, the dreams.

I find it hard to let it go It was such a magical place for me. Its history is rich, and although this story came out of my imagination, much of it is true. And it all could have happened. It could have and did happen, and so much more. I have only touched a small bit of the surface. The story will continue in time. Young Josh and Michael will grow up and have a full life, fall in love, get married, maybe fight in a war, maybe not. But one thing is sure. The 20th century is going to be a time for them to make their place. The land will remain the same, but the generations will continue. The Indians and the buffalo left the Bayou Salada and the miners and ranchers came. Some have stayed. It is now, and will always be, the land of the 190-Degree Horizon.

Oh yes, the loyal dog at the Salida Depot, Duke, he passed away in 1902 as well. In 2006 I watched a little blue heeler named Shadow walk by his grave.

In 1906 professional hunters cornered Ol' Mose and killed him on Black Mountain, that foreboding looking piece of real estate that stands in the south end of Park County and looks just as it did when Marsh rode The Buckskin by it. It ended is Ol' Mose's immense reign of terror.

There will be a story about Marsh Redman as a young man and a trail drover, a prequel to this story, as well.

This is such a small story about a very big place. Do yourself a favor this year. Load up your family and go to Colorado and drive the back roads of Chaffee, Fremont, Park Counties and watch for the ghosts of those gone before. Go sit on the side of a hill and listen. Walk down to Badger Creek and look for those miners silently panning gold. And drive by Whitehorn late some afternoon after the sun has set. Pull off to one side and go look down at the old town site. Maybe that old African American lady will be walking the streets singing

Amazing Grace

Whitehorn

A cloudless night in a woodland park
A dark meadow with tall pines outlined stark.
A moon so bright, you might think its day,
It wakes me up, keeps dreams at bay.
To the west, where the winds begin,
Mighty mountains seem to have no end.
They reach to sky, thousands of feet,
Like mighty soldiers are slow to retreat.
Across the sky, like a jeweled belt,
The depth of a milky way is less seen, more felt.

I walk alone in a dreamscape wood,
A halo of light is my covered hood.
I turn to look out in the light,
A cabin, now empty, in moonlight bright.
What story could it possibly tell?
A family stood round it, a maid at the well.
And around the corner, near to the back,
A band of assassins, about to attack.
I turned to warn them, to cry "*look out!*"
But alas, to warn them, I could not shout.

For you see, in that moonlight vision that night,
It had already happened, their day of plight.
Back in the forest, a lonesome call,
The lobo's howl, to gather them all.
Then, from all corners, an answer for him,
From valley low, to canyon's rim.
As I walked on through the night,
The soil below me gleamed silver in light.
And then falling upon my ear,

The sounds of digging, a pick rings near.
Then I saw the men, digging a drift,
A mining tunnel, they erected a lift.

As I watched their toil and sweat,
They faded from view, their dreams unmet.
For in this new land, a dream to get rich,
Was just as elusive as any itch.
But to scratch this one sore,
Required toil and luck, and a whole lot more.
For you see, in this valley at high elevation,
Was doomed to never create a sensation,
But would steal dreams from men
And not reward their efforts, or even begin.
And this small town, built in this place,
Would fade from this Park, and leave nary a trace.

So as I walked through Whitehorn, that starry night,
I could see all their ghosts, alive in the light.
The old black lady, walking the street,
Singing her songs, with voice so sweet.
I saw the merchant, sweeping his deck,
With produce all stacked by bushel and peck.
And with a rumble and a clatter out loud,
The stagecoach arrived and drew a crowd.
And all about town people walked with a hustle.
Men in work clothes, and ladies with a bustle.

Oh what dream that night did appear?
I look at its emptiness now, in my eye, a tear.
Where once a center of men and their dreams,
Herds of elk and deer crowd a tiny stream.
I will never forget my hypnotic moon,
I hope I be able to return there soon.

Made in the USA
Columbia, SC
05 November 2018